THE VANISHED BIRDS

SIMON JIMENEZ

DEL
REY

NEW YORK

2021 Del Rey Trade Paperback Edition

Copyright © 2020 by Simon Jimenez
Excerpt from *The Spear Cuts Through Water* by Simon Jimenez
copyright © 2022 by Simon Jimenez

Published in the United States by Del Rey, an imprint of Random House,
a division of Penguin Random House LLC, New York.

DEL REY is a registered trademark and the CIRCLE is a
trademark of Penguin Random House LLC.

Originally published in hardcover in the United States by Del Rey,
an imprint of Random House, a division of
Penguin Random House LLC, in 2020.

This book contains an excerpt from the forthcoming book
The Spear Cuts Through Water by Simon Jimenez.
This excerpt has been set for this edition only and may not reflect
the final content of the forthcoming edition.

LIBRARY OF CONGRESS CATALOGING-IN-PUBLICATION DATA
Names: Jimenez, Simon, 1989– author.
Title: The vanished birds / Simon Jimenez.
Description: First edition. | New York: Del Rey, [2020]
Identifiers: LCCN 2019034925 (print) | LCCN 2019034926 (ebook) |
ISBN 9780593129005 (paperback) | ISBN 9780593128992 (ebook)
Subjects: GSAFD: Science fiction.
Classification: LCC PS3610.I54 V36 2020 (print) | LCC PS3610.I54 (ebook) |
DDC 813/.6—dc23
LC record available at https://lccn.loc.gov/2019034925
LC ebook record available at https://lccn.loc.gov/2019034926

Printed in the United States of America on acid-free paper

randomhousebooks.com

2nd Printing

Book design by Elizabeth A. D. Eno

Praise for **THE VANISHED BIRDS**

"Highly imaginative and utterly exhilarating . . . [*The Vanished Birds*] already feels like a science fiction classic."

—Thrillest

"This extraordinary science fiction epic, which delves deep into the perils of failing to learn from one's mistakes, is perfect for fans of big ideas and intimate reflections."

—Publishers Weekly (starred review)

"A lyrical and moving narrative of space travel, found families, and lost loves set against an evocative space-opera background."

—Booklist (starred review)

"Reminiscent of Justin Cronin's *The Passage,* yet the journey itself evokes Bryce Courtenay's *The Power of One,* creating crossover appeal for readers who enjoy a bit of emotional attachment with their time travel . . . The story takes on a tone and depth that recalls an N. K. Jemisin novel."

—Library Journal

"This powerful, suspenseful story asks us to consider what we'd sacrifice for progress—or for the ones we love."

—Kirkus Reviews (starred review)

"*The Vanished Birds* strikes a breathless balance between the conceptually dazzling and the emotionally resonant, and it's in that balance that a bright new voice in genre fiction is born. Simon Jimenez has announced himself as a graceful, spellbinding storyteller."

—BookPage (starred review)

"*The Vanished Birds* finds an intimate heartbeat of longing in a saga of galactic progress and its crushing fallout. . . . A novel of vast scope that yet makes time for compassion, wonder, and poetry."

—INDRA DAS, author of *The Devourers*

"The future world-building is rich and smart, the prose assured, and the story both intensely personal and a blistering commentary on capitalism and colonialism. . . . Highly recommended."

—KATE ELLIOTT, author of *Black Wolves*

For Mom and Dad,
the strangest people I've ever loved

I

1

Six Harvests

He was born with an eleventh finger. A small bead of flesh and bone beside his right pinky. The doctor calmed the worried parents and told them the nub was a harmless thing. "But still," he said, unlacing a small cloth pouch, "a farmer needs only ten fingers to work the dhuba." He coaxed the child to sleep with the smoke of torched herbs, and sliced the nub from the hand with a cauterizing knife. And though the mother knew her baby felt no pain in his medicated sleep, she winced when the flesh was parted, and clutched him to her breast, praying that there would be no memory of the hurt when he woke, while her husband, unable to resist indulging in his hedonism even then, breathed deep the doctor's herb smoke, and was spelled by a vision of the future—in his dilated pupils his son, a full-grown man, handsome and powerful, with a big house at the top of the hill. The new governor of the Fifth Village. To commemorate this vision, he had the finger boiled of its flesh, and its bones placed in a corked glass jar, which he shook on wistful days, listening to the clack of good omens as he whispered to his baby, "You are going to run this place one day." The boy burbled in his arms, too young to recognize the small and varied ways life was contriving to keep him put.

They called him Kaeda, the old name of this world.

Kaeda grew up proud of the scar on his right hand, the shape of it changing over the years. When he was seven, the healed tissue rippled down the side of his palm like a troubled river. He was happy to show the other children the mark when he was asked, and he giggled as they stroked the skin with furrowed brows, at once impressed and unnerved by its texture. Some children called him cursed; those were the children who learned from their parents to distrust the unusual. To them, he shoved his scar under their noses and confronted them with the fact of it, repeating the words of his father: "I'm going to run this place one day!" and through sheer force of will convinced them that the scar on his hand was a lucky thing.

He had a natural charisma. The caretakers doted on him, and the other kids played the games he wanted to play, believed what he believed. Everyone but a girl named Jhige, who never missed an opportunity to push back against his wild declarations, matching pride with pride as she countered his wild theories on why the sky was red, and why the smell of the air changed during the day; why everything smelled soft and sweet in the morning and sour as a kiri fruit at dusk. "And your scar isn't special," Jhige shouted. "It just means you were born wrong!" They wrestled in the yellow grass until the caretakers separated them. They fought like dogs most days, but despite the bruises he might nurse on the way home, he always emerged from the fights unbothered, certain that she was only jealous that it was he who was destined for greatness, and not her, though what greatness that was, he did not know, and would not, until the day the offworlders arrived.

Before that day, he was only familiar with the stories his parents shared: how every fifteen years the offworlders broke the sky with their cloth-and-metal ships and landed in the plains east of the village to collect the harvest of dhuba seeds. His father told him that this special day was called Shipment Day, and that on every Shipment Day, a great party was held for both the offworlders and the farmers. "A party you will never forget," he promised.

His mother laughed from the other room. "Unless you drink too much."

"The drink is half the fun," his father countered.

Kaeda was unable to sleep the night before his first Shipment Day. His mind was too alive with the stories; the new faces he would see, the new hands not stained purple from the dhuba fields. He gazed through his small bedroom window at the black sky littered with stars, with no regard for the late hour, as he imagined what it would be like to leap from light to light. What places there were, on the other side. When his mother came to collect him in the morning he was exhausted, all his energy spent the night before, conjuring these fantasies. He dragged his feet into his sandals and complained loudly as they marched with the other villagers to the plains east of town, begging for rest until his father sighed and carried him on his back, where he drifted in and out, unaware of time or location, only the warm and thick smell of the man's shoulder, like the embers of a dying fire.

He slept.

And then the sky cracked and he woke up with a shriek and his father laughed and pointed upward and he followed his father's finger up to where, against the slate of red sky, twelve thin green lines arced above the horizon line, the end points gaining in size until, not two minutes later, the giant metallic beasts touched down on the carpet of grass with ground-shaking thumps, one after another, the vibrations attacking his heart, swollen now as it occurred to him that he had never seen such large creations, nothing as intricate as their cloth wings and the hull panels that gleamed under the sun, or the sonic boom of their hangar doors that dropped onto the dirt like jaws mid-shout, or the people who emerged from within of every variant shade of skin, some lighter than his, others darker, dressed in clothing that seemed woven out of the stuff of starlight. With a nauseous rush the scope of his world telescoped outward to accommodate the breadth of these awesome quantities. His whole body shivered. And then he pissed himself. His father cursed and lowered him to the ground, cringing at the stain on his back.

The offworlders were shown to the banquet cushions in the center of the Fifth Village. Bowls of spirits and plates of dhuban pastries—long, purple, and flaky—were served on wide platters. Kaeda could not see the offworlders from where he sat—a minor disappointment, as he stuffed himself with sweet breads and bowls of juice, feeling warm and content between the motions of his parents' bodies, pleased by the sound of hard snaps when his mother cracked open nuts with her muscular fingers, and the bellow of his father's drunken, joyful laugh. He felt a satisfaction with the world so complete he even smiled at Jhige, who was with her own family on the other end of the long table, and she, startled, returned his smile with a small wave of her own before turning back to her uncle, who was in the midst of another tall tale about the Butcher Beast of the southern forest—horror stories with which the young would startle themselves awake later that night, and stare into the dark corners of their bedrooms, waiting to be devoured. The adults exploded with laughter.

After the banquet, when the hard drinking began, the caretakers and new parents brought the children back to their homes. But Kaeda wasn't finished with the night—he had yet to meet an offworlder—so he planned his escape from the group. He told his friend Sado to lie to the caretakers and say that he had run home ahead of them, and before Sado could so much as nod, the boy was gone, hugging the side of the squat buildings, back to the bonfire and the harsh scent of liquor.

It was there, at the end of the alley, before the path opened up into the plaza, that he saw her: a woman, alone on a bench, silhouetted by the fire.

She held a wooden flute to her lips. Her fingers spidered up and down the length of the instrument, playing music that reminded Kaeda of the sound of wind whistling through a cracked-open door. He watched her from the shadows. Even sitting down, she seemed tall. She was black-skinned, her hair shaved to the scalp, and was dressed in an outfit simpler than her friends: a white top with a collar cut down to the chest bone and dark bottoms that hugged the curves of her legs. Each note she played on her flute made the bonfire ahead of them dance, or maybe it was the fire that was influencing the music, or the stars, or all of it, working in concert, together. The song was the night itself. It was in his people's laughter as they danced by the fire, and it was in the smell of fruit and smoke in the air; it was in the light, caught in the beads of sweat on her collarbone. It was everywhere. The woman's breath flumed through the wooden tube, and bellowed heat into his belly, gladly mesmerizing him, until her large eyes shot up and saw him.

The music stopped.

She spoke with two voices, one in a language he did not understand, and the other his own. It sounded as though she were haunted by her own ghost, she her own distant echo. He was too young to recognize the doubled voice as a quirk of her translator device, believing instead it was a kind of offworlder magic.

"Did you like it?" she asked, referring to the music.

He nodded. She stood up and approached him. Her shadow was long; it ran past him, into the dark fringe at the end of the alley. There was an instinct in him to run, as though some part of him knew that if he should stay there would be no turning back, but he ignored this instinct and planted himself to the ground, stubbornly so. She crouched before him, eye to eye. Close enough for him to smell the flowered chemistry of her skin.

"Take it," her doubled voice said, handing him her flute.

Their fingers grazed as he took the gift. He held the flute to his chest with a knuckled grip as she looked down at him with the smile that only adults were capable of—one both happy and sad—and he watched her turn away and stride toward the bonfire, while the shape of her branded itself to the back of his skull. He did not know at the time that the shape would remain there for years, only that he was at once pleased and frightened by the heat he felt when he watched her go.

He pressed the flute to his lips, the mouthpiece still wet.

In the morning, the fire pit was cold ash and the travelers were gone, taking with them the seed his people had harvested. The flute stayed by his bed. He told his parents that it was a gift, which, much like his eleventh finger, his father interpreted as a sign of good things to come and his mother accepted as yet another weary fact of the world. He played it when he was feeling lonely, lying on the stalked roof of their home, blowing into the mouthpiece until he was hoarse in the throat, never getting the notes quite right; filling his nights with clumsy, earnest melodies. Songs that repeated themselves, maddeningly.

First began the dreams of innocence; him showing her his land, teaching her the rules of the games he and his friends played—"keep one foot above the knee and a finger on your nose and sing the harvest night song backwards." In those dreams, she was the listener, and never talked down to him. She liked his finger scar and told him he was very brave. Then came the other dreams; the quiet, wet dreams, of her sitting on the foot of his bed, a finger pressed against his big toe, then sliding up the hill of his foot, up his bare leg, trailing a path of electricity, until the short circuit, the explosion.

And then he was fourteen.

Kaeda began to work the dhuba fields. He worked alongside his parents, who taught him how to squeeze the gelatinous purple seeds from the heart of the stalk, to cradle the fragile things inside the woven bowl, to hack the emptied stalk down with a machete, at the base, with three precise strikes. When he was more capable, he was assigned his own field farther down the road, where he worked alongside Jhige and others he knew in passing. The work whittled the youthful dough off his body, replaced it with hard and useful muscles that pressed against his skin like many little fists. Women noticed; some men. Jhige noticed. Their childhood rivalry had by then eased into a playful camaraderie. The jokes they shared tinged with something unknowable and exciting, as each would sneak glances at the other through the rows of stalks they worked, watching the way the other's body moved.

Late in the moisture season, on their way back to town, she asked him—quickly, as if to overcome her own nervousness—if he was attracted to her. He tripped over a knot in the dirt. He said yes. And he was. But that night, as they groped each other behind one of the storage shacks and sucked skin bruised, it was another woman that Kaeda kissed, the heat of the bonfire licking his face as she whispered with her doubled voice the burnt secrets of this world.

His relationship with Jhige was short-lived. It was obvious to both of them that his mind was elsewhere. He looked past her when they lay together, would hold her hand limply when they walked through the village to meet their friends, and when they fought, he would be the first to walk away, as if he could not be bothered to come up with a retort, much less a resolution. The end was quiet, and sudden. In the plaza he saw her holding hands with another boy, who worked another field. Yotto. A kind boy, and, in Kaeda's opinion, a stupid one, with a clumsy blade swing. A poor choice for Jhige. But he said nothing to her about this, and walked past the two of them without comment. It would be years before they were on speaking terms again.

He had other lovers in the interim, none of whom he stayed with for longer than a month, always finding them wanting in some aspect; not tall enough, not strong enough, not clever enough, but always the true reason remained the same underneath it all: none of them were *her*.

Lying on the thatched roof of his home, staring up at the stars, he could convince himself that somewhere far away, she was thinking of him too.

They cracked open his first jug of spirits on his fifteenth birthday and poured the contents over his head, a sour baptism that shepherded him into the world of adults who drank at night and floated to the purple fields in the morning. "This is when your life begins," his father cried, gripping the boy's face in his callused palms, kissing him again and again on the forehead, drunk, along with the old refrain, "You're going to run this place one day." It occurred to Kaeda under his father's smothering kisses that all these good omens were always in some distant point in the future, never now.

"Just you wait and see."

He waited.

Kaeda was twenty-two when the next Shipment Day arrived. He was working in the fields, squeezing the last of the seeds from the stalk, when Sado elbowed him and pointed up at the sky. Twelve green lines cut across the clouds, disappearing behind the horizon of tall stalks to the east. "They're here," Sado said. Kaeda nodded, his hands now trembling as he stripped the skin off the next stalk, anxious to finish off his quota. They dragged the wheeled containers of seed back to the village. His friend warned him not to get too excited, that even if she was there, the chances were good that she would not remember him, to which Kaeda grinned and replied, "I hope she doesn't," for he did not want her to see the boy from years past, but a man worthy of her night.

"After she turns you down," Sado said, slapping him on the shoulder, "come drink with me and all the other lonely bastards."

Kaeda laughed. He let out the first holler of the song of home-coming, and smiled as the song spread down the marching line of farmers, their voices full-throated in anticipation of the coming cel-ebrations. They brought the wicker containers back to the collec-tions building to be weighed and stored, and once the last container was delivered, they ran to their homes and dressed in their good breeches and dress robes. The bonfire was well under way when they arrived. Kaeda picked up a jug from the long table and took a great swig that burned courage down his throat before he went in search of her. The shadows of the dancers by the fire made the whole plaza pulse, shifting the ground beneath his feet, and as faces flashed by, none of them hers, the fear gnawed at his stomach that maybe she had not returned—but then, in the corner of his eye, he saw the alley, thrown in light, and her, on the bench, watching the dancers and the fire with a calm smile.

He knew time moved differently for her, but still it shocked him how much she resembled his dreams of her—how little she had aged. He straightened his posture and pushed out his chest, a show of bravado that was undercut when he introduced himself and stumbled over the simple syllables of his own name. Still, the off-worlder smiled at him, the light caught on the curve of her soft lips, and his chest cracked open. Everything he had been holding in for the last fifteen years came tumbling onto the ground by her feet. A tangled mess of want.

"Hello," she said.

Her name was Nia Imani. She told him it was an old name from back when Earth was whole, but when he asked her if it was her mother or her father who gave her the name, she smiled and spoke instead about her work.

He already knew the basic nature of her travel. The governor covered the subject with every tired welcome speech he gave in the fields. But still he listened with rapt attention as she described the sensations her body experienced when her ship departed from this reality and folded into another. She told him it was called Pocket Space. The place where time moved differently. He imagined what she asked him to imagine: a black ocean, with currents and eddies and rapids that stretched the seconds into hours into years. Some currents stretched time infinitely, and other currents not more than moments. But always, there was an imbalance of time. "We can travel long distances this way," she said, "but every time we return, things are different. The route we're taking now, we arrive on the Assiduous Current and leave on the Diffident. These currents have a specific time differential. It takes me eight months to bring your harvest to its destination and to return here for the next shipment, but for you—"

"Fifteen years," he finished, knowing the number well, having walked slowly through each of them. "And what is it like, when you go home and your friends are older but you are not?"

"Sometimes sad," she said, then, smiling, "but sometimes good." She told him she was hired by the Umbai Company for six shipment cycles; this was her second.

"So you will be back four more times."

"Yes," she said. "Just four." Then, "Are you sure we haven't met before?" and he assured her that yes, they most definitely had not, afraid that the truth would catch him; that the spell of the night would shatter and she would pat him on the head like the little boy he was and say good night. But she pressed no further, and instead asked him about the nature of his work. He puffed out his chest again. "I'm the best on my field, fifth fastest in this village." He told her about the moisture seasons, when the barren fields were covered in a thin layer of white mist, the best time to replant the stalks, and how the roots fed on the wetness in the air and the sugar in the rutted dirt. "We harvest the seeds when the sky sucks up the moisture. A day of work will turn your hands purple." He showed her his palm, the mauve patina that stained it, and when she glided a finger across his hand, he shivered.

"You're proud of your work," she said. It wasn't a question.

"I am," he said, which wasn't always true. Most days he found the work mundane, sometimes tedious, never exceptional; but tonight, as she listened to his every word, the work seemed important; bigger than himself. He spoke until there were no more words to say, the topic exhausted, but the air between them still violent with energy. Her hand lay next to his trembling fingers on the bench. He swallowed.

"You are very beautiful," he said.

The words fell out of his mouth like rocks.

But she picked them up anyway, one at a time, and she told him that he was beautiful too, and there, in her eyes, he saw the same want. He followed her through the dancers, past the long tables where people ate, past Sado and the other single men who drank and comforted one another and who bit their lips in jealousy as he and the offworlder walked away from the party together. Past Jhige, who held his gaze for only a moment before turning back to her husband, twining her arm around his thick waist tightly.

They walked down the shadowed road, his feet drunk and stumbling on the ruts in the dirt, while Nia strode beside him, straight-backed and poised, eyeing him from the side with a beguiling smile. He wanted to stop, to take a moment to memorize her against the backdrop of his town, but she slipped her hand down the front of his breeches, gripping his erection, and pulled him down the slight hill, behind a large rock, where she ground him into the earth with her hips, her hands pressed firm against his chest, forcing him to stay right there, his hands cupping her breasts, her waist, anything to keep him anchored to this dream, until it was over, and they lay together on the grass, naked and spent. She lay her head on his chest, a hand on his navel, her weight pinning him to the ground in a way that he liked. Both of them adrift on this moment. From a place of utter satisfaction, he began to hum a song. The song reserved for the end of a long day. When she asked him what it was he hummed, he told her about the song of homecoming. "It's what we sing on our way back from the fields when the work is done," he said. His fingers stroked the grain of her scalp. "The song of bargaining. *Take my day, but give me the night.*"

"It's pretty," she said with a sigh. "Sing it again."

And he did, looping the song onto itself like a string around his finger, a rope that hugged their bodies together, until she fell asleep. And as she slept, he listened to the night. The crackle of bugs. The breeze that whistled through the fields and lifted up into the sky. Her breath. The incoherent mumble of her dreams.

And he knew what it was he wanted.

He nudged her shoulder till she stirred.

"Can I come with you?" he asked.

Her eyes opened just enough to see the haze of him.

"Where?" she asked.

His heart galloped. "Anywhere."

She blinked once, and shut her eyes.

"Maybe," she murmured. She turned away, and pressed her back against his chest. "We'll speak in the morning."

"Okay," he said.

Kaeda listened to her snore in loud, rumbling breaths, but this too he loved. *They weren't just dreams*, he thought with pride. And soon, he drifted off as well, with his hand on her hip, where it was warm.

He woke to laughter.

It was midday. The sun was hot on his naked body. Two farmers, both men he knew, kicked his feet and told him it wasn't healthy sleeping outside with no clothes on. "You'll get bugs up your crack," they said. More laughter. Blearily he looked around. She was gone, the only proof of her the depression in the grass beside him. He yanked on his pants and sprinted toward the fields—"Bugs!" the farmers cackled—and arrived just in time to see the last of the ships lift off. The crowd of villagers that had come to see the departure waved goodbye at this last ship as it faded to a prick of light in the sky, before disappearing. The children shouted "Goodbye!" in chorus, as Kaeda's hands dropped to his sides, his heart unspooling beneath him. He didn't see his mother approach, not until she knocked his bare shoulder with a baffled expression. "Where is your shirt?" she asked. "Go put on your shirt, you stupid child!" And the other families chuckled as she pushed him out of the fields, back to the village, while he stumbled forth, knuckling his wet eyes.

He disappeared into his work. Two thumbs choked the dhuba seeds out of the stalk's throat. A machete cracked against the spine of the stalk; the beam bent at an angle; body weight took it the rest of the way. One hundred kilos of dhuba seeds spilled into five containers, the containers wheeled back to town, half the number placed in cold stasis, the other half sent to the mill, where callused fists ground the jellied seeds for hours into fine paste in a vaulted room filled with the sound of wet smacking and volleys of dirty jokes. The broken stalks were shaved of their sharp ends and painted red, bound together, and used to build houses for new families, of which there were more every year.

Jhige gave birth to twins. Kaeda was there, wetting the towels, studying the devotion of her husband, Yotto, who bowed penitent by her bed, whispering, "Soon, soon, soon," to her, shouting, "Now! Now! Now!" The babies came eventually. Healthy girls, seven pounds, each a proud owner of their mother's sharp nose. Kaeda congratulated the new parents, and as they cooed over the next generation, he stepped outside the doctor's hut and rang the bell to signal the success of the new birth. The toll was heard throughout the village. Candles were lit by dark windows. He glanced into the hut at Jhige and Yotto, and he sighed. Every week it seemed another friend was sprouting children of their own. The town spread down the hill, the houses spilling into the valley below. And every week, an old one dying, making way for the new.

Kaeda's father died one year after Nia left. It was a drunken accident. A friend had given him a playful shove, and he, in a stupor, lost his balance and snapped his neck on the edge of a wooden table. The man who killed him walked out of town that same night, overcome with guilt. He never returned. He was presumed dead when the next moisture season arrived, and with it the jawed beasts that stalked the surrounding hills and woods. "Good," Kaeda's mother said when she heard the news of the man's disappearance, and that was all she had to say on the matter. She returned to the dhuba stalks with her machete and curled lip, for there was still more work to be done. Stoic around the other villagers, she thanked them for their kind words, but refused to entertain their nostalgia, or their prayers. It was only after the fieldwork was done, and she was home, just her and her son, when she let loose her sorrow. She shouted, and she wept in Kaeda's arms, and filled that house with such mourning there was no room for her son's own grief, which he let harden like sediment on the bottom of his heart as he attended to his mother's tears. He curled into himself under his blanket at night, and retreated into memory. His father's warm shoulder the day they went to see the ships. A finger pointing up at the stars. He found his own places to cry. Places only Jhige was privy to, for they had begun to sleep together again.

The affair began a month after his father's death. Jhige had switched assignments with a friend, and for the first time in years worked alongside Kaeda in the fields. "To make sure you don't fall behind on your quota," she said when he asked her why she had switched, and though he tsked and told her he didn't need a caretaker, already he felt better. They worked in quiet, and with time, they began to reminisce about the games they had played as children.

"You convinced everyone that the night smelled sour because the moons were made of kiri fruit," she said.

"You knew the truth," he said.

"It didn't matter." She wiped the sweat off her chest and chuckled. "They preferred the lie." She picked up her bowl of seeds, then let out a long sigh, the weight of their history pressing all the air out of her lungs. "It was lonely, growing up around you."

"You were my only friend."

He said this more to himself. A quiet realization.

"That," she said, "I will never believe."

But she smiled anyway.

It was inevitable: days later, before they parted ways on the road back home, she grabbed his arm, and told him a time and a location, without saying what for, she did not need to. He was there, and he was ready. The fumbling of their youth was gone, now the measured movements of adults who knew the dance, and where the hands and feet must go. His hands fell through the bristled curls of her black hair and they made love on a bed of rumpled clothes. The moons were red that night. He told her the moons were red because they were burned by the heat of the sun, and she laughed, and shoved his bare shoulder, and whispered into his salty skin, "Shut up, shut up, shut up."

Three seasons of love passed.

Jhige's husband found out about the affair, whispered in his ear by a friend who had seen the two lovers one night in the millhouse. Yotto gave her a choice, and when she chose Kaeda, he marched to his challenger's house, pounded on the door, and no sooner was it opened than he threw Kaeda to the dirt, where they wrestled each other bloody until his mother stormed out of the house with a machete gripped in her right hand. The light from inside threw her broad body into harsh relief. She held the blade against Yotto's veined neck. "Let him up," she said. When the two men were on their feet once more, she lowered her blade. She told Yotto he was allowed one good hit, and no more, and before Kaeda had a chance to protest, a fist knocked him back on the ground with a spout of blood, and the husband walked away, throwing the rage off his shaking shoulders. Kaeda's mother stood over him and dropped the machete by his feet. "Fool," she said, and knelt, and with her sleeve rubbed the blood off his chin.

She brought him inside. Fed him.

"I loved your father," she said from across the table, her arms crossed over her chest. "But he died an idiot's death. I never forgave him for that. Promise me you won't make the same mistake, or your spirit will never be welcome in this house."

Quietly, he said, "I promise."

She gripped his hand.

And that was the end of it.

A month later, another house was built in the valley, where Kaeda and Jhige lived with her two daughters. From his old home, Kaeda moved his clothes, some furniture his mother insisted that he take with him, the glass jar of finger bones—he felt too guilty to leave them behind—and one wooden flute, which he told Jhige was a gift from an offworlder he had once met. He was thankful when she didn't pry further into its history. The instrument was kept out of sight, in one of the drawers of his bureau, and taken out when he was alone and feeling melancholy—but even then, it was never for long. He never played it.

For all their childhood, Yana and Elby would live in two homes, one at the bottom of the hill, and one near the top, never understanding the polite tension between their three parents when their father came to collect them on his free days, not until they were older. They got along with Kaeda. He couldn't have children—some bodies just can't, the doctor had said—but he treated them like they were his own. He never hit them or raised his voice, and he made them laugh with his silly faces. This excused the times he was distant; the nights they'd hear his footsteps wander throughout the house; the frantic pace of them, as if there were something he'd forgotten to do, but he couldn't remember what it was, or where.

When he was thirty-seven, the twelve green lines boomed across the red sky once more. He was there, in the crowd with the rest of the welcoming committee, as the violent gusts of wind heralded the ships' arrival. Jhige's girls, now eight years old, ran in circles around their mother while the offworlders emerged from the bellies of their ships. "Just look at the governor," Jhige said, nodding at their leader, who bowed before the offworlders as though they were gods. "He is the first to greet them, yet he almost never walks the fields, he never visits the homes; he is oblivious. Look at how low he bows. Like he is made of jelly." When she got no response, she turned to Kaeda. "What is it?" She touched his hand, breaking his gaze. "Where are you?" she asked, in a whisper.

He smiled too wide.

"I am here," he said.

It was easy enough to get away that night, for the girls never took long to tire and needed to be brought home early. Kaeda threw an arm around Sado's shoulders, drinking and laughing with his friends, playing the part of the reveler who was having too much fun to go home. When Jhige came to collect him, he told her the party was just beginning, and he considered himself a brilliant strategist when she relented and suggested that he stay, while she brought the girls back by herself. After he was certain she was gone, he excused himself from Sado's company under the guise of fetching more drink, and lost himself in the crowd. He crossed the bonfire plaza to the entrance of the alley. On the bench, Nia sat, watching him approach, studying him calmly, her face unmarked by time. She wore light-red clothes that fell over her body, as though she had washed herself under a melting moon. She was, as ever, beautiful. His stomach boiled just looking at her.

"You never said goodbye," he said.

Her eyebrow lifted, and her second voice said, "You're a handsome sleeper. Would've been a shame to wake you up." The second voice had by then lost its magic—he knew the truth of her technology. She shrugged, and her beaded necklace clinked against itself. "It didn't seem necessary, considering I'd see you again so soon."

"I've spent the last fifteen years hating you."

Her smile fell, her expression hardened. "Keep your hate," she said. "We spent one night together. Just one." She made a gesture with her hand he didn't understand, then looked away, into the fire. He saw something in her face he never thought he'd see. Exhaustion. "I'm not a god," she said. "I'm not here to answer your prayers."

He sat down beside her. The anger was there, but quieted.

"Why do you sit alone?" he asked.

"I like parties," she said, "but I don't like crowds."

He nodded, but he didn't understand.

"Do I look different?" he asked.

"There are mirrors for that," she snapped.

He sucked his teeth.

"I'm sorry," she said. "The journey here was hard." She rubbed her face, making valleys of her skin. "I said I was sorry."

"Fine," he said, too proud to say it was okay.

"I'm tired, Kaeda. I leave in twenty hours. I need to have a good time. Please make this easy for me."

"What do you want?"

"To spend the night with you."

He laughed.

"I do," she said. "You're attractive. More than those men, at least." She nodded toward Sado's table, the bachelor heads rotating slowly whenever a woman passed by. They both laughed, the laugh cut short when she put her hand on his. "And I like you."

His breath hitched.

He hated that.

How one touch from her could undo him.

They didn't walk through the celebration like last time. On Kaeda's suggestion, they walked farther down the alley, away from any eyes, and went off the main road. They headed toward the millhouse. Inside, they walked past the rows of troughs where the seeds were mashed, up the steps to the loft, behind bound piles of purple stalk spines. It was different from last time, or the same, with Kaeda noticing new aspects of her; like how she refused to make eye contact when he was inside her, as though he was not there, or she was not there, she on some other planet, loving some other person. But despite her distance, still he gasped and bucked and held her like she was his own beating heart.

"Look," she said when it was over, and they lay together, exhausted. She stretched his pubic hair between the comb of her fingers. He asked her what was wrong. "You have some gray," she whispered.

She sounded almost sad.

In the morning, he offered to walk her back to the plains, but she touched his arm and told him she would prefer to go back alone. So he returned to the plaza, where he helped clean the trash from last night. He beat the cushions free of crumbs and fell in step with the others as they carted the bowls to the river to be washed. When overhead he heard the sky crack, heralding the departure of the ships, he did not look up. Wouldn't. Not until the last of the green lines had faded away and it was safe to miss her again.

His mother passed away in her sleep at the end of the moisture season. It was her heart. A neighbor found her with one of his father's old sandals gripped in her fist, which she had up until that night kept by the front door, as if at any moment the old man might return from the fields looking for them. Kaeda lit the pyre and tossed her ashes down into the moisture pits, and with those ashes his guts followed like lengths of rope, whipping into the dark below.

He slept that night with his head on Jhige's lap. She stroked his hair as she hummed the old songs they used to sing as children. The songs children learn from their mothers, to help them make peace with the dark.

The dead were remembered, and the living went on. Soon their daughters were old enough to work. Elby, the stronger and more serious of the two, joined the hunters, and Yana, the talker, cracked her knuckles and set to work in the millhouse.

They were not the only ones with new assignments. After a back injury had rendered him useless in the fields—thrown out after he'd carried a heavy container of seed—Kaeda was assigned to the collections building, where he manned one of the seed scales, tallying the weights of the containers the farmers brought him. He worked around the growing paunch of his belly, distended from large plates of meats and pastry, his sweet tooth another new discovery with age. Yotto visited often, the violent past between them now settled. They were even able to joke about the time, years ago, when they fought in the dirt for Jhige's love.

It was late into the moisture season when Yotto sat on Kaeda's work table, fiddling with his hands, and asked him about their daughters. "Have they said anything to you? About . . . men?"

Kaeda shook his head, finding the man's worry amusing. He told Yotto there was nothing to worry about, even though he knew Yana had her eye on one of the hunters; he saw no reason to trouble the man with things he could not change. "Best you keep your mind on other things," he said.

Comforted, but not ready to leave, Yotto picked at the gray in his beard and asked how much longer Kaeda planned on working in collections. "You shouldn't be here," he said. "You were born for the fields. Everyone knows it."

"Soon as my back is ready, I'll be out there again," Kaeda assured.

But when his back healed a month later, he remained with collections, having discovered that he liked being able to sit and rest. There he made the tallies while Jhige continued to squeeze the fields, her body a livewire network of muscle and tendon. When she lifted her containers up onto Kaeda's scale, she would prop her elbow on his desk and brag about how long she had outlasted him on the field. "One year and five days," she said, when he was forty-nine. "Two years and twenty," she said, when he was fifty.

"Three and eighty," he said, cutting her off with a smirk, when he was fifty-one.

She leaned across the desk and kissed him on the corner of his mouth. "I win," she whispered, for even after all this time, their rivalry was still strong.

When he was fifty-two, at the end of the dry season, he sat on a bench in the plaza, alone, while the others attended Shipment Day in the fields. He wanted Jhige, Yotto, and their daughters to enjoy the event together without him, for once. In the plaza he watched the propping open of the long tables, and the building of the fire pit, and he wondered what Nia would think of him, now that his hair was a thick shock of white and his once work-hardened muscles were now hidden beneath a layer of sedentary fat.

Later that night, when the fire was at its peak, and they sat together at one of the long tables, still easing into conversation, he asked her this. She was younger than him by sixteen years now. Never had her youth been more apparent. Perhaps that was what she was thinking about as she studied him while rubbing her smooth cheek. "You look very distinguished," she said.

"And you," he said, "like yesterday."

She smiled. "How long have you been waiting to use that line on me?"

"Five years," he admitted.

They laughed, and after a toast, drank their bowls of spirits.

That was the last night they slept together. He had enough in him for one bout. As they lay in the chill night, clothed, he too cold to be naked, he wondered aloud how difficult it must be, to always be moving, always arriving at a place where your lovers were either old or dead. She told him it wasn't difficult at all. And as her left hand formed and re-formed a fist, she said that the day she stopped moving would be the day that she died. She turned her head toward him, her brow knit, and asked him why he was laughing. He wiped his eyes and told her he didn't know, though in truth he did, but didn't wish to share the reason for fear of insulting her: that her words were absurdly dramatic. She was content to let the moment pass. Come the next morning, they parted without saying goodbye; both knew they would meet again soon.

When the governor passed away from a stroke the following dry season, it was time to hold the ruling elections. It surprised no one but Kaeda when he was elected. He had unwittingly begun his political ascent during his tenure in the collections building, where as he tallied the container weights the farmers learned his name, and spoke with him, and trusted him as one of their own, whose purple palms told the story of his field experience. He ran against the son of the deceased governor, an ineffectual man who ran solely out of the familial pressures of his aunts and uncles, who were hungry for a dynasty. It was clear from the outset which way the vote would swing; the governor's son bowed out of the race before the final votes were even tallied, and spent the rest of the night in the bar claiming that the election was rigged from the start, buying drinks for anyone who would listen, though the few who entertained him were either not convinced or didn't care. "My father was right in the end," Kaeda said to Jhige the day they moved into the governor's house on the top of the hill. "This place is mine." He tossed the jar of finger bones into the moisture pits that afternoon, where it joined the rest of the dead, the prophecy fulfilled.

As governor, he made annual visits to the other villages to meet with the other leaders to discuss trade agreements and field borders. Monthly coordination meetings with the appointed heads of the millhouse workers, the hunters, and the traders, paired with weekly one-on-one meetings to listen to gripes the heads had with one another and with him. And daily, at seemingly every hour, there was someone knocking on his door, a villager in need of mediation for whatever neighborly territorial dispute was waged that day, his house the new temple of grievances. All this he attended, including the walks through the fields, the first cutting of the hunted flank, the harvest speeches and benedictory words for all the newly born children. By day's end he was drained, as was Jhige from her work in the fields, and when the sun was down and the air was cool, they would sit together on the porch and say nothing, staring blankly out at the village that was theirs, Jhige gazing at the sections of field still to be tended, while Kaeda's gaze was lifted higher, at the field of stars, tired beyond measure, and wondering what could've been, had he been wiser in his youth—had he chosen his words with more care.

Months would pass without his noticing.

On Nia's penultimate arrival, he gave his speech to the gathered crowd on the sacrifice the offworlders made, traversing time and space to spread their harvest. When the sky cracked and the green lines arrived and all the children whose names he didn't know gazed up at the approach of ships with widened eyes, he was overcome not with nostalgia but an intense worry for these children, and the years of reckoning that lay before them. He wanted to warn these children that time was not their friend; that though today might seem special, there would be a tomorrow, and a day after that; that the best-case scenario of a well-spent life was the slow and steady unraveling of the heart's knot. But he held his tongue. He let them enjoy the lights. "Let us welcome them with open arms," he said.

Nia almost didn't recognize him when she emerged from her ship, not until she was close enough to shake his sixty-seven-year-old hand. Her eyes widened, but only just, at the liver spots.

"It's nice to see you," she said.

They spoke by the fire like old friends. Commiserated about the difficulties of leadership. How draining it was to run a ship, a village. Took turns refilling each other's bowls. They fell into an easy quiet, as they enjoyed the heat lick of the flame, and the bitter-strong taste of their drink, the anxiety Kaeda had felt earlier in the day settling down as he sat beside her and admired the dancers and the bonfire as it wavered through the hours. And when it was time, she gave him a brief hug before she returned to her ship, the warmth of it remaining even after she had left him.

He returned to Jhige at the long table, a little startled when, as she rubbed the lobe of her right ear between thumb and index finger, she observed that he and the offworlder seemed close. But she said this with no jealousy in her voice, the smile she wore one of amusement. A simple, matter-of-fact statement that cleaved him in two.

"No, not close," he said, stealing a last glance at Nia as she walked away from the fire. "We've met only a few times."

They would meet only once more, on his eighty-second year.

The year the sky broke, and the Fifth Village received an unexpected visitor.

It was the moisture season, and still many months to come before Shipment Day, and with it, Nia's last cycle. The village was quiet but for the wing-rattle of night bugs and the distant howls from the forest. Kaeda was asleep in the governor's house, his eyelids fluttering, dreaming of the day his father took him to see the ships, when he woke to a sonic boom that rattled the shutters. He sat up, dazed, unsure if he was still dreaming until Jhige's trembling hand found his in the dark. He grabbed his cane by the bed. When they stepped out onto the porch, they saw it—a ball of fire peeling across the sky. The two of them watched with stolen breath as the ball arced downward and landed in the fields south of the village with an impact so great that it shook the earth.

A crowd had already formed in the plaza when they arrived. Amid the crying children and the parents who demanded answers Kaeda found Elby. He sent her and the other hunters to investigate the crash, the smoke of which he could see rising above the roofs in the dark distance. Elby sprinted off while he and Jhige went around to each family to calm them and assure them that they would be safe. The wait for news was endless. He sat on one of the benches, rubbing the ache from his knees, worried for his daughter, until she and her hunters returned through the village gates, carrying with them the body of a naked child.

It was a boy. His body was the only one they found at the site. All else was hot and black. "He was just there," Elby said, "lying next to the rubble."

Bruised and bleeding, but not broken, the boy was brought to the doctor's house, where his glancing wounds were cleaned with wet cloth and wrapped in soft bandages.

He was a small, skinny thing—no older than twelve. Cheeks gaunt, his flesh so emaciated Kaeda winced, worried that if the boy tried to stand, his leg bones would snap in half. But there was no fear of him standing, for the boy was in a deep sleep, unstirred even by the loud and frantic conversation of everyone around him.

For three days the boy slept in the bed of the doctor's hut while rumor spread through the village of his identity, be it demon, demigod, or harbinger of war; rumors born from nothing but fearful imagination, gaining weight and truth as they spread throughout the homes, from mouth to ear. Kaeda paid little mind to the rumors, and continued his visitations to the doctor's hut despite the warnings of his advisers. "They once called me cursed," he said to the sleeping child, holding up his scarred hand for proof. "Best not to listen to what they say. There's no end to the stories that cowards tell."

On the third day the boy woke from his long rest. Kaeda heard the toll of the doctor's bell from across the village and shouldered his way into the hut, moving people aside with his cane, into the sickroom, where he found the child curled into himself at the foot of the bed, arms hugging his knees to his gaunt, brown chest, as the leader of the millhouse bombarded him with questions of where he was from and what he wanted. The boy was unresponsive. He sat with his back pressed against the board, peering at the strangers from above the ridge of his smooth forearms with eyes as wild as his knotted black hair. The millhouse leader's voice rose with each question, red-throated, until Kaeda had had enough, and he ushered everyone outside, where he was swiftly surrounded.

Every villager was in attendance. All of them shouting variations on the same theme: that the boy was trouble and that he did not belong here. Shouting, until Kaeda raised his hand and silenced them. He looked out into the crowd. Of course they were frightened, he thought. This was their village's first unexpected arrival since the time before Shipment Days. Even he did not know what to do. "I understand how you are all feeling right now. I feel the same way. I assure you that the child is only a temporary presence. Come Shipment Day we will hand him over to the offworlders. But until then we must remain calm, and remind ourselves that he is only a child."

"Shipment Day is three months from now," Goro, one of the fishers, said. "Who'll keep him till then?"

The villagers exchanged glances while the dry grass skittered against the hot breeze.

"I will," Kaeda said.

Jhige was less than thrilled when her husband returned to their home with the offworlder at his side. She gestured for the boy to wait in the living room and pulled Kaeda into their bedroom, where she let him know through whisper-shouts how furious she was that he had not consulted with her first. She listened to his apologies without expression; the explanation of his frustration with the others, and how they were so quick to judge the character of an unconscious child. And when he was done, she made a hard line with her mouth, and he worried that his words had made no impact, until she muttered, "Go see if he's hungry."

In truth he had always intended to be the one to take the boy in, ever since the night of his arrival, as he had a difficulty resisting anything that came from the sky.

Living with the boy was an adjustment for them both. He did not seem to understand their language, and never spoke in his own; a mute presence in their home, deaf to their attempts to help him. The first time he had to go to the bathroom, he relieved himself in his bed. Jhige washed the sheets while Kaeda showed him to the outdoor pots and pantomimed how to use them. He was unlike any child Kaeda had met. His movements were small and exact, his footfalls almost inaudible. It was easy to forget he was there at all, Kaeda remembering only when he would hear a small cough from the corner of the room and would see the boy covering his mouth with both hands, his shoulders trembling, as if expecting a beating.

They had fewer guests those days. Yana refused to pass the threshold of the house. Even Elby, fearless hunter that she was, made a point not to linger in the same room as the boy for too long. "The others are right," she whispered, as she glanced into the living room, where the child stared out the window at the sky, as if he had never seen a sky before. As if it were impossible. "There's something not right about him."

"He's a little odd," Kaeda conceded. He rubbed the old scar on his hand. "But odd isn't bad."

The boy's oddness was intriguing. Kaeda took the child with him on his long, rambling walks beyond the village, both to give Jhige some air, and to scratch at the mystery of him, and see if he could not make some connection. It was a game of sorts. The boy followed him without resistance, almost unconsciously, snapping from his trance only when Kaeda would reach into his satchel and hand him a sweetcake.

During those walks, Kaeda spoke enough for the both of them. First there were the gentle, probing questions. Questions of where the boy was from, if he had family. And then, when it was clear that the boy would offer no answers, Kaeda spoke about himself. He started with the simple facts. As they climbed the foothills with his cane and the quiet boy's careful footstep, he shared the names of his parents, and how he had known Jhige since he was a child. How he was governor, and that it was his job to keep everyone safe. Over the days, and weeks, the longer they walked, the more he shared, as if the boy were an empty bowl that he was pouring his memories and thoughts into, all with the knowledge that the bowl did not understand, or nod, or question. In the twilight hours above the fields he indulged in sentimental thoughts; thoughts Jhige often teased him for, but that the boy took in as he did the breeze and the light. Childhood adventures in the yellow fields. The difficult harvests. And quietly, at dusk, in a murmur, the fears he'd carried with him over the years.

"This is the only sunset I've ever known," he said one afternoon, smiling as he pulled grass from the dirt and twirled the dry blades around his fingers. "I'm lucky it's a pretty one." Words that glanced off the boy without impact as he chewed his cake and stared past the red sky at a point Kaeda could not see.

It was late in the afternoon, the two of them sitting on the cleft of a hill, watching the deep red approach of night, when they heard the music.

From beyond the tree line came the farmers, marching down the dirt road with the containers of dhuba, singing the song of homecoming. They seemed to march directly from out of Kaeda's memory. He was swiftly caught up in himself, wracked with emotion as he listened to the melody's swell, delivered by farmers young and strong, his eyes tearing up at the words *Take my day, but give me the night*. He sniffed, and wiped his face. It was only then that he glanced at the boy, remembering that he was not alone, and he saw something surprising: the boy's eyes were shut, and his ear tilted toward the song, as if he were basking in it.

"So you like music," Kaeda said with a smile.

When they returned home, he brought the flute out from its dusty corner of the bureau. The boy was confused by the object until Kaeda demonstrated for him a trill of notes, inspiring in the boy a startle of widened eyes, his hands reaching out toward the instrument.

This was how the flute lessons began. Kaeda taught him how to play when he had the time; how to hold it, how to purse the lips, and as he taught, he would remember with winces of pleasure and regret the image of Nia at the entrance of the alley, her musical silhouette. He taught the boy the old songs.

He was a quick study, even with the language barrier. It was clear he was an experienced hand with music, if not with the flute. It wasn't long until he exceeded Kaeda's skill—a matter of days, much to the old man's delight and jealousy—and was able to play new songs, ones that Kaeda had never heard before, and were beautiful in their own right. Jhige was touched when the boy played for her a sweet and sad tune one evening, and when Yana stopped by with a fresh supply of food and she heard the music coming from the boy's room, for the first time in months she crossed the threshold and sat at the table to listen for a while.

Kaeda had only intended to lend the boy the flute. It was not a gift. But the flute remained on the boy's lap when they ate, and he took it with him into his room when he slept, and as the house swelled with his song, Kaeda's mood darkened with the petty thought that the flute had betrayed him, that it had used him to get to its true owner. He knew this to be true the day Jhige referred to it as "the boy's flute."

"It's not his," he snapped.

Jhige stared at him.

The music infiltrated his ears at night. It brought forth nightmares of Nia, at the foot of his bed with tears in her eyes as she asked him where the gift she had given him had gone; of him assuring her that he had kept it with him for all these years, and that he could prove it, if he could just find the damn thing; nightmares of him upturning his house, ripping out the floorboards, scoring the mattress with his machete, until he woke up with his hands clawing at the air. On the worst of these nights he stumbled out of his bedroom still half dreaming, using the wall for support as he limped down the hall, and had gotten so far as to twist the knob of the boy's bedroom door, thinking he just wanted to see the flute, to hold it one last time, make sure it was safe, before he was stopped by the sound of muffled weeping from inside the room, and he emerged from his half-dreaming state and backed away from the door. He returned to his bed empty-handed, hoping that his acceptance of the situation would bring easy sleep. But in the morning, he felt much the same. Tired.

His pockets empty.

He did his best to hide his distress from the boy. Forced smiles when there was no reason to, and he cooked up many sweetcakes for him to eat while his own appetite shrank. During meals he shuffled his extra food onto the boy's plate and watched him eat. And at night, as Jhige stroked his hair, she asked him the question she always asked when he was in such a mood; where he was, and where he was going. To which he would give the same answer he had always given.

I am here, I am here.

The flute song wafted through the moisture season, and brought down the dry, until the dirt crumbled and the stalks turned brittle under the hard sun; the village holding its collective breath for the approach of the offworlders, and their release of this stranger, while Kaeda waited out his days in dread.

When the sky cracked and the green lines broke across the wisped clouds, he knew this was most likely the last Shipment Day he would ever witness. The last time he would meet Nia Imani. In the fields, after he gave the welcome speech he had rehearsed on his walks the weeks leading up to this moment, he coughed phlegm into his sleeve and wondered why now, at the end, he wanted nothing more than to get on one of those ships and leave with her; why this desire still lay dormant in his heart after all this time; why it still flared bright. Nia hugged him when she left her ship. She was younger and stronger than ever, and he felt so small in her arms. When she released him, he made his request, and was surprised when she told him, without a moment's thought, that she would take the boy. "Interesting," he said, smiling a little. "I was expecting more resistance."

"And why is that?" she asked, returning his smile with one of her own.

"You never struck me as the generous type."

Her smile wavered. The old hurts were returning, and he could not help himself. "I'm sorry," he said finally.

"It's fine." Nia shifted her bag over her shoulder and walked toward the village, where the party would soon be held. "Consider it repayment for the company."

Come the bonfire, they spoke only briefly—plans of where to meet tomorrow for the handoff of the child. Nia kept her company with the other offworlders while Kaeda remained with his own at the long tables, glancing at her from the other side of the fire, hoping that their eyes would connect and give him an opening to apologize for his behavior earlier that day. But she never looked at him, not once, and was gone before he could find the courage, or the time, to approach her on his own.

He did not sleep that night. He paced the halls of the house, passing the door to the boy's bedroom, until morning.

It was a brutally hot day. The heat like a weight on his back as he made his way to the village plaza, where Nia waited for him. The villagers sweeping up the ash pit and clearing the tables snuck glances at the two of them as he approached her. He nodded to her, and she nodded back. And though now he had her full attention, he did not know what to say. A whole night of thinking, preparing for some grand speech, some resolution, but the words were gone.

"Where is he?" she asked.

"This way," he said.

They climbed the steepening path to his house. He struggled with his cane, but refused the assistance of her offered arm. He was short of breath when they reached the top, his heart full and pushing against the lax muscles of his chest. He showed her to the living room, where the boy stood with the travel bag at his feet, packed with spare robes, some cakes, and other things Kaeda thought the boy might like to own. He was about to ask Nia if she would like a drink, but before he had the chance, she picked up the boy's bag and headed for the door with a hand on the child's back. Kaeda followed them. She spared a glance at his cane, and said, "You don't have to come down with us. We can say our goodbyes here."

"No," he said. "I will come. I can manage."

"If you're sure."

The three of them walked through the village, past the wary eyes of the other villagers, while Kaeda struggled to keep up with Nia's quick pace. The boy didn't so much as look back at him to make sure he was still there. Kaeda grimaced through the joint pain.

It was all falling through his hands.

In the field of yellow grass, where the ships waited, and where the last of the dhuba was carried off, the two offworlders turned toward him. Nia told him it was time. Kaeda nodded, and put his hand on the boy's shoulder, and told him he had enjoyed their brief time together. He smiled at the boy in a way that only adults were capable of, one that was at once happy and sad and full, his grip on the boy's shoulder tightening as he told him how lucky he was to go with her. The boy stared at him blankly, the old man's words beyond him; words that were increasingly choked with tears as it dawned on Kaeda that he had never stood this close to the hangar doors of Nia's ship before.

He had never felt the cool air seeping out of the ship's dark maw. Never smelled that peculiar lace of fresh metals, or heard the idle rumbling of its belly and the snap of its folded sails as the posts swayed in the wind. Nia asked him if he was all right with such startling kindness that he was seven years old again, and he was twenty-two, and he was thirty-seven, his whole life sandwiching into this one moment, startling him with a powerful need to take her hand and walk into the ship and fly away and live the dream of his youth. He slapped the wetness from his eyes. *No!* he thought. *I'm happy! I'm happy!* He gave the boy a pat on the head and he shook Nia's hand and wished her safe travels, words chipped carelessly from a mountain of impotence, before returning to his home, his namesake. A long walk punctuated by the sound of the ship smacking the sky, its green trail dissolved by night, no remnant of its passing, only the red moon swollen with kiri juice when Kaeda shut the windows and eased himself into bed beside his old friend. He gazed at her. The dream was gone, and only now, at the end of the day, was he awake. And as Jhige wondered aloud where the boy had gone, he took her hand and pressed his face into her coarse palm, comforted by the skin callused by the days of work. The sweet smell of the harvest. The taste of a banquet. And he told her, "I'm here, I'm here," and he kissed her like they were young again, behind a storage shack in the conspiratorial dark, no lick of flame to distract him. Nothing but the two of them, while in the vaulted dark above their sky, in her ship of cloth and metal, Nia opened the boy's travel bag and found among the folded clothes and wrapped pastries a long-forgotten object—unable to breathe as she held the flute in her trembling hands, and felt in its cracks the decades.

2

The Flute from Macaw

"Sneaky bastard," Nia muttered, as the flute slipped from her fingers and dropped into the travel bag. She stood up from her crouch with a smile even she did not understand, and palmed the sweat off her brow, her skin hot to the touch. Feverish. It was when the pressure began to bubble behind her eyes that she knew what was happening. She gave the quiet boy in the corner of the room a curt nod before she stumbled out of the hatch, gripping the causeway railing for support as she made her way to the ship's lav, the veins thick in her neck. She slammed the door shut behind her and doubled over the toilet. Counted out the beats in her head as she breathed, and with each breath returned the paste in her veins to liquid, and the drumbeat in her ears to a melted drone, until the Compression Panic left her system and she was able to smother it, this sudden sense of lost time.

She grimaced, ashamed that, even after her many routes through the fold, time loss could still get to her; that it could still startle her from behind and squeeze the air from her lungs. She cleared her throat and spat into the toilet. Flicked on the faucet. Splashed cold water on her neck. The walls were throbbing, but she told herself it would soon pass; that the ocean waves would settle and she would stand on solid ground again. This was known territory.

But for the rest of the afternoon the effects of the attack lingered. A ball of fingers in her gut as she moved through the ship, checking in on her crew while they prepared for the coming fold into the Pocket. She nodded through a joke Durat had learned from the dhuba farmers the night before, and she made use of the railing as she walked herself across the ship to the medica, where Nurse was performing her diagnostic tests on the boy and delivering him any needed vaccinations.

The boy was perched on the edge of the metal table, with the flute gripped tight in his right hand while Nurse asked him simple questions about his health and history. He nodded, and shook his head, to the questions.

Yes. He felt fine.

No. He did not know where he was.

Yes. He had a name.

No. He could not write it.

No. He did not know how to write.

No.

No family.

Outside the medica, she and Nurse spoke in hushed tones about their newest crew member.

"So he understands Station Standard?" Nia asked.

"Yes," Nurse said as her eyes fixed on a bead of sweat trickling down her captain's temple, "but he seems unable to speak it. Or won't."

Nia thumbed away the sweat. "Won't?"

"Might be he just needs more time. He's been through a lot. Long past of broken bones: legs, arms, even his ribs. Signs of repeated fractures, none of them caused by the crash. Too healed for that. Nothing is broken now, nothing physical, but mentally"—she glanced at him through the hatchway—"the only person who knows how bad it is, is him." She leaned against the wall, as if weighted by her own sense of empathy. "He might speak, he might not. Some trauma patients take a while to find their voice again."

"They found him months ago. How much more time does he need?"

"You know I can't answer that." Then, "Captain—Nia, are you all right?"

"I'm fine," she said, self-conscious as she wiped her shirtsleeve against her damp face. The boy played a quick note on the flute. A piercing F. She winced.

"I would suggest not worrying about him too much," Nurse said. "There are facilities on Pelican. He'll be taken care of by people trained for such situations. And in the meantime, the flute should keep him occupied." She hummed. "It's funny. You have one just like it, don't you?"

"I did. I gave it to him," Nia lied. She was in no mood to explain the story of Kaeda. "I thought it'd be something he could play with."

Nurse smiled. Surprised. "That was kind of you," she said.

Kaeda's words rang in her ears: *You never struck me as the generous type.* "I can be kind," Nia said.

"I didn't say—"

"Captain," Durat interrupted over the intercom, "ship's ready to fold on your order."

"I'll be right there," she told him. Then, to Nurse, "Can you bring him back to his room when you're done?"

"Of course," she said. "And Nia. About tonight?" She made a subtle drinking gesture with her right hand.

Nia placed a hand on her stomach. "Later this week, maybe."

Nurse chuckled. "Now I know you aren't feeling all right."

An understatement. It was like she had swallowed a bag of glass. With a hand on the wall railing, she made her way to the cockpit and sat down in the copilot's chair, leaning back with eyes shut as Durat told her all the things he would do, and the people he would do, during their furlough on Pelican Station. "Did I tell you the joke the dhuba farmers told me?" he asked. "Yes," she said. But he told her again anyway. One-armed man goes hunting with his nephew, it began. And as he explained to her for the second time that day why it was funny that the nephew ended up in bed with the one-armed man's wife, she rubbed one hand against the armrest of her chair, centering herself on the tactile sensation, and told herself that what happened in the boy's room was just a trick of body chemistry, an explainable thing, and because it was explainable, it was something she could control. She told herself this, and many other stories, as she gave Durat the go-ahead, and he in turn gave Baylin confirmation to pull the rip cord, and the ship began to sandwich in on itself, like an infinitely folding sheet of paper, until they had left that reality and entered the next, where the sails billowed open in great swells and rocketed along the energetic waves of the Diffident Current.

Let me finish this contract and move on, Nia thought sickly as her boat rode the black waves. *Let this last leg be easy.*

But then, like a curse answered, the music began.

It started an hour after the fold. The crew was still shaking off the wobble effect, stretching out their jaws, vomiting in the lav, when they heard the thin, reedy notes of the boy's flute coming in through the vents. It was fine in the beginning, most of the crew agreeing that the boy was very talented. The problem was the music didn't stop. Their guest played regardless of the hour, and since the *Debby* was an old gossip of a ship and carried sounds from hatch to hatch with giddy talent, nowhere was safe.

The flute song had a life of its own. It seeped into the kitchen from behind the cold-stasis container, and drifted across the counter into the common room, where it lay over the sofas and the shelf filled with old books. It fell through the grates to the engine room, following the tendrils of thick cable that ran straight to the heart of the ship, where the fold-core clicked its brassy gears, and where the engineer sat on the workbench, so distracted by the music that he stripped the wrong wire and killed the backlights under the causeway grating. It flumed through the c-path vents, into the cavernous cargo bay, around the twenty crates stuffed with purple seed and the veteran who sat cross-legged on a mat, scowling at the music as it kicked her out of her meditations. Leaked into the cockpit, where the pilot leaned back on his throne, his legs kicked up on the console, eyelid twitching as the music disrupted his dreams of sexual exploits. And it whispered through the cracks of the paneled walls, into the captain's quarters, where it found Nia sitting at her desk, staring up at the air around her as she listened to the music that haunted the *Debby*, wondering why the notes put her at ease, and how it could be that she did not hate it.

It was in the cargo bay where the music was loudest, and where the veteran was most tormented. The sounds of the *Debby* trended downward, collecting like sediment among the crates and catwalks of the bay; an ecosystem of sound, amplified by the concave walls and the cathedral ceiling. Footsteps and plate clatter and muffled causeway conversations—the white noise of ship life the veteran had no problem phasing out when she rolled out her mat, sat with pretzeled legs, and fell inward, unfurling in her mind the bloodied knots of her post-trauma. This was the hour in the day Sonja most looked forward to. The hour she could breathe. But with the white noise now came the music, and she soon found she could not phase it out, for unlike the step and clatter of the crew, the music had shape, and story. It had pain. It shattered the temple of peace she made for herself in her meditations, and left behind only her agitations. She cursed. She stormed the causeways, proclaiming her displeasure as she banged plates in the kitchen when she was making her meals. She went further. When Nia got word that she'd kicked the boy's door one night to get him to stop, she confronted her in the cargo bay, interrupting her railing pull-ups with a single warning. "I'm only going to tell you once. Do not kick our guest's door again."

Sonja let go of the railing, her boots thudding onto the grating below. "I was trying to get some sleep."

"You have plugs. Use them."

"Plugs. I have plugs." Sonja slapped her towel over her shoulder, her face screwed up like she was about to let fly some choice words, before she saw Nia's humorless smile and checked herself, blunting her sharp tone. She was nothing if not respectful of hierarchy. "It's not just me, Captain," she said, looking away. "The others won't say it, but they're just as pissed as I am."

"None of them kicked his door."

"Someone will."

Nia knew she was right. The proof was in Durat's sleep-deprived eyes, and Baylin's skittered mind as he fumbled through his repairs of the rotting ship. When she met with Baylin to discuss his work for the week, she learned of all the tasks he had fallen behind on; the tertiary lav door that was still jammed and the fried sublights of the causeway. "And the Grav?" she muttered. "Please tell me you haven't forgotten about the Grav."

"I didn't forget," he said. "But it's not fixed."

Nia breathed through her nose. "I thought you said you'd fix it."

"I tried. But it's old—can only do so much. We'll need to buy a replacement when we get to Pelican."

"Will we be safe till then?"

The young man nodded, playing nervously with some small oblong tool in his gummed-up hands. "Worst that should happen is some light carbonation—zero-G bubbles popping up around the ship. Expect a few lunches to float off your plate, but that should be the extent of it." In a small voice, he added, "I hope."

She sighed. "Add it to the requisitions list."

"Yes, Captain."

Before she walked up the steps that led out of the engine room, she turned. Said, "You're the most important person on this ship. We don't fly if you don't."

He blushed. "I understand."

"So be honest: Is the boy's music distracting you?"

He smiled confidently. "I've lived in loud places all my life," he said. "This is nothing."

But she saw the truth behind his words. The hesitation before the smile. She climbed the steps with a sigh, knowing something would have to be done about the music, and that it would have to be done soon.

But not yet.

She was still listening.

The music played while she made him his meals. Before they left Umbai-V, Kaeda had told her the boy liked sweet things, so she served him a bowl of sweet rice for breakfast, and flavored nutrient porridge with zucar for lunch. Dinner was reconstituted vegetables and vat-meat slices, with a candied fruit for dessert. Three times a day she brought him his meal, and would lean against the wall and observe him as he ate his food one-handed, his free hand gripping the flute. They wouldn't speak during these meals, or make eye contact, and when he was done eating, she would gather his plates and slot them into the kitchen wash like giant coins while from the vent above her head she would hear the opening notes to his song. The terrible, insistent beauty of it.

The music was her constant companion. It was there when she exercised with Sonja, or chatted with Durat in the cockpit, or read old books in her quarters. Sometimes she would stop what she was doing and just listen. Would allow the music to seep into the folds of her and bring forth thoughts of Kaeda. Would relive the midnight memories of sweat on skin, and the taste of his mouth sweetened by a lifetime of dhuba—memories that were paired with the dark suspicion that he had returned the flute to her as an insult.

No one knew about their affair, not even Nurse, who prided herself on being the captain's closest confidante. During their clandestine drinking session near the end of the week, when the lights were off and they were the last two women awake within millions of kilometers, sipping bourbon from tin cups and playing a few hands of Tropic Shuffle by the light of Nia's desk lamp, Nia made no mention of Kaeda. She let Nurse lead the conversation.

"I'll deal," Nurse said, shuffling the cards.

The games were played in quiet as Nia worked through troubling thoughts. And though Nia knew all of Nurse's obvious tells— the way she rubbed the material of her sari between finger and thumb when she had a good hand—that night she was too distracted to use this knowledge to her advantage, surprising them both as she lost each of the rounds. "You've lost your edge," Nurse said as she poured herself a winner's cup.

Nia smiled weakly. "Just giving an old woman her due handicap."

"How kind you are. Another round then." She gave Nia the warning look. "*Without* help."

After the last hand was dealt and Nia had lost for good, she swallowed the rest of her bourbon, held the glass to her lips, and said, "You're staring at me."

"You have a face worth staring at," Nurse said.

Nia smiled. "Say what it is you want to say."

"Even if it's the obvious?"

"I could use obvious right now."

"Something has to be done about the music," Nurse said. "We all know this." She slid the cards back into the box. "There are compassionate ways of putting a stop to it. The boy may not be able to speak, but he understands us well enough. We can set up certain times in the day that he's allowed to play, decide areas in the ship where the sounds don't travel so far. But I know this has already occurred to you." She tossed the box of cards onto the desk and looked into Nia's eyes. "You're stalling."

"You're right," Nia said.

"So she admits it," Nurse said playfully, "but she doesn't say why."

"The why is . . . difficult." Nia was about to pour herself another glass, but stopped as soon as she touched the bottle. "I realized something recently."

"What did you realize?"

"I'd forgotten what day my sister had died." Nia smiled, embarrassed, but Nurse was attentive, and nodded for her to continue. "Something I should remember, right? I checked once, years ago. Saw the day and date on the Feed. Thought I'd carry that number with me till the end . . . but I just let myself forget." She gazed into the lamplight, the burn of bulb on her retina, the echo of a young woman's shout as she begged Nia not to leave. A little sister who grew up without her; an entire life, spent and emptied, while Nia whittled away the years in the Pocket, running as far as she could from home. The day she learned her sister had died decades her senior was the first time she experienced Compression Panic. She thought that day would stick to her heart like a tumor. But somehow it receded, became just another shadow in the attic. One among many. She sighed. "I've let myself forget a lot of things."

"Like what?" Nurse asked.

Like the flute, she wanted to say, but the moment was over, and her heart's door shut without ceremony. "I'm sorry," she said with an awkward smile. "I don't know where that came from." When Nurse reached out to touch her hand, she pulled away. "I think I'm going to call it for the night."

At the hatch, Nurse stopped the door from closing with her hand.

"Please," she said. "For my sake, if not yours. Take it easy on yourself."

"I will," Nia promised. "And congratulations on winning the game."

"I don't think my wins tonight count." Nurse walked down the dark causeway, back to her hatch, a hand raised in good night. "Save your congratulations for when I earn it."

Nia returned to her desk, rubbing the bourbon throb from her brain as she flicked on the lamp. She opened a fresh notebook, in the mood to write. During their last voyage to Pelican Station, she had struck up a conversation with a historian in one of the greenery pubs on Schreiberi Wing, who with wild red eyes taught her the craft of the haiku, claiming such art would open her senses and make her more receptive to the spirit channels that were woven into the station transmission signals by beings they could not see. Now there were journals on her desk filled with practice poems, some better than others, and most, in her opinion, terrible. But regardless of skill or spirit channel, she'd discovered that she liked writing the damn things. The words helped her organize the hurricane. And so, that night, she put pencil to paper, and wrote:

The flute from Macaw,
Cheaply made and out of tune,
~~Was a terrible~~
~~Was without~~
Had no

She tore the sheet from the notebook, ripped it up into many pieces. Dropped the confetti into the wastebasket. She had started a new piece when she noticed in her periphery the shreds of paper rise up, and hover over the rim, suspended in air. They twirled in the lamplight like sprites.

For a moment she feared the haunting of old ghosts before she remembered the malfunctioning Grav that Baylin had yet to fix. With a sigh she waited for the bubble to pass, and when the shreds of paper drifted back down into the basket, where they were meant to be, she undressed and slipped into bed, the writing mood gone. She lay staring wide-eyed at the ceiling, no closer to sleep than she had been at the desk, her legs so restless they could've gotten up on their own and walked out the hatch had she let them. As she had with the panic attack, she told herself the feeling would pass, that it was just the alcohol, and that, as with all her nights, it was just a matter of waiting it out. But it didn't pass. She lay with her fists curled tight against her eyes, pressing against the boil of troubled thoughts in her head, the what-ifs and should've-beens, all the bad things she was made of, until she heard from the vents the notes of the boy's music.

They were soft, the notes; barely audible, but there. She didn't know the song, but she knew the feeling. Took comfort that there was at least one other person who was kept awake by the past. Her shoulders relaxed. Her fists bloomed into open palms, and the blood returned to her knuckles. From the back of her throat, she murmured along with his melody. Their voices in a tentative dance as she hummed her way into a calm and dreamless sleep.

For a week the boy played his flute.

And then someone broke it.

It was the morning of the eighth day in the Pocket. A distant, omnipresent rattle in the *Debby*'s bones as it sailed the rapids of the Diffident Current. With his breakfast balanced in the crook of her arm, Nia opened the boy's hatch, her eyes widening when she found him sitting on the floor by the cot, with the two broken halves of the flute laid out before him. She put the bowl of sweet rice down on the table and crouched at his side. "Did you break it?" she asked.

He limply shook his head.

"It's okay if you did. It's okay if it was an accident."

But still he shook his head.

"Did you find it like this?"

He nodded.

Nia silently gathered up the flute halves and gave him a curt gesture to eat. As he lamely played with his spoon, she walked across the corridor, and let the anger fly as she punched the ship-wide channel.

"Everyone to the kitchen. Now."

They knew better than to delay. In five minutes, her crew filed into the communal seating area, trading confused murmurs. The confusion was cut to the quick when she tossed the broken flute onto the table, the pieces skittering.

"Who did this?" she asked.

Bodies stiffened. They traded suspicious looks as they decided the likelihood of who was to blame, a silent play of one act that ended with all the actors pointing at Sonja. The veteran let out a harsh laugh. "Yeah, I get it. I do. But this one wasn't me."

"Of course it was you," Durat said. "You've been threatening to break it ever since we folded."

"Fuck off. It was a joke." There was a rare panic in her voice as suspicions sharpened on her—if there was anything Sonja could not abide, it was someone thinking she had broken the captain's rule. To Nia, she conceded, "I hated the music. You knew that. Everyone knew that. But I knew it was the only thing the cracked kid had." She sat back in her chair and crossed her arms. "I'm not a damn monster."

"'I'm not a monster'—fantastic defense."

Sonja glared at Durat.

"I can't even imagine doing something like that," Baylin said, his legs jouncing under the table. "Not like I'd have the time to go and break his flute; like you said, Captain, I'm the busiest person on the ship—"

Durat rolled his eyes.

"Unlike others," he continued, staring pointedly at Durat, "who do nothing but play games in the cockpit."

"Dexterity exercises," Durat said. "They're dexterity exercises." His grin wavered. He patted his hands on the table. "Regardless. Captain, I'm not sure why this is an issue. I doubt there's anyone here who wasn't at least a little bothered by the noise. Maybe we should just let it go?"

She slammed her palm on the table; the flute halves jumped.

"My ship," she said, her eyes as cold as moons. "Nothing happens on my ship without my say-so. You disrespect our passenger, you disrespect me."

Durat lowered his head, cowed.

Nurse, who had up until that point been leaning on the wall, listening, said, "The captain's right. Someone acted way out of line. There's no disputing the point. But"—her arms uncrossed, then recrossed—"the fact of the matter is it happened. The flute's broken. This minor inquisition isn't going to reverse that."

"'Minor inquisition'?" Nia bared her teeth. "You think I'm being unreasonable."

"Of course not," Nurse said. She brushed a lock of gray hair from her eyes. "All I am saying is that you have made your point. Unless you plan on jettisoning the culprit out the airlock for a moment of stupidity, I think Durat's right. We should move on."

The two women stared at each other.

"I'd like to speak to you alone," Nia said.

The crew scattered. Within seconds, only Nia and Nurse were in the dining area, staring at each other from across the table, their faces half-lit by the bulbs that hung above the counter. Nurse put on a brave face, defiant even, but Nia could see she was anxious; how one hand rubbed the hem of her red sari as if to furrow a hole through the fabric.

"Did you do it?" Nia asked.

"Yes," Nurse said.

Nia smiled, not believing any of this. "Why?"

"Does it matter?"

"I wouldn't have asked if it didn't."

"We have four months till we reach Pelican Station," Nurse said. She spoke quickly. It was obvious the words were rehearsed beforehand. "Four months stuck in this ship, together. I've served in many ships, I've seen crews fall apart. You know what I've seen. That I know what can happen when . . . it's never because of any one thing, but an accumulation of tiny cuts. I felt that the boy's flute was a cut. So I did my job and I healed it."

"You broke it."

"For the better, Nia."

"Captain," she corrected, "and what's for the better is not for you to decide. That's my job." She stepped toward her. "I'm docking your paycheck by ten percent."

Nurse scoffed. "That seems extreme. What I did was in the best interest of the crew and endangered no one."

"Ten percent."

Nurse opened her mouth.

Closed it.

"Yes, Captain," she replied with a tight smile, then walked out of the kitchen.

Nia let out a breath. She rolled her neck, her bowstrung muscles.

She scooped up the cracked halves of the flute and tucked them into the drawer of her bedroom desk, believing it was better the boy did not see it again, not like this.

His bowl of sweet rice was empty when she returned. He was scraping the spoon against the bottom of the bowl, scooping whatever grains still remained. She was never good with children. Comforting them was a skill she'd never had any cause to practice. So with an awkward lightness, she patted him on the shoulder, and hoped that would suffice.

The spoon stopped. He went still at her touch.

She almost admired his disquieting ability to remain silent. Even as he cried.

For three days, there was no music. The hatch to the guest quarters remained shut. On strict orders, no one but Nia was to enter the room—she made it clear that should they disobey, they would be discharged upon arrival at Pelican. The crew complied; they had no more business with their guest, their moods having lightened considerably with the newfound silence.

For those three days, only Nia was privy to the boy's slow retreat into the corner of the room. She sat with him when she had the chance, would read to herself while he lay in bed not moving but for the soft rise of his breath. And every lights-on, as she blinked herself awake, and fixed his breakfast, she asked herself what she was doing, what difference she was making with her company; asked herself why she cared. As angry as she was with Nurse, she knew the woman was right—once they arrived at Pelican, the boy would no longer be their problem. All she had to do was keep him eating, keep him clean. There was no need to attempt these clumsy jabs at comfort. But still she would find herself coming back to his room, pulled there as if by the force of empathy, or something else, a responsibility, maybe; oblivious that every now and then the boy would look up from under his blanket, like a small animal from its burrow, to make sure that she was still there.

On the fourth day, his room was empty.

Nia gripped the frame of the hatchway, but she stopped herself before she conjured up worst-case scenarios. She searched the ship, starting with the most dangerous areas first, the engine room and the cargo bay, but neither Baylin nor Sonja had seen him. Nurse hadn't seen him either in the medica. She offered to help Nia look for the missing child, but she declined, the betrayal still too fresh. "Thank you," she said, backing out of the medica, "but it's fine. I'll find him."

And she did. With a breath of relief she discovered him in the cockpit, seated in the pilot's chair, dressed in one of the field outfits that Kaeda had packed for him—a magma-red, one-shouldered robe that cut across his torso diagonally, cinched at the waist with a black rope belt, dropping into a skirt that touched the tops of his small knees. His hands were enmeshed in the cat's cradle of taut strings that were the *Debby*'s controls, while Durat stood behind him, instructing him on which string to pull for the back thrusters. In truth the boy piloted nothing, the cat's cradle locked in autopilot, the strings dead to his touch, but his eyes nevertheless focused straight ahead at the shuttered viewport as he listened to Durat's instructions and pretended that in each movement of his agile fingers he commanded the fate of a ship and her crew. Their lessons ended at the sound of Nia's cough. Durat turned, saw her standing in the hatchway. "Captain," he said with a grin.

The spell was broken. The boy returned to himself. He pulled his hands from the well of the ship's controls and slipped off the seat. His sandaled feet slapped across the floor as he went to stand by Nia's side, staring up at her.

"I found him in here," Durat said. "Kid almost gave me a heart attack."

Nia cracked a smile. "You taught him to fly?"

"The cursory basics. Years to go till he's good as me."

"Maybe not. Maybe I just found myself a new pilot." She grinned, the whole situation strange but welcome. She looked down at the boy. "Are you available for hire?"

The boy shrugged.

Her ex-pilot dropped his head. "And so I die the quiet death of obsolescence."

"Doesn't seem that quiet," Nia said, chuckling. "I didn't mean to interrupt. You two can keep playing if you want."

"This is no game."

"Right. Dexterity exercises."

She turned to go, but she got no farther than the steps to the causeway when she heard the sound of the boy's sandals in pursuit. He stood there, looking up at her again with that penetrating gaze, like it was a matter of course that he would follow her.

"I wouldn't recommend coming with," she said. "My routine isn't as exciting as flying through the Pocket. Stay here and play." She led him back into the cockpit and sat him in the chair. "Keep playing with him," she said to Durat firmly.

She was halfway down the steps when the sandals slapped up behind her.

"Sorry, Captain." At the head of the steps, Durat smiled in a way that suggested he wasn't sorry at all. "Unless we strap the kid down, I think you're stuck with him."

"I'm realizing this," she muttered.

So it was that she had a partner for the day. Their first stop was the back of the ship, where Sonja was performing her post-workout ritual of disassembling her gauss rifle and polishing the pieces over a sheet of tarp. While Nia asked her if she had updated their food inventory like she'd asked her to do days ago, Sonja raised her eyebrows as the boy appeared from behind her captain's back and wandered the cathedral hollow of the cargo bay like a cat, pawing at everything: the netting on the wall, the thick black straps that lashed the containers of seed to the grated floor, the ammo clip to her rifle—she slapped his hand away. He looked at her, affronted. "I'll do inventory today," she said, unnerved. "Just get him out of here."

On their way to the common room, they ran into Nurse, who was headed in the opposite direction. Nurse brightened with what seemed to be genuine delight at the boy's presence, opened her mouth to say something about this, but Nia continued on without stopping, the boy close on her heels. In the common room they moved the couches against the paneled walls, rolled up the rug, and brought it to the catwalk. They draped the rug over the railing and beat the dust with brooms while, below them, Sonja sneezed. It would've been quicker to run the rug through the vac, but Nia thought the boy might enjoy the activity, and took pleasure in it herself, reminding her as it did of home; how her sister would watch the clouds of dust bloom from the fabric as Nia beat their mother's rugs on the balcony railing, the City Planet skyline their view, the little girl delighted by how the particles glimmered against the chemical orange light of the false sun. Unlike her sister, the boy paid no attention to the play of dust. As he was with the flute, every ounce of his focus was directed on the task at hand. A single-mindedness that Nia found endearing.

After they unfurled the rug on the common-room floor, she gave him a tablet and stylus, and let him doodle while she read one of the old books in the shelf, the sweeping epics from Old Earth her mother once loved. While on the page the warrior queen Faydra Faneuil fought for the freedom of her principality, Nia's gaze drifted above the brim of the book, and she watched for a time as the boy drew long, spiraling lines on the tablet's screen—lines that didn't cohere into any particular picture or shape, but spiraled again and again, each intersecting with itself until the screen was one large black coil.

The boy stopped drawing when the lamp on the coffee table rose from its platform. The lamp held its position in midair, as if it had gotten up on its own, only to forget where it had wanted to go. He looked to Nia for an explanation. She told him that the ship was old and that there were parts that needed to be replaced. She got up and clasped the lamp's body with both hands and was about to remove it from the zero-G bubble when the boy stood and gazed at his warped reflection in the lamp's brown, oblong body; the wide, dark eyes; the black hair that fell over his head in long, frizzy bangs. When he reached out and touched the reflection, the lamp dropped into Nia's hands, safe.

For dinner, she ripped open a foil bag of jerky and plumped the strips in the boil. She fanned them over a bowl of sweet rice and observed the way he ate, his deliberate movements, not one grain of rice dropped or left forgotten on his lips, the bowl polished clean by the end. His body so still and controlled he blended in with the furniture, nearly unnoticed by the crew that filtered in and out of the kitchen. Baylin didn't see the boy at all, giving Nia a polite "Captain" as he grabbed some protein noodles from the fridge, going on about leaking engine filters as he walked back out. When he was gone, Nia looked at the boy with a wry smile, impressed by his uncanny ability to disappear.

"You'll have to teach me how to do that," she said.

The boy held up his empty bowl. Looked around.

"It goes over here," she said, showing him the wash.

She waited outside the lav as he showered, and helped him dress for bed; a white sleeping shirt that swallowed most of his body, a hand-me-down from Durat, as the clothes Kaeda had packed were not suited to the cold nights aboard the ship. She leaned against the frame of his hatch as he lay in bed, his small body curling into itself under the thick woolen blanket. Despite herself, she smiled at the sight.

"Sleep easy," she said.

His hand lifted up in a small wave as the nonessential lights switched off throughout the ship and brought them the night.

Weeks passed with the boy as her shadow, he stitching himself slowly each day to the soles of her feet. He helped her do loads of laundry, dropping them into the mouth of the vac, waiting ten minutes for the *ding!* and the clothes that smelled like steel flowers. He sat beside her as she played Tropic Shuffle with Durat and Sonja, studying her hand of cards, and with each game picking up the convoluted rules as they explained to him why certain birds beat others, and what the difference was between a gaggle and a flamboyance; why Sonja insisted that Durat keep his hands above the table at all times.

"Cheat once, always a cheater, apparently," Durat said bitterly.

During the afternoons he listened as Nia explained why there were handlebars running along the walls and ceiling. He listened to her stories in the common room, old contracts like the Roman treeplant they shipped across three systems, not realizing the treeplant was in its fruiting season, and was pollinating their ventilation system with neurotoxins, giving the whole crew a delirious and happy high for a few hours before they had enough wherewithal to grab the gas masks and move the treeplant into the sealed airlock. "We found Ponchi in the kitchen massaging rice into his face," she said, mushing her face in her hands in demonstration, which made him smile. He listened to the fun stories, for those were the only ones she shared. And when, one day, she and Durat brought him to the cockpit and placed the headset over his ears, he listened to the sounds of the Pocket, his eyes widening to the symphony of crackles and finger snaps. Nia studied his tranced expression, wondering what thoughts were going through his mind as he listened to the black materials rush past the hull sensors of the *Debby*; and after that day, when she would sometimes find him in the cockpit in the early morning, asleep with the headset on, she would carry him back to bed, his arm limp and swaying, and would ask herself what it was that strange boys dream of.

But most mornings, he was awake, and waiting for her. In the fringe of lights-on, Nia would lie in her bed and listen while outside her hatch she heard the familiar slap of his sandals make their eager approach. She would smile and find it strange that she was smiling. She would get out of bed and dress, leisurely, her pants first, her tank top last, drawing out the moment when she would throw open the hatch, delighting in the fact that on the other side was a person who could not wait to see her. Sometimes during this morning ritual she would stop, and would think of Kaeda, standing at the edge of the purple-stalked field, staring up at the sky as he gripped the flute she had left behind, and she would feel shame as she remembered how good it felt each time she left him, a throb of dark satisfaction in her heart for every ounce of her he was left wanting. And though the relationship between her and the boy was different, the notion remained: he was sustained by her presence, and she knew it.

There were the rare days when she exploited this, when she told him she was busy and locked herself in her room to write her haikus or write nothing at all while she indulged in the youthful vanity of withholding. But there would come the hour when she saw herself from the outside, and knew that she was too old to be playing these games. She would go to find him—there, sitting at the kitchen counter, staring hard-eyed at some unknown memory in the corner of the room. Smiling at the sight of her. The cloudbreak, and a nod.

Yes.

Let's do something today.

She learned his mannerisms. How his right foot tucked itself behind his left leg when he ate, and how he picked at his nails when he was nervous. How he tugged at his hair with impatience—hair that they had by that point sheared off, leaving an inch of black on top—and how, when he dropped a plate or bumped into her or messed up whatever small task she had assigned him, his shoulders would hunch as if braced for a blow. And in these moments, she would catch a glimpse of his past. A history of silence that existed long before the trauma of the wreckage. A learned pain.

On the third month and third day, after she had put the boy to bed, there was a knock on Nia's hatch. She knew who it was even before she opened it. The talk was a long time coming. "This is absurd," Nurse said, standing in the dark corridor, fuming. "Can we stop this now?"

For a while now they had been civil, their conversation in the causeways light and without meaning. They had made feints toward reconciliation, but they never made it past the awkwardness of casual conversation. Nia had been so preoccupied with the boy that it wasn't until now, seeing her friend standing outside the door, that she realized how much she missed Nurse, even though her pettier side still considered shutting the door in her face. She stepped aside and let the sari flit past her. There were four fingers left of the bourbon. She poured two cups and dropped the bottle in the wastebasket. "How've you been?" she asked.

Nurse laughed as she sat on the bed. "Lonely," she said.

They drank.

"We're almost out of Sonja's injections," Nurse said. "You'll want to add that to the requisitions list, unless you want her leg to fall off."

"Maybe we should let it," Nia said with a sigh. "Maybe then she'll stop kicking in all of my doors."

Nurse nodded. "Speaking of: When is Baylin going to fix the door to the tertiary lav?"

"He says he can't. Says the door needs to be replaced at Pelican, though part of me is convinced he doesn't know how."

"That curtain he set up . . . every time I sit on the toilet, that's when the ventilation decides to restart and the curtain blows open and somehow Durat is always passing by just in time to see me." Nurse shook her head as Nia laughed. "Every time. It's humiliating."

"I'll fire him when we land. Him and Baylin. Sonja for good measure. We can start again with a fresh crew."

"Fresh crew. Fresh start. That's exciting."

They drank again. During the quiet that followed, Nurse played with her fingernails, which Nia could see were recently chewed, though she made no comment about it, knowing how sensitive she was on the matter. "But I didn't come here to talk to you about the door, or Sonja's medicine," Nurse said almost in a mutter. "I came here to say that I acted out of line. I recognize that."

Nia leaned forward. "Why did you do it?" she asked.

"I told you why. The flute was affecting crew morale, yet nothing was being done about it."

"I mean why did you break it? Why didn't you just tell him to stop? Isn't that what you suggested I do?"

Nurse hesitated. "I wasn't clearheaded that night," she said.

Nia knew what she was getting at. "A flashback?"

"Yes."

It had been five years since Nia found Nurse in the wreckage of a derelict in fringe space, and though the starved body had by now filled out, and the mouth remembered how to smile, and the mind rediscovered its wit, there were still the flashbacks of the time be-fore, when the food had run out, and the meat was the bodies of the volunteers she'd served with. "I make no excuses for how I be-haved," she said, "only an explanation: that at two in the morning, in the state of mind I was in, I felt there was no option but to break the flute in half."

"I understand that," Nia said. "I do. Just so long as you under-stand that what you did was in direct violation of my command."

"With clarity," she said.

Nia nodded. "Okay then."

A third drink. There was something else on Nurse's mind; Nia could tell by the play of her hand on her sari. "He is a sweet child," she said. "And I'm glad that despite my best efforts, he's getting on well here"—she put her cup down on the nightstand—"but I'm worried about how much time you're spending with him."

Nia gave her a funny look while she drank. "He's a guest on our ship. I'm entertaining him."

"You know you can't keep him."

Nia put her cup down beside Nurse's. "No one said I was going to."

"No one needed to. It's obvious you've become attached."

"Why are you talking about this?"

"You know exactly why," she said. "The moment we reach Peli-can Station, Umbai is going to take their cargo. That includes the boy. He trespassed on their property. They have first rights."

"He crash-landed. Intention counts for something."

"And they might let him go and that will be the end of it—but if it isn't, if there's something else going on, you won't see him again. You know this."

Nia held up her hands. "Then we all go on living our lives as happy and legal citizens of Allied Space."

But Nurse wasn't finished. "Even if they let him go, what then?

Are you going to adopt him? Raise him on this ship and make this tin can his home?"

Nia's lip curled. "This tin can saved your life."

"I will never forget that, Nia." Nurse shook her head. "Never. Which is why," she continued, leaning forward, beseeching, "I'm telling you now, in no uncertain terms, that this child is just that—a child. He's not your pet, he's not your plaything. He's a child who needs a home."

"This is a home," she said.

"It's a cargo ship. Barbet Class. Carries fifty tons and upward of ten passengers. A mercenary's den. My savior. This ship is many things, Nia." Nurse grasped her hand. This time she did not let Nia pull away. "But it is not a home."

The trip was almost over. The end of the fourth month approached, and with it, an excitement that electrified the recycled air. For the last crew meal of the trip, Baylin pulled a trout from stasis and grilled the fillet on the crosshatched element until the skin blackened. He unzipped the belly with a knife, and served the fish whole on a platter, with stewed tomatoes, spicy gurcoli flowers, and fist-sized florets of sautéed cauliflower. The crew applauded. After reconstituted meat and vitamin pellets, everyone was ravenous for something substantive. Their eyes were close to tears as their tongues rediscovered taste.

Spirits were high. Durat and Sonja were at a cease-fire, the barbs they traded blunted by good-natured smiles, even when there was one last strawberry on the platter and the teeth came out. The boy sat between Nurse and Nia. He had no taste for the fish and ate the cauliflower with his sweet rice, his usual stillness not as guarded, his feet letting out a playful kick under the table. Nia served him more rice. She did not think about the coming days as she watched him eat, just listened to the sound of his thoughtful chewing, and the clink of the glasses around her as a third toast was made to a safe journey. It was a nice, uneventful meal, until the end, when Sonja had launched into one of her old war stories, a time she was hunkered in a diamond trench while green gunfire serrated the air, and her story was interrupted by the lights flickering above them, and the trout's skeleton rising from the plate as if by fishing wire. Conversation stopped as they watched the fish fly up to the ceiling. Nia sighed, and asked Baylin how expensive a new Grav would be—but before Baylin could answer, the zero-G bubble expanded, and with it, a kick in the ship that threw it all up into the air, the last of the tomatoes, the cups of booze, the table itself, and, with a yelp, the crew; Baylin, Sonja, Durat, Nurse, the boy, and Nia, all of them floating off their chairs—with their chairs—Sonja cursing as they twirled, the tail of a fish smacking Durat in the face, Nurse fighting to keep her sari over her legs, none of them close enough to the walls or ceiling to gain purchase on the safety rails, struggling, red-faced, to reach a hard surface until, one by one, they stopped struggling, their attention caught by the sound of laughter, and they craned their heads and looked at the boy drifting in the center of the madness, his small body framed by a sea of floating bones and silverware as he clutched his sides that ached from hiccupping laughs, his joy so vicious it made Nia's heart leap, and she gazed up at him, until the gravity returned and they crashed to the floor.

After they cleaned up the splattered food, the cracked plates, and upturned chairs, grinning at what had just happened; after the boy was showered and put to bed; after he sighed under his blanket, and she told him that she would see him in the morning; only after all of this did Nia return to her quarters and finish the haiku she had scrapped months ago.

The flute from Macaw,
Cheaply made and out of tune,
Still plays.

* * *

In a matter of days they would emerge from Pocket Space. To curb the nauseous effects of the unfolding, they stretched each morning and night, ate nonacidic foods, and drank as much water as their stomachs would allow—things that wouldn't stop the nausea altogether, but would round it into bearable. As Nia and the boy pounded glass after glass of water and followed Sonja's exercise routines, she told him about Pelican Station. What the nexus station of Allied Space was like, and of the days she spent on its east wing, watching the half-light of the Perseus sun. And as he listened to her stories and together they prepared for the coming arrival, ten million kilometers away, on the wings of their destination, the people of Pelican Station underwent preparations of their own for a celebration that was centuries in the making.

Nerves were frayed from the stress. Umbai representatives oversaw the construction of the fairgrounds in Izuni Park, and they coached the different culture groups performing in the Avenue Parade, going so far as to critique the act of a famous starlet, telling her to resist her usual flourishes and sing the notes on the page and no more. When she told them they could not hobble inspiration, they replaced her with a second-tier singer who was willing to follow their directions. In the schools, the teachers told their students the whys of the celebration: why it was important for them to dress well, and why they must have fun while also being respectful of the festival's significance. On the quicksilver screen, they traced for the students the lineage of this historic day, and led them back through the centuries, to the time before the province of stars. Back to when Earth was old, but not yet done, and Fumiko Nakajima was still dreaming up her stations.

3

Nakajima

Like most babies of her time, Fumiko was designed before she was extracted from her mother's womb. Unlike most babies, she had been designed to be ugly.

It was her mother's doing. As one of the figureheads of the post-vanity movement, her mother requisitioned for Fumiko an off-kilter nose, crooked teeth, a slight overbite, eyes spaced close together, and satellite-dish ears too large for her small, heart-shaped head. Later, when Fumiko was famous in her own right, and interviewers would ask her why she didn't undergo facial reconstruction to undo the damage her mother had done, Fumiko would tell them two things: first, the question was offensive, and second, this was her face, the only face she knew, and she would have none other. But after those interviews, when she returned home alone, she would remember how desperate she was as a child to be as pretty as the other girls in the park, who danced under falling cherry blossoms with their faces perfect in their symmetry. She would remember shame.

A man at a signing once told her that yes, it was a shame her mother had made her ugly, but at least she was a genius.

"Thank God for small mercies," he said.

It never ceased to amaze Fumiko, the things people would say to her face with a smile.

The initial germination of her idea for the stations implanted itself long ago, at eight years old, when her mother took her to California to visit the last preserve of birds. Her mother, Aki Nakajima, was a once-famous actor who, after a series of cinematic flops, receded from the public eye and devoted her time and energy to various causes—the bird preserve was one of them.

The preserve itself was a glass enclosure the size of two football fields, its terrain varied to simulate natural avian habitats. There was a forest, tributaries, even desert. As her mother performed for the news crew, Fumiko leaned on the railing that overlooked a false river, where the pelicans stood in the shallows, scooping water into their bucket mouths. There was one pelican in particular that caught her attention. It had a gimp foot, swaying when it moved, its body covered in bald patches. The thing looked diseased. She watched with amusement the bird's splayfooted walk, thinking of how funny the creature looked, until the pelican perched itself on top of a boulder and unfolded its wings, drying its feathers in the light. Its wings open in presentation to the sky.

As an adult she would struggle to articulate the transcendence of this moment, the sudden shift she witnessed when that ugly bird became beautiful, the words turning the moment into something small and quaint. Impossible to capture the awe she felt as a child. The top of her head tingling as she gazed at the drying bird while her mother finished her interview. The light on its feathers.

The feeling that at any moment it would ascend into some holy form.

When the news crew was gone, a hand gripped her shoulder, and her mother flatly told her it was time to go. Fumiko glanced at the bird once more as she was shepherded away.

Its wings like boomerangs.

On the four-hour SeaTram from the California preserve to Yokohama, her mother loaded math problems onto Fumiko's Handheld—Fumiko was another one of Aki's causes, determined as she was to have a daughter with a mind finely honed, for intellect was the most prized attribute of the post-vain. As they tunneled through the murk of the Pacific, passing the derelict wreckage of old oil tankers and other vestiges of the past, Fumiko balanced equations on her device, solved polynomials, scribbled her algebraic proofs with her stylus, while a part of her mind segregated itself, created a place where the pelican could perch and spread its wings under a beam of light that was always amber. When her mother left her seat to use the bathroom, Fumiko minimized the homeschool app and opened Doodle, and with the five or so minutes of free time she had she drew a quick sketch of the bird, accentuating its strange features, its sagged mouth, its tuft of cowlicked feathers, even gave it a speech bubble that said "BWRAAK"—

Then remaximized the homeschool app, her mother back from the bathroom, brow knit with worry as she regarded her Handheld. "You've been on question five for a few minutes now. What's confusing you?"

Fumiko came up with a quick lie, said she had blanked on the quadratic formula; an unconvincing excuse, as she had performed the formula with ease just the other day. But her mother didn't push the matter, and recited the formula for her again—though, by the time her mother arrived at "$4ac$ over $2a$," Fumiko had solved the problem, and moved on to the next, the packet done by the time they reached Japanese seaspace. They passed through the ruins of the old city. Fumiko opened the camera app and snapped a picture of the watery grave—the algae blooms on the frames of shattered windows, the bicycle frame suspended on telephone wire, which swayed with the current, and the blown-out homes swallowed by the risen tide. She uploaded the picture to her mother's Handheld, her insides twisted with stress as her mother regarded the picture with a stoic face, until she nodded, and said, "Good."

Fumiko devoured the praise.

From Yokohama, they took a smaller, slower tube to Okinawa, where they lived at the top of a high-rise. It was just the two of them. There was no father. Aki did not see the need for one.

The sea was their view.

At the behest of her mother, Fumiko showered. Once her allotted ten minutes were up, the timer clicked, and the water guttered out. When she stepped out of the stall, she did not dry herself as she normally did, working the towel from ankle to head; instead, she draped the towel onto the floor, and stood on top of it, with arms spread open under the mirror's band of fluorescent lights. She let the water drip off her body one bead at a time, until her mother rapped on the door and asked what was taking so long. She hurried the towel over herself and dressed for dinner.

She waited at the table while her mother measured out the rice on the calorie counter, plucking grains out one at a time until the number fell to an even three hundred, and then measured the broccoli, the paper-thin slices of steak, the fifteen salt-dusted edamame pods. The girl's mouth salivated, until finally her mother brought her the plate, holding it just out of reach as she asked her daughter, "What is the quadratic formula?"

The rice steamed.

"X equals negative b, plus or minus the square root of b squared, minus $4ac$, over $2a$," Fumiko answered.

The dish rested on the placemat.

They ate.

After dinner, when she was sure her mother was asleep, Fumiko snuck into the kitchen. With a chopstick and a paper clip, she jimmied open the locked drawer that contained her Handheld—darting glances over her shoulder each time the coastal wind rattled the shutters—and she sat in the dark with her face lit by the screen, her back resting against the skillet cabinet while with a finger she stroked her ugly drawing of the ugly bird, its big wings, its fat beak; her pelican.

The pelican, and the other rare birds she soon grew to love, remained with her as she studied and flourished in academia. Despite her mother's status as a has-been actor past her prime, she still wielded great influence in the public eye, which was why no door was closed to Fumiko, and no expense spared for her education. She graduated magna cum laude from Okinawa University with an engineering degree, and from there, the California Institute of Technology, where she earned her PhD in aerospace engineering—the field most bright minds were funneled toward as Earth was becoming a less viable home with each passing year, despite the solar-panel fields, the gullies stuffed with banned diesel vehicles, and the dirigibles that were always overhead, everywhere, spitting vapor coolant into the too-warm air. Able to perform complex mathematics without the aid of a Handheld or PrivateEye, Fumiko was in high demand. After a stint at JAXA, where she pioneered the development of massive hull structures able to withstand the fold into Pocket Space, she moved between various private tech companies with footholds in the aerospace industry, leaving behind her a wake of accomplishments, her name whispered in circles in the know—she, who was notoriously difficult to work for, who succumbed to bouts of intense depression, and who demanded perfection of her teams, no matter the time of night, and who always finished the jobs she started.

During her time working for Cybelus Chicago, she took one of her subordinate engineers to task for his lazy mathematics. She broke down the numerous points where he went wrong in frantic proofs on the wall screen, not realizing that a snickering colleague, who had been waiting for this particular engineer to be chewed out, was recording the whole thing through the squint of his PrivateEye. The scene was uploaded onto the public Feed with a wink, where it went viral in a matter of minutes; the story of a furious genius, of a woman so brilliant she needed no technological crutch, her hand a slipstream font for the intricate and impenetrable workings of the universe. The man she disciplined lost his job soon after. He was hounded off social media, and from there, out of the state he lived in. There were rumors later that he had gone into the woods and mouthed the end of a hunting rifle, but no one cared enough to verify.

As for Fumiko, she began to see her face displayed on her co-workers' screens—photos from the past, of vacations and events; her hunchbacked graduation photo with her horse's smile. The personal et ceteras of her life that were revived for popular entertainment. Her mother, now post her post-vanity, called her from Okinawa to congratulate her on the viral success. "This is it, Fumiko. This is when your life starts."

"My life," Fumiko repeated, dumbfounded, as she received yet another notification from the Feed of a recent story about her.

Her mother was not listening. She was too busy listing the steps her daughter had to take to hold on to the fame, to make sure it didn't gutter out. "Fumiko." Her voice from the speaker was textured with static. "Opportunities like this come along so rarely. Do not be foolish and squander it."

But the public eye was restless. Fame tended to burn out bright in those days, and Fumiko's fame was no exception. Notwithstanding her mother's best efforts—who went so far as to resurrect the old article written years ago about one courageous actor's choice to thumb her nose at bought beauty and manufacture an imperfect daughter—the noise quieted over the next few weeks. Every day there was a new viral, billions of people pumping their PrivateEye stories into the Feed, to the point where it was impossible for anyone to remember the contemporary folklore for too long unless the subject of the viral made an effort to remain under the spotlight, which Fumiko refused to do. Her coworkers were in awe of how the social-media flare-up glided off her back like water; how she didn't even smile or frown when it was brought back up in passing conversation; she who would just nod and say, "Yes. It happened."

But the biggest surprise arrived in spring when, one day during a meeting in Cybelus's conference hall, Fumiko's Handheld went off and she excused herself to take the call in her office.

Two days later, her office was empty.

There were no goodbyes. Only a two-sentence letter of resignation on her desk, printed on paper, with ink. It was an old-fashioned gesture that no one knew what to make of. One of the men stole the letter, framed it, and sold it on the Feed market, made enough money to buy groceries for a year, but spent the money instead on a trip to the Arctic, where with his children he watched the last of the icebergs sweat. And so it was that, for a time, Fumiko Nakajima disappeared.

It was the viral that put her on Umbai's radar. The ping that led them to call, and offer her the once-in-a-lifetime proposition: to design for them a series of space stations that would rival the best of their competition. She said yes without hesitation. They allowed her one month to get her affairs in order before she joined them in their Malay headquarters. They told her she would be working there in isolation for a number of years, the isolation a safeguard for their intellectual property. They told her it would be best if she took her time to say her goodbyes.

Out of familial obligation she packed a suitcase and visited her mother in Okinawa. She took the trolley from the port, amused by the cherry blossom trees that passed the window. She had forgotten it was spring.

When Aki opened the door, she did not hug Fumiko. She shuffled out of the way so that she could enter, and told her to be ready for dinner, which would be in an hour. After her mother ladled rice into the calorie counter with varicose hands, and prepared the plates still hot from their steam bath, Fumiko half expected her to hold her dinner ransom and demand a recitation of formulae. But the woman gave the plate to her without a fight, and they ate as they had always eaten, as strangers. She didn't tell her mother about the new job, or that she would not exist for an indeterminate number of years. It was no longer her business.

"The university called," Aki said.

"What did they want?" Fumiko asked.

But her mother shrugged, squeezing open an edamame pod with her spidery fingers.

Word had gotten around that Fumiko was back home. When she returned the call to her alma mater, an old professor of hers, M. Toho, asked if she would come attend a panel on massive wing dynamics that Friday. Fumiko was in no mood to participate in the talk—she never liked performing for the public—but she didn't turn down his offer, because in the other room she could hear Aki watching one of the old movies she'd once starred in, laughing at the jokes she and her onscreen partner told, and when she was not laughing, reciting the lines along with the characters in an eerily youthful voice. The routine depressed Fumiko; she needed out.

She asked M. Toho what time they needed her.

Two days later, the silhouette of a dirigible drifted against the white moon as many meters below, in the auditorium of the university, the panel finished to a carbonation of applause. Fumiko stood with her fellow speakers, her curtain of black hair falling forward as she bowed, wondering all the while what she was doing there. During the reception she drank her glass of water while her former professors spoke about her as though she were not present, praising her many accomplishments at such a young age—*Only thirty and she has access to more grants than I've had in a lifetime!*—and curbing those praises with subtle, and not so subtle, suggestions that she might be in over her head—*I've seen many brilliant young minds burn out from the pressure, Fumiko. Please do your best to not lose control*. She thanked each person for their suggestions, her patience for such pleasantries wearing thin, regretting having come at all, until M. Toho waved a stranger over from across the room and shepherded her into the group. Fumiko stood a little straighter, correcting the slight hunch in her back, for the stranger was one of the most beautiful women she had ever seen in her life.

"This is Dana Schneider," M. Toho said, beaming. "She's going to save the world."

Dana laughed, showing off her brilliance of teeth. "I wish you would stop introducing me like that." She bowed to Fumiko. "It's a pleasure to meet you, M. Nakajima."

Beauty was cheap in those days. Like Fumiko's mother, parents with access to good hospitals had to go out of their way to not have a child who was at least conventionally attractive. Billboard models were the new average. Some bucked the trend, creating children that were alluring *because* of their defects—Fumiko had a few suitors who fetishized her asymmetry, which made her more self-conscious of the fact—but then there were parents who made art of their children. Parents who considered the ears, the eyes, the mouth, the nose, the discrete parts of the face and how they melded with the whole.

These were the people who created new variations of beauty. Dana was a new variation. There was a story in Dana's face—a forgotten myth, of a deer who for one night turned into a man and made love to a human woman by a cold-water brook, in the dark heart of a forest. A strange ancestry that revealed itself in the dramatic contours of Dana's cheekbones, her jaw—the way the lower half of her face projected forward just a nudge, a hint of a snout, and on that projection, a flattened nose, positioned just above the wide set of her lips. She was the tallest woman in the room by a head. Her hair was cut short, with blond Nero bangs that fell evenly across her brow. Her ears were sylvan, pointed at the tip, and her lips full and red, without makeup. On her cheek were five freckles, each freckle a point of some invisible star, just below her right eye; an eye that was large, luminous, its iris purple and flecked with gold, which reflected nothing but Fumiko's post-vanity face. Fumiko shut her eyes, unnerved by the spark in her heart, and returned the bow. "Are you a student here?" she asked.

Dana nodded. "Eco-friendly tech. Solar-panel fields, bio-farms. Nothing that's going to save the world," she said, giving M. Toho a playful look, "just make the end of it a little slower to arrive."

"A realistic goal," Fumiko said.

"An honorable one," M. Toho added. "Sustainability is important work. Go on, Dana, tell Fumiko what you and your group are working on."

"Strictly preliminary in its stages. I wouldn't want to bore her with our half-baked ideas."

"Nonsense. Fumiko is a scholar first. I'm sure she'd be delighted to listen. She might even provide some keen insight, and, if you're interested, Fumiko"—and now M. Toho had taken her aside with a conspiratorial hush—"it would be a great help, to not just us but the project itself, if you spread the word about our work among your circles."

"You need funding," Fumiko said.

"We need people paying attention. And yes," he admitted, "like every academic institution, we need funding. But I do genuinely think you will be interested in the work. So please," he said, "as a personal favor to me, listen to Dana while I show M. Takahashi to her car—I think she's had a bit too much free Champagne." And like that, M. Toho walked away, glancing back at Dana with an encouraging smile before he helped up a woman who was drooling on one of the tables.

Dana sighed. "He's a subtle one."

"I won't be able to help you," Fumiko said. Her eyes were trained on the carpeted floor. "Sustainability isn't my field. I can't provide much insight. And right now, I'm not in a position to pass your work on to those who might fund it further. Your pitch would be a waste of both of our time. I'm sorry."

Dana considered this for a moment, then said, "I'm hungry. Are you hungry?"

Startled, Fumiko looked up from her feet.

"There's a great curry place on the boardwalk," Dana said. "We should go. Unless you wanted to stick around here and have more student projects thrown at your feet."

"You mean now?"

"Right now," she said, smiling. "Before M. Toho comes back."

Fumiko surprised herself when she agreed, never one for impulsive decisions, the acceptance of Umbai's job offer notwithstanding. She chalked it up to the fact that she was in no hurry to return to her mother's apartment, though she was self-aware enough to know that there was more to it than that; knew by the fast pace of her heart when she looked at Dana that there was so much more as they pushed through the double doors and left the auditorium together. Outside, where the air was warm and dry.

Somewhere, she heard a child laugh.

They walked down to the shoreline; a long strip of boardwalk that stood above the surface of the water, the true shore, the sand and dirt and trees gone under the tide. During the ambling walk, Dana explained to Fumiko how M. Toho brought her out of the lab anytime he needed to "seduce" someone into giving his department more funding or notoriety. "'Seduce' is the wrong word—more a distraction tactic. I charm them with my purple eyes and they open their wallet, or their contacts page."

"I see."

"I'm sorry if M. Toho's 'salesman mode' was off-putting," Dana said. "He really does think highly of you. It's a rare day when you don't come up in conversation."

"It's fine. No apologies necessary."

Dana relaxed. "I'm glad."

"How much farther is it?"

"A few more blocks."

"And what is the project you are working on?"

"Oh, I was being honest earlier when I said it's all preliminary. We're working on alternative light sources. Luminescent bulbs that don't require electricity. Not much more to say than that. We're still brainstorming." She laughed. "I'm not sure what 'pitch' M. Toho was expecting me to give."

"If you don't have a pitch, why did you invite me to dinner?"

"I wanted the company."

She sounded so genuine, Fumiko wanted nothing more than to believe her—that anyone would want to be with her for her company alone—but it was difficult to quiet the neuroses in her head as she followed Dana across the intersection, unable to escape the feeling that this woman was working some sort of angle; an impromptu dinner date disguising a hard sell. They walked through the manufactured public garden and onto the planks of the concrete boardwalk, where they could hear the water lapping against the struts.

The "great curry place" Dana had referenced was a food stall manned by an older woman, who heaped steaming rice into biodegradable containers, draping the rice in ribbons of thick brown sauce, fanned with slices of fried chicken. They brought their food to a bench by the water.

What Fumiko noticed first about Dana was her gift of talk; how without any perceptible effort she segued from topic to topic, dipping into her reservoir of personal history—her parents both worked for a lunar fracking company, which proved a major point of contention between them and their eco-conscious daughter during holiday get-togethers—then back to the present, the people she worked with, her small apartment below a pianist who played dirges nonstop from two to four in the morning, and to Fumiko herself, when she admitted with appealing shyness how taken she was with the panel that night, and the intelligence with which Fumiko spoke. There was an ease to Dana's presence that was contagious. Fumiko spoke with hesitance at first; brief descriptions of her career thus far, then a clumsy, self-deprecating reference to the viral vid of her dressing down her subordinate—"The worst part was I got some of the math wrong, but no one noticed. Yell loud enough and no one cares what you're actually saying; you're always right." Soon they were walking down the pier, with Fumiko comfortable enough to complain about what it had been like, living with her mother again. "And it's unbelievable that she's still using that same calorie counter. They discontinued the model a few years ago. It miscalculated caloric percentages and had people thinking they were eating more than they actually were, but she insists on keeping it. I think she likes the deception."

Dana laughed. "I thought my parents were difficult, but I can't imagine what it must've been like, growing up with her."

"I take it you know about my history."

She grinned. "Just what's been made public. Did the post-vanity ideals stick?"

"Only until I threatened to become famous, and she started treating me like an actual daughter."

Dana sighed. "You deserved better."

Fumiko slowed her pace when she heard this trite sentiment. "How do you know I deserved better?" she asked.

The question caught Dana off guard. "I just meant a child deserves someone who loves them unconditionally."

"I've made my peace with it." She continued walking. "And if it wasn't for her, I wouldn't be where I am now."

"I suppose not," Dana said.

"I'm done talking about her," Fumiko said.

Dana was quiet. "All right," she said.

They walked through an avenue of cherry blossom trees. It was a quiet night in the city. There were couples out, and families, but still plenty of space to walk. Fumiko stewed, regretting the swiftness with which she'd shut Dana down. A pink petal fell before her, twirled until it landed on her shoe. She chuckled, which she knew wasn't like her at all—something in the air.

"What is it?" Dana asked.

She almost thought better of sharing the story, but she knew that if she didn't, the night would end and she would be back where she started—alone in a room not speaking to her mother.

"It's a trivial story," she said, a lightness to her voice to make the telling easier. "When I was a child, my mother and I went to a park once to sketch the trees. Lessons in taxonomy. While we looked for interesting leaves, there was a boy in the park who was tucking cherry blossoms behind girls' ears." Fumiko shoved her hands in her pockets, not knowing what else to do with them. "It was just a thing he did for the ones he thought were pretty. The girls would line up like attendants and wait for their turn. One by one he would slip a flower onto their ear, and they would say *Thank you, Koji* so sweetly. I wanted a flower too, so I joined the line before my mother had realized I was gone. But when the boy got to me, he just looked at my face and said, 'No.' That was all he said. No. And then he walked past me like I wasn't there." She laughed when she said this. It was all so ridiculous. "My mother saw all of this, and she had a—let's say a 'conversation' with the boy's mother. His mother made him give me a flower. The face he made when she told him to go back . . . I'll never forget it. The anger he seemed to feel at the unfairness of it all. *Why, Mother, why do I have to give a flower to the ugly girl?*" She laughed again, but this time she was shaking. "The worst part is, I was still happy to get my flower, even though I hadn't—that the criteria wasn't met."

It was the first time the story had ever left her lips; the act of re-telling it made her wince, the hurt still fresh. She waited for Dana to say something, to segue into happier conversation, but Dana just regarded her with her purple eyes that caught the moon, until she knelt down, picked up a fallen blossom, and tucked it behind Fu-miko's right ear.

All it would've taken was a touch for Fumiko to crumble apart on the sidewalk. But there was no touch when they parted ways that night, just an exchange of Handheld numbers. "You're here for a month, right?" Dana asked.

"Yes," Fumiko said.

"Then we should make the most of it. What are you doing to-morrow?"

She lifted her shoulders. "Nothing."

Dana nodded, and put away her Handheld.

"Then I'll see you tomorrow," she said.

Fumiko returned home with her heart in her pocket. She lay in bed but did not sleep. Troubled by her strange need to shout from her window, to grab someone by the neck and whisper the possibility of miracles. But by her own design she had no one in her life she could call. No one to whom she could describe the encounter with that beguiling and beautiful woman; no friends, or even good acquaintances, her lifetime of distancing herself from others now taking its vengeance as she tripped in and out of purple-eyed dreams.

The next day she walked the sunbaked streets that overlooked the green waters of Nakagusuku Bay with her hand in her khaki pocket, gripping her Handheld while waiting for the telltale vibration, afraid that she would somehow miss the call if she did not keep a hand close by. She regretted never investing in a PrivateEye—it would've been impossible to miss a retinal notification. She ate a slice of sponge cake on a park bench while she considered her regrets, and when she was done, she brushed stray crumbs off her lap and walked to the Museum of Earth Sciences. She paced around the Grand Hall, studying the enormous magmatic sculpture that was suspended by wire above her. A fast reader, she sped by the many digital plaques that contextualized the exhibits until she had experienced the majority of the museum in a little under an hour and a half. It was toward the end of her private tour when Dana finally called.

"Are you still free tonight?" she asked.

"Yes," Fumiko said, pausing at the display on tectonic shifting. "What would you like to do?"

"There's a new exhibit on supervolcanoes at the Museum of Earth Sciences. I heard it's pretty good. Have you seen it yet?"

She had. In fact, she was there. Behind her was the blue-red holographic display of cracked earth crust. A child shrieked as lava spewed from a digital fissure. "No, I haven't seen it," Fumiko said, covering the mouthpiece so Dana wouldn't hear the display. "When do you want to meet?"

"My last class gets out at three, so an hour after?"

That was five hours from then. "That works with my schedule. I'll see you then."

"Perfect! Can't wait."

Fumiko lowered her Handheld. The crying child was escorted out of the dome by his harried mother, who glanced at Fumiko in apology before turning the corner to the bathrooms.

The wait for Dana was excruciating. Fumiko kicked around the neighborhood. Was both frustrated and thrilled by the hours of waiting, the long rehearsal of what she would say and how she would smile and if she should shake Dana's hand or give a friendly hug. When Dana finally arrived, it took everything Fumiko had to not explode from all the collected potential energy. Dana gave her a brief hug, and said, "Shall we?" before leading her back into the museum, and though it was exhausting for Fumiko to pretend it was her first time experiencing the exhibit, she would have done it again in a heartbeat, if only to see once more the dazzle in Dana's eyes as the holographic projection of Earth's insides expanded and swallowed their bodies in its bright fires.

After dinner by the pier, they made plans to meet the next day. Dana suggested they ride on a gondola—insisting against Fumiko's misgivings of tourist attractions that it was the best way to see the city. Most of Okinawa City was built upon struts lifted above the water, the city's geography crosshatched with canals, the canals populated by tourist gondolas that drifted between the backs of buildings and beneath arched bridges.

The sky that day was overcast, threatening rain, but they risked the boat anyway. The ride started off well. Dana pointed out various land-marks while Fumiko let her right hand fall over the side of the boat, dragging along the cold water as she gazed up at the birdless sky and listened to the reverence with which Dana spoke the names of architects she admired. But twenty minutes in, the clouds broke, and the rain began to fall, forcing the pilot to dock downtown. They sprinted through the downpour to a café across the street, Dana giggling as she squeezed water from her thin scarf. The café was a warm place made of wood and carpets. At the counter, students chatted with the barista and in one of the booths a man muttered into his Handheld while scrolling through the news Feed. They sat at a table by the window, ordered tea for Dana, and orange juice for Fumiko, which she felt the need to explain, even though Dana didn't pry. "I can't drink caffeine," she said. "It wreaks havoc with my system." On the wall screen, the volume dialed down to the last bar, a news station played a story on the recent certification of the Desiree, the station that would begin construction next year in the Eridani system. "There they go," Dana said during a wide shot of engineers shaking hands below a congratulatory banner. "That's the third one this year, isn't it?"

"It is," Fumiko said, wiping her wet neck with her napkin. She thought about what Desiree Station would look like—the cylinder, beautiful in its simple geometry. She wanted to tell Dana about her new job, about how one day she would accompany Desiree with a beautiful creation of her own, a statement to the world of what she treasured; but she knew that would break the NDA, and so said nothing.

Dana sighed as she stirred her tea. "Shame I'll be gone by the time Desiree is done."

"You could buy a ticket on an Ark," Fumiko said. "A half century of cold sleep, and you could see it and all the other stations."

She laughed. "Not on my student allowance. And even if I could," she said, quieter, "I wouldn't."

"Why not?"

Dana glanced out the window, at the rain. "I was born here. For better or for worse, this is my world, a world I'd have a hard time saying goodbye to." She shrugged with just her left shoulder. "Besides, who else is going to build those solar farms and lightbulbs if not me?"

"In two generations this planet's surface will be uninhabitable."

"Most likely."

"So your point is a nonissue. Building solar farms on Terra is useless. All it would do is collect energy for the empty cities. You should put serious thought into traveling offworld. The frontier could use more good minds."

"It's not useless." Dana was frowning. It occurred to Fumiko she had had this argument many times before. "The world is billions," she said. "At most—and I'm being generous with this estimate—twenty percent have the means to leave. Eighty percent have to stay behind. They're going to be trapped in hell until the Arks return for a second pickup—if there's a second pickup, and even if there is, there's still billions left over. Maybe by then more Arks will have been built. The numbers go down but we're still in the billions, and the odds are they won't make it that long—will live underground for a few decades while the surface cooks, and all they'll have left is the moisture that collects on the walls of their caves. Not everyone gets to leave. The least I can do is give them some working lights to read by." It was then that the screen played a commercial for teeth-whitening markers. A parade of nice teeth and beautiful faces. Dana watched the screen, expressionless, her cheeks still flush from the rain. "The people who leave always forget that the world doesn't end once they're gone," she said. "They forget about the decay."

"'Useless' was the wrong word," Fumiko said.

"It was," she replied before offering up a smile. "But that's okay."

They drank. The quiet that now passed between them was not the same quiet that Fumiko shared with her mother at dinner—that was a silence, a void. This was a cushion between moments. Beneath their table, Dana's foot rested by Fumiko's, their ankles touching.

Neither commented on this. "You haven't seen my apartment," Dana said, with no suggestive quality at all, more as if she were observing a quaint fact about the café, how lovely the décor; but the suggestion was there, in the small, but significant, contact of their feet.

"I haven't," Fumiko confirmed. She moved her foot away from Dana's, fearing she'd sense its mad tapping.

"We could go there, if you want. Watch a movie on the Feed."

"We could," Fumiko said.

They left the café once the rain died. The walk to her apartment wasn't long, a few blocks east, toward the shore. Dana chatted with the doorman before calling the elevator, but Fumiko didn't hear their conversation, her mind preoccupied—an exposed wire, sparking thought after anxious thought, terrified because she knew what was going to happen. Something new. The elevator doors shut and the box drifted up, humming. Dana leaned against her. Fumiko counted the lights. Fifth floor. Sixth floor. Her breath snagged when Dana's hand reached up and touched the side of her face. "Is this all right?" she asked.

"Yes," Fumiko whispered.

Dana held her cheeks like the sides of a chalice, Fumiko's eyes widening as she leaned forward. Their breath mixed. Their eyes shuttered. Their lips pressing together as soft as folded wings. She could taste the lemon from Dana's tea. The doors wound open on the tenth floor, and they parted. Dana took her hand. She flicked the keycard against the reader, and the automatic circuits switched on the kitchen counter lights, the lamp by the plush sofa. She never told Dana she was a virgin. She didn't need to. It was clear from the way she took off her clothes, the pausing before every action, looking into Dana's eyes as if to ask, *Is this too allowed?* A question that repeated itself when Dana kissed the inside of her thigh, and her consciousness tunneled, until she was only aware of certain things—the rain drizzling across the bedroom window. The black screen with the digital read-out of the time. *Thursday, 4:30 p.m.* The electric pleasure of Dana's finger tracing circles around her nipple. There was nothing else.

No one else.

They spent every day together. On Friday Dana excused herself from class so she could go with Fumiko to California to see the International Bird Preserve, a place Fumiko spoke often about; it would be her first time visiting in many years and she was eager to return. The layout of the preserve was unchanged, the only proof of the passing of time the number of birds that still populated the glass enclosure, significantly fewer than when Fumiko was a child. She remembered flocks overhead, and the dizzying movement in the trees and the rivers, the cacophonous echo of squawks from the man-made gully. But now much of the enclosure was quiet apart from the manufactured wind that rustled the grass. A lone tern sat on a metal strut by the glass wall, observing its own reflection. One of the keepers told them that the last of the pelicans died a year ago. There were only geese in the river now.

"This place used to be impressive," Fumiko said.

"It's still an amazing construction," Dana said.

"I wish you could've seen it." Fumiko placed a hand on the railing, gazing at the birdless tree branches and tall rocks. "There used to be so many of them."

It was then that Dana kissed Fumiko, without warning.

A goose kicked up from the water and flew east, toward the gully.

She was amused by how much she enjoyed Dana's surprise kisses, and the impromptu hand-holding; displays of affection she had been averse to in other couples, finding it trite and ostentatious, as if the couple were trying to prove to the rest of the world how in love they were. But now she knew why they did it—how it was like having a secret; a language only two people shared.

There were other less intimate surprises. When Dana returned

from the canal market with a bag of noisemakers, she waited for
Fumiko to emerge from the bathroom, and threw one of the noisemakers at her feet, the loud pop making her jump like a frenzied cat.
Dana howled with laughter as Fumiko chased her around the apartment, grabbing the bag, each woman throwing noisemakers at the
other, until the landlord called and informed them of the many complaints from downstairs. They apologized to him, killed the call, and
fell into bed together, red with exhaustion. Fumiko crawled on top
of Dana, hungry for her. She believed she could fall into that woman's bed every hour of the day for the rest of her life, sustain herself
on nothing but the taste of Dana's fingers the way the starved suck
water from a rock.

They lay entwined while Dana dreamed up fantastic scenarios of
the future in her arms. "A planet of our own. Just the two of us by
the shore. We can take a boat out to sea on weekends."

"What will we do with potential invaders?"

"Fend them off, of course. You can build the weapons. Make
sure they're automated, I don't want to hold a gun."

"As you wish. But do you have a fail-safe in mind, for when they
destroy our turret army?"

"Why, darling, we've wired the whole place with explosives."
Dana nestled into the crook of Fumiko's neck and whispered, "If we
can't have what is ours, then no one can."

It was a month like none other. Some mornings Fumiko could barely
breathe because she felt so lucky. Her heart smiled with teeth. Skin
electric and giggly when their hands met and their fingers twined.
Stomach cradled in a basket of feathers.

But it was all tempered by the fact that soon she would have to
make a choice: whether to leave for Umbai or stay with Dana, one
of the few good things she had in this world. As Dana slept, Fumiko
weighed the pros and cons of each decision. She risked losing Dana

during her years of isolation if she left, but if she stayed, risked losing the career opportunity of a lifetime, and might lose Dana anyway to the natural, inevitable currents of failed relationships. They had known each other for a handful of weeks. They were strangers. There was not enough substantive evidence Fumiko could draw on to say they would stay together long-term, despite the many hints Dana dropped that she would like to continue this relationship even after Fumiko had left Okinawa, for wherever she was headed next.

Things were made more difficult on Thursday, when Dana brought up the topic of their future together after their sixth curry dinner by the boardwalk. Dana said she felt that there was something strong between them. The hope in her eyes was too much for Fumiko. She decided to break a minor clause in her NDA that night, and told her the truth: that when she left, she would not be able to contact her, or anyone, for a long time. When Dana asked her how long this period of silence would last, all Fumiko could tell her was until the work was done. What work that was, Fumiko couldn't tell her. Dana took in this news. Her eyes on the water. "Can you at least give me an estimate of when I'll see you again?"

"A number of years."

"A number of years," she repeated.

"How many, I can't say," Fumiko said. "That depends on how development goes."

"What are you developing?" But before Fumiko could say NDA, Dana held up her hand. "Right, you can't say." Dana stood up. She paced around the bench, her skirt whipping behind her. "If you want to break things off, I understand. I do. I won't be happy about it obviously, but I'll understand. Just, please, please don't lie to me."

"This is a stipulation of the contract I signed with the company. On their premises, I'll have access to research networks, but nothing in the social-media cloud—no Feed. Not until the project is finished and made public."

"I wish you would've told me this earlier."

"Would you have stopped seeing me if you knew?"

There was a time when Dana didn't answer. But soon her shoulders relaxed. "No," she said. "I just would've liked to have been prepared."

"I'm sorry."

"I called my parents yesterday." She laughed. She hated her parents. "Calls to the moon are expensive, but I did it anyway because I wanted to tell them I met someone special—and before you even think it, yes, I do still think you're special, despite this wonderful surprise you've given me." She sighed. "And once you go, you can't leave at all?"

"No."

"If you didn't have this job, would you still want to see me?"

Without hesitation, Fumiko said, "Yes."

Dana brightened. "Then it's simple." She clapped her hands. "Here's what you do. You get in contact with them, and you renegotiate your contract. You tell them that you won't work for them unless you have the *bare minimum* of time off to go do what you want, and then you can come visit me. It probably won't be for long, but we can make do with the time we have. I have a lawyer friend we can get in contact with—he's a bit of a jerk, but he's good at his job and besides he owes me a favor so we can probably get him to look over your papers pro bono, and then—what? Why are you shaking your head?"

"There is no debate with them." She pressed her hands to her knees. "If I want the job, this is what it is."

"You won't even try?"

"There is no trying."

"Impossible. You're impossible." Scowling, she sat back down. Behind them, two teenage girls laughed at a vid on one of their Handhelds. Water lapped the struts while a dirigible whirred far above, but this time, it was more lonely than romantic. Dana didn't look at Fumiko as she played with her chopsticks, pecking at the remnants of rice in her container. "There is a PO box," Fumiko said. "You can send handwritten letters there. I'd get them."

"But you won't be able to write back."

"I'm sorry."

"Please stop apologizing. I know you're sorry. I know. I know." She rubbed her face. Then she shook her head. "I just don't know if I can wait that long."

Fumiko had expected this answer, prepared for it, but there was only so much preparing she could do for the punch to her gut. As she cried, Dana wrapped her in a hug and accepted the full weight of Fumiko's body as she leaned into her. "I won't promise anything," she whispered, "but when you come back out, and you find me, and the circumstances are right . . . then maybe. Maybe we can do this again. Properly."

"I want to stay," Fumiko said.

Dana laughed, despondent. "Words," she said. "Those are just words."

On their last night, they made love. Dana asked Fumiko to wake her up if she fell asleep so that they could have a proper goodbye, but that never happened. As Dana breathed, her eyes shut, her fist curled against her parted mouth, Fumiko slipped out of bed, dressed, and left her apartment. Much like she had done when she resigned from Cybelus, she left behind a note, weighted under the saltshaker on the kitchen counter. The note thanked Dana for the past month, and left the address of the PO box, should she wish to write.

With gratitude,
Fumiko Nakajima

It was the only goodbye she knew how to make.

Back at her mother's apartment, she packed her suitcase. Stuffed it with her clothes, her pd-console, her notebook filled with bird sketches. There were three missed calls on her Handheld, all of them from Dana. She did not return them.

Aki was asleep, her body so small on her queen-size bed, a mask over her eyes and plugs in her ears. Though Fumiko felt no particular affection for this woman, she did feel a responsibility to make some gesture of farewell now that the time had come. She kissed her mother on the cheek, the skin soft, tender, whiskered with fine hairs. Fumiko thought it interesting, how lovely even terrible people could be when they slept. Aki stirred with incomprehensible murmurs as Fumiko gently shut the door behind her. The car waited for her outside the building.

By three that morning, she had left Japanese seaspace. She was in Malaysia not long after dawn. Umbai Company Headquarters towered like a great tusk at the edge of a sea cliff, its many floors going both up toward the sky and tendriling down into the earth. Before she entered the glass expanse of its lobby, she called Dana's Handheld, but there was no answer. Fumiko believed this to be karma. She made no further attempts, and pocketed the device as the greeter at the doors approached her and led her through the first security gate.

At the end of every workday, Fumiko would go down to the lobby and ask the attendant if there was any mail, and each time the attendant would apologize profusely, as if this were some personal failing on his part. It became a routine of sorts, an occurrence so frequent that, after a few weeks, she would only have to walk past and meet his eyes to get her answer; that solemn shake of the head. Soon she stopped expecting any correspondence, finding the ritual of going down to the lobby and confirming her suspicions with the attendant comforting on its own, which was why she was surprised and even a little unnerved when, a month into the work, the attendant didn't shake his head, but smiled with enthusiasm.

"For you," he said with a dramatic flourish, handing her the sealed envelope, addressed in fine ink to one M. Fumiko Nakajima. It took all she had not to tear it open in the lobby. She returned to her penthouse on the thirty-third floor. Silhouetted against the neon-blue sky, she whittled the letter open with a pen, and read.

Fumiko,

I would apologize for taking so long to write to you, but you must understand that when you left without saying goodbye, I was very disappointed. No. I was fucking furious. I still feel both of those things. I hope that, wherever you are, you are refining your interpersonal skills. I do not need to tell you that they are sorely lacking. That said, I will apologize for my clumsy handwriting. My skill with a pen has atrophied drastically since primary school.

I am not sure what I should write, considering I don't know any specifics about what you are doing, and can't ask you any questions, since you have no way of answering them until your "prison sentence" has been served. M. Toho asked about you the other day, asked if I had any news of where you are, what you are doing, etc. I wish I knew, so that I had something to write in this letter other than about myself . . .

We are making some progress with our bulb. Right now we're studying the properties of naturally occurring luminescence, like glow worms and fireflies, figuring out a way to extend the life span of photobacteria. Honestly, I doubt much will come of this project, not with the time we have left. In two months I will graduate. I've sent a work application to Arboreus, an NGO that oversees various sustainability projects around the globe. They're not as big as the for-profit tech companies, but they're pretty well regarded. With luck, they will hire me, and I will not be on the streets or worse, living with my parents on the lunar colony—I hear living there is like how the Vegas Strip used to be. But I'm sure things will work out one way or another.

I am still angry at you, but I hope you are doing okay. I hope that your work is what you hoped it would be. I wish you were here. I miss your seriousness. Maybe your work will not take too long. I hold on to the chance that we will see each other again before the year is out. I have a lot of yelling to do.

Dana

The letters came with some frequency, about every two to three months. Fumiko pored over them again and again, for days after their arrival, listening to the Dana in her head speak the words in that warm whisper of hers. Fumiko's subordinates never knew why there were those rare days when she was made of light.

The next letter was sent after the brainstorming had finished, and the first preliminary drafts were sculpted in Umbai's enclosed virtual space.

I am, from here on in, an employee of Arboreus. My first assignment is in the Federated States. I leave Okinawa in three weeks. I thought I would be sadder to leave this place. It's frustrating that my love for the city has been colored by our time together, as if somehow the mere fact of you has changed the chemistry in my brain, and all I can think about is what might've been.

You'll be happy(?) to know that M. Toho still sings your praises—it's like I can't escape! He goes on and on about your discipline and focus. And while I know that both of those things are true, I can't help but think about the vid of you that went viral last year. I never told you this, but the first time I saw that vid, when I saw you shouting at your subordinate, I was put off. You seemed cruel. I wasn't sure why M. Toho was so enamored of you before we got to know each other. Geniuses are born all the time, but kindness is rarer, these days especially. The world could use more kindness. I'm rambling. I'm not trying to tear you down. I just want to vent.

Take this letter as evidence that I am still thinking about you, and that, despite my self-interest, I am still waiting.

With each letter, Fumiko became more certain that she had chosen well—the sacrifice she made, for the creation of a place where new love could bloom. Between the arrivals of the letters, her most treasured time was folding the headset over her eyes and disappearing into virtual space. She liked the power that was at her fingertips, the ability to mold the lines and shapes before her into comprehensible, even beautiful, objects; with a few practiced gestures, the wings of the first station took shape, and folded out from the main body as if in flight.

This is my first time in Louisiana. The people here are decent, but many of them are unused to designer babies. My face startles them, even my eyes. You can tell the difference between colored contacts and true pigment aug-

mentation. There's a group of children who follow me every afternoon while I patrol the panel fields south of town. They call me Sister Angel. I think one of the girls has a crush on me. Every Friday she gives me a rose from her father's garden—or rather, she leaves it on top of my backpack when she thinks I can't see her. It's adorable. Her name is Huck. I asked her if she was named after the literary figure, but she didn't know what I was talking about.

I'm worried about the solar field itself. My boss and I discovered that someone had wired illegal jacks into the panels of the eastern quadrant. Following the jack lines, we discovered that there's a suburb a few miles away that has been siphoning off more than their allotted share of electricity. People's homes are going dark because of them. The frustrating thing is that we can't do anything. When we contacted the authorities, they stonewalled us, told us there was nothing that could be done. This is of course bullshit. It wouldn't surprise me at all if they're being paid under the table by the thieves. Sustainability is great in theory, where there are no humans involved.

It was decided that there would be four stations in total: Pelican, Macaw, Barbet, and Thrasher, each modeled in the likeness of its namesake.

The first eight months of work were devoted to Pelican Station, which would act as a template for the other three. There was some difficulty in fulfilling Fumiko's vision, the massive articulated wings, the vacuum elevators that would pipe through the belly of the station like arteries, the kilometers-long strip between the wings, where principal commerce would take place, but it was done. Umbai had spared no expense on the quality of its personnel, or its technology.

Fumiko was in awe of the resources at her disposal, as though the company had been preparing for this project for a very long time.

> *New border lines are drawn each day. My friends and I used to drive to the nature preserve fifteen miles east of here every other week to see the tree tunnels and hike through the protected bog areas, but a month ago we were stopped by a guarded tollgate. They told us the land now belonged to St. Abner—the suburbs I told you about before. They haven't stopped at just stealing power, now buying up land from the government, expanding their acreage. Families evicted from the homes they've been living in for years. Some of my colleagues are resigned; say this is the history of our species, and the best we can do is win the tiny battles and hope for some sea change. The more I see, the more difficult it is to disagree with them. But a part of me still revolts against the notion that this is our basic nature; that we are, in essence, self-serving creatures. That love is an explainable construct and souls are a pretty feint to distract ourselves from our own cruel emptiness. I just reread that last sentence. What the hell am I turning into?*

The first vertical slice of Pelican Station was completed. There was a celebratory party in the conference hall, which Fumiko did not attend. One of her subordinates brought a flute of Champagne up to her apartment on the thirty-third floor. She accepted the drink, and after she shut the door in his face, she poured the alcohol down the sink drain, refilled it with cool water, and sipped it on her balcony as she gazed up at the night sky. She imagined a possible future where she and Dana would ride out on the Ark ship, sleep away the present, and arrive in time for the coronation of Pelican. She imagined how beautiful Dana would look, standing on the tip of the station's wing, suspended below the ceiling of stars, silhouetted by the holy white sun. How they would escape this place, together, and perform their own ascension.

There are refugee tents along the western border. We've been building new panels, but it's not enough to accommodate the population. Many live by candlelight now (in fact, wax is melting beside me as I write). Huck has been helping me on the weekends. In the morning we go to the tents to help feed those who have no homes, and after lunch, we go out to the fields and solder the wiring the wild animals have chewed through during the night. I've met her parents a few times. Decent enough people, if a little dazed. They smile like they're not sure what year it is, or what day. It is a marvel that their daughter is so in tune with her surroundings, so aware. With a few cursory lessons, Huck has picked up the foundational principles at work behind the panels. She even helped me fix one! It hasn't been easy living here, but her friendship has been invaluable.

The mosquitoes bothered me at first, as did the extreme heat (it's 32 Celsius on a good day), but I've learned to appreciate the beauty. Louisiana is one of the few places left in the world where you can stand in one spot and not see any buildings, aside from the Colombian Elevator, but even that is just a thin vertical line on the horizon. It disappears if you squint. You can convince yourself that you are surrounded by nothing but earth and sky and willows. I find myself doing this more and more, as new sectors of the panel fields fritz out, and more power is stolen by those who cannot be stopped.

It is a comfort, of sorts, to phase it all out.

In the days leading to the completion of Barbet's vertical slice, Fumiko sat alone in her room during her free time, plugged into the virtual ecosystem. Like Dana, who stood in the middle of the Louisiana plains to disappear for a while, Fumiko had taken to escaping inside this private world, where there was nothing but black and light, and a grid of malleable lines. Sometimes she would raze these lines, and construct out of them a woman's face, with short hair and pointed ears. For hours she would create these abstractions of love.

Eighteen people were gunned down at the gates of St. Abner. They went to protest the town's devouring of land and power. Started as a peaceful protest, but someone in the group drew a pistol, and the guards in the tower fired back with automatic weapons. Huck was there. I told her how important it was to fight for what was hers, and now she's dead. It's my fault. I went to see the body. I felt I had to. Her parents were there in the morgue. Her mother told me to look at what they did to her daughter so I looked. Her jaw was blown off. She was thirteen. This world is on life support, Fumiko. With every day, I am more convinced that maybe the plug needs to be pulled. I am angry and frustrated and sadder than I've been in a very long time and what I wouldn't give to be in Okinawa again with you to watch the cherry blossoms. But unless the project you are working on is a time machine, there is no going back. We're stuck in today.

There were more discussions to be had, more work to sign off on, more version numbers of component systems. However acute Dana's pain was, Fumiko was unpracticed in the ways of long-distance empathy; aside from the clumsy reconstructions she created of her in virtual space, it was difficult to spare a thought for her as her responsibilities fractaled every week and demanded more of her attention. She told herself this was just as well, that there was nothing she could do for Dana anyway—no way to get in contact and tell her to hold on, that she was still coming, one day.

And then the last letter came.

It was January. They were midway through the development of Thrasher Station. The attendant handed her the letter with a smile, oblivious of its contents.

> *I've met someone. She is a colleague of mine. We met during a summit in DC two months ago, and she has been visiting me in Louisiana every few weeks. I would tell you her name, I would tell you all about her, but I'll spare you those details. The reason I'm telling you this is so you don't expect me to be waiting for you on the other side of your project, on the off chance that you were still expecting me to. That wouldn't be fair to either of us. There was a time in my life where I would've waited for you, but now, seeing how everything is falling apart, I no longer think of time as a luxury to be spent. I needed someone, so I found someone.*
>
> *My time in the Federated States will soon be over. I will be flying to Iceland next, to observe the magma wells. This will be my last letter to you. If you get this—if you have been getting any of my letters—know that I will always treasure the brief time we spent together, and that I hope you are happy, or at least feel complete in some way.*
>
> *Dana Schneider*

Fumiko did not tear up the letter, or burn it, or toss it off the balcony. She was never given to melodramatic gestures. Instead she folded the paper back up, placed it back in its envelope, and left it on her desk, as though it were meant for someone else.

She left her penthouse.

Yes, she thought as the elevator plummeted toward the offices. *Back to it.*

Four years.

That was how long she lived in the Umbai Building before she emerged in the public sphere with her plans for the completed stations. The draft was displayed in the gallery alongside the other designs from other companies in the Louvre. The crowded room, brimming with the well-dressed elite, toasted her and her project, and they applauded as she gave the draft her final assignation, with a quill dipped in rich, black ink.

> *Four Stations*
> F. Nakajima
> Feb. 23, 2136

PrivateEyes snapped the occasion, surrounding her with hundreds of uncanny winks.

Umbai commissioned a renowned biographer to describe the creation of the stations, though much of the information was, in the end, redacted. As per her contract, Fumiko attended the book signings and gave interviews. During the last few months of her time with the company, they trained her in the art of public speaking, and though she was still a bit clumsy socially and often regressed to blunt or overly technical answers, her mother told her she'd made noticeable improvements.

Aki was still alive, her thin body still sustained on her calorie counter. She was not upset with her daughter for not saying goodbye, not after she learned that Fumiko would be stepping out into the public arena. She attended whatever signings were physically possible for her to attend, dressed in full regalia, pushing herself into view of the Feed. "Let my daughter be a lesson to the world," she said to the many PrivateEyes recording her, "that society's idealization of physical beauty is wrong—that beauty comes in many forms, the most wonderful being the brilliance of the mind." It did not escape Fumiko, how her mother's freshly tightened skin would blush when people asked if they were sisters.

The first few weeks of PR were exhausting for Fumiko, but she was surprised to find that once she had given enough interviews and talks and signatures she somewhat liked the attention. Though there was still the odd person who commented on her physical appearance, most of the attention, and praise, was directed toward her work. It pleased her that her birds were getting their due rewards, even if their namesakes were, by this point, near extinction; at least they would live on in some way.

Dana was never far from her mind. When she looked into a crowd she would sometimes see blond bangs paired with ostentatious purple eyes and her heart would skip before realizing it was a stranger's beauty-standard face that gazed back at her, starstruck. In time the public circuit did its job of distracting her enough to make her think she had moved on, only rediscovering the pain during the moments before sleep, when she was most aware of how alone she was, in bed, with no body beside her. She would pick up her Handheld, her thumb wavering over the contact address, but she would never call. She was too afraid, and still too hurt.

Soon the year was almost ended. Umbai's plans were well under way, and Fumiko's victory lap was drawing to a close. She was on the rooftop of a residential tower in Cape Town, attending an early New Year's party in mid-December, when her Handheld vibrated in her back pocket. She almost didn't pick up when she saw the name on the screen, but her hand moved on its own accord, and she answered.

"Congratulations," Dana said, with such collegial warmth, it was as if it had been only days since they had last spoken.

The sound of Fumiko's world dimmed out. She stepped away from the crowd and the trays of flaky hors d'oeuvres and rare meats, and leaned on a railing from where she could see the slanted roofs of the city below, and the dirigible above, which floated close enough that she could hear the whirring of the coolant as it was pumped from its ventilation. Moonlight gilded all. "Where are you?" she asked.

"Mongolia. I was served spaghetti with ketchup the other day. The waiter said it was a local delicacy, but I'm dubious."

"I wasn't sure if I would hear from you again."

Dana laughed. "That was the original plan. But then I saw your face on the cover of a magazine, and I thought, *That can't be Fumiko. Fumiko doesn't smile!* So I thought I'd call and find out if you were replaced by a robotic facsimile during your time with Umbai."

Fumiko didn't want to smile, but she did. "I'm not a robot. Not yet."

"Good. It's . . . really nice to hear your voice. I'm sorry if that sounds weird, considering how long it's been, but I needed to say it. And I wanted to let you know that, for what it's worth, I am so impressed by the work you've done. I haven't had a chance to see the plans in person—one day I'll visit France—but I've seen shots on the Feed. The designs are beautiful."

Though Dana's voice was staticked by the distance, she felt so close to Fumiko that, if she shut her eyes, she could smell the fresh wheat of her hair. She felt she had no choice but to ask, "Are you still with her?"

There was a pause. "Yes. We are still together."

"Are you happy?"

"I am." There was a sigh. "Are you?"

"I thought I was."

"I shouldn't have called. This was a mistake. I'm sorry."

"No." Fumiko almost yelled it. A few people even glanced at her, worried. She whispered, "Don't hang up. Please."

". . . I won't. Is there something you wanted to say?"

So many things. She fell quiet as she gazed out from the balcony. "Tell me it was worth it."

"I've told you, the designs are exquisite. I mean, I have literally no experience in your field, but aesthetically—"

"No," she said, the Handheld pressed so firm against her mouth the skin began to redden. "Tell me I made the right choice."

"I— Fumiko. Only you can tell yourself that."

There was a hollowness in Fumiko. She needed to feel. She needed Dana to hurt, to react in some way other than professional courtesy. "You're so wise. What self-help Feedboard did you steal that line from?"

"What the hell is wrong with you?"

"Why didn't you just wait? If you waited, everything would've been"—she shut her eyes—"it would've worked out. We would've been happy."

"I *am* happy. Did you even get my letters? I met someone, and she's fucking wonderful, and if she asked me to marry her tomorrow, I'd do it in a heartbeat. I'm sorry you're feeling lonely right now, but don't you dare try to tear me down—and thanks, by the way, for not calling me as soon as you left Umbai, for not making sure I was okay after I saw Huck's—after I . . . You have no idea, do you? You didn't even think about the hell I'd been living through, trying to forget what I'd seen. You didn't think at all. You know, I used to think of you as a genuinely decent person, trapped under a hard shell, but obviously I was wrong. For all your pretensions, you're just as self-involved as your mother. I can't believe you'd even think—"

Fumiko hung up.

Once she let out a breath and she had steadied her nerves with a sip of wine, she was surprised by how little she felt. She pocketed her Handheld, and ordered another drink; she rejoined the party.

The crowd was happy to receive her.

Umbai's Ark departed from the Colombian Elevator two years later, in early June. It was the third to leave Earth, followed by twelve more, from the Singaporean Elevator, and the Kenyan, on their way to other stations, which belonged to rival companies. The stations were still in active construction, but the trip would be long enough that they would be habitable once the people arrived. It was the leaving that was unpleasant. There were revolts, battles over rights to board the ships, all of which were lost by the rebels under the salute of gunfire, and the vague promises on the Feed that one day the Arks would return for a second pickup. They did not.

In five years, more than one billion people rocketed into the stars under the time-stopping veil of cold sleep, their lips frozen in prayer for their eventual reawakening in a safer time, a better place. It was a sleep that lasted decades, until, pod by pod, the families woke up and pressed their noses to the band of windows, mouths agape at the sight of the massive birdlike structure silhouetted by the white sun; the two gracefully articulated wings in full spread against the light. Pelican Station. Their home borne on wings, with the stars their canopy. The transition was long and difficult for the first generation of settlers living so far from Earth, their dreams haunted by their lost north star, but with time, and the arrival of children who had no emotional connection to blue skies, Earth became only a story; a story shared lightly between strangers rich enough to afford passage between worlds while over the serving of hot drinks they traded speculations on the old ways of travel; if this was what their ancestors felt, when they boarded a boat and kicked away from shore, this dread excitement.

Life spread—to Macaw, to Barbet, to Thrasher. Desiree and Palatian. To the outer reaches and the worlds with skies yet unscarred by man-made contrails, and the City Planet Capitals, whose every block, every turn, had been planned decades in advance. The routes were paved by corporate mapmakers who voyaged the yet-uncharted currents of the Pocket, cataloguing the distance and time debt, before signaling the colony ships, and then the company traders, who looped the systems together in the binding web of commerce. The ships dragged behind them the years, the contracts signed and stamped in undying digital ink, and the spires of City Planets were borne upward with the swiftness of bamboo, and, as it had been since the beginning, the steadfast tradition of hierarchy was continued in this fashion, the wealthy living above the clouds, and the unlucky down below. And though it was lost on no one the strangeness of this progress, of how humanity had come so far but still there were people who never saw the Stations, or even the sun, no change was made to the structure. They lived and died in the Minotaur's labyrinth of the City Planet substrata, deep in the shadows of the glass towers, the steam plume underworks, the vomit of trash flumes, where there was no time, no progressive sign of the turn of the century or the millennia. Only the heat, and the daily stench of corpses wedged in the ventilation chutes beneath the streets, where they would be flashed into ash come next month's heat cleaning, and soon forgotten, as Allied Space stretched its jaw and continued its swallowing of the stars. Its enlisted soldiers diving in and out of the Pocket, skipping over the eras of its history as they brought back the contracts of newly acquired planetary systems, and the noble wealth of their Resource Worlds.

After a four-month journey through the interstellar currents, a flock of ships unfolded into reality like paper napkins. There were twelve in all: the *Roendal*, the *Greenery*, the *Cedarcrest*, the *Helena Basho*, the *Brightband*, the *Solus*, the *Rock on Water*, the *BGT*, the *Mandolin*, the *Bittedank*, and the *Ghost Dog*—ships that had been traveling alongside the *Debby* all this time but unable to speak or be seen through the frack of Pocket Space, flying together deaf and blind with their cargo of dhuba seeds. "We've done this so many times," the old captain of the *Rock on Water* said over the link, "but there's something about crawling out of the dark that makes me cry when I see your faces again."

Nia grinned at the fuzzed image of the old man on the console screen. "If you cry, I'll start crying too, and that's something no one needs to see."

The old man laughed loudly.

"Agreed, Imani," he said. "Agreed."

There were still a few more hours until they docked with Pelican Station. Nia sat with the boy in the common room until they arrived. He was still dressed in the red robe, with his hands in his lap. She told him what would happen when they landed. How there would be Yellowjackets waiting to take him to Nest. She told him that she would stay with him for as long as possible and that she would make sure he was safe. She told him that beyond this she did not know what the future held, but that she had enjoyed their time together. And after she told him all this, he nodded, somber.

She hoped he understood.

Baylin took final inventory. Nurse and Sonja surveyed the cargo bay, checked the temperature of the seed crates. Durat threw the ship code out to the Nest authorities for verification, and told them over the comms that the boy was well and fine. "Looks like everything's in order," the authority man said. "Yellowjackets will be waiting for your ship on the dock to take the boy and look over your manifest. Shouldn't take more than a moment."

"Great. See you guys soon."

"Very good. And Happy Nakajima Day."

Durat raised an eyebrow. "Sorry?"

"Nakajima Day. Thousandth anniversary of the stations' completion. Tell your crew they're in luck." The authority man's mouth grinned underneath his visor. "They're about to see the largest party in the galaxy."

As the *Debby* arced toward the station's waiting maw, the celebration long in the making was already on full display—a parade on the Avenue Strip underneath a virtual blue sky, populated by the dazzling projections of ancient animals whose roars and squawks were so loud even the adults flinched a little. Company bands with their twanging lyns and bellowing chufflahs playing the "Anthem of the Wings." Delicacies from a hundred worlds slung from float carts: Adizan apples dipped in black sauce, fried billyduck tongues, and thirty-layer cakes—rich, sweet smells that were sold for too many iotas, which was fine, for today the people of Pelican Station and its visitors would allow the price gouging, the bumping and kicking, the incessant shouting and cheers, because they were electrified by the sight of her, the one without whom none of this would be possible—Fumiko Nakajima, standing on her float made of dust and light, waving to the roar of the crowd with her youthful hand, smiling for them, she their beacon of where they had come from and where they would soon be going, the crowd enraptured by her smile; a smile that fractured only once, only for a moment, when the first of the fireworks bloomed in the sky, pink and red and loud, and she saw in their fleeting shapes cherry blossoms in spring.

4

Departures

In flowed the clamor of the Pelican docks—the spray of extinguishers that fought to contain a spontaneous fire in the *Rock on Water*, the shouts of crews negotiating the seed crates from their berths with thudding loaders, arguments over manifest numbers, the whirl of witness drones overhead, and the disciplined boot-stomp of Yellowjackets cutting across the immense space of B-3 with their sheathed batons, headed for the *Debby*. When the boy saw them, he gripped Nia's hand; she could feel his rapid heartbeat through his palm. "It's all right," she whispered as the Yellowjackets scaled the ramp. "You'll be all right."

He squeezed her fingers.

The line of Yellowjackets stopped a fair distance from Nia and her crew—a neon wall of armor that blocked the *Debby*'s exit. The shortest of them stepped forward. "Captain Nia Imani?" The Yellowjacket saluted, rapping a gloved hand against her chest. "My name is Andetwa, first ser of Nest Security. Happy Nakajima Day to you and yours. May I be the first to offer my congratulations on completing your shipment cycle." The beaked visor covered Andetwa's eyes and nose. Nia could see only her thin-lipped smile. "Is this the boy you found planetside?"

"It is," she said.

"If you would."

The Yellowjacket held out her gloved hand like they were exchanging a pet's leash. Nia restrained the instinct to slap that hand away, and moved between the jacket and the boy, her arms crossed over her chest.

"Nia," Nurse said, tense. "Don't."

The first ser's smile flattened. Her fellows placed hands on their baton handles. "Is there a problem?" she asked.

Nia's jaw tensed.

Durat laughed. "Uh, Captain?"

She silenced him with a glance, and said to the first ser, "Where are you going to take him?"

Andetwa seemed caught off guard by the question. "We will escort him to the security offices on the thirteenth strut for arrivals processing. If we get an ID match we'll return him to his rightful guardians. No match, we'll put him into the system, bring him to Child Services on fifteenth." The ser looked between her and the boy, and, as if she understood the situation, her smile softened. Her hand moved away from the baton on her belt. "I assure you, he will be taken care of the entire way."

"Will you contact me with news?"

A brief moment of hesitation as Andetwa scrolled through the pages of traveler's rights on her visor. She nodded. "If there are pertinent updates."

Nurse put a hand on Nia's shoulder.

"It's time," she said.

Nia shrugged her hand off and lowered herself so that the boy could see in her face that this was not the parting she wanted. "I'm not going to say goodbye just yet, okay?" she said. "We'll see each other again. Do you understand?"

Suddenly, he hugged her.

He smelled like her ship.

It was a brief hug. He stepped away before she could even think to return it. She walked with him and his escorts to the dock elevators, her heart twisting when the doors slid shut between them. His hand pressed against the glass. His eyes were wide, like he was waiting for her to rip the doors open and save him. And she reached out, to do what she did not know, her hand touching the glass when the vacuum pressure shot the platform upward, into the belly of the station. The boy gone. Her reflection wincing back at her.

"It has been a calm fifteen years on Pelican," their orientation leader said. The delicate tattoo of the bird's wing on his cheek spread its feathers as he smiled. "There was an incident last year, station standard time, with the promulgation of floric leaves in the lower struts, which is why that product is now illegal contraband in station-space, and will be confiscated with a large fine if Nest Security finds any on your person. Retinal supplicants as well. But it is not all bad news. Umbai has opened new trade routes between the stations and the Grammaton-owned planets, so expect to find an assortment of new spices, clothing, and approved tech in the market—a personal favorite of mine is DanSen Tea, which comes in a glass bottle and is sprayed directly into the nostril. The misted caffeine is very cleansing.

"As always," the leader continued, "the Umbai stations retain strict control over linguistic infection. You'll find that all the residents and most of the travelers still speak your version of Station Standard, with a few minor additions and changes, none of which should impede the enjoyment of your stay. The Avenue Strip on the upper strut remains the locus point for travelers, especially today, and for the following week, while we celebrate Fumiko Nakajima's great work. And as thanks for *your* great work, Umbai has booked rooms for you all at the Travillion Suites for the next thirty days—station standard time—which, aside from its excellent view of the Strip, also includes free access to the worlds-renowned Travillion Spa. Please enjoy the perfumed baths and massages at your leisure."

In honor of Nakajima Day, and the Old Earth era during which Fumiko lived, each of the crew were handed their own private Handhelds for personal use for the duration of their stay on Pelican. The devices were served to them off a metal tray, like hors d'oeuvres, as thin and flexible as playing cards. Through the Handhelds, Umbai transferred the pay to Nia's account, which she then dispersed among her crew's accounts. She remembered to dock Nurse's pay by ten percent even though she no longer wished to, for there were few things more important to her than keeping her word. Nurse made no expression when she saw the updated pay on her device. Nia suspected this would come up later, a midnight argument she would be ready for.

After orientation, it was a ten-minute ride on the elevators to the top of Pelican. The crew's excitement for their return was dampened by Nia's Handheld call with Nest Security during the ride, her quiet, tense replies into the receiver—the call ending with her grunt of frustration after the secretary on the other end of the line gave her the vague assurance that her contact information was catalogued, and that the first ser would reach out if there was any relevant news.

"He'll be fine," Nurse said.

Nia ran her hand over her scalp.

The grains were coming in.

When the elevator doors spiraled open, they stepped into the twelve-kilometer-long canyon of commercial enterprise that ran down the length of the Pelican's back, the crew so used to the sight they were no longer dazzled by the many shops and playhouses and meeting spots that projected the bright ghosts of words like DEALS and LUXURY PRODUCTS. They headed for the Travillion Suites. During the walk, Nia saw that little had changed since her last visit—or rather, everything had changed, but those changes were all expected, and easy to pass over. Shops gone, devoured by the competition, subsumed into larger entities, with long chaining names that asserted their predatory lineage. New holos of unfamiliar celebrities that gazed longingly at her below entertainment loglines. But the feel of the place was the same—the sidewalks still lined with photorealistic trees from fir to red maple to mountain birch, all of which swayed in time to the artificial breeze; the vaulted ceiling that was still a precarious span of digital glass, the pane now faded to a royal purple to represent evening and pricked with white dots that would in an hour resolve into stars. The only notable difference was the presence of flapping banners that declared the thousandth birthday of the stations and the various planetary and corporate flags that proclaimed their allegiance to Umbai and Nakajima—so many flags that Nia recognized only a fraction of the logos. She wished the boy were there, so that she could point out the ones she did know, and tell him why it didn't matter.

In the warmly decorated lobby of the Travillion the crew discussed how they planned on celebrating the first day of their furlough. Nurse intended to visit the station hospital and offer her services. Durat teased her for being so predictable, before he surprised no one with his plan to scout the new drug pubs and to see about the dances. They spoke with enthusiasm about these plans, but when they were done, no one moved, the five of them standing in the middle of the lobby while other travelers moved around them, because after four years of being in one another's company, it was strange to now go their separate ways.

One by one, they left to begin their vacation with their nods and their see-you-soons, until only Nia and Sonja remained under the Travillion's twirling chandelier of glass and dancing pictos.

"So what are you doing?" Nia asked her.

The vet side-eyed her. She accepted Nia's invitation to dinner, not seeming to care one way or the other, her shrug noncommittal. They found a place a half kil away; a snow globe of a restaurant, with holographic white specks that flurried about, and tables that circled the projection of an acacia tree. Birdsong played from unseen speakers while they took their seats at the table in the back, the song interrupted by an announcement on the Feed that at 1930 there would be a performance in the Grand Hall on Schreiberi Wing by a singer whose name Nia did not recognize, but who she figured was very famous if the eruption throughout the restaurant was any measure. "So some asshole designed this station," Sonja said, her voice raised against the din. She waved a white speck from her face. It reacted to her movements, and swam away. "You know anything about this Nakajima?"

Nia said she didn't, not really listening as her thumb described the outline of the Handheld in her pocket, waiting, waiting. When the bowl of kurim berries was placed on her mat, she moved the berries around with her spoon, not eating, and ignored the wet sounds the vet made as she swallowed the strips of flowered meat whole, like her throat was a well that dropped into nothing, and the meat the wishing coin. She knew this was a mistake. She should've stayed in her room at the hotel, or her ship, somewhere quiet where she could wait for the call from Nest. All she needed was a few words—a simple confirmation that he was taken care of. She sighed. Hadn't realized how long the table had been quiet till Sonja broke the silence.

"Never liked kids," she said. Her eyes were on her meat, her expression severe as she cut through the coarse, vat-grown grain. "My brothers were little shits. Didn't listen to good advice, didn't care who they hurt." Her knife stopped cutting. "But he was all right. That kid." She looked at her captain in the way Nia imagined she would've looked at a fellow soldier who had lost their friend in battle. "Sorry you guys got the short of it."

The words were so unexpected Nia could think of no other reaction but to laugh. A short, abrupt laugh. She picked up her glass of ojai liquor and toasted Sonja's cup without waiting for her to pick it up. Shotgunned its contents.

Her stomach bloomed from the drink; that blindside of kindness.

She returned to the station elevators after dinner rather than the hotel, preferring her ship to the Travillion's opulence. Some of the dockworkers gave her the eye as she walked past the unmanned loaders and the empty crates, wondering what a captain was doing in the docks at this hour, away from the celebrations, the lights of the upper strut. One of the workers nodded at her and winked, and flicked his details to her Handheld. She passed him without comment.

The *Debby* was dark. The corridors dead. She stopped by the boy's old room, half expecting to see that little hand waving good night. The room was empty. She made the linen on the cot and fluffed the pillow before continuing on to her quarters, where she sat at her desk, her face half lit by the lamp, her hand holding the pen above the paper, the ink tip drawing circles in the air, unsure of what to write. Something that would capture her dark mood. Trap it on the page instead of in her head. But that transition was never made. She fell asleep with her head propped up on her fist, the pages beneath her blank and unattended.

While she slept, and dreamed of flute song, Durat entered the Schreiberi Grand Hall, his arms cast over the shoulders of the friends he had met in the sauna of the Travillion Spa—a couple who were traveling together, retracing the famous pilgrimage of some monkish figure whose name was in their eyes a revelation. Durat had little interest in the performer singing that night in the Grand Hall, and it was difficult for him to keep up with his new friends' conversations as they often segued into topics that referenced events he had missed during his time in the Pocket—what the Pompadour Fleet was and why they were important was beyond him—but he was enjoying himself anyway, because after four months stuck in the *Debby*, it was exhilarating just to hear talk that had nothing to do with ship maintenance or flight plans. To be around so many unknowns. Flush with new money, he bought drinks for his entire row, and he absorbed with almost manic glee the attention this brought, and he told himself that this was going to be the best vacation of his life, which is what he told himself every time they landed, and was almost always proven wrong, because even he recognized the wild impossibility of his fantasies.

As Durat drank himself into joy, Nurse patrolled the milk-white corridors of Pelican Hospital's central branch. Her sterilized booties padded past the patient quarters while her mouth chewed the nails on her right hand; an old, stress-induced habit that had returned ever since the boy had boarded their ship. A pair of gloves was stuffed in her back pocket, which she would put on to hide her nails when she entered a patient's room, resuming the chew when she knew no one was watching. During her rounds she argued with Nia in her head about the ten percent pay cut, and explained with sober clarity why the punishment did not fit the crime, and how it was necessary to take into account the fact that the boy's presence had hobbled her ability to reason. She refined these arguments and made knives of them until an alert signaled on her retina. Room 23. She hurried to the patient in distress. There would not be a day she would let pass unguarded. When the worst arrived on its fiery hooves—and she was certain that it would, could feel the vibrations of it on her feet—she would be ready to tear out its throat.

While Nurse cleaned the soiled thighs of a man who would never wake again, somewhere on Gracilius Wing, in the small alcove of a local park, Sonja sat with a group of fellow veterans as they shared with one another the names of the dead. The ages of the soldiers vacillated, from a ninety-year-old woman to a nineteen-year-old boy, the one commonality between them their inability to forget the smell of a body after it was toasted by a railgun. They didn't swap war stories, didn't relive the glory days of terror; those stories they saved for civilian ears. All they did was say the names of those they had lost, one at a time, clockwise, giving the dead the space to live again for a night. Parda. Suchong. Jura. "Norrin," Sonja said, when it was her turn. "He was from Edelweiss. He saved my life, once."

"Norrin," the nineteen-year-old repeated.

"Norrin," the ninety-year-old repeated.

During the rehearsal of the dead in this park on Gracilius, kilometers away, on Pelican's alternate wing, in the same Grand Hall where Durat sat with his friends, Fumiko Nakajima took her seat up in the private balcony. She sat beside the woman chosen to be her companion for the duration of her stay: a young woman with hair cut short into blond Nero bangs, and eyes that were dyed royal purple, none of these attributes coincidental. They held hands from across chairs, Fumiko stroking the consort's soft palm skin with her index finger, tracing the identity lines, trying to unearth a long-forgotten name. The consort was not her only companion that evening—to her left, by the balcony curtains, sat one of the Pelican consuls, his presence required by Umbai for the PR. Fumiko ignored him until midway through the performance, when she heard him speak to an indeterminate third party through his neural, his tone hushed and secretive. When she asked him if something was wrong, he assured her with a too-quick smile that it was but a small security matter. Fumiko smiled and turned back to the performance, while with her custom neural she traced the call the consul was making to Nest Security. To her evening partners it looked as though her attention was solely on the elliptical aria, but within her dilated eye there was a whole play of action, her neural flipping through dozens of different windows, combing through recent station acquisitions, until the pages stopped, and she discovered the boy from Umbai-V, who was at that moment sitting alone in a holding cell in the thirteenth strut. It didn't take long, twenty seconds at most, for her to research the whys of him, and to see that she had been waiting for someone like him for a very long time. Her hands gripped the sides of her chair and she excused herself from both the consul and her blond companion, telling them that she was tired but that she hoped they would have a fantastic evening. She was gone before either one could convince her to stay, the man and woman looking at each other with uncertainty across the now-empty chair.

And while the Millennia Woman rode her private tram back to the main body of the station, far below, in Pelican Dock B-3, Baylin stumbled into the bay of the *Debby*, unable to remember why he had returned to the ship instead of his heated bed in the Travillion. It was the fault of the greenery pub. The weed had wreaked havoc with his senses, he too young and inexperienced to know when he was about to smoke his way over the edge until he already had. He moved through the darkened ship, one foot in front of the other, thinking it odd and tickly that he seemed to be experiencing time with a ten-second delay, his neurons wading through molasses as his brain told his foot to rise up and step forward. It was a nice change of pace from the anxiety he felt most days, but detrimental to finding his way back to his bunk. He tripped over his own feet like a toddler as he navigated the main causeway. Found a nice place to sit, on the grating between the door to the lav and the common room, where he listened to the dark and the quiet. Strange to be on a ship that wasn't flying. Was it still a ship then? He giggled, until he heard the approach of footsteps from behind. When he turned his head, he gasped—the Goddess of Shadow towered above him, Nelho, She who would ascend all into the night, and he cursed himself for not believing in the family stories, his sisters' insistence that the old myths were real, until the goddess laughed, and her gentle face resolved into Nia's hard eyes and sharp cheeks. "You're high," she said.

"I think I'm high," he said.

She helped him to his feet. Led him back to his room. He stopped before a three-step staircase, for despite Nia's assurance that it was only three short steps, those steps were eighty feet tall and would take years to climb—entire generations of his descendants would die before the lineage ever reached the top. And then what would they do? The climb was fruitless, the pride of effort a holdover from the old days. Who was the first person to climb a mountain, and what god did they expect to witness at its peak? What truth?

His spiraling quest for answers was interrupted when Nia sighed and scooped him up like a baby. She carried him the rest of the way.

"This is nice," he murmured against her warmth. When she chuckled, to his addled senses each chuckle was an underwater detonation, distant and percussive. He thought he heard her say something along the lines of *Don't get used to it*, but he couldn't be sure. He shut his eyes, with comfort borne on the strength of her grip. In a murmur, he said, "I know why he looks up to you." She did not ask him who he was talking about; such an answer was unnecessary, when the boy was everywhere around them. She only asked him what made him think that. He told her the simple truth he'd known since he'd first met his captain.

"Because you're strong."

For a time, there was only the sound of her footsteps.

And then she thanked him.

When Nia lowered him onto his cot he melted into the pillow with the vague awareness that she now sat beside him. He clutched his blanket to his chest as if it might be taken away and smothered it over his head until his world was as dark and warm as the engine belly of his parents' generation ship—and in that dark, there was a glimmer. A number. An important number. "Thirty thousand," he mumbled. "New Grav. Costs thirty thousand." Beyond his blanket he could hear the air whistling through the circulation vents, and could feel the mattress shift as Nia stood up. She asked him a strange question. If he liked living on this ship. He always thought the answer was obvious. "Yes. . . . yes," he said, drifting. "I do." The dark was warm.

"Would you call it a home?"

But he never answered her, for he'd fallen asleep.

And as the young man slept, Nia smirked, denied the answer to a question that had been plaguing her for a while now. She had hoped that Baylin, as young as he was, would be able to share his perspective on the matter, but he was too far gone for that, and come morning, when he was sober again, she suspected it would be too awkward to ask. So she left him to his dreams, and went to the kitchen for a glass of water, her throat dry and scratched.

Her eyes were still adjusting to the dark when the Handheld lit up and shot a notification straight to her brain.

This is a personalized invitation for Captain Nia Imani BC2890 to attend the Canopy Dance in celebration of Fumiko Nakajima and the Umbai Company.

The party will begin at 2300 on the 14th of March, Station Standard Time, on the Canopy Deck of Pelican Station.

Directions are provided below.

Please wear appropriate attire for the occasion.

Resell/recoding of this invitation is illegal, and will result in immediate expulsion from Pelican Station, as well as further disciplinary measures.

—UMBAI REPRESENTATIVE COMMITTEE

The captains of the twelve commercial transport vessels convened in the dining hall of the Travillion for breakfast. The activity was suggested by Baruk of the *Rock on Water* as a way of commemorating the four years of travel they had spent together, even if much of it was spent in their own isolated bubbles of Pocket Space, and because Baruk was the eldest, and had helped the other captains out of various rough patches in the past, they felt they had no choice but to accept his invitation, even though there was much else they would rather be doing than entertaining his nostalgia.

Nia joined them after she made her fruitless visit to Nest Security. The secretary had turned her away almost as soon as she had arrived, telling her Andetwa was not in the office and that she would be contacted when and if the ones in charge of the case "deemed it appropriate." She was in a foul mood when she met the others, and was itching to complain about something. Once they were each served the first course—a perfumed broth that was milky white, with a swirl of blue, which tasted to Nia like drinking straight from a sour teat—she brought up the topic of the invitation she had received the night previous, and asked them if they were going to bother attending the event, having assumed the invite was a cursory gesture from Umbai to all the captains; the belligerent reaction of the ever-temperamental Toral Anders of the *Solus* proved that assumption wrong. "Is this a joke?" he cried. "*You* got invited?"

"No offense was intended," she said. Firm. "I honestly hadn't realized it was such a big thing."

"It's a privilege," he said, with acid.

The captain of the *Helena Basho* swept an auburn bang from her eyes and explained, "From what I've heard, of all the parties that are happening this week, the Canopy Dance is the most exclusive."

"The rarefied air of the elite," said the captain of the *Ghost Dog*. "I wouldn't have gone even if I was invited. Glad I wasn't. Can't imagine a place more suffocating."

"I'm not glad," Toral snapped, close to slamming a fist on the table. "We all did equal the work, we should get equal the pay, and *equal the benefits*. None of this is fair."

Baruk stroked his gray beard. "Few things are, my friend."

"Save your wisdom for the pilgrims."

The captain of the *BGT*, the name of which stood for nothing but was chosen because the captain liked the sounds of the letters B, G, and T jammed together, leaned her small head forward, and said in a low voice, "I heard even the Primark Prince wasn't invited."

"That's because he spoke out against the station's policy on language control," the captain of the *Helena Basho* corrected. "Less to do with him not being special enough to attend."

"Still," the *BGT* captain said, "he wasn't." Her big eyes regarded Nia. "And you were."

Baruk's eyes twinkled. "I'm not surprised. Nia is a great captain."

"And what about us?" Toral asked.

"It was a compliment, Toral, not a slight. If I must save you from my wisdom, you must save us from your hurt feelings."

To that, Toral stood up, his chair teetering from the abrupt movement, and excused himself to the bathroom.

"His crew are an unlucky bunch," the *Helena Basho*'s captain murmured.

Baruk sighed. "Don't let him get to you, Nia. Whatever reason you were given the invite, I am sure you've earned it fairly."

The other captains nodded in agreement, and though Nia was touched, she wasn't convinced the invitation was a meritocratic gesture. It made no sense that the Umbai Company would pick her, and her alone, because as much as it hurt to concede Toral's point, she knew they had all done the same amount of work. The only difference between her and them was that she was the one who delivered to the company the fallen boy.

She was certain he was the reason.

It was then that she decided that tomorrow night she would attend the dance. She would be among the great, and see if she could once and for all get some answers, even though she bristled at the invitation's mention of *appropriate attire*, which almost never meant comfortable. "Just be careful," the captain of the *Mandolin* warned her. "Those nobles are some of the most powerful in Allied Space. You cross one of them, you can find yourself executed on some backwater planet."

"Or ejected out the airlock one night."

"Or thrown down an elevator chute."

"Or just shot in the back of the head!"

These were supposed to be jokes; Nia gathered this when everyone at the table broke into laughter.

That night she paced around the *Debby*, moving things, rewashing dishes, polishing panels in the cargo bay, having learned from her father that the best way to curb anxiety was to pour herself into busywork and not give her brain a chance to consider the captains' playful warnings. It was when she was elbow-deep in the lighting circuitry that she laughed at herself, realizing both that she had no idea which wire led to the causeway lights, and that the hours she lost trying to figure it out had been lost in vain, for her heart was still punching her chest in anticipation for the dance that was still more than twenty hours away. With a sigh she finished off the last checks on her list, submitting the requisitions list to Dock Acquisitions and solving the weird rattling problem in the tertiary lav shower—it was a loose bolt—and then she called Durat on her Handheld to ask him if he was busy that night. She'd been thinking about Baylin, the image of him blissed out on pipe smoke, and decided that was what she needed—the old days, when the days were still cheap. Durat asked her where she wanted to meet.

The greenery pub—sea blue and pastoral orange lights that shifted against the smooth concave walls while a quartet of synth artists played warblers on a raised dais for the people who smoked their pipes inside the many discreet recesses. The air was dank, and laced with the artificial flavoring of smokes both citric and sweet. Nia smiled when she entered, the seductive vibe of the pub loosening her wound-up neck muscles, asking her to sit back and remember her twenties. Durat had booked a private alcove in the back, with enough plush couch space for a dozen people. She didn't ask him how much of his paycheck he'd blown since they'd arrived. Just took a seat. "Welcome to my ship, Nia Imani," he said with arms splayed out along the spine of the couch. "Tonight, you are not a captain. Not even crew. You are my valued passenger." He gave her a toothy smile. "All you have to do is point, and that's where we'll go."

They ordered a quintet of pipes. The first hit was a sour mix of berries and nose-numbing granite spice that hit Nia in the face. After they took their first, second, fifth drag, she relaxed into the cushion of the seat, feeling at once weightless and gravity-bound, her muscles taffy and her smile loose as Durat described with his hands the shape of a perfect ass that belonged to a man he'd met the prior night in the Grand Hall. They played two games of Tropic Shuffle with the pack Nia had brought from the ship, until their minds were too floaty to remember who had just gone, and who had rights to the flamboyance. When the pipes were emptied they climbed the twirling steps to the club above, into the pulse of light and gyrations, a roaring beat that shredded the last of her hang-ups. Nia swallowed a fist of spirits at the bar before she stepped into the crowd and synched her neural to the pub's Movement, her eyes shut while her body obeyed the Movement's command, the modulated electrical pulses carrying her into the mosh of bodies as they writhed together as one synchronized, beating mass.

There was a time when she could lose herself in the Movement; find that neurotoxic nirvana among the swimming limbs and strobe lights. But that night, after the best of the smoke fluttered out of her head and the dizzying heights of her sensations turned grossly nauseous, she experienced no holy revelation like she was accustomed to in her reckless youth—just a cold finger down her spine as she looked around at the travelers who tore up the floor, their red joy, and knew these nights were no longer hers. With a wink she left the Movement. Stumbled to the counter, muscles numb as they remembered control, her finger held up, signaling the bartender, who then fixed her something small and sharp.

The pipe smoke fleeting, the dancing ineffective, she looked around the room for someone to sleep with. Saw a man, alone at the fringe of the club, nursing a beer. He was postured like someone had jammed a stick up his ass. *Toral*, she thought hazily. He didn't look half bad. Full head of fiery hair. Strong jaw. She could do without the perpetual scowl on his face, but still, he was handsome enough to satisfy. She grabbed her drink and wandered over to him, half a mind to chew him out for being such a bastard during the captains' brunch, but when she arrived at his table—a journey that, in her mind, took hours—he had the nerve to look bashful, lowering his eyes when she took a seat without asking for permission. He muttered something, but it was drowned out by the pounding drums of the Movement. She shouted for a repeat. "I said I want to apologize for how I behaved earlier today!" he shouted back. "I know you weren't trying to . . . flaunt your success. I forget myself sometimes. Something I'm working on."

"Accepted," she told him, and when she saw that he seemed genuinely relieved, she thought, *He'll do*. Her eyes wandered along his biceps, the contour of muscle described beneath the snug shirt he wore. It occurred to her that the last person she slept with was Kaeda, and she wondered if maybe that was part of the problem— that she needed to sleep with someone who wouldn't die of old age the next time she saw him. After some aimless conversation with Toral about the finished delivery of seeds, and listening to the many gripes he had with his crew, all of whom he believed were too lax with inventory protocol, she silenced him with an invitation to her bed. He asked her if she was serious. And he smiled when she said yes. They left the bar together, back to his room in the Travillion. She shoved him onto the bed, grabbed his hands and slapped them to her waist. He was proficient, she would give him that. Adventurous in a way that many men were not. But no matter the joy she felt in the moment above him, and underneath, the act of it was much like the pipe smoke—fleeting, over before it really began. Two hours later, she was left in the same state she had been in before, only this time with Toral drifting off beside her, murmuring about abstract pleasures while she sat against the headboard, watching her minutes clip into hours. The fringe of day as the wings of Pelican Station unfurled, and sunlight broke through the glass ceiling of the Avenue Strip, the window blinds scoring her tired face.

She was not in that room. She was not on that station. She was in the *Debby*, walking down the causeway. She was listening to the sandaled footsteps that followed her. The leather snapping between sole and metal.

The snap of it like an awakening.

In that Pelican morning, as her fellow captain slept beside her, she believed she would do anything to hear that sound again.

Two hundred twenty-six attendees were invited to the Canopy Dance. Those planning the event were surprised by the last-minute addition of Captain Nia Imani to the guest list, but the order had come from up the chain, so they did not question it, and placed another chair at a banquet table. The kitchen was alive leading up to the party, a crash of preparation as off-station chefs shouted at their charges for more salt and finer slices, each dish made by hand and not, as was usually the case on Pelican, by automation. As they mashed and baked the sweet-smelling seeds into delicate art, and the members of the orchestra tuned their instruments and went many times through the night's set list, the invitees prepared for the event. In her hatch in the *Debby*, Nia fitted herself into her dress. The red silk draped down her body in rivers. Nurse looped the back straps together, telling Nia to please be still for one goddamn second. Despite the rocky state of their relationship, she was glad that Nurse came by to help, even though she was obviously exhausted from her night shift, her gray hair undone in long, frayed curls, and her eyes sagged. Nurse tightened the final knot and stepped back, appraising her work with a frown. "What's wrong?" Nia asked.

"The dress looks good," she assured Nia. "I'm just worried we've prettied you up for the firing squad."

Nia chuckled but let the comment lie. She smoothed some lint off the hem and grabbed her bag.

"I think this is a mistake," Nurse said.

"I know."

Nurse didn't sigh, though it was clear she wanted to—she held it in, along with the many other things Nia imagined she wished to say.

No public communication devices were allowed on Canopy Deck. Handhelds and other neural extensions were handed off to the Yellowjackets guarding the doors to the tower elevators. As Nia stepped in line for the elevator, she glanced warily at the crowd gathered behind the cordon applauding the ones chosen for the dance. Her crew was there, everyone but Nurse—Durat and Baylin leaning far enough over the cordon a Yellowjacket shoved them back, the two of them shouting incomprehensible words while Sonja, who stood between them, gave Nia a subtle salute from the hip, a salute that Nia returned before she gave her Handheld to the Yellowjacket and entered the pod.

Four others shared her pod ride up the tower's neck—nobles, if their impossible dresses were any clue. For the duration of the ten-minute climb, she stood apart from them, their clothing of liquid crystal and spectral shapes and patterned ideograms. She was unsure if she should try to make conversation with these people, until one of the women eyed Nia's outfit and asked what company she represented; when Nia told her she represented no company but was the captain of a commercial transport ship, the woman's smile wavered and she offered vague compliments in regards to her service of Umbai, then returned to her companions. When the pod hushed to a stop and the doors spiraled open, Nia let the others step out before her, waiting until they were a good distance ahead before she followed suit, her step staggering slightly at the awesome sight of the Canopy Deck.

The scale of the deck was overwhelming. Large enough to house a guest list of thousands, let alone the curated gathering of hundreds that now occupied the space, the dance hall of the Allied elite made Nia feel claustrophobically small, as if the vast and empty space above and around her had omnidirectional weight, slowly crushing her into a diamond as she made her way to the cloth-draped tables in the center of this social arena. Beyond the glass dome, engine trails of distant ships scored the black of space with chemical streams of color, painting intricate patterns that she soon realized were various company logos. Within the dome, clusters of nobles and company officials chatted under a riot of automaton birds—a peacock strutted past Nia, its brass-and-diamond plumage arrayed as its talons clicked between the tables. A child dressed in a suit of thousands of tiny black crystals giggled as he fed a thrasher the crumbled appetizers in his hand, the bird twittering at him before taking flight, back to the mechanic to have the food it had no way of digesting extracted. But beyond the automaton birds and the people dressed like abstractions of thought, Nia noticed something else—a difference in the gravity, lighter than in the rest of the station, subtly so, promoting a kind of glide when she moved. The furls of her dress swayed, suspended in the air just long enough to be noticed, and like everything in the canopy, moved as if underwater. Overwhelmed, she sat down at one of the empty tables and gathered her bearings. It was impossible to suss the difference between Umbai personnel and average royalty, for there was no conformity of dress, each outfit as spectacular and diverse as the last. There would be no way to know who was relevant to her goal until she got up and started talking to someone. As she decided on a target, a man asked her if the seat beside her was taken. She tossed her hand at it.

"How is the gravity treating you, Captain Imani?" he asked.

The man was smiling. He was shorter than most in the room, his face pleasantly round, and smooth of any facial hair, his brow shaped by a prominent widow's peak. He wore a conservative black suit, a small winged brooch pinned to his heart, and in his hand was a napkin with a small purple pastry inside, the smell of which was more than familiar to Nia, considering she'd carted the ingredients to and from the station for the past four years. Her thoughts were knocked askew by the aroma and the memory it carried—the night she inhaled Kaeda's scent, behind that rock, on that hill. The man beside her regarded her with a light in his eyes, something close to amusement, as if he had some sense of the warm place where her mind had gone, but not its exact coordinates.

"Have we met?" she asked.

"Not yet." He put down his napkin and brushed the crumbs of dhuba off his palm, the work of decades discarded in a thoughtless instant as he extended his hand in introduction. She shook it a bit too firmly. "I'm Sartoris Moth, the architect of this soiree." He beamed with pride at their surroundings while under the table he massaged the hand she had crushed. "What do you think? The birds were my idea. They felt appropriate, considering M. Nakajima's preoccupation with the creatures." He gazed at the mechanical thrush that had landed on the floor by their feet, pecking at the purple crumbs he had let fall. The bird chirped, electric, once it finished cleaning the mess, its jade eye glancing at Nia before its wings erupted in flight. "You were a last-minute addition to the guest list. When I found out you weren't connected to any company or noble family, my curiosity was piqued, and I thought, *I must know everything about her!*"

"Do you know who added me?" she asked.

"You don't know?" His eyes twinkled. "Now, that's interesting. Unfortunately I cannot say. It was all a rather sudden, but welcome, interjection."

She clenched the cloth on the table between her thumb and finger and rubbed out her anxiety. Someone in this room had brought her here. "Can you tell me what I should expect tonight, M. Moth?"

"Sartoris, please." He had resumed eating his snack. She noticed he ate with one hand, while the other remained in his left pocket. "After the opening course and drinks, there will be a speech from the head consul of the station, followed by the seven-course entrée, after which Fumiko Nakajima will initiate the Canopy Dance. From there, a series of smaller events will open up, all of them optional, but available, should you be in the mood to partake—interactive presentations of life on various Resource Worlds. The people's way of life, what they wear, the produce they cultivate on these unique habitats. Give the people a thrill, as it were." He gestured to the dhuba pastry on his napkin as an example. "If I were given to gambling, I'd bet on your seeds winning the night. They have a sweetness like none other."

Nia wondered how strange it was going to be to see actors play out the harvesting of dhuba stalks, and hoped she wouldn't have to stay long enough to see it. She leaned closer to the party architect. "Can you tell me something else?"

He mirrored her lean forward, enjoying the conspiratorial shift in conversation. "If I am able."

"Are there any representatives from Nest Security here?" she asked.

"Now, that is a question." He gestured to a cluster of guests on the other side of the dome, at an older man with a thick gray beard and a posture that not only suggested he had served time in a private military company but that this was the last place in Allied Space he wanted to be. "Guard commander of the station—a chore and a half, convincing him to attend." Sartoris let out a put-upon sigh. "He's not one for socializing, which I find amazing, considering his social standing. His presence here is my second greatest accomplishment of the night."

"He's very striking," Nia said, hoping he would get the hint.

"Do you think so?" Sartoris grinned at her. "Well. Would you like me to introduce the two of you?"

Nia pretended bashfulness, made a show of fighting back a smile. "I'm just a transporter. I doubt he'd be very interested in me."

"My dear captain," he said, "we live this life only once. We must live it bravely." She noticed in the man's pearly eyes a hard-cut gleam, a boldness behind the pomp—an earned boldness, from someone who fought for his seat at the table. She liked him for that.

"You're right," she said, standing up. "Let's be brave."

He clapped his hands like a child.

But once they had weaved through the crowds and Sartoris had introduced her to the guard commander, it was clear from the way the man's once-unfocused gaze sharpened on her name that he was already well aware of her. "Congratulations on completing your shipment cycle with Umbai, Captain Imani," the tall man growled. "You served this company well."

"Thank you," Nia said. "It was a long few years. It'll be nice to be stationary for a while."

"If the two of you will excuse me"—Sartoris backed away—"I believe I am being called. I'll have more drink sent over. Please, enjoy, you two." With a wink, he was gone, and Nia was alone with the guard commander. He gave her a thin smile before he moved his gaze toward the transparent wall of the dome. She followed. A ship cut across the horizon like a diamond on black glass, underlining the winged insignia of the Umbai Company. "I'm aware that you've been asking about the child you've brought to us," he said. "I admire your persistence. But whatever you think is going on, it's not. The boy is fine."

"I just want to see him," she said.

"And you've been told you cannot." He gazed down at her. "How many more times must you be denied before you stop?"

"I've yet to find out."

She grimaced at her silly choice of words, but the guard commander smiled. It was a tectonic shift of a smile, as if his face were unused to such an expression. "I am impressed you somehow got your way into this party to talk to me," he said. "That's an achievement in and of itself. Be proud of that. But as I said before, you are wasting your time. I suggest you take Sartoris's advice and enjoy what is around you." He placed his empty glass on the table. "Bother me again and I'll have you thrown out."

With that, he turned heel and joined another group. The group accommodated him swiftly, swallowing him into their conversation, their backs turned to Nia, the borders made clear. It was a disheartening moment, but she took solace in the intel she'd gathered from the guard commander's words—that Umbai had not invited her, but rather a third, yet unknown, party.

The evening wore on. She spoke with the other guests, which proved a futile endeavor. Always they would be sweet at first, interested, until she introduced herself as the relative no one that she was, and they, seeing that there was no advantage to be gained in conversation or disadvantage to be had in snubbing her, would almost invariably shut her down with a pitying smile before moving on to more fruitful quarry. After the fourth snub, she retreated to one of the buffet lines, snacking on the kebab of a pillaged Resource World, feeling more depleted than before. The most information she could gather was that people were irritated that Fumiko Nakajima had yet to arrive to her own party. She wondered if she was wasting her time.

A glass was clinked and the people gathered in the center of the room for the head consul's speech. The consul moved through the crowd in her dress of many geometries, up the steps of a raised dais, where she began her speech about the continued expansion of Umbai. The words were inert and uninspiring to Nia, and yet the nobles clapped at the end of every sentence as if it were the new gospel. She remained at the fringe of the crowd, half listening to the speech, when a hand grazed her shoulder. "I'm sorry it didn't work out," Sartoris whispered. "The guard commander can be blind to extraordinary beauty at the worst of times."

"You did your best," she said.

The consul was gesticulating to the stars.

"Please don't let one foolish man ruin your night. Let me know what you need, and I shall attend to it."

But she told him it was fine, and walked away. She headed back to the elevators to regroup. The light gravity was getting to her head and she needed solid footing. *So I say again*, the consul shouted behind her, *thank you for all of your continued support, and please enjoy the rest of the night. And let us celebrate together a millennium of progress!* The crowd broke into applause, the sound like thunder in Nia's ears as she waited for the elevator. When the door opened, she stepped aside to let the woman inside pass, but instead of joining the dance, the woman halted midstep and turned toward her.

"There you are," she said.

It took a minute for Nia to recognize her—she had only seen Fumiko Nakajima's face in passing on the Avenue Strip banner-lights.

She was much smaller in person, not only in size but in significance, dressed in an opal blouse and black pants—a simple, professional outfit; almost comically underdressed when compared to the nobles. Her hair was black, tied into a bun that hung loose at the nape of her neck, and her face—average, with some features too large for her small frame—held two dark eyes that gazed at Nia with startling clarity. She was waiting for Nia to speak. Only one question came to mind.

"Why did you invite me?"

Fumiko considered this question for a moment before she leaned forward and whispered in her ear, "He's in my loft. Endure these fools for a few more hours, Nia, and I'll take you to him." And then, without another word, she led the stunned captain back into the heart of the crowd, who applauded her entrance, the crowd whispering among themselves theories of how the captain of a small commercial transport ship knew the most famous woman on the station—and later, once the dancing was done, why the two of them left together, and where. Not even the head consul had the answer, and, when asked, shrugged with a look of amusement, and told the people how difficult it was to predict M. Nakajima.

Fumiko's loft was halfway down the station's neck. Like its owner, the place was unspectacular. There was a small kitchen area, partitioned from the living room by a marble counter, and from there, a hallway that led to an office, and a single bedroom, for one. "It was modeled after an Old Earth apartment," Fumiko said as she drew a circle in the air, and piano music began to play from an old speaker system by the couches. "Go on, sit. Make yourself comfortable. I'll go fetch him."

She did not sit. As Fumiko walked calmly down the hallway, Nia stood by the counter, steadying herself with a hand placed on the cool marble. The situation was fortuitous to a degree that was impossible, and she wondered if maybe she was dreaming. There was movement down the hall: the sound of a door opening, the quiet murmur of voices. She wiped her arm across her brow as she heard footsteps on wooden flooring, preparing herself for the possibility that Fumiko would return alone, this night an elaborate prank orchestrated by a woman driven mad with power. But this was not the case. When Fumiko returned, she was followed by a blond woman, who in turn ushered forth the boy.

He wore a plain shirt and cotton pants. His cheeks were flush, as if he were freshly showered, and his big dark eyes, once narrow, uncertain, now brightened like suns when he saw her. Nia's heart swelled as he let go of the blond woman's hand and walked up to her. She put a hand on his shaven head, rubbed her thumb on the buzz.

"It's good to see you," she whispered.

He sniffed, nodded.

The reunion was short-lived. "Come to my office, Captain," Fumiko said from the hallway. "We have things to discuss."

The job, as Fumiko explained it from behind her glass desk, was simple. Nia was to take the boy on board the *Debby*, and bring him to fringe space, outside the territorial regions of Umbai and its Allied partners. Once there, they were to wait for the day when they would rendezvous with Fumiko at an arranged time and place.

Whatever Nia and the crew of the *Debby* chose to do in fringe space during the wait was inconsequential to Fumiko. "As long as it does not place the boy in physical or psychic harm, you can do as you please." They were not to leave fringe space. They would be able to visit stations owned by companies who had neutral or antagonistic relationships with Umbai, but even then, only for a few days at most, before they must move on—as for where, it didn't matter, just as long as they kept moving. "As a safeguard against possible interference from these stations, you will have to register as the boy's permanent guardian." Fumiko pushed the contract across the glass. The wording was different from Umbai's, short, with terms stated clearly, and directly, in a numerical list.

One, the boy could not die.

Two, the boy could not be abandoned.

Three, the boy must be returned to Fumiko, at the specified coordinates, at the determined time.

Four, Fumiko Nakajima must have access to the *Debby*'s folding logs, so that she could adjust her own travels accordingly.

Five, if, for whatever reason, the *Debby* must be abandoned and they fold on another vessel, Fumiko Nakajima must be notified.

Six, the boy's nature could not be disclosed to anyone not preapproved by Fumiko Nakajima. "The gist is," Fumiko said, "any action that prevents you from meeting me when and where I tell you, with the boy safe and unharmed, will constitute a breach of contract. If you breach contract, you will be in violation of company law. Your captain's license will be revoked, you will be forbidden from entering the stations, and your accounts will be frozen."

Nia flipped the contract over, her brow furrowed. "This mentions nothing about how long the job will take."

"It will be a number of years, but how many is dependent on the boy."

"Why is that dependent on the boy?"

As Fumiko stared at her, all the reservations that Nurse had disclosed were now percolating, and Nia was suddenly unsure of who it was she had been chasing after all this time, and why this woman had a vested interest in his future. It amazed her that she was considering the offer at all—any other suspicious job, given by any other suspicious employer, she would've walked out on, moved on, and lived satisfied with the knowledge that she hadn't been irresponsible with her livelihood. But the responsibility she felt for the boy compelled her to stay in her seat.

"What is he?" she asked.

"After you sign the contract." Fumiko pointed at the sheet in Nia's hands, as if to emphasize the point. "All you need to know right now is that the boy is of no danger to you or your crew, and that it is in everyone's best interests if he is allowed time and space to develop outside the purview of federated space."

The contract sat on her lap like a granite slab. It pressed into her with insistent force. Nia had fantasized about what it would be like, to take the boy in, to raise him on board the *Debby* and teach him the life of the stellar traveler, but in these fantasies there were no caveats, no contract explicitly stating the consequences should she fail in her appointed task. Up until now, she had thought of the boy as a window outside of herself. Now he was a prison sentence.

"How long do I have to decide?" Nia asked, dry-mouthed.

Fumiko glanced at the cuckoo clock on the wall. It was an elegant construction, made of real wood, with smoothed surfaces and tapered edges. A hollow click for every second that passed.

"Not long," she said. "An hour, at most."

She left the office to give Nia space to consider the offer.

The cuckoo clock ticked musically, and on the desk, a miniature rock fountain burbled with cold water, spilling into a well before being vacuumed back up and spilled out again in an unending cycle.

Nia rested her face in her palms. Once she signed the contract, there was no going back. Her life, the life she had scraped together, would be gone, and as frustrating and lonely as she often found that life, it was hers. Once she signed the contract, she would be tethered to the fate of a child who, as Nurse had pointed out many times, was in essence a stranger.

He was a stranger.

Nia paced around the table. She considered the possibility that Fumiko had lied, that the boy would in fact be a very real danger to the livelihood of her and her crew. She considered the possibility that, even if Fumiko had not been lying, the boy would grow into an unbearable presence; that he would develop into the sort of person she would despise. Someone capricious and cruel. Selfish. Stubborn. There were no hints of these traits now, but she knew that anything was possible, knew from experience that people could change into any sort of sloth or monster. But most of all, Nia was afraid that at the end of the contract, when the job was done, however many years that would take, she would look back and realize that it had all been wasted time. That the boy offered nothing more than a distraction from her late-thirties rut. A dangerous, reckless distraction.

Nia knew what she had to do. She had to go to Fumiko and decline the offer. She had to tell the boy that she was sorry, but that she could not help him.

She had to leave.

She made it to the door, had her hand wrapped around the brass handle, when, with the startling abruptness of curtains thrown open to light, Deborah's face flashed in her mind, overwhelming her.

She let go of the knob.

I've been here before, she realized.

Nia signed the contract. She did it in one quick scribble, afraid that if it wasn't done furiously, she would lose heart. The paper shimmered with new data and then went dead, the course of her life now set. She sat down in her chair and breathed out, fighting the shake of her hands as the door behind her opened and Fumiko walked in, expressionless, as if she were not at all surprised by the outcome. She sat on the other side of the desk and thanked Nia for her amenability. She told her that she had made a wise choice. That she looked forward to their partnership.

And then she told her of the future of interstellar travel.

It was six in the morning when Nia made the call. She waited in the common room of the *Debby* while, over the following hour, her crew arrived for debrief. Durat was hungover, his neck peppered with love bites. Baylin was blinking away sleep. Sonja was alert, smirking as she did when something curious was about to take place. And Nurse was frowning, as though she had already divined the motivations for this early-morning meeting, and had steeled herself for the worst. After the crew were seated, Nia took a moment to look at them all, for a moment questioning whether this truly was the best course of action, even though she knew there was no going back. She had already signed away her rights. "A few hours ago, I signed a contract for the *Debby*'s next job."

The room was quiet. Durat knuckled his red eyes. When he spoke, his voice was rough from a phlegm-coated throat. "Wait. Weren't you just at a party?"

"That was where I was hired."

Nurse folded her hands on her lap. "What's the job?" she asked.

There was no point in delaying it. Nia sat down and told them what she was able to. "Fumiko Nakajima hired me to escort the boy out of Umbai corporate space. For a period of years, a maximum of fifteen, real-time, I'm to provide the boy a safe environment where he may live and mature. During that time, the *Debby* will be on the move within unfederated fringe space, taking jobs where available, until the day comes when the *Debby* is to rendezvous with Fumiko Nakajima, completing the contract. To reiterate, there is a chance that the job will last for fifteen years, lived time." She cracked a smile. "There's a close to one hundred percent chance I'll turn fifty before the contract is completed and I can dock at a federated station again." She paused, letting the first dose of information sink in. Durat's hangover evaporated. Baylin blinked. And Nurse stared at Nia as she continued: "There are severe penalties for failing. Should the boy die, or we fail to bring him to the rendezvous point when the time comes, we will be exiled from station space, our financial accounts will be frozen, and we will be stripped of our licenses. I'll lose the *Debby*. None of us will be allowed to work on a vessel again."

Somewhere in the vents, there was a click as the conditioner reset its cycle.

"What's the pay?" Sonja asked slowly.

"Two billion iotas for each signed contract."

No one breathed. It was enough money to last three decades of vacation. The room was silent as everyone considered the potential windfall. Nurse chewed her nails.

"There is no one I would rather have with me than the four of you," Nia said. "You are some of the best operators I've had the pleasure of working with, and I would consider it an honor if you served again. That said"—and here she looked at all of them—"I only want you to accept if you are one hundred and ten percent sure you are up to it. You were paid a good amount for our last job. The pay should last you a number of years' vacation on a pretty rock somewhere, and should you want for another transport gig, you'll have your pick of ships to serve on under my recommendation. You have options. I signed my contract with Fumiko. There's no walking back, for me, or for this ship. But there is for you. You have three hours to decide if you want to follow." She drummed her fingers on the table. "That's the short of it."

"This is crazy," Baylin muttered.

"Fifteen years lived time . . ." Durat shook his head. "I'd be forty-five by the time I saw Pelican again."

Nurse asked, almost in a whisper, "What is he, Nia?"

The question was a virus. It worked its way into the others' systems as their eyes narrowed, they too beginning to question the boy's identity, the suddenness of the contract, the incredible paycheck waiting at the end of the years-long stint in fringe space; a place to which Nurse never wished to return. "Why does the contract pivot around the boy's development?" she asked, and then, more insistent, "Nia, what *is* he?"

"I can't tell you that." She was not about to breach her contract hours into the job, even though she wished she could tell them that he was in all likelihood just a kid caught up in a thousand-year-old psychopath's game. "Only those who have signed the contract can know the full details. What I can tell you is that he isn't dangerous, mentally or physically."

Durat groaned. "That's reassuring."

"The job will be skirting the law, but we won't be breaking it. All we would be doing is creating a bubble of privacy around him in the less-visited regions of the galaxy."

"A nice euphemism," Nurse said. "I almost died in that 'less-visited region of the galaxy' when the ship I served on went derelict and there was no one to pick up our distress beacon."

Baylin grimaced. "None of this sounds right, Captain."

"I know," she said. "Like I said before, and like every job we've ever signed up for, if you aren't certain this is for you, then this is where we part ways."

"But this isn't like the other jobs," Nurse said. "The other jobs were within federated space. They were signed with companies and approved businesses. They had safety nets. And if we failed, there wasn't the threat of exile." Her voice was raised. Baylin was nodding as she went on. "Stop talking to us like this is fair, because it isn't. You throw this job at us with countless unknown variables before morning while we're exhausted, promising everything and nothing, like this is just another day, like we're just coworkers in an office on some City Planet. Like this ship isn't our home."

This made Nia smirk. "You said yourself this ship isn't a home."

Nurse slapped the table. "Because I was making a goddamn point! A point I stand by. Which is that this isn't a home, not for a child who has no real choice in the matter. A child, by the way, who you keep hinting is special in some way, yet you refuse to trust us with any specifics about his identity. And while I understand you're under a nondisclosure agreement, I wonder if even *you* know what he really is." Her cheeks were flushed. "You say he's not dangerous, but considering the absurd amount of money on the line, how do you know that Nakajima hasn't lied to you? Baited you with this paycheck to keep you distracted from what's real? For all you know he's a science experiment that could erupt into a nuclear explosion if he eats the wrong kind of sweet. And don't you dare accuse me of being paranoid again, because nothing about this situation is normal."

It took everything Nia had not to bring down the hammer and tell Nurse to shut the hell up and listen. She would not win them with impatience. She even agreed with the consensus: that she had put them in an unfair position. That to sign the contract was to go against all self-preservation instincts, but that to walk away would be saying goodbye to what was, for all intents and purposes, their home, for however many years they had served. "You're right," she said. "You are absolutely right."

Nurse blinked. And then, the spell of tension broken, she shriveled. "Nia," she moaned. "Why are you doing this?"

"Because I need to." The words came out cracked; clumsy things that dribbled out of her lips, delivered with barely any conviction.

Beneath the table her hands fought. The job was ludicrous, but that was, in the end, irrelevant. She would be with the boy. She had to remind herself that that was all she wanted. The boy, the boy. "I've made my choice," she said. She stood up. "You have three hours to make yours. Come to my hatch when you've decided." And then she exited the kitchen, leaving behind her a hard silence. She left the hatch to her quarters open and sat down at her desk. She didn't take out her notebook, didn't even make the pretense of writing. Just sat and waited, her stomach roiling with angry acids, eager to eject the alcohol she had consumed at the Canopy, which by now seemed like years ago. *You've made your bed*, she thought to herself. *You have no control over what happens next.*

Baylin was the first to come. He stood at her hatch, his answer clear by the contempt on his face. "Nurse is right," he said. "What you're doing isn't fair. This was my home." He stared at the floor, his mouth working itself over difficult thoughts. "You're my first captain. Don't want you to be my last."

"I respect that," she told him, though it still hurt to hear it. "I'll send your stats out to the other ships. The *Helena Basho* is looking for a second engineer. You'll have a place by the end of the week."

He took this in and nodded. Glanced once at Nia's outstretched hand, and shook it begrudgingly.

She watched her engineer leave.

Durat was the second. His hangover was no better when he walked in; his large cheeks sallow, his brown hair a greasy mop that kept falling over his eyes as he brushed the bangs away. "I love flying, Captain," he said, his foot rabbiting, "and I love the stations. And I love eating in nice restaurants and drinking." When she told him in jest that this was news to her, he chuckled, but even that was half-hearted. "Did you know I also love sleeping with pretty people? And that I love being the age I am?" The last dregs of forced jovial-ity dropped out of his voice. "And that fifteen years is too long to be away from the things that I love, and that while I love you, it isn't enough to—" His voice hitched. He laughed as he turned away and rubbed at his eyes. "Sorry. It's hard to say this shit out loud."

"You're doing good," she said.

"I'm a coward," he muttered.

"You're not a coward."

"If I was brave, I'd trust you." He knuckled his eyes. "I've served under six different captains. Some were great, one was a real bastard. But you, you are the one who'd make me even consider signing this contract." He smiled, a tear falling from his reddened eyes, and pointed at her. "When you come back two billion iotas richer, come find my ass and tell me how stupid I was."

They bear-hugged. His snot dampened her shoulder. On any other day, she would've called him out, told him he was messing up her good shirt, and he would remind her that she had no good shirts. Not today though. Today, she let him melt into her.

"I'll miss you, Nia," he whispered.

And she watched her pilot leave.

Sonja didn't even give a reason when she came by and told Nia that she'd sign on. Just said, "Let me know when we're leaving," and walked off, leaving her captain speechless for the second time since they'd landed. This was a welcome reprieve.

The hardest of the meetings was yet to come.

The three-hour deadline was almost up when Nurse arrived. She didn't walk through the hatch, not right away. First she leaned against the riveted frame, looking in, still wearing her sanitary gloves from her night shift at the hospital. Hands on her elbows. Distant eyes.

"There's not much more to say, is there?" she asked, her voice sober, cold. "We've talked, and talked. And fought. And fought some more." It was then that she walked inside, observing the blank gray walls, the uncarpeted floor, the simple bed adorned with a single pillow. "My opinion of your room has changed over the years. When you first took me on, and we shared our first drink in here—"

"Marbury Cider," Nia recalled.

"That's the one. A bit too sour for my tastes." She almost smiled. "Anyway, that night, when I saw how . . . sparse your decorations were, with that beautiful desk and nothing else, I thought, *Wow, this person has absolutely no personality.* Or that you were wildly depressed. Or that you had no conception of beauty. But then I got to know you." Her hand touched the wall, as if in benediction. "You were just single-minded; owned what was necessary; a desk to write on and a bed to sleep in. I even thought it was enlightened, the way wise ones perch on a mountain and consider the changing winds."

Nia looked away and said with a lace of bitterness, "Never knew you thought of me with such poetry."

"Flowery, trite, but it's what I thought." She withdrew her hand from the wall, stood there with her back to Nia. "But I've changed my mind. I see how empty you are. And you see it too. That's why you're clutching for anything that will fill you up, even if it's a shadow."

"I'll tell you now, I won't miss your constant dissection of my psyche."

"Yes, you will," she said. "But as always with you, it will be when it's too late for you to do anything about it."

"And what is it you think I'm doing now?" Nia asked. "The boy was almost taken away from me. I stopped that from happening before it was too late. I made a choice to help him."

"You were led by the nose by your childish impulsiveness."

Nia stood up. Fire coursed through her veins. If this was the last fight they were to have, she would make it one Nurse would never forget. "On impulse I folded this ship out of Pocket Space in a fringe region and discovered your shit-covered body. On impulse I gave you a place to become yourself again."

"And you've never let me forget it," Nurse shouted. "Not for a second. Praise be to Captain Nia Imani for her stalwart instincts. Her benevolence! Let me know how much longer you expect me to play the role of cowed and thankful so I can warn the boy of what he has to look forward to—the many years of kissing your feet on this goddamn ship!"

"I keep reminding you because you keep undermining me with every decision I make. You say you keep me honest, but it's never been about my leadership. It's always been about you. Your pathetic need to make yourself feel important. But I know you. Coward. You hid while your crew cannibalized itself. And you're doing it again. Abandoning the people who need you when things get tough."

"How dare you," Nurse snarled. "Is that what you want? You want us to throw our tragedies in each other's faces? You want to talk about abandonment? You want to talk about Deborah? Your sister—"

"Shut your fucking mouth."

"Your sister. Corpse in the street, your sister. That's your doing. No one but you left her alone in that house full of debt. I never believed you, you know. You moaned that you had no choice but to leave her behind, leave her to pay your father's debts like they weren't your responsibility too, but I know you could've found another way. If you gave a shit to try. But you loved it. You loved to leave. How free you must've felt, shrugging off her love for you. Leaving her to the money wolves. Paint her name on your ship all you want, dedicate your misery to her ghost, but don't you dare talk to me about abandonment like you're a guiltless saint. Like you're doing any of this from the heart. You have no heart. If you did, you wouldn't have started this disgusting game. But there! I played my round! Is this the dead you want to revive?"

"No!" Shaking, Nia staggered backward, sat back down. The bed hiccupped under her sudden weight. She pressed the back of her hands against her eyes. "No," she said, quieter. And then she said the two words she rarely said, proud as she was, stubborn as she was. "I'm sorry."

"I loved you," Nurse cried, "but you chose the boy over us." She sniffed. "Over me."

Nia pressed the tears into her hands, the pressure hot, forcing them back into her eyes. "Meena," she whispered, but Nurse did not answer. She didn't have to look up to know when the woman had gone.

She felt it.

The void ripped in the air.

The departing crew were silent as they gathered their belongings from their respective rooms. Sonja had retrieved a driftcart from the docks to help them move the heavier boxes. Nia placed a call to the Travillion, and within minutes, four attendants arrived to shepherd the belongings up to the hotel.

She sat on the ramp of the *Debby* and watched the departure. The entire experience was surreal. Different members had left her company over the years, for many reasons, but it was always one at a time, always amicable; parties separating with some certainty that all was as it should be. As each box was rolled down the ramp, Nia reconsidered the choice she had made, the reasons for it, wondering if the selfless act she thought she'd made was really that, or just another feint powered by some dark desperation within; if it mattered. When she looked up, she saw Nurse pass by with her last piece of luggage, rolling it down the ramp, the wheels dancing along the grated surface. Her old friend stopped at the bottom but didn't turn around, her gloved hand rediscovering its grip on the handle of the suitcase before continuing toward the elevator, where, without another thought, she and her sari were gone. There was no goodbye.

Durat sat beside her.

"I'll stay till you guys leave," he said.

"That's not necessary," she told him.

He laughed. "I know," he said. "But I will."

She gripped his hand, and they sat together on the ramp of the *Debby*, with Sonja standing behind them as they waited for the new crew members to arrive.

The elevator doors flowered open, and the blond woman from Fumiko's apartment stepped out. The boy was with her. His large eyes fixed on Nia and her ship, a silly grin on his face. The mere sight of him settled her anxious heart. Behind him were two Yellowjackets and four other people, all of whom Nia assumed were to be her replacement crew members. "They look serious," Durat whispered before leaping off his perch and pulling the boy into a rough hug.

The blond woman was wearing a long, billowy yellow dress that shimmered like sun on water. "I'm sorry it didn't work out with your crew," she said, sounding like she meant it.

"It's fine." Nia was in no mood to speak of it further. She eyed the two Yellowjackets at the bottom of the ramp. "Should they be here?"

"Nest Security is a fractured beast," the woman explained. "These two are loyal to Fumiko. You needn't worry about them." Then, with a flick of her finger, the group of four stepped forward. "Allow me to introduce you to your acting crew. This is Pilot Vaila Jenssen, Engineer Em Reese, and Medical Tech Royvan Hollywell. Each of them are exemplars of their respective fields. They can be trusted well." The trio bowed when the woman called their names, but already Nia was looking beyond them, the wounds of departures still fresh, unable and unwilling to make friends with the scabs just yet. She was more curious about the fourth member of their group, yet to be introduced, his diminutive frame and widow's peak striking her as very familiar. "And I believe you've already met Sartoris Moth."

It took a moment for Nia to remember the man from the Canopy Dance. He made a deep bow in his fine black jacket. "We meet again, Captain Imani," he said in his dilettante way. "It'll be a pleasure working with you, I'm sure."

"It's nice to see you too." She was confused as to why a party architect was being added to her crew. "I didn't realize I needed a fourth."

"Sartoris will be acting as Fumiko's intermediary," the woman explained. "If there are any issues, he will be able to contact her and send for help."

"And tattle should you misbehave," he added with a wink.

While the new members boarded *Debby* and made themselves at home, the last of the goodbyes were said. Durat and Sonja clapped backs. With a smirk, she muttered, "Later, cheater," and he responded in kind, thanking her for all the money he had won from their card games. And after he pulled the boy in for a last quick embrace, he turned to Nia, and when they hugged, it struck Nia how strange it was, to know this was in all likelihood the last time they would touch; that hours ago, she had not once entertained the notion of his leaving the *Debby*, but now it seemed inevitable, as though this was and had always been the moment he parted from her world. He blinked.

"Good luck, Nia," he said.

From up in the cockpit she saw him wave as the engines kicked to life and his replacement spoke in codes with the operator on the other end of the comms channel. Nia held up a hand, waved to her old friend. And as he began his walk back to the Travillion, she wished him many drunken and happy nights, and wished she would be there to see them. As delusional as she believed Fumiko to be, she had to concede her theory about the boy was a pretty thought—the idea of him, traveling across the galaxy in mere seconds like an emblem of light. Fumiko had called it something stupid, like "the Jaunt"—the name the mysterious first man had given it—but to Nia, if it was real, and true, the power was more than that. It was no more goodbyes.

Her new pilot looked up at her. "Everything's ready, Captain," she said.

Nia nodded.

The boy was waiting for her outside her hatch. He was wearing Kaeda's one-shouldered robe. It was strange to see him now that Fumiko's knowledge had been imparted—aware now that behind his devoted gaze was a network of thought; a bank of memory she had no access to. She wondered if he knew the truth about himself—if he knew that one day, years from now, he would be able think of a place, and be there. But these thoughts soon evaporated as he smiled at her approach. He is only a boy, she thought. And he will be safe.

While the strangers aboard the *Debby* prepared for the fold, she walked him down to the cargo bay to bother Sonja, who was now the one person they both knew on the ship. There they spent the hours, perturbing the vet with their company until it was time for lunch, and then for dinner, the long day settling to a close, the lights in the ship switching off systematically as Nia tucked him into bed.

"I'm glad you're here," she said.

He looked up at her, the blanket up to his neck. And when the light of the hatch went out with a click and cast them in black, Nia lost him—could only hear the slight rise of his breath, and the rasp of his voice, as he whispered, "Good night."

*   *   *

"I met a man, many, many years ago, who claimed he had Jaunted from the Nodal Straits of the fringe to Grammaton Station, without boarding a single ship. There was alcohol on his breath when he grabbed my arm and told me this—I could've had him shot for that, but I was more interested in watching him humiliate himself. So I listened, and I told him, fine, if you have this power, then show me. Show me how you traveled decades across the stars on just your feet. And then he smirked, and he was gone. The ground where he stood was smoke and ash. The air was humid, waved. I don't have many regrets, Captain Imani, but to this day I regret not asking for his name, some way to find him once he had gone. I stood two meters from the future, and let him fall through my fingers.

"My eyes remained open after that. I've lived a long time. There is little I do not have access to. I wink, and planetwide demographics, the people's rumor, their mystery, are at my disposal. I see the mosaic in its entirety. The unaccounted disappearances. The people gone as if by spontaneous combustion. Lone survivors from cratered wreckage. Naked bodies undamaged in the brimstone, who wander amnesiac before disappearing once more, never to be seen again. A pattern revealed if you know where to look. I believe the boy from Umbai-V is one of them—a step in the mutation that binds us further to our galactic destiny." She paused here with the creep of a sly smile. "And I believe you think I've lost my mind."

Nia had the face of a woman who just realized she had been conversing with delusion—it was rather attractive, Fumiko thought, how swiftly the captain regained her composure. "It is a lot to take in," the captain said with care.

"Yes, it is. And I could very well be wrong," Fumiko admitted. "But this is not a chance I am willing to take again. Not with the power at stake here."

The captain nodded. Her back remained upright, as though the chair she sat on were made of needles. "Why me?" she asked.

An expected question. Fumiko rolled her shoulders. "For a number of reasons. The first," she said, with a held finger, "the technology of today isn't capable of detecting whatever quantity the boy's power is composed of. It would take time to develop this technology, too much real-time to risk."

"Risk?"

"Umbai. They've been looking into my extracurricular projects for some time now, and I'd rather they did not find out about this one. They do not know how to handle good things without breaking them." She smiled. "I need the boy far from here, from me, until we not only have the tools with which to study him, but we know for certain that he is the one I've been looking for. You have a ship. You have experience traveling the fringe. And from the data available, I know you are calculating and make informed decisions.

"Which brings me to the second reason"—second finger, a peace sign—"that aside from your credentials, it is obvious the boy is attached to you. Of all the case studies I've observed over the decades, the common thread that bound all of the supposed Jaunters is that they never returned. Once they were gone, they were gone. Smoke and ash, as it were. If the boy has the ability, then unless I knocked him into a coma, I couldn't guarantee his continued presence. Since I would rather not do this to a child until necessary, I would rather he remain with you, who would give him a reason to stay, and reason to return, should he one day disappear."

"Disappear," the captain repeated. There was a slight pain to her expression—the same expression Fumiko herself wore when she had to bear with some poor soul's incoherent rambling.

A headache overcame her. The headache would always be there, that dull and persistent throb, a consequence of her long stretches of cold sleep, along with the gaps in her memory, the names long forgotten. It would be so easy to refuse this woman an explanation, but for some reason, she needed her to understand. Maybe because she saw in her files a kindred spirit. "I accept that it is a possibility that what I saw was not real," she said. "And I accept that the research I have done over the centuries could be nothing but a vain gesture toward confirmation bias. But I will be sure. I must be sure. What you must understand, Captain, is that I have nothing to lose, sending you to the fringe with the boy, and everything to gain if I am right. Whether you believe in me, or my eyes, is irrelevant. Whether you think me psychotic is irrelevant. You are now a participant, and you will help me erase the distance between the stars."

Nia stared at her. Fumiko was so startled by what the captain said next that she lost her train of thought—the words out of nowhere, spoken with certainty, as if the fact was something to be observed on the table, beside the small and endless fountain.

"You've lost someone," she said.

The words stayed with Fumiko, as she waited for the consort to return to the apartment with news of the *Debby*'s successful departure. She was seated at the marble counter, stroking her bottom lip, wondering what it was on her face that had made the captain think such a thing, when the consort knocked on the door, and confirmed that the boy was now far from the station. She pushed aside her wonderings and set to work, notifying the private vessel that waited for her in the Pelican's reserved dock to be ready to set off within the hour. In her bedroom she packed the clothes she would need for the trip—the simple blouses, the quartet of suits she fancied and which people often commented were wonderfully archaic in their cut but were to her only normal work clothes. As she packed, the consort waited by the door, her hands folded behind her back, patient and quiet. Fumiko snapped the bag shut and, on her way out, stopped before the blond woman. "Thank you for the company," she said, and kissed her fully on the lips. The consort let out a small moan, but Fumiko felt only an ember; somewhere in the ruin of her memory was the name of the woman she had once loved, but that name had been sanded away by the years spent in cold sleep. Even she did not know why, when she visited Pelican Station, she hired a consort for the duration of her stay—why she demanded they dye their eyes purple and color their hair blond, and cut it short, lightly mussed, or why, when they smiled, it must be as if in benediction. All she had was a distinct sense of relief when she was around these imperfect facsimiles, as if finally, after a long day at work, she had come home.

You've lost someone.

"It was a pleasure to serve, M. Nakajima," the consort said.

Fumiko transferred the payment for services to her account, which inspired a thankful smile, but when the woman leaned in for one more kiss, Fumiko moved past her and out of the apartment. She rested against the railing as the elevator pod dropped down the Pelican's neck. She thought about the drunk man who had once disappeared before her eyes. The unexpectedness of his act. The beauty of this unseemly man suddenly revealing to her the impossible. A gimp pelican, drying its wings in the light. She sighed through her nose as she gazed through the curved elevator window at the passing sight of the Gracilius and Schreiberi wings, and the Avenue Strip, which ran down her bird's back like a river between rhomboid mountains; down, at the small abstractions of people partying in the night.

There it was, her pelican.

There it went.

Her jaw tensed as the elevator descended.

None of this was real.

The pilot and crew welcomed her aboard the schooner. A man took her suitcase, a woman her coat. Fumiko thanked each of them for their hard work, and the work yet to come, and they with stars in their eyes told her they would not let her down, to which she nodded and asked them to prepare her stasis chamber.

It was as the winged doors of the chamber folded over her and encompassed her body that she thought of edamame—a bowl of them, dusted with sea salt, on a marble counter.

She grimaced. These images haunted her in the strangest moments; images with no time or context, slipping through the cracks of cold sleep to taunt her of a past she could not remember. Ribbons of curry and a boat in a canal. A thousand winking eyes. She squeezed her eyes shut and willed these images away, threw the bowl into the dark and tossed the curry into the water and stilled the winks until the crowd was eyeless and silent. The temperature dipped, and the static electricity dribbled across her skin. She readied herself for the long sleep. Believed she had found peace. But before she froze, she was visited by one more image—was confused by how moved she was by it, the tear on her cheek flashing to crystal as she gazed at the silhouette of a woman sitting on a bench by some distant shore, waiting for her.

II

5

The Pinch Point

The Pocket was charged with purpose. Down the Languid Current the *Debby* went, its radiation sails open, and borne on the slow drift of the tide's namesake. It was the first true day of the trip. The crew at work, accommodating to this new space, their new circumstance, busying themselves with this difficult adjustment; none more so than the middle-aged man locked away in his quarters, who with brow caked in sweat wrote in an old journal, one he packed away in haste, along with his other most treasured effects in his apartment, once M. Nakajima had given him his new assignment.

His new, very long assignment.

THE LANGUID CURRENT

DAY 1

The journey has begun, this grand adventure, & I lay in bed, dying.

I have been sprawled for most of the day recovering from the fold into the Pocket. The good doctor Royvan has informed me that those of a certain age are more susceptible to the symptoms— queasiness, headaches, pinched nerves, cold sweats, etc.

On the silver side, I have now had the chance to become well acquainted with my quarters. It is a bit small, not much larger than a cheap booking at a substrata hostel. There is enough room to pace in a small circle between the hatch, desk with lamp, & firm cot. The alloyed wall by the bed has a worrying amount of give when the ship hits current turbulence, rattling against the forces of the Pocket, threatening to sandwich me in my sleep. The room is colder than I would like, but alas, the Debby's temperature regulation is central-ized. No adjusting the climate for private comforts.

I am honored to have been chosen for this mission, but I am al-ready homesick for my old apartment on Gracilius Wing. Good memories, sharing a drink with good friends on the balcony, look-ing down on what you created. I will hold these memories close, as I crawl back in bed, & hope for a healthier tomorrow.

DAY 2

I felt marginally better this morning, though the numbness in my right foot persisted. Breakfast was a sparse affair. Protein noodles, with my choice of brown or yellow dipping sauce. Since I woke a bit later than the others, I ate alone, with only the sound of the running dishwasher for company.

Apparently I missed a great deal during my convalescence yester-day. For a belated orientation, the captain had private, one-on-one meetings with each of her new crew, & a shared meal at the end of the day, cooked with fresh ingredients culled from stasis. My mouth was watering as the good doctor Royvan described the steamed trout to me after my breakfast of tasteless noodles.

I spent the day becoming acquainted with the ship at large, while also observing how the old members & the new were getting along. Interactions are polite, professional, & stiff. This is as predicted. Many of us are strangers to one another, with only you to bind us in common history. That said, it is heartening that Vaila is with us. It was good to see her again during debrief on Pelican. It had been too many years since we'd last worked together. The feeling was mutual, though she was—& still is—understandably morose about this whole enterprise. She's eager to be back by your side, I think.

The only outlier in crew politics is the boy. True to what I've been told about him, he is a strange creature. Small, quiet, & with a singular way of navigating the space, as if he has rehearsed his movements before entering the door, his path one of maximal efficiency. Most of the time he is with the captain, their attention solely on each other, or the mercenary Sonja in the cargo bay. The new crew avoids eye contact with him. They behave strangely when they are in the same room, acknowledging him with a glance, but conversing with one another as if he is not there. It is only the second day, so there is little reason to be concerned, but crew integration is something to keep an eye on. I am eager to see how the captain plans to smoothen the transition of us scabs into the ship's daily routine.

DAY 3

I crossed paths with the boy in the causeway. He was alone, with neither the captain nor Sonja looming over his shoulder. An opportunity to strike, & make friends. I stopped walking & smiled with cheeks & said good morning. I think I frightened the poor boy. He seemed uncertain how to respond, & bowed slightly before he sped off to the captain's hatch. Nothing makes you feel quite so monstrous as when a child runs from you.

He is not the only one avoiding me. The other crew members, both old & new, evacuate the rooms I enter—kindly, with a thousand excuses, but obviously, & clumsily. This is not so surprising. Expected even. I am, after all, your eyes & ears. It is only natural they fear incriminating themselves in my presence, however incidentally, via unguarded complaints, or statements that could be construed—by one much less understanding than I—as treason.

It is lonely here.

Dinner tonight was heated gruel with savory chunks. I dashed it with some spice to make it marginally tempting. Still rueful that I missed that trout & a bit peeved that no one thought to save some for me. I tried to strike up conversation with Engineer Em, who was already at the table when I arrived, but I received only monosyllables in reply before he had had enough of me, & left the room with his bowl.

Add him to the tally.

DAY 4

Not much for this one to do aboard a commercial transport vessel other than to wander, & there is only so much wandering to be done on a vessel this size. It takes about four minutes for me to walk the ship from end to end at a normal clip. I believe I have walked the main causeway's length about fifty times since departure, each walk progressively less interesting than the last, the only new details that I notice are ones that inspire some amount of fear, as I realize slowly just how old this ship is.

It is curious that you did not start us off on a newer model of ship, though I understand the reasoning, letting the captain keep her comforts.

That said, there is no getting around the fact that the Debby *is a messy assemblage of outdated parts. The kitchen still relies on an old form of cold stasis, so produce will keep for a measly few months before the rot. Laundry vac gives clothing a metallic odor. Hatches groan in pain when opened. The temperature of the lav showers vacillates between hot & cold at random. Many times there is no hot water. Something is always rattling within the walls—a loose bolt about to fall off its thread, perhaps, & let this unstable house of cards collapse on itself. & then there is the engine. I am still feeling the remnant queasiness from our first fold into the Pocket— right foot is still tingly! According to Vaila, newer engine models have corrected for fold-nausea. Of all the parts that need replacing, surely this would be a priority for the captain! But no. When I asked her why she hasn't upgraded, the captain's eyebrow rose. She was quiet for a beat, & then shot me a curt reply about expenses & time before returning to her inventory list. It seems she has little tolerance for critiques of its handling, however well-intentioned those critiques may be. Will be more tactful in the future regarding this topic. If I remember from her file, the ship was named after her sister. Must choose words with care when speaking of the dead.*

DAY 5

Today I chatted with the only person willing to speak to me at length. Vaila is different than when we last worked together. I have never known her moods to be so dark. Her thoughts so scattered. She talks about the job as though we will be turning back any day now, convinced that the fifteen-year contract must be a test of loyalty for us, on your part—that you will call us back before we enter the fringe. I did not encourage or dissuade her conviction. From past experience, I've learned it is best to let realizations come on one's own terms. Instead I played the part of sincere listener, & observed her manual rotation of the radiation sails to catch an on-

coming swell. Let her believe what she must, if it helps her do her job.

DAY 7

Right foot was still somewhat numb this morning, so I decided to go visit the medica & ask the good doctor's advice. We had a pleasant chat commiserating about the boredoms of long flights, but what was most interesting was what he told me before he left: that on the second night of our journey, while I was ill at sleep, Royvan had gone for a midnight water, on his way to the kitchen, passing by the captain's quarters, when he heard the muffle of voices behind her hatch. One voice he recognized as hers, but the other—he had not heard the other voice before. Or since. Many of the details of the voice were lost in transit through the metal walls, but he was sure of one thing: that it was the voice of a child.

DAY 9

If it were not for Royvan, I do not think I would have noticed this certain curious thing these past few days: that, for one hour, shortly after their dinner, the captain & the boy sojourn to her quarters & shut the door. They do this regularly, as if keeping to an appointment. & for the duration of this hour, the merc walks up & down the main causeway, her movements casual & her eyes alert; a walk that I originally thought was nothing but her evening constitutional, but now, through the suspicious narrowing of my eyes, seems more like a patrol.

I made a mistake in confiding my observations with Vaila this morning. The pilot was already discontented with this assignment & I'm afraid that my suggestion that something was amiss only made things worse, swiftly igniting her dry & oiled sticks of conspiracy. She has now talked herself into the captain's villainy; that somehow this woman has hoodwinked you, & this is all part of some grand scheme of hers, either as an informer for Allied Security, or as a casual trickster hungry for a windfall. In a matter of minutes she both spun out this improvised narrative & bought into it whole-sale. She gathered up both Royvan & Engineer Em, & the four of us convened in her quarters & shared all that we had seen on the ship thus far. This was an ill-advised move—I knew it then, & I am only more certain of it now. Having all of us suddenly disappear for twenty minutes while we spoke among ourselves in Vaila's room was sure to catch the attention of either the captain, the merc, or the boy. But the others were set on meeting in private, I could not dis-suade them, & I felt that I must join them, to both temper their wild theories & suspicions, &, if I am to be candid, to quietly indulge in my own.

Has the child had the ability to speak all this time? Why did the captain hide this from us? Why is the merc stationed outside her quarters for an hour after dinner each day? & why, if Engineer Em is to be believed, does the boy walk the ship alone at night? Where is he going & for what reason? Can he already Jaunt?

DAY 10

Portentous quiet. The causeways are as silent as the moment before the sermon. Everyone keeps to their own company. Muscles tense, & eyes watchful & wary. I am in my room, where I have been for most of the day, attempting to cheer my mind with old entertain-ments that I have stored on a Data-D. It did not work. My attention was snapped away from it regularly by a sound in the vents above me. I hear it now, even. Like a pebble in a can. My finger twitches, itching to rip out the grating & shine a light on my irritation.

An hour ago there was a tense exchange between Vaila & the captain regarding our future travel plans. It seemed almost perfor-mative, on both their parts. As you are aware, the original plan, the route Vaila herself had drafted before we departed from Pelican, would have taken us directly from Bran-Neruda to the hub world of Fujimoto-Set—which I hear is the most Allied-like fringe world there is, due to its close proximity to the border. It also falls within the Sullivan Trade Route, which means it would have the necessary supplies should we require intensive ship repair or medical treatment. But this also means that it has close ties to many Allied companies, including Umbai. There were rumors on the Feed that it would be the next fringe world to be subsumed by Corporate & transformed into a City Planet.

The captain has decided this route would not do. After Bran-Neruda, we are to instead circumvent Fujimoto-Set, & ride the Austere Current to the world of Black Rock Drannon. Farther out, where it dwells alongside a lesser trade route. I've heard little of the place myself, but the captain claims she has been there before; trusts that we can keep a low profile under the shadow of its hard edge. Vaila retorted that we must keep to the plan that you approved. Silenced, as the captain reminded her with a firm, unyielding tone, that under the contract the only approval she required was her own.

Our pilot smiled with no small amount of condescension, & said that she would carry out her captain's wishes, despite her many reservations. Later went & found Vaila in the cockpit. Told her that I understood her concerns, but that it was in everyone's best interests she not test our leader's patience.

"Our leader is not on this ship," she said, & turned her chair away from me. Took my cue, & left her to her silence. Bran-Neruda Station approaches in four days. The end of this weary prologue approaches, as does the start of the first chapter of our long journey. Skeptical that we will even make it that far.

Breakfast was a boiled tuber of some sort.

DAY 13

The door to the captain's hatch was ajar tonight—not wide enough to see through, only hear. Her voice was dialed low. She was speaking to the boy about what sounded like something urgent. I paused briefly to listen. It was too quiet to hear most of what she said. I caught only this:

". . . needs to happen soon . . ."

& then Sonja walked out of the lav. I jumped into the common room, breathing hard. Waited until I was clear to amble casually back to my room, where I now write, & debate with myself whether or not to tell the others what I heard. There is not enough context to make an accurate guess as to what "needs to happen soon" could mean. Telling the others could add fuel to an already growing fire. But it could also be the bucket of water that stops the house from burning down.

I know too little to take action.

Will wait; tomorrow we dock at B-N.

BRAN-NERUDA STATION

DAY 14

Stylus heavy in hand as I write this entry. Still thinking about all I learned today. Taking all restraint available, to not start at the end.

So, the beginning. We made our uneventful dock with Bran-Neruda Station. I think we were all happy to leave the ship for a while. A necessary release in pressure. The crew enjoyed themselves in the last Allied marketplace we will visit in some time, spending what iotas they could on things that might make the long journey easier; music compacts, imagers, pipes, physical games. The captain made sure everyone followed your rules—no neurals or delvers, nothing traceable with access to the Feed, though there were those who were less enthused with settling for the more analog entertainments. Sonja the mercenary was made to stay on the ship to keep watch on the boy. The captain said it was too dangerous for him to enter the station (Umbai-owned, with many Yellowjackets & plainclothes operatives scanning crowds with neurals for potential disturbers). Though I think the boy understood her reasoning, he made a sorry picture as he watched us leave the ship without him.

It was good to stretch my legs after that eternity aboard the Debby. Though Bran-Neruda is not the most extravagant station, after being cooped up in that ship, I was still overwhelmed by the many glittering storefronts, the throngs of people coming to & from Allied Space. I soaked in the noise as I shopped, keeping in mind that beyond this station, I would be in unfamiliar territory for an indeterminate number of years. I discovered a treasure trove of classic literature in an Old Earth shop & have thus added a few dozen books to the captain's collection in the common room—histories, adventures, & travel narratives whose authors have inspired my own writing, & will no doubt keep me in good company during our journey, much as they had in childhood.

When we were all back on the ship, about to depart, the captain called us into the common room. We thought it was to be a standard debrief before our departure into the fringe. The requisite rousing speech. Em sat cross-legged on the floor, Royvan & Vaila on the sofa, Sonja on a chair pulled from the kitchen. I perched on a stool, by the counter that divided the space, recording all that I heard, to be synthesized into this report.

The debrief was surprising, to say the least. The captain regarded us all, & said that shortly after we left Pelican Station, she discovered that the boy could speak. For the past two weeks, in her quarters, she has been learning who he is, & where he is from. He has had a difficult life, she told us. Speaking is a skill he is still learning. As is trust. To respect his privacy, she had originally left it to him to decide when he would trust us enough to talk. But the captain saw now that this process would have to be expedited before we entered the fringe, where it would be essential for all of our cards to be placed firmly on the table, faceup. She gazed about the room, lingering on Vaila, when she said that it was important that we trust each other, & that like the boy, she herself needed time to size us up. To understand just who she was working with. Her speech ended there. She stepped outside to fetch him. This moment brought to mind the opening act of a play; the curtain drawn, as the principal actor steps onto the stage, & we, the hushed audience, waited for him to speak the first words of this recital.

Enter, the boy.

Words were still new to him.

Understanding words, he could do. It was the saying that froze his nerves, his tongue fighting to remember the shapes it was supposed to make. In that moment, his mind was a cloud of words, crashing into one another, broken and entangled.

His hands clenched at his sides.

Before she gathered the crew, Nia had taken him aside and told him that for the next hour, he was in charge. She smirked as she said this, as if to let him know this was all just play. Nothing to be scared of. She told him he didn't need to answer any questions he didn't wish to answer. He could stop the proceedings at any time if he got too uncomfortable. He could even leave the room mid-thought, and that would be that.

"For the next hour," she said, "you are the captain."

He looked at them all; to the new ones whose names he was still learning, and to those he trusted. Sonja. Nia.

He unballed his fists.

And he told them where he was from.

* * *

Our silence in the common room was a solid thing as we sat there, listening to the soft rasp of his unused, adolescent voice. He relayed his story in curt, halting statements, & with the aid of intense gesture & facial expression.

A Quiet Ship.

That was where he said he came from.

He covered his mouth with his hand, and he shook his head.

"None," he said, through his fingers.

Speaking was not allowed there.

He mimed the act of playing musical instruments, playing a bow against an invisible violin. He gestured to people taller than himself. His masters.

"They speak. I follow," he said. "They tell. I do. They play music. I—" He stopped. Struggled for the word. He looked to Nia for help, as he tapped his ear, clueing her into the word he searched for. She understood.

"Listen," she said.

"I listen," he said.

He served at the pleasure of these masked musicians as they played ancient symphonies in a grand hall of red curtain. It was a ship of castes, of which he was the lowest. His days spent attending his masters with their bowls of rosin & polish sponges, restringing of violins & cellos & mandolins & the sanding of new instruments.

"Bowl," he said, holding an invisible tureen. "Once, I drop." He opened up his hands, and let the tureen clatter to the floor. Rosin, everywhere. "Make a . . . mess. Oh well."

The crew laughed at this choice of words.

"For this, they hurt me." They fell silent as he touched his arm and traced the ulna with his forefinger. "Bone," he said. He always liked that word. The strength of it.

He held out two fists, side by side, as if the ulna were in his grip.

He snapped it.

For every mistake, a beating. A breaklet wand thrown against the rib, cracking the bone & re-fusing it in moments, leaving behind only the memory of the fracture, the body still able to perform its due tasks. A beating, for not breathing properly. It was a world that valued self-control in all aspects.

Even now he could hear it: the peculiar click when the wand extended from its sheath. The red light on its tip, like an eye, and the buzzing sound, like a chitinous bug.

When Nia asked him if he was okay, he flinched.

"Yes," he said.

A Quiet Ship, swollen with music & suffering.

There were many more details, each more gruesome than the last. Tongues that were clipped from the mouths of crying babies— his voice disturbingly matter-of-fact, & even touched with a hint of pride as he showed us his own tongue, pink & fully intact, & told us that he was one of the good ones.

There was a slight smile on his lips as he remembered pride. The ecstasy, when he perfectly polished the cello, and the Mistress gave him her rare nod of approval; a nod barely noticeable, unless one were looking for it, which he was. And which he found. This was a good memory.

We live in an era where ships can slip into the opaque folds of the universe, & sail along the fringe ripples of time. We can generate muscle tissue, & spool the threads into new limbs. Sunder conti-nents with a single YonSef explosive device. Life has changed, but not our capacity for absurd cruelties. For all my complaints of how my parents kept a house, I recognize that I have had a privileged childhood. Albeit poor in laughter, ours was a family never in want of food or security. I have no love for that old home in the Aerie of the station, but I cannot dispute that it was, by definition, a home. One that was mine. All the boy had was hell.

There were many reactions. The man with the big beard whom they called Doctor mumbled his disgust with the Musicians. The man who was dagger-thin, and whom they called Engineer, looked at Ahro with an appraising look and a slow nod, as if they had more in common than either had realized. And the woman with soft, round features and the careful hair, the one they called Pilot, stared into the corner of the room, avoiding his gaze completely.

As for the other one, the older man at the counter who had no title or honorific, he was at work, writing notes on vellum, with lips pursed in focus.

The galaxy is strange, & its terrors varied. Hundreds of generation ships still remain unaccounted for. I'm sure you have seen the stories on the Feed; unique cultures that gestate in these behemoths during the long passages through the Pocket. I for one am willing to believe that one of these ships is the baroque hell that the boy has described.

There are holes in his tale. He does not know how he escaped from the Quiet Ship, & was without explanation for why dhuba farmers discovered him naked & unconscious in their crop fields, among the black ruin of what I now suspect were the remains of an escape pod.

What he did have an explanation for was how he learned to speak in a ship where speaking was not allowed. He struggled for a

time, organizing the chaos of unused words in his head, before he
settled on "Kind One."

It was this Kind One who showed him the nature of words, in
secret, their clandestine meetings taking place in random rooms
throughout the ship while the other musicians slept. The Kind One
taught him the words for Please, Help, in preparation for the day
that he might quit that place. & they taught him the way of names.

"No name," he said, tapping his chest. "We have no name. Kind One
teaches. Shows me." He gestured before him, to an imagined window.
He reached in, and grabbed something. "I find name. Give to me."

The room was quiet.

"What is your name?" Sartoris asked him.

His arms lowered.

"Ahro," he said.

He pronounced it Ah-Row. The spelling is my own invention, as he
does not yet know his letters. Ahro is not a word that I have heard
before, & by the blank expressions of the others, unfamiliar to them
as well. Even to the boy himself, who could not say why he chose
this name, only that he had, the word plucked from the Kind One's
tutor screen.

It is tempting to imagine this moment in full: him, sitting before
this screen, flicking through topics during their covert nights, filling
his mind with details of the outside worlds—until he stops. Discov-
ers in this grand encyclopedia some forgotten language, & sees
there, before him, this word.

Ahro.

Perhaps he has the Kind One speak it for him first, before he tries
it out on his own; smiling over the syllables, the sound like a sweet
on his tongue, rhyming with the word of his soul; a discovery of not
only his new name, but a guiding philosophy on life. That this is

how everyone should be named: a hand, thrown into a bag of words, in search of that singular & fitting shape.

Royvan was the first to stand from his seat & extend his hand to the boy in partnership. Engineer Em followed his lead, & I after him, the three of us telling the boy it was a pleasure to finally meet him. Only Vaila did not rise. She looked to the boy, & then the captain, in confusion & lace of frustration, before she asked if he truly had nothing to tell us about his supposed ability. When the captain confirmed that he did not, Vaila got up & left the room, leaving behind an almost inaudible "Nice to meet you" to the boy on her way elsewhere.

Once the debrief was over, the crew set to work preparing for departure, quietly, all of us in an interior sort of mood as we thought about what the boy told us, & what he did not. Though I believe Vaila's concerns could've been spoken with better timing, & tact, I cannot deny that those concerns are valid. How inextricably our lives are bound to this child's, on an uncertain route to nowhere.

A strange, sobering day.

But I should not forget to make note of the music.

After I finished shopping in Bran-Neruda, I was making my way to the docks when I caught sight of the captain through the window of a repair & requisitions shop. Like any good busybody, I made my way in & inquired about her business—made it look as though I had my own matters to attend to there; a fiction she saw right through, & one I had no evidence with which to back up. But she did not seem too concerned about my presence, & told me she was there for a gift. She showed me what it was that she had come to get repaired. Told me who it was for.

A flute. She had purchased it years ago, back in the days when she made her rounds between Macaw & Barbet. When she first met Ahro—only "the boy" then—she gave him this flute to play with.

She told me he was quite taken with the gift, until an incident rendered it unplayable; snapped in half "on accident," though what
accident this was, the captain would not be more specific.

We both gazed down upon the repaired object. The fissure was
fused with an inlay swirl of gold & silver, & at the base, she had his
name inscribed in small, neat lettering. It was beautiful work. I told
the captain he would love it.

But after hearing his story, I wondered if a flute would make an
appropriate gift for a boy whose history with music is also that of
pain on a dark & Quiet Ship. That the flute might trigger some horrible flashback, rather than bring him joy. But it was not my business, the gifts she gave, or the thoughts in his head. I know more
today than I did before, but there is still much about him that is a
mystery. One day, I will ask what it is he hears, when he hears the
notes of music: the infernal, or the celestial.

Judging by what I hear now—that flute song through my open
door—it is most likely something in between.

A fiery heaven all its own.

We have ten minutes till we fold again, from where we shall
rocket along the Gracious Current to the fringe world of Drannon.
When I asked the captain for strategies to curb the fold-nausea, she
said it helps to have something to focus on; an object, like a worry
stone, to distract from the nausea. Last time we folded I tried gripping one of the safety rails embedded in the wall, but still vomited
all of my lunch, much to Sonja's amusement. But I am nothing if not
resolute—this go-round I will use something of more sentimental
value: the comb in my pocket, which once belonged to my father. I
will rub my thumb along its worn tines & remember how cross he
would be should I embarrass the family name with my unpleasant
retching. & should the comb fail me, I will be positioned near the
causeway lav, ready to make use of the toilet. But faith, Sartoris!
Believe in your own strength!

THE GRACIOUS CURRENT

DAY 16

The second fold was somehow worse than the last. A true punch to the stomach. For two hours was doubled over the toilet in painful evacuation. Gross exaggeration of the body no doubt heard throughout the ship. My status has shifted from dedicated transcriber to village joke. Not a moment goes by when Engineer Em is not teasing me for my "weak" constitution.

That aside, there is a noticeable change in atmosphere on the Debby. The air is not quite the brittle glass it once was, the awkwardness between us less palpable. There are now even jokes.

Some funnier than others.

For instance. Today, I had gone to the medica to see about the numbness in my foot, only to discover that the mercenary Sonja had beaten me there. She was propped on the metal table wearing nothing but her undergarments while she answered the good doctor's questions monosyllabically. When they noticed me, I asked if I should return later, but the doctor said they were almost done, & the merc seemed completely comfortable wearing so little clothing around strangers. Experience from her soldiering days, I gather. I sat to the side & observed their appointment. Learned that the merc's left leg is vat-grown, the real one blown off by a party mine during a poorly strategized skirmish—though I am well aware that you probably knew this already. There is a darker hue to the vat leg than the rest of her body. Apparently the muscle threads were woven in a time before the science of it had been perfected. Every two months she requires a reacclimation injection, right on the line where the new tissue starts, lest the limb revolt, & break off her hip like an old branch from a tree. Sonja said all this matter-of-factly, through sweat & gritted teeth, as she endured the slow push of the doctor's needle, & the neon-blue fluid that flooded her veins.

When she was done, the doctor asked what ailed me. After hearing the merc's story, I felt more than silly coming in with my tingly foot, & thought I heard Sonja snort when I explained my symptoms to him. Royvan had me sit on the metal table. The merc dressed herself at the side of the room while the doctor gently squeezed his way down my ankle & sole. He then stepped back with a sudden & severe expression, & told me the foot would have to be amputated. The blood drained from my face. I sputtered some nonsense that not even I could decipher, much less repeat here. Royvan & Sonja shared a glance. & then he laughed, & confessed that he was only joking. The merc chuckled. I felt the fool. He unscrewed a bottle & tapped out two small gray pills onto my palm, assuring me this would cure my affliction by the start of the next day. Noticed the doctor look after the merc as she exited the room, sensed a glimmer of attraction, but was too peeved to take further note. I slinked back to my quarters, humiliated.

To the doctor's credit, he came to see me later in the day to apologize. I of course accepted. Eventually. Not before jousting with a prank of my own, when I told him I would write to one M. Nakajima & recommend his execution.

So, things are progressing. Jollies abound. It helps that we have not only a name but also a context for the boy—Ahro, need to get accustomed to no longer calling him "the boy"!—& there is no longer that requisite awkwardness when he steps into a room. & although there is a beguiling quality to his stilted approach to language, it is a vast improvement to his impenetrable silences.

When I said hello to him in the causeway, he stopped, & said hello back! That was a good moment—offset slightly by the moment after, when we both stood there, not speaking. Luckily for both of us, he mercy-killed the interaction with cold swiftness as he walked off without another word or gesture.

Small progress, great goals, Sartoris.

DAY 17

It seems I have just received a promotion—not one of monetary value (alas), but one of trust. Near midday, the captain knocked on my hatch & requested that I continue from where the "Kind One" left off, & tutor the boy Ahro in the art of speech & writing. She acknowledged that this was outside the realm of my responsibility, & that there would be no hard feelings should I decline. I said yes immediately, not only because I was immensely flattered to have been asked at all but also recognizing the added benefit of making my way into the inner cloister of the Debby—*the tight-knit trio of Captain, Merc, & Star Child. I suspect there is much to learn there. As an added benefit, with developed language skills, the boy might be able to share more of his past with greater precision, & perhaps reveal further clues to his latent ability.*

We begin the lessons in earnest tomorrow. Anxious to start, & to have something close to a routine on this ship.

DAY 18

Had our first lesson in the common room, with the captain joining us to observe. It was a brief introduction, didn't want to overwhelm him. As he already understands speech rather well, & can read simple sentences, we do not have to start from the very beginning. Most of our preliminary work will be in writing, & practice in articulating syllables.

He has a curious way of listening to instruction. Doesn't quite meet my eyes when I speak. Thought at first that he was uninterested & that I lacked that engaging touch all successful teachers have—but it was not long till I realized that because of his history, he is still uncomfortable with meeting adults eye to eye. With his stylus he wrote the first letters of the alphabet as I clued him in on tips for where to begin the shape, & where to end. He enjoyed writ-

ing the letter Q. Made so many of them I had to interrupt his trance & insist that we move on to the next.

DAY 20

Routines are necessary out here.

When she is not with the boy Ahro, the captain likes to write haikus, which I found to be surprising & rather endearing, though she refuses to share the poems with me, claiming that they are not very good. The boy Ahro has his exquisite music, which he plays according to the schedule of allotted time the captain has drafted for him. Sonja the mercenary spends much of her time exercising in the cargo bay, dismantling & polishing her vast collection of weaponry of which I hope we never see the need for, attending them with the care of a supplicant at an ancestral grave. She of course has names for all of them. Her favorite is a bell-nosed rifle she calls the Buffoon. Em has taken it upon himself to furnish & upgrade various parts of the Debby that have till now gone unattended—with Royvan's help. Those two are thick as thieves with their many private jokes. The captain was pleased when she discovered the door to the tertiary lav was finally fixed & that one no longer needs to fasten the curtain to achieve some sense of privacy on the lid. Vaila is still distancing herself from the rest of us, our albatross in the cockpit, keeping watch on the route ahead. I hear her praying on her ladeum beads when I pass by her on the rare occasion. The prayers seem more fervent with each day.

I've been making my way through the literature I purchased on Bran-Neruda. Currently absorbed in the autobiography of Luca Assaya, former corporate mapmaker of the Blessed Currents. Wonder what his routine was, during Pocket doldrums; how he passed those incredible stretches of time. At his young age, no doubt frantic masturbation.

DAY 24

We have moved on from the alphabet to writing & speaking simple words. He understands the difference between nouns & verbs, but is confounded by conjunctions. Has no difficulty speaking closed-vowel syllables like "rot," but struggles with vowel teams that require subtle modulation, like "south," or vowel teams that mesh into a single note, like "reading," which he pronounced, strangely, as Ruh-Deen.

DAY 27

Made a surprising discovery today—the captain owns the complete collection of Six Kingdoms! She didn't strike me as the type to enjoy historical romances. When I told her so she laughed, said she favored the books more for their sentimental value than for their content, as the quartet was once a favorite of her mother's, who was an Old Earth historian. I asked her if these books were handed down to her from her mother, but she said they were not & with sudden distance in her eyes said her mother's books were gone before she changed the subject. Detected a story there, but did not press the matter.

We spoke for quite a while about the books. The collection itself was written by a long-deceased author by the name of Samuel Palen, who was known in his time for his dense & indulgent epics. The story of Six Kingdoms takes place in a parallel Old Earth, & centers on a young peasant woman's rise to power, becoming the first queen to rule over the southern principality of the fictional continent Shumar. A large pleasure in reading the series is watching this woman grapple with the terrible position of political power, its slow corrupting influence on her. Though I know you hate it when I compare you to great figures both historical & fictional, I cannot help but see a little bit of you in her, or her in you. The captain & I sat on the common room sofa as we discussed the plot, the difficult choices Faydra Faneuil had to make between her greater responsibilities & the men & women she loved. The captain said she liked the author's portrayal of Faydra's love life: the freewheeling, polyamorous nature of it. I agreed, though had to admit that when I read the quartet as a young boy, I did not take much interest in the many love scenes—of all that has changed about my countenance, my disinterest in the physical side of romance remains intact—but relished the devious machinations of the warring civilizations. My father & I are very different people—he of the school of thought that life's successes are measurable quantities—but we both have a weak spot for the histories of grand strategy.

The conversation with the captain was stimulating & absorbing. Hope she feels the same way. Before I left, she lent me the first book in the collection, & added that she was happy with how my lessons with the boy Ahro were coming. Feeling very good about our prospects.

Behold the work of my eager pupil, who has skipped ably from letters to words to full sentences.

Worksheet—Sentence Practice
My name is Ahro. I am thirteen years old. My friends are Nia and Sartoris and Sonja and Vaila and Royvan and Em. Nia is my best friend. She is strong and pretty. Sartoris is my friend too. He is old and he has no hair.

Our next lesson: the value of tact.

DAY 33
Drannon nears. I dread the moment we unfold. Already I have been hounded relentlessly by those who will not be named—Em, it is always Em—for my weakened states.

A few days ago the captain, recognizing my worries—& perhaps tired of hearing me expel my insides into the shared lav—gently sug-

gested that the mercenary Sonja lead me through yogic poses to prepare my lungs & muscles for the reality shift. I accepted, naively assuming the workout would be adjusted for my body type & age (how wrong was I). I also made sure to invite Vaila to attend, but, as expected, she declined, continuing her impressive solitude in the cockpit.

The workout is two hours every afternoon, until we arrive. Two hours of Sonja folding me like laundry, twisting my body in such grotesque contortions it is as though she expects me to breathe out of my anus. Some of the crew have joined us, whether in solidarity or to curtail their own nausea, I do not know. I continue to struggle through most of Sonja's exercises, my hands nowhere close to touching my toes, or my knees, for which Em takes great delight in needling me. This is to say nothing of our diet, one that is almost purely liquid. Water, water, more water than I have ever imbibed. It is almost enough to curb my excitement for arrival completely.

Almost. Apart from the captain, none of us have ever traveled outside Allied Space. This is our first opportunity to see how the fringe-dwellers lived with visions unclouded by company bias. During the boy's lessons, I told him what I knew of Drannon, & what I imagined it might be like—cultural nexus enlivened by its position so near the Allied border, a waypoint through which travelers pass, multiple histories accumulating on a single world, a single city, building on one another to create forms both new & beautiful; a human coral reef. Was happy to see that the boy took so well to my vision & that, like me, he was compelled by mystery, the anticipation of discovery. Wouldn't be surprised in the least if he has as much difficulty sleeping tonight as I no doubt will!

Ahro was awake most nights.

Because of the bad dreams.

Because of many things.

He walked barefoot, without sandals, in fear that the slaps would wake the others, the metal grating and paneled flooring cold against his soles, inspiring bodily chills, but this was okay; he even took pleasure in the vibrant sensation, reminders they were that he was awake, and in this place he loved very much. He walked with an outstretched arm, his finger grazing the walls as he went. Walked with fingers running over the rivets as he passed the entryway to the kitchen and common room, the hatches to the private quarters, Nia's quarters—he paused here before continuing on—up the corridor that connected the body of the ship to the cockpit, where he always found himself on such nights, and where his walk always ended.

He sat in the copilot's chair and placed the large headset over his ears. He listened to the Pocket as its strange materials rushed past the hull sensors of the *Debby*. The spackle-frack. The white noise filling his mind like water, drowning out the worries and the bad dreams, until he was heavy against the chair, and lulled back to sleep. To a place where there was no symphony and no broken bones, only soft whispers and finger snaps. The rich void over which he was suspended. And there he stayed, until the fingers slowed their snapping, and the lips shut mid-whisper, and it was quiet again as the ship emerged from the Pocket, dripping from the fold.

When he woke, his mouth was dry, his tongue as coarse as old fabric. He licked his lips, gathered himself.

Vaila was beside him in the pilot's chair with her hands enmeshed in the cat's cradle, and beside her, Nia, who leaned against the console with a mug of something hot in her hands. They did not speak to each other. He watched them for a time with eyes half-lidded, the odd quality of their silence, until Nia noticed that he was awake.

She nodded at the viewport.

"We're here," she said with a gentle smile.

FRINGE PORT DRANNON

DAY 34

The ship has only just switched to lights-on, & already I have been awake for two hours, in anticipation of our arrival. Heart now arrhythmic as I hear the captain call us to the cockpit. Here it comes, my first fringe world. I feel as Assaya must have felt, arriving at the end of the Blessed Currents after so long a journey—eyes open & eager to drink in the new quantities before him.

We are circling the skies above the city, about to land. Cannot see much through the raised viewport—only wraithlike clouds, gray & foreboding. Rain. Fingers of water streaking upward against the glass. Em is the only one not in the cockpit with us. He is in the engine room, tightening a loose panel that popped out when we broke atmosphere. The boy is strapped into the copilot's chair, with the captain standing beside him, as Vaila articulates the cat's cradle & brings us down.

Am sitting on a chair in the Port Authority lobby hall, beside three unsupervised children who are slapping one another's hands rather violently. I hope it is a game. Across the way, the rest of the crew meanders about. Sonja keeps an unwavering eye on the boy as we wait for the captain to return. Can see her now, speaking in confidence to one of the attendant guards at the dock entrance gate. Suspect this will take some time. Will describe what occurred when we landed half an hour ago, & the loading ramp dropped open.

We smelled it first, on the bitterly cold gust that rushed through the Debby's cataract—the smell of the dead. An odor so powerful it was electric. Vaila buried her face into the front of her coat. Even Sonja, so often boastful of the grotesque circumstances she'd lived through during her military days, turned her head away from the wind, teeth gritted into a furious smile. With tears in his eyes the boy asked the captain in his deliberate manner what the smell was. She winced a smile & told him that it seemed like someone had gone fishing. This confusing statement was understood by none of us, not until we exited the ship & saw the carcass. It was at the end of the docks, past the dozens of other landed ships—a massive sea beast, at least half the size of the Debby, *strung up by the tail via a large metal hook. The gelatinous belly sacs punctured by workers' lances while their fellows caught the viscous liquid in upheld buckets. Observing them, I was struck by images of Old Earth whalers. Quite the way to start our stay here on Drannon.*

Port Authority is crowded. Many grumpy people—young girl selling some fried unknown at the end of a stick, man pacing in circles shouting at digital projection of what one assumes was an old lover. The three children beside me continue to bray. Looking around, I see no one who could be their guardian.

Finally, a chance to sit after hours of marching. We are inside the city's travelers' bureau. Odd place. Neat little microcosm of this city. The bureau is a wide, vaulted space; dark, with many shadows, lit only by the domed ceiling strung with dull glimmerbulbs, & the circular skylight, which casts an eerie haze on the arena we now sit along the circumference of.

This, the captain has told me, is the pit. Where travelers looking for temp work meet those who are hiring. Negotiations—a kind word for it—are carried out in red-throated screams in the pit. Elbows shoved firmly into neighboring stomachs as the prospectives shout to be heard. The captain is now shouldering men & women out of the way, shouting the qualifications of her & her crew, her ship make & model, her years of experience, pausing in between shouts to listen for the response to her volatile queries. Surprisingly analog way of handling things. The air is congested with various smokes & body odors. A noxious heat opens the pores, lets loose my essence in vital globs of sweat that wet the vellum I now write on. The boy does not mind the heat or the smell. He is enraptured, leaning far over the balcony as he watches the captain work the crowd of the pit. Even when she is below us, there is still the sense that the boy is looking up at her.

The others fare better than I, though only marginally so. Royvan, Em, & Vaila are deep in a card bout, while Sonja remains upright as a statue, Buffoon at the ready, as she creates a bubble around the boy through which no one dares trespass.

For years I dreamed of what life was like beyond the controlling grasp of the Allied Standards. & here it is, all that I had ever wanted: a grab bag of architectural design, no uniformity among the buildings, harsh juxtapositions without purpose; twirling helix spire standing tall beside a low, one-story, flat-roofed hovel. Homes on top of homes, & some built at a slant, leaning on their neighbors like tired lovers against all reasonable code of safe construction. Makeshift bridges of corrugated metals & scrap wood connecting the tiers of the city, blotting natural light. No consideration spared for line-of-sight vistas, pleasing symmetries, or purposeful reveals when turning a corner. Everything a City Planet is not, almost purposefully so, as though the grand designer made a deliberate choice to invert every sense of Allied aesthetics. A perversion. But I know this is not the case. It would take a genius of the highest order to create such a place of chaos.

The captain returns. She says she has a job.

She is looking at Sonja & her gun.

DAY 35

The merc left today with the caravan she is meant to guard, on the way up the mountain pass with a cargo of musky spices. She is ex-

pected to return tomorrow, which left us a full day to explore the city at our leisure.

Joy, thought I.

The group of us went for a walk through the city. By the captain's command we were to stay together, which provoked a slight eye roll from Em, who must be used to such difficult places, & disliked the coddling, but gladdened me, as I was still nervous of returning to those wild streets. I hoped that yesterday was but a fluke; that it was too quick of a submersion into the new, much like an inarticulate gasp one lets out when jumping into a pool of freezing water. Perhaps today would be easier.

It helped to see the place through Ahro's widened eyes. With nothing to compare his experience to but the bloodied hallways of the Quiet Ship, every person & every object was a frightening delight to him. For the better part of an hour he stood outside a cracked shop window & pointed at objects & listened as the captain explained what each one of them was.

& I was charmed, when I noticed the way he glanced at her as we walked, & how he slowly began to mimic her confident stride.

But I am sorry to say that the city itself has rebuffed me yet again. To wit, I have seen no pedestrian walkways or quickways or verti-tubes or dumbbots to clean the refuse on the streets, no helpful screens with which to draw open a map & reorient oneself in the miasma of . . . streets, illogical streets that end without notice, streets with sharp inclines that can be traversed only with aid of the railings, streets that have no unified naming convention, some numbered but in no discernable pattern & some with words long & confusing in multitudinous languages I could not read, for I was without the aid of a neural. Occurred to me during our long walk through this Styx that, in all my life in the Allied territories, I have never been lost before—that I was a stranger to that dread sensation *of not knowing where the next street will lead. Desperately miss my neural mini-map. Have no sense of orientation here. In hindsight, I am embarrassed by my behavior—how closely I huddled to our little group, afraid of losing them in the noise. They must have thought me quite the coward, if Em's withering stares were any evidence. He commented offhandedly that I must be having great difficulty, being so far from the temperature-controlled paradiso that is the Pelican Aerie, to which I made no retort. What more is there to say in the face of truth than silence?*

Night descends, but I cannot sleep. The city is awake as well. I sit on the Debby's *ramp & listen to the noise & bustle, at once annoyed & intrigued by it. Repulsed by the smell of piss & oil, yet salivating for the lace of savory that wafts alongside the refuse. I am miserable & I do not know why.*

What is it that I am still holding on to, that prevents me from being here? What sense of myself am I afraid to discard? I wonder if I am truly that much of an Allied creature, & what it will take, & how long will it take, to let that world go.

DAY 36

It is morning. A smog had descended the night prior, & has remained. Sonja was due back two hours ago, but she has yet to return with the caravan. The captain has gone to the travelers' bureau for any news, while the good doctor paces madly before me along the perimeter of the Debby, *asking me—anyone—what could have gone wrong with the merc's mission. Despite my assurances that nothing had happened to her, he remains tense & casts eyes toward the gates every other minute, in anticipation of her arrival. The boy sits beside me. I can tell he is worried too, by his constant smoothing of his clothes. & though I have not yet had the opportunity to truly know her, even I must admit to some worry that she is not safe, for without her, we have no guard.*

Sonja has returned to us. We all sat in rapt attention, listening to her relay the comic horror of her story while the good doctor cared for the bullet hole in her right arm.

It was an overnight round-trip between Drannon port & the neighboring town up in the black mountains, where the caravan was delivering its stock of spice worms; & for two days, Sonja said she suffered. It wasn't the bitter cold at the high altitude. Nor was it the corpses they discovered along the climbing road, with both throats & pockets opened. It wasn't even the magnificently slow crawl of the eight-wheeler or its nauseous back & forth cradling as it navigated the damp & bulbous rocks. It was the company. The two high-pitched hyenas who hired her. Two men who did not know the meaning of silence as they commented on every rock & shrub & corpse they happened upon. But even this was fine—she could zone out through most irritations, she said. But not if one of the hyenas thought he saw an attacker emerge from behind a rock & shot his flechette from the hip without aiming, ripping a hole through her arm while the other hyena chuckled, & said no, it was not a brigand, only a three-legged mongrel.

She gave the one who shot her a broken nose.

The other one screamed.

It was all sorted in the end, the delivery made, the ride back blessedly silent. She was paid an extra rations crate for the gunshot, & docked a bushel for the broken nose. There had been worse jobs; there had been better.

There had been war, she said.

She did not know how to react when, at the end of her story, the boy took the hand of her wounded arm, & touched it to his fore-

head. None of us understood this strange blessing. But she grunted her thanks all the same, as she did to the captain when she told her she did good, & that she was sorry things went sour. Soon after, we left Sonja in the care of the doctor, who worked in solemn silence on her spilled blood. Walking away, I thought I heard her chuckle gently, in response to his warmly chiding voice. There was a strange air between the two of them when they later emerged from the ship; an electricity that we all let pass without comment. I did my best to avoid eye contact with her wound, for just the thought of it threatened in me a fainting spell. But I did gaze at her, our injured knight, impressed by how undaunted she was by the gash. There is a lesson here, Sartoris. It concerns our ability to accommodate.

As of this moment, we are watching the workers finish off the remains of the sea beast, while the captain completes her business at port. The skeletal remains have been dropped from the hook, the last of the fat scoured off the bones with wire scrubbers. In celebration of the hard job done, the workers produced shot glasses & dipped these glasses into the buckets of sac fluid. I watched them toast one another, & down the liquid in wince-inducing gulps. In jest they offered these drinks to passing travelers & laughed when the travelers would hurry away from the stench with faces blue & stomachs churned. They've been drinking the stuff for a while now, & continue to do so, daring one another to take yet another cup. One of them has fainted. Money is thrown, bets placed on who is next. In my periphery I notice Em shudder. So. Not even he is above his revulsions.

Interesting.

An idea strikes me—perhaps if I were to approach these workers, & accept one of their gruesome shots, this would endear me to the rest of the crew. Sonja's injury & her triumphant return has only stoked my desire to live up to their standards. Up till now, I have proven only that I am at best a dead weight aboard this ship. A frail body unsuited to the life of travel. What better way to show them otherwise than to dive headfirst into that sour baptism squeezed from the pustule of that disgusting creature?

Upon re-read, no. That is a terrible idea.

I did it. I am in my room aboard the Debby, wondering where my instincts for self-preservation have fled to.

Flashback. I headed down the docks & approached the workers. There were six of them in all. They paid me little mind at first, one of them glancing my way before turning their back to me, as if that was all the time he needed to decide I was no one of interest. Swallowing my fear, I invaded their circle & through my translator unit asked if I could bother them for a shot of their . . . intriguing essence. This provoked a hearty laugh. "Wouldn't recommend it, foreigner," the tall one said. "This stuff, it's not meant for drinking." I pointed out that they had no issue with it. "Years of practice," they said. More laughter. I asked them again for a drink, let them know I was serious & soon their laughter died. The game was on. The tall man nodded to the one with the shot glasses. He dipped the glass into the bucket & handed it to me. The cup was slick in my fingers. Could taste the bile in my throat. But found that hidden reservoir of strength within & held out. Told myself none of this was real. It was a performance. So in the spirit of play, I turned toward the Debby, from where the crew gawked in horror, held the glass up in toast to Em, & tossed the contents down my throat.

Hard to describe the drink, only its effects. Spasmed neck. Kick of the leg. Colors of new & beguiling shades shattering across my eyes. My stomach punched my chin. Coughed as I handed the glass back to the man, managing somehow to thank them as spittle quit my lips. Back at the Debby, the reactions to my stunt were varied. The boy Ahro understood neither the importance nor the grotesqueness of my actions. Sonja let loose a startling laugh. As for Royvan, *he minced no words. He called me a "dumb bastard" & commanded me to the medica for immediate stomach expulsion.*

Em said nothing.

Dutifully I went to the medica, where the good doctor insisted I throw up, & even attempted to jam his finger down my throat despite my protests. In the end my stubbornness won out. I crossed my arms like a child & after some argument the doctor relented & told me that whatever happened next was on my head.

He leaned against the counter & sighed, as he must've done with many difficult patients in the past. He told me it was no matter—that it would exit my stomach when we folded. But I have no intention of that.

When we fold, I will hold in every last drop.

THE VOLCANIC CURRENT

[UNMARKED DATE]
The drink was a mistake.

[UNMARKED DATE]
I do not know how long this moment of lucid thought will last so I will record what I can before I cannot bear to any longer with no guarantee that this entry will see its end. I am drowning in sweat. Sweat that reeks. Consciousness comes & goes without pageantry. I am visited by the crew. They rotate keeping watch on me & I suffer through bedside conversation & then, like that, I am alone, the ship hibernating during lights-off, just the hushed sound of the air recycler to keep me company as an invisible needle digs into the soft flesh behind my eyes. Royvan said there is little risk of my dying, but that the next few days will be worse than any I have lived through, & he said this with a bastard of a smile. This is what happens when

you do not listen to your doctor, Sartoris. He says I will not die but my body is on fire & I cannot escape the fear that my heart might stop in this small room so far from home. Where is [UNDECI-PHERABLE TEXT]

[UNMARKED DATE]
I miss my old apartment on Gracilius Wing. Cute place. Wish you could've seen it. Comfortable seating, spacious balcony overlooking Avenue Strip. Pots of everblooming brunias hung from the railing. My favorite flowers. They're gone now, most likely. We have spent in total a month & a half in the Pocket since leaving Pelican, & because of the Volcanic Current's differential, this means a year lost in real-time (for my clarification, not yours). There is no question that my home has been sold to new residents. New residents who have by now settled in, hosted parties, celebrated corporate holidays with good wine. I bet they called that place home without feeling strange about it & have had fights late into the night & made love in the living room, maybe even had children, if they were ambitious. I see them so clearly in my head as I die in bed. Overwhelmed by the silly fear that they have thrown out my flowers. Brunias are not fussy plants. Easy to care for. Damn it all, I should have left them instructions. Something handwritten & tied to the vine with nice string to show that it mattered. One hour of light & a toss of water, the note would've said. That was all they needed for their purple hues to keep, even in winter.

[UNMARKED DATE]
My old life is gone. My flowers are gone. All I have now are fifteen years on this fucking ship. I suppose I have you to thank. For all of this.

[UNMARKED DATE]

Memory is water through fingers. Sometimes able to grasp half a remembrance. The boy coming to show me his sentences, play his flute. That beautiful song, the inverse to his unconfident & raspy voice. Em visiting, telling me about his days in the substrata of Galena, his boxtown alley. Hangdog stories as he shuffled through old haunts, glaring up at the noble streets that blocked the sun above his head. Something about a cat. & then, Vaila's shadow by my bed, the sole light in the room the soft glow of her ladeum beads while she whispers prayers I do not understand.

These strange rotations of faces. Trapped in my room, there is no way of knowing when it was lights-off, no markers of time, apart from when I would visit the lav, or when my hatch would groan open, signaling a new visitor. The crew, checking to make sure Sartoris was not a corpse. Their visits are pragmatic, this I know. But still. I cannot help but be moved by their presence, shepherding me through the dark.

[UNMARKED DATE]

The dregs of sickness still cling to my stomach lining. But something happened today—made me feel . . . unburdened. Vaila asked me why I had acted so stupid. Why did I imbibe that awful substance? The answer came to me upon a hallucinatory sunbeam. Drink, or go thirsty, I told her. Eat, or starve. For the journey is long, & cannot be survived on hope alone. She looked at me as though I had gone mad. & perhaps I have. So with madness I looked into her chestnut eyes & told her the truth she had been avoiding since departure: that we are not going back, & she will not see you again, not for a very long time. The words struck their target. Her fingers curled over her rosary of ladeum beads. & before she stood up, she wondered aloud when I had become so cruel. Left me to wonder the same thing, alone in this makeshift hospice, as I glimmer in & out of this nightmare.

PERADA

DAY 54

The hurricane is over. Open your cellar doors & emerge into light, for Sartoris's illness has finally broken! Apologies for his brusque manner during his convalescence. Here he stands now, in the verdant wash of Perada, breathing deep the freshest air he has ever had the pleasure to experience.

What a relief it was when the loading ramp dropped & we were greeted by nothing less than a cool pine breeze. Royvan played doctor at the local medical facility while the rest of us were free to explore this forested region of the fringe. On the recommendation of one of the locals in the travelers' bureau, the captain, Ahro, Sonja, & I went on a vigorous constitutional up the main hill to visit one of the largest trees on the continent. Vaila stayed behind to perform some maintenance work with Em. She surprised us all when she wished us a nice walk. First kind words from her since we had left. This did not go unnoticed by the captain. I'm glad Vaila is starting to come around, however slowly.

It was a beautiful path, the leaves around us a vibrancy of colors—every green you could imagine, then doubled. I was surprised by my own energy, keeping pace with captain, but not the boy, who jogged ahead with Sonja, matching the soldier's technique. By the end of the hike we all were sweating. The day was hot, moist. On our way back, the captain & I smelled change in the air.

In him.

No, not the Jaunt. Sorry to say it was nothing more spectacular than body odor, though no less noteworthy. His scent was of an old, wet rag summoned from the drain of a gym shower. None of us made any mention of it to him until we were back in town & the captain procured from market a deodorant for him to use. She showed him how to use the spray, but I don't think he quite understood the why of it, for the next morning, at breakfast, the adolescent smog had made its return.

Ah, the throes of puberty. I don't envy him this time in his life. The time when the body undergoes its mutations & lights the mind on fire & makes a mess of one's perceptions. The days too long in the living & too short in the retrospect.

I would warn him if I could of this phenomenon; tell him to do his best to enjoy & savor each second. But I know all too well that one has to actually experience the phenomenon for oneself to understand how quick it all goes—how like days spent in delirious illness, you turn your head, for but a moment, & realize that a whole period of your life has gone.

Like that.

YEAR 3, DAY 22

The black spires. Sounder's Outpost Kai. Networked streets of Suda-Sulai. The icescapes of Gallahad. We've performed countless jobs in places both large & small. Delivered vaccinations across continents. Escorted three wealthy sisters as they pilgrimaged to the old temples of their religion. Diagnosed the mysterious ailment that plagued the son of a Primark Prince, an ailment that would go on to take his life. We've traveled circles & zigzags across all of fringe space, rambling behind us years of stories. We've journeyed as lions. & yet, after all of this, all of this moving, & waiting, the boy exhibits no signs of his ability. I no longer expect that he will. None of us do. Only Vaila, who misses you dearly, cares that the task has taken this long, & even she has calmed over the past few months, resigned to the fact that this was all but a lark.

& that is fine.

Outside of my tent, the embers of the fire dwindle. It is quiet & warm. I can hear the wind tousling the large leaves in the trees. The water lapping the sand. The soft play of Ahro's flute.

Today is his sixteenth birthday. We spent the day lounging in the sun in this temperate region of Hodas. While the others bathed in the cold waters Vaila & I sat in the shade of a palm, where she shared with me the secret histories of certain ships she loved & would love to see; the Umbai warships she dreamed of as a young girl in her father's study. We built a bonfire at dusk. We enjoyed our crew meal to a blood-red sun melting over a horizon of limitless water. Saw the lines that bound us. The easy friendship between Em & Royvan. Vaila's bemused chuckle at Sonja's blue jokes. & Nia, watching over all, with Ahro by her side.

As we fetched clean water from the ship, Nia observed that it was amazing how much the boy had grown. She was right. He is not a boy any longer but a young man. He is not very tall, about my own height, but moves with a grace usually not afforded ones his age, settling into the new developments of his body, his movements similar to that of the bending of willows. He keeps his hair in the style of the youths of Suda-Sulai, the sides shaved, with a black road that runs down the center of his scalp. Filling the gallon container of water, Nia watched him laugh brightly with Royvan, & she said, unprompted, that her boy had become very handsome, a statement under which I detected a lace of something that smacked of fear. When I told her so, she laughed, & told me that she wondered how long it would be until the day would come when we arrived at a place & the boy became infatuated with another. "I won't be able to let him stay," she said sadly. "He's going to hate me that day." I told her that while that may be so, there would come a day in the future when they would not have to keep moving; that after the job's time limit had run its course, she & Ahro would be free to do as they pleased. But this did little to settle her. There is no assuaging the fear that things end & people leave. The day when this will be true for Ahro, however far from now, still approaches.

Outside Sartoris's tent, Nia listened to Ahro play his flute by the dying bonfire, wondering where the time had gone. It had just been morning, and now it was night—now the stars were out, and the birthday was almost over. It wasn't long ago that she had discovered her first gray hair, above her right temple. It wasn't long ago that the young man who now sat beside her was a boy. He no longer fit in Kaeda's one-shouldered robe. Where had the time gone? The young man played a high note, a calm smile on his lips.

She shut her eyes.

Remember this day.

The moment was done. It was already a quaint snapshot, ready to be discarded for more useful memory, stronger regrets. That was how her mind worked. It was so hard to remember the good things, pushed out as they were by the fear of troubles to come. Here before her was proof that time was moving, and quick. Here was this child who had already survived so much, but was still naïve about the way of things. Here was a small fire that must be nursed.

"Did you like it?" he asked, when he had finished the song.

"I did," she told him.

He smiled.

Shield the fire from the wind. Feed it with old branches. Time was slipping, and he needed to learn the important things, learn them before it was too late.

That was the night she decided the lessons would begin. Plans formed in her mind as he continued to play. She would teach him how to negotiate a contract, how to come out of a trade with the advantage. The crew would train him in their fields of expertise. Vaila would show him the cursory basics of flight, enough to lift off and land without too much damage. Royvan would teach him how to tend to physical wounds. Em would outline for him the organs of the ship and the art of rudimentary repair. Sartoris would continue with his generalized lessons of galactic life and history. And Sonja would teach him how to protect himself from harm, with violence, if necessary. She decided all of this in the space between his songs, told him none of these plans, not yet, for she did not wish to stress him on his birthday. Instead she nodded for him to play once more.

"The happy one," she requested.

With a grin, he obliged her.

Tomorrow the lessons would begin.

A passage from Six Kingdoms comes to mind. It appears toward the end of the last book. Faydra Faneuil has been captured by the opposing principality. After a month of deliberation, the govern-ment decides that she will be beheaded before the crowd as a warn-ing to the civilians who might still consider uprising. Upon seeing the chopping block, Faydra says, "I've warped reality, sundered empires, & built from nothing a legacy that will be remembered for millennia—but now, the work is done, & I think only of my empty youth in Arcadia. The idleness of summer. The sun on my back, & his hand, stroking the hair from my eyes."

I expected many things from this trip.

I did not expect a family.

Fumiko. Your mind as ever remains a mystery to me, & though I am certain you will in all likelihood be unmoved by what I have to say next, I feel it is nevertheless my duty to write it: If the Jaunt is real, it does not reside in the boy. He is but a boy like any other. This task is a fool's errand. After three years, we have made our peace with the notion, & I ask that you make peace with it too. I beseech you to find it within yourself to cancel the contract, & let these people, all of whom I have come to care for deeply, return to Allied Space, or any destination of their choosing. They deserve their lives unbound by the strict terms of contract. They deserve freedom. Please, let this flight of fancy go, & do what you know in your heart of hearts is correct.

Our next destination is the satellite moon of Ariadne. Nia has visited once before. Supposedly it is a musicians' enclave. She wants Ahro to meet people like himself there; people he can talk to about the craft before we inevitably move on to the next of our many landings. Perhaps I will buy myself an instrument while we're there. Never played before, so will start with something easy. A drum, or a two-stringer. Start with a ditty, challenge myself with a scale. Maybe in time, a song of my own composition.

We will see where we go from there.

6

A Long-Term Thing

Morning draped over the empty houses of Ariadne, but no bugle played, for the musicians were gone. No sound but the scatter of lizard things on warm rock as they prepared themselves for the sun that was about to break over the eastern dunes. No sound but the snore of a hundred dogs as fingers of red light crept through the alleys of the conspicuously silent fringe town.

The dogs were everywhere in the former artists' enclave. They were beached along the dusty side streets, and curled in piles on the porches of the abandoned prefab houses. Most of them were asleep; it was still early, still dark. Their collective breaths rumbled the air. A carpet of rising bellies. Of the few that were awake, only one now moved: an overweight mastiff, ambling down the main street.

The smell of her, the Oldest, roused the others, and one by one their heads rose as she passed, a procession soon following her. She stopped in front of the town's gate, which had been shut for days. The others remained at a respectful distance while she sat on her haunches and trained her rheumy eyes on the transmission tower that sat on the high dune, beyond the gate. The tower was many meters tall and cleaved the bruised sky in two. The mastiff knew, if not explicitly, then by feeling, that once first light broke above the ridged horizon and filled the highest of the tower's many dishes, made a bright moon of it, the Man would arrive. It was always morning when he came and brought their food. The other dogs knew this too, their mouths watering in anticipation as morning came, and with it, the gray-white light that draped down the span of the tower.

The barking began when the black speck crested the far hill, trailing behind it a plume of sand.

The Man was coming.

His name was Gorlen. He was the only human who lived on this moon. And he feared he would be the last.

He kept his days to a strict schedule. Hour-long segments of different activities to stave off the madness of being alone, or worse, in his eyes, the boredom. But today, he fed the dogs for a bit longer than usual, did not rush the feed into the trough, for the visitors were enjoying themselves with the dogs, the young man who was with them smiling widely, but with hands petrified to his chest, as a Dane shoved her weight against him.

Gorlen witnessed them for a time.

He scratched at the scar behind his right ear.

After the ravenous dogs were fed their pellets from his truck, he whistled at the mastiff, who then clambered into the passenger's seat for the day's ride. Their work here done, he shut the gate to the dead town and began the steep drive up to the transmission tower. He drove with one hand on the wheel. The other hand rested on the sill of the open window, the tanned index finger tapping the beat of the music in his head. On the usual days when he drove, he would be singing along with the music, but today he spared the visitors his rusty voice. He glanced at them through the rearview. The three of them were quiet. The captain gestured for the young man to drink from his canteen, while beside them, the cheekboned engineer slept with his head resting easily against the rattling window. Gorlen bet he had a history of sleeping in uncomfortable places.

When they landed the night prior, he agreed to lend them supplies for their journey if they would help him with his day's chores, though in truth he didn't need any help feeding the dogs or checking the status of the tower and realigning the dishes knocked askew by the weekend storms.

The company was nice, is all.

He parked the truck by the first strut of the tower and the young man woke the engineer with an elbow nudge. Gorlen asked them if they had any questions about the work, but they did not. The captain told him they remembered his instructions, and would be done soon, and she gave him a smile of reassurance that he was tempted to interpret as one of flirtation, though he knew that whatever ounce of charisma he used to have was long gone in the intervening years of being alone on this rock; unless, on the off chance she was into a man with three missing teeth. "Good," he said. "I'll be here if you need me."

As they ascended the rusted steps of the tower, shaking loose the sand that clung to the metal, Gorlen climbed out of the truck and stretched his arms and legs while the mastiff shark-circled him. Together they sat in the shade of one of the struts. She flopped on her belly close, but not too close, beside him, while he massaged the corns on his feet. When she yawned with all her rotted teeth, he looked at her, thought, with amusement, *We are one pair of ugly,* and was overcome with fondness for her.

He felt this moment needed a song. So he shut his eyes and stretched his neck, and with a pained wince, activated the memory drive nestled under that scar behind his right ear. From the listings in his left eye he plucked the night he heard "Lover's Quarry," years ago. A simple ballad, sung in a duet between two youths who had, by now, most likely moved on to better things. The memory of that concert played out in the limbic theater of his brain, the sounds as clear as yesterday. Slowly, he smiled. And after he glanced up to make sure the visitors were a good ways to the first dish, and well out of earshot, he cleared his throat with the warm dregs of his canteen, and began to tentatively sing along.

And as he sang, and the notes quit his lips, it happened: many meters above him, up where one could hold both the town of dogs and the landing base in both sides of one's periphery, the youngest member of the visiting party paused mid-step, sensing in the air the subtle vibrations that should have been impossible to detect—a chill, from the base of his spine to the top of his head, and a tickle as his heart opened like a hand.

"You all right?" Nia asked from behind.

The moment ended, the sensation evaporated.

Ahro blinked, and then shouldered his pack. "Yes," he said. "My apologies."

They continued up the steps. The impressive height to which they climbed was enough to distract him from the echoes of what he had felt moments before. And by the time they reached the first dish, it was as if it had never happened.

The updraft buffeted their loose clothing as they worked, threatening to tear the bag of tools from his grasp, but he held on and handed the needed tools to Em when requested, guilty that Em was the one doing all the hard work, though Nia had made it clear he was there to just observe and pick up what he could. From a few steps up, she recounted what this moon used to be like when she last visited over a decade ago, her time. The place where the dogs now lived used to be a real town back then, she told them. Like Gorlen had said, when the colony failed, the people moved on. "There used to be a lot of musicians here," she said. "Some of them I called friends, but I guess they left too, or passed away."

"Before," he said. "This place. What was it like?"

"Bigger. Beyond the prefabs there were large-volume tents, enough to hold a few thousand people, most of them traders—like me, before I moved to corporate shipping. I'd just left home, was still figuring things out. Thought the freedom of the fringe would save me. I had a different ship then."

"What was the name?" he asked.

"Also the *Debby*." She chuckled. "*Debby One*. Cheap Pelican model with a snub-nosed cockpit. Ugliest fucking thing you'd ever seen. But it was all I could afford. Soon as I bought it, I shot straight out of Allied Space. Spent a few months trading. Did the runs through here; food and other necessaries for the artists' works, which were pretty valuable back then, when Ariadne was a name people cared about. This place lived on trading." She sighed as she looked out into the empty distance. "Died from it too, I guess."

"There was music?"

"Everywhere." Smiling now. "An entire hall, two kilometers long, just to sell the instruments. Bassos and lyns and cellos. Street concerts. Nightly choruses out in the dunes. It was good. It was really good."

There was much about Nia that still confused him. Mostly it was in the way she spoke about her past. Infused with so many conflicting emotions that it was hard to know how she truly felt about something. "If it was good, then why did you leave?" he asked.

Nia went quiet in all ways. For a moment Ahro feared he had said something that upset her, but soon realized she was only thinking about the words she would use to explain a difficult thing. "I was happy, but I also wasn't. Something was missing, here," she said, tapping her chest, her heart. "Or not missing, but sleeping. But nothing here could wake it up. It made me feel alone. I don't know how else to explain it."

She didn't expect him to understand; was surprised when, after some thought, Ahro nodded. "I have felt this," he said.

"You have?"

He tapped his chest, where she had hers.

"Something asleep," he said. "In here."

An updraft kicked through the grating beneath them, tousling their hair. She stared at him for a beat, as if thinking about how to interpret what he said. In the end, she simply smiled. "I'm glad you get it," she said. "It's a lonely feeling, isn't it?"

"Yes," he said.

She glanced down at the engineer. "How's it coming, Em?"

"It's coming. Going." The engineer was elbow-deep in the terminal, the wires cascading around his shoulders; sweat cascading down his face. "The heat sure isn't helping."

"Echoed. I wonder how Gorlen deals with it every day."

"No cool. No people. Empty bed. Sand fucking everywhere. Surprised he hasn't lost it yet." Em stopped for a moment and looked up at her. "How long could you manage it, Captain?"

Nia sighed in thought. "I could do a year—two, if I got something for it. You?"

"One month. At most."

"Just a month?"

"That's if I was by myself the whole time." He reached for something in the terminal. "Change the parameters, give me a special visitor every now and then, you could convince me to stay longer."

"Those poor women."

"Then I'd see the benefit of an empty planet," he said, ignoring her jab. "You could be as loud as you like"—he grinned at Ahro—"no fear of waking anyone up in the middle of the night." Ahro shifted his feet, very aware of what Em was referring to, and regretted having let the man wheedle that particular story out of him.

Nia leaned against the railing and asked Em to clarify.

"His room is right next to Sonja's, you know."

"I'm aware," Nia said.

"You hear all sorts of sounds when two people are neighbors. Sounds like, say, a vigorous late-night checkup by the good doctor."

Gathering the gist, she pressed a hand to her eyes.

Ahro was sheepish as he admitted, "They weren't very quiet."

"Can't fault them for that," Em said. "Gotta celebrate that third anniversary hard."

Nia fought off a grin, and failed. "I'm sorry they woke you up," she said. "I'll tell them to be more discreet, that's not something you should have to deal with. But if you are disturbed again, don't tell the town gossip"—Em rolled his eyes at this—"and tell me instead, so that I can take care of it. We want to be respectful of the crew's privacy, right?"

"Right."

"A gossipy ship is an—"

"An undisciplined ship," Ahro finished, having by now memorized all of her favorite sayings.

"I'm glad you've been listening," she said. She nodded at Em. "How much longer will you be?"

"Almost done." He snapped his fingers at Ahro, who at the signal dug into the bag and handed him the canister of spacklegum, and the connexion-nut. A few clacks later, the servos whirred to life, and with great pageantry the dish on the side of the tower shifted a few degrees to the left. Em shut the lid of the terminal, and with a nod Nia led the way to the next terminal a few flights up. They took breaks between the arrays for water and reconstituted snacks from her pack, enjoying the view of the desert, which seemed limitless from their height. "That's where we landed," Nia said, pointing to the right. While they worked, Em explained his process to Ahro; the best practices for spacklegum application, the steps he was taking to ensure his heart wouldn't explode from electric shock, and the stories of fools from the past who learned the hard way about these things. And though Ahro didn't have much interest in the technical details, he listened, because Nia had asked him to; the lessons were important to her, so they were important to him.

They spoke no more about Royvan and Sonja's nighttime trysts, but it remained in the air between them: the image of the boy wide-awake in his room, trying to block out the muffled sounds of slaps and moans. It was an image that stayed with them even after they had finished the work and had climbed back into the truck, Em playing with his chit, Ahro leaning his head against the cool window, following the swell of the passing dunes with his finger, thinking of that strange moment up in the tower when he thought he saw infinity; the both of them startled out of their private thoughts when their captain broke into laughter.

Through the rearview Gorlen observed how the laugh spread from one person to the next. He was envious of it, and wished he knew the reason and the context, so he could join in. It seemed he was always on the outside of these things.

It was a twenty-minute drive from the tower to the compound. When they crested the last dune, they could see the tiered landing pads, the *Debby* docked on the topmost pad like a bee on a petal.

After he parked the truck in the lot he showed the captain to the storage building, where the promised rations waited. He pointed out the boxes that were still good, the ones not chewed through by the rat-things. The captain fetched the strongest of her crew, the big woman he had met the night before, along with a loader, and moved the boxes into the elevator, and from there, the berth of her ship. When the last of the boxes had been delivered, he thought their business was done, was at once dreading and looking forward to the solitude again, exhausted as he was by the new, but the captain said they wouldn't be leaving till the morning if that was all right with him, and then asked if he would like to join them for dinner.

It had been a long time since he had received such an invitation. There was once a day when those things were taken for granted. No longer. He savored the moment as she waited for his answer. "Is it all right if she comes too?" he asked, gesturing to the mastiff while the dog relieved herself in the sand.

The mastiff watched Gorlen shave before the meal, dragging the blades upriver, tapping the hairs out into the sink. He was an irregular shaver, there was little reason to clean up these days, and his hand was clumsy; he made a few undesirable nicks on his chin, which he pressed with a towel to stanch the bleeding. He opened the locker, rummaging through his clothes. He sighed when he realized the only presentable outfit was the last one he wanted to wear. He flattened the jacket over his desk, and for ten minutes set to work removing the winged insignia of Umbai from its breast with one of the blades from his razor. He tossed his shame in the garbage and pulled up the pants he hadn't worn in years. They were two sizes too loose. A belt carried it the rest of the way. He asked the mastiff how he looked. She stared at him, her expression an incurious one, as though she had seen all of this happen in some prophetic dream and was now playing her humble role as dispassionate observer. "I know," he said, rubbing his jaw as he looked into the mirror, the cuts made from the dulled blade. "I'm not fooling anyone."

At the appointed time he and the mastiff rode the elevator up to the *Debby*'s pad. The young man was outside with two others—the engineer and the broad-shouldered woman. They were hosing down the ship's radiation masts, chatting as the black gunk of Pocket Space pooled at their feet. He wondered if he had come too early, but when the young man saw him, he waved, and said, "The food is almost ready. We have to finish this, but you can go inside if you like." They resumed chatting while he headed up the ramp, his hands wrestling with each other as he walked through the vaulted cargo bay, and up the stairs into the main causeway, nervous for the coming meal.

Voices echoed from the lit doorway down the corridor. He touched his armpit. He was sweating. He could barely remember "hello." To calm himself, he activated his memory drive again. Played out the memory-record of the Salt Flat Heights concert.

Percussive drums coronated his march forward, the strength the music lent him fleeing as soon as he stepped into the light of the common room.

He stood in the doorway, his posture awkward. The captain was on the sofa, speaking to a bald man whose name he could not remember. In the kitchen that abutted the common room a severe-looking woman was setting plates on a table while a stocky, bearded man was at work at the stoves, throwing spices into the fire like a crazed alchemist. It was the bald man who noticed him first.

"Our guest!" he cried. Everyone turned. Gorlen gave them a small wave. The bald man stood up and gestured for him to enter. "Please, come in, sit, be at home. Yes, any seat you like. Royvan is putting the finishing touches on the meal. It should be a few more minutes. And my God, I haven't seen a dog in, well, I don't remember, a very long time. A mastiff, if memory serves. Is it all right if I—?"

"She doesn't like to be touched," Gorlen said.

"Sartoris," the captain said, embarrassed. "Give them air."

"Of course." Sartoris blushed. "My apologies. It's just that it's been a while since we have had guests and I— Oh, Vaila, no! The napkins are a mess!" The severe woman setting the table gave Sartoris a death glare. As they argued over proper utensil order, the captain sat beside Gorlen on the sofa.

"He was a social organizer in another life," she explained. "He's been needing an outlet for a while now. Apologies if you find him intense."

"It's fine," he said.

The mastiff sniffed at a dropped piece of vat meat beneath the counter.

"What's her name?"

"I don't know," he said. "She's not mine. Her owner left her here, like the others."

He felt a small shiver when he saw how the captain looked at him—the intensity of it. "This place," she said. "What happened to it?"

He told her the thing between truth and lie. "Same as what happened to a hundred other worlds. An Allied company wanted to acquire it. This system is at a crossroads between five different currents. A good foothold on the trade routes. So the company made an offer. And the people refused."

The captain nodded. She knew how the story went, it seemed. But he made it explicit anyway; maybe for his own peace of mind, he wasn't sure. He winced and turned off the music-memory in his head, and he told her what happened next. "When they refused the offer, the company went the long way around. Ariadne lived on trade, the food that was brought in from offworld, the tools for repair. So the company took away trade. They diverted the trade route that ran through here. Flooded the market with cheap duplicate works 'inspired' by the original creations. Started rumors of crime and infestation. Bribed big-name traders to take their business elsewhere. Slowed things down to a trickle over twenty years while one of their representatives whispered in the ears of Ariadne's governing body. Told them it wasn't worth the holdout. And then they left, along with everyone else."

"Food's ready," the bearded man called out.

"Thanks, Roy," the captain said. "Can you go get the others?" As the cook left the room, the captain glanced at him. "Why did you stay?"

Gorlen shrugged.

"Someone had to take care of the dogs."

She smiled.

The three crew members he'd seen outside now entered, with hands sticky and stenched by the mast work; Sartoris told them they had to clean up in the lav before they'd be allowed to join the others at the table. The former party architect directed Gorlen to a seat between the broad-shouldered woman and the engineer—he wished he was better with names—but before the eating could begin, Sartoris stopped the eager hands. "Etiquette, people! The guest must be served first." Gorlen wanted to tell him that wasn't necessary, but he couldn't find the words, managing a quiet thank-you as the young man ladled him the stir-fry. "If I may, Nia," Sartoris said, standing up with a raised glass, "I wish to make a toast."

The table groaned.

"Try to keep it under a minute this time," the captain said.

Sartoris's soliloquy on the merits of good food and greater company was longer than a minute, closer to five. Gorlen thought of making a joke about this to win over the table, but once the toast was done the eating began and his moment had passed. He used to be good at this. Could command a soiree of Pelican nobility with a king's confidence and a prince's charm. But that was another man.

A younger one.

The one he loved, and hated.

There wasn't a lot of food; enough to comfortably serve four at an Allied dinner party. He was reintroduced to everyone while they ate their meager offerings, but the names left his mind as soon as he heard them. He was in a daze as they all spoke to one another in a crackly manner, chuckles, snaps, laughs, stop-eating-off-my-plate, at ease in the way makeshift families are. It was so hot in this room. He could smell his own body odor. The broad-shouldered woman beside him seemed unaware of the smell, but he worried anyway. To calm himself, he flicked on the music-memory of a time he and a date had gone to see the performance of Take Me Down, out in the theater dune. Could feel the softness of her hand in his as he drank the greywine that was offered him at this table, the cup refilled by Sartoris every time he put it back down. "Food portions are small, yes, but we bought crates of these bottles at the last station," Sartoris said. "Fire sale. We had to take advantage. Please, drink as much as you like." He did, though the drink didn't help him keep track of the multiple conversations that were happening at once. "Can we get a refill?" the captain asked, holding out her cup. "It wasn't like I had any choice," the bearded cook said to the broad-shouldered woman, "so I said to them, look, the arm must come off." Beside them, the young man was carefully ladling out portions of vegetables onto everyone's plate until the captain told him to stop serving and start eating, for God's sake. Gorlen's date in his music-memory smiled at him as the next song started, whispering that this was the good one as the ship conversation went on without him. "We need more rice." "I got it," the severe woman said. "Where's my fork?" "Then the guy looks at me with the most serious expression on his face, and he says, that's fine, Doctor, you can take the arm, but can you leave the fingers?" The broad-shouldered woman boomed with laughter. "It's Em's issue, not mine," the severe woman said to the captain, "the suspension is supposed to wear out after so many landings. It's the engineer who's supposed to do something about it." "I sense being turned into a scapegoat." "Tell me that's not true, he really said that?" "Who has the bottle?" "Are you from here originally?"

It took a moment for Gorlen to realize that Sartoris was asking him a question through the noise. He quit the music-memory, the only trace of it the tickle on his earlobe, where his date had begun to nibble.

"No," he said, his face flush. "I was born on Falstaff."

"A City Planet?" The bald man turned this fact over in his head. "You've come a long way."

"I did." He could tell that Sartoris was socially trained, the way the man looked at him like he was the most interesting person here. Still, even after recognizing the technique, he liked how it made him feel. He would've told him anything. Almost anything. "I heard the stories about this place. So I came. And I stayed."

"And you said you aren't a musician?"

"No. But I"—he caught himself, voice trailing off—"just a fan. Used to go out to town and listen to the concerts, back when there were concerts." And between the concerts, enacting the company plan that would stop the concerts from happening.

"That must've been nice."

"It was." He smiled, pushed his glass out, and let Sartoris refill it. He co-opted the story of someone he used to know, and made it sound like his own. "I was an operator here in the landing base. Had long shifts, ships coming and going, illegal dockers, fussed-up reservations, they always needed us on call. Took a lot to keep going. But it was worth it when I'd hear them play."

It was a subtle shift in energy. He didn't notice the others had gone quiet until he really got to talking. Momentum carried him the rest of the way, along with the food, and the wine.

He told them how the town used to be, before the dogs ran the place. Told them that there was no music so beautiful than what you would hear each morning from your bedroom window. There was an old saying, he said, of how the ear hears but the heart listens, and those were the days his heart was sated. He told them of the hours of nodding off in his operator's seat and the weekends he spent in town in the company of strangers as they applauded the new sounds onstage. He told them about the drinking. How he found himself in that audience, a part of him he didn't know was there until he left Allied Space.

He used to dream of playing with the bands onstage, but he'd missed his chance now that the musicians were all gone.

Gone, but not quite.

He tapped the scar behind his ear. "Thousands of memory records on my drive. Performances I've captured. Name a song. It's probably in here."

They played a game of music. Someone at the table would call out the name of an old treasured song, or a song they believed too obscure to know, and he would search his database with a clenched fist and toe twitch until, almost every time, he found it, for this was once the city of musicians, and they were many, and there was not a day that went by on Ariadne when he was not in the audience, listening to them. And he would translate these memories through his humming of the tune, singing for them the words he could catch, and would take great pleasure in the crew's nostalgic delight and surprise. He would know what it was like to be on that stage.

"I bet I know a song you don't have," the captain said.

"Try me," he said with a challenger's smile.

The crew hollered.

"A song from a Resource World," she said. "Umbai-V. The farmers would sing it at the end of the day. Think it was called the song of homecoming."

He shut his eyes and searched.

Nia crossed her arms.

"I think you stumped him," Royvan said.

But Gorlen smiled.

"No. I have it."

He was in one of the smaller venues. Nayla's Tent. A hollowed-out fruit was in his right hand, filled with weak, sugary drink. The man to his left had a whistle in his nose that was very distracting. And on the narrow stage was a woman in a gold-shimmer suit, who claimed the next song was one passed down to her by her mother, and from her mother, and so on. The translation was her own. Gorlen winced as he remembered how impatient his younger self was— the dragged-out sigh he let loose at this long-winded performer. *Get to the song.* She did, in time. And as she sang, Gorlen, from this place in his past, echoed out her words in the *Debby*'s kitchen.

> *"The fields are empty of their fruit*
> *My basket heavy with their seed.*
> *I walk the road back to our home*
> *This song my light by which I lead.*
>
> *Take my day, but give me the night,*
> *Take my day, but give me the night.*
> *Feed the hearth and pour the brew,*
> *A drink for me, a drink for you.*
>
> *The road is long and does not end*
> *The rocks below now bruise my feet.*
> *But up the hills I march tonight*
> *For by the gates you wait for me.*
>
> *So take my day, but give me the night,*
> *Take my day, but give me the night.*
> *Feed the hearth and pour the brew,*
> *For I am coming home to you*
> *I am coming home to you."*

It was a lackluster translation. Gorlen's younger self cringed at the hokey rhythm and childish rhymes, while his older, present self had a more generous view of the lyrics' earnest qualities; opinions that were, in the end, irrelevant, for the crew was so drunk they would've applauded if he pissed on the floor. They gave him a standing ovation, led by Sartoris, not only for winning this impromptu game but for the performance, which, while strewn with false notes and nervous warbles, was sung with great emotion. Only two remained seated; the captain and her boy. Nia clapped without energy, the song having put her in a melancholic mood, as she remembered the night she spent with her head on Kaeda's chest, sweet and long gone, and thought how unlikely it was that she would ever have a night like that again.

As for Ahro, what he felt now defied his own explanation. He was too startled by these sensations to have a coherent thought or theory; could only let the feeling envelop him, as from his chest an invisible line tugged at him—upward, breathlessly, to the sky that swirled like an oil painting of many colors, as the sleeping thing within now fluttered its eyes.

Not long after the performance, the meal was finished and the last cup emptied, and it was time to say good night. At the entrance of the cargo bay, Gorlen thanked them all for the wonderful dinner and stumbled his way back to the landing pad's descending elevators, believing he would treasure this memory till his last day, only to curse himself after he returned to his room and realized he had recorded none of it for later recollection.

It was just as well. The memory drive was old, and he had used it cavalierly that night. He sat on the frayed sofa, clutching his head, massaging away the throbbing ache as the drive did a brief short circuit and threw clipped music-memories at him like a series of wrathful slaps. The mastiff watched him from the dark of the other room while his face twisted into a grimaced smile. Due punishment, he thought, for using the ghosts of the world he'd ruined as a cheap parlor trick.

Tomorrow, and the next day, he would continue to play guardian to the abandoned dogs, and the transmission tower, until the day Umbai would call and let him know the construction fleet was on its way. He would not be the last human on this satellite, but he would be the last to remember the concerts. He would drive to and from the town, and while away the years listening to his memories. And for a time, he would find peace, and reconcile the way his life had turned out, until the day would come when he approached the gates and there was no dog left to bark.

He saw all of this before him as he fell asleep that night.

And still, he smiled.

Once he was gone, the crew set about cleaning the table, talking about other matters, the sole reminder of Gorlen's presence Roy-van's impromptu review of the performance, which he said wasn't bad for a beginner, but that the man had a long way to go if he had any hope of drawing people back to this world by music alone—a review Sonja rolled her eyes at before knocking him affectionately on the elbow. Soon it was only Ahro who still thought of the man and the song, his brow furrowed as he remembered his physical re-action to the music—the dance of nerves on top of his head, the wind-rush of a sudden opening in the air.

Feelings he did not know what to do with.

He picked up the mastiff's plate and brought it to the wash, thinking about the song. He glanced at Nia from across the room. Studied the lost look in her eyes.

She was troubled too.

"I'm going out for a smoke," she announced as she backed out of the kitchen. The women and Sartoris followed her outside, where they would share a pipe.

Ahro stood in the entryway to the common room and watched them go, unable to follow, for Nia had told him it wasn't good to indulge in such a habit. He wandered back into the kitchen and joined Em and Royvan at the table, even though he wasn't in the mood to play Tropic Shuffle. He didn't want to be alone. He rested his cheek on his fist and watched a few rounds of the game, two perches, a whole nest, before he went back to his room, and brought his flute to the table, figuring out the melody the man had trapped in his head while Royvan ran circles around Em in their game.

While he rediscovered the notes to the song, the women and Sartoris put out the fold-out chairs, near enough to the edge of the landing pad that they could see out into the desert black, the *Debby*'s floodlights on their backs. This high up, there was a cool breeze that dried the sweat off Nia's brow and made pleasing swirls of her pipe smoke. The melancholic mood was still strong. She passed the pipe to Sartoris, and, in the last dregs of her sobriety, remembered the conversation she'd had with Em and Ahro on the tower. She rolled her neck muscles and asked the others how long they thought they could live on a world like this, where there were no people. Sartoris coughed smoke from his mouth, sounding like a squeeze-toy, and asked if he was allowed any books; when she said no, only the desert and the dogs, he said, "A few weeks then," and passed the pipe to Sonja, who gave no qualifications for her answer and said, "Five years," and left it at that. Sonja presented the pipe to Vaila, but the pilot didn't grab it, or answer the question—her thoughts far away from them, while in her hands her ladeum beads embered. "Sorry, Captain," she said, when she saw how they all looked at her. "What was the question?"

"How long could you live on this world, alone?"

In the dark Nia had to squint to make out Vaila's smile.

"As long as I was asked to," she said.

In the *Debby*'s kitchen, the last card was played, and conversation turned to work. Royvan was leaning back in his chair, and Em leaning forward, his chin resting on his cup. Ahro was between them, his flute on the table, listening intently as Royvan told him why he'd joined this crew. "I joined because that was what Nakajima requested that I do. Same goes for Em. Right, Em?" Across the table, Em nodded, his eyes on his hand of cards.

"That was the only reason?" Ahro asked.

"You're dubious. I get that. Fifteen-year job is a big ask. But what you have to understand, Ahro, is that all you have to do is lose one patient"—he laughed, without humor—"one well-known and talented and loved patient . . . and they will ruin you. They will punish you for acts of whatever god was beyond your control, and throw you down the chute with the trash. That's what happened to me. In one day, I went from being one of the premier doctors on Thrasher Station to living in the slums of the orbiting City Planet." A sigh. "Lived like that for a while."

"We were probably neighbors," Em said.

"Box buddies." Royvan smiled, rubbing the whiskers on his cheek, recalling old memories he would rather not speak of. "But then Fumiko found me, just before I ended things. Offered me a way out, in her service. When one of the most famous women in the galaxy visits your awful little box of an apartment and offers you a new life, you take it."

Em's story was briefer. "I tried to steal her ship. She caught me, said she was impressed with my work. Hired me after."

Royvan chuckled. "It wasn't that simple."

"No, it wasn't," Em said, but he didn't elaborate, which didn't surprise Ahro, for he'd by then figured out that as much as the engineer loved to gossip, he was quiet when it came to his own matters.

"Fumiko does that kind of thing a lot," Royvan said. "Pulls the wayward into her gravity, breeds loyal servants for a cause only she's aware of. Deploys us when necessary. She has access to so much information, she knows when to strike." He drank, gritted his teeth. "When she found me, I thought I was so goddamn special, until I learned there were hundreds of others she'd 'saved' like me." He sighed. "So now I do what she tells me."

"Do you not like her?" Ahro asked.

Royvan laughed. "I love her," he said. "But I don't know her at all."

"Who knows anyone?" Em muttered into his cup.

"Well said, idiot."

"What about Vaila?" Ahro asked.

The two men glanced at each other. Neither spoke. For a moment Ahro was worried he had spoken out of turn, until Em said, in a murmur of a voice, "She was one of the consorts."

The scramline in Sartoris's pocket danced. He twirled it open, and when his expression turned grave, Nia sobered, as did the other women, all of them sitting up in their fold-outs.

"What does it say?" she asked.

"'Your request for an abbreviated contract is denied,'" he read aloud. There was a pause. The hollow sound of the rushing breeze. "'You will continue to travel until the boy exhibits his ability, as stated in the contract. Expect penalties in full should you or any of the crew return before this, or before the contract's fifteen-year ceiling. All future reports should address the boy's development, and his development only. Extraneous details will be duly ignored.' Signed, Nakajima." He sighed as he put the device away. "That was about what I expected her to say."

"You think we'll return before fifteen years pass?" Sonja asked.

"No," Nia said, the night catching up with her quicker than she expected. "I don't."

None of them believed the Jaunt was real. The topic was by then a long-running joke. Nia had once pretended she left a toothbrush behind in some city—she couldn't remember which—and asked

Ahro if he would please Jaunt over and get it for her, and when he shut his eyes as if in intense focus, everyone in the room went quiet, each of them wondering, *Was something about to happen?* until he pressed his fingers to his temples and farted, which was as definitive an answer as any of them expected to get. So when she heard Fumiko's latest transmission, Nia let it make a glancing blow before she sighed the smoke from her mouth. Her eyes shut, she opened one, when Vaila, in a strangely calm voice, asked Sartoris, "Did you tell her I missed her?"

A pause.

"Yes," Sartoris said softly. "I did."

She nodded. "Thank you."

Nia regarded her through the curl of smoke.

There was context that had to be explained. Royvan started at the beginning. "Fumiko visits Pelican sporadically, sometimes twice in a year, sometimes in the space of decades. It's always a big thing. And whenever she visits, one lucky woman is chosen to be her consort during her stay. They get their hair dyed, their eyes too, the works." He took another drink. "Vaila was one of Fumiko's favorites. When a consort's week is up they're paid enough to live off of for a few decades, and they never see Fumiko again, but Vaila, she hired Vaila, took her in like she did us."

"Vaila was special," Em said.

"Very special," Royvan said. "She was Fumiko's personal pilot, living the life of travel with the most famous woman in the galaxy."

"But not that special," Em said, and whispered to Ahro, "Fumiko still had her consorts."

"So what?" Royvan said. "I saw the 'graphs. Vaila looked like she didn't care. She looked happy."

Em snorted. "Look where that got her. Dropped her here, with us. Forgotten in the fringe."

"Diamond in a tin can," Royvan said.

"That should be a song title," Em said.

"It is, idiot."

They fell quiet when they heard the others coming down the causeway. Ahro feared they'd heard their gossiping, but his worry was short-lived, as Nia sat at the table and told them the reason they looked so somber; the news from Nakajima, and the years ahead of them that were now a certainty. That this was, in her words, a long-term thing. He knew this news should've made him happy, that he would be in this place he loved very much, but as he listened to the strung-out quality of the others' voices as they said their good nights, he was overcome with a heaviness that dragged his step. Besides, his thoughts were scattered. He lay in bed thinking of that inexplicable tug of the chest and dance of the head he had earlier felt. Sensations much like what he'd felt when he listened to the white noise of the Pocket, only emphasized, underlined, greater than before. He touched his chest, suspicious of what these sensations heralded, what they meant.

From the room next to his, he heard the sounds of love—sounds that were quieter than before, but still audible; the short, knifelike gasps, whether Sonja's or Royvan's he was not sure; the rustle of a hand moving across sheeting and up a lover's arm. The whispers through the wall. Sounds he was tranced by, like he was most nights, lately. Nia told him that this was the year he would learn to take care of himself, but that night, as he listened to the sounds of love, he saw there were some lessons he would never learn on this ship. Lessons none of this crew could teach him.

He imagined what it must feel like, to be so close to someone. And as he remembered that tug he felt toward the swirling sky, he wondered how far he would have to go, to be in such good company.

7

His Year of Learning

They were waiting for him in the cockpit the next morning. Vaila in the pilot's chair and Nia standing beside her, she the most awake of all of them, waving for Ahro to come closer. "You're going to watch the liftoff procedure," she said. Her hand kneaded his shoulder into pliable clay. "Vaila's going to talk you through it. Like with Em on the tower, we don't expect you to pick it all up the first go. All you have to do is look, and listen. The doing will come later."

He took his seat in the copilot's chair, wondering what Vaila was thinking as she gestured to the console—if even now, as she began her lesson, she was dreaming of Fumiko. "There are five safety checks all good pilots run through before takeoff," she said. "Fuel. Thrusters. Strings. Gears. Sails. Even in an emergency, you run through the checks. Any of them are compromised, your flight is compromised." She narrated each of her actions as she flicked the switches on the board above them, twirled a small wheel beside an imposing lever, and when she was done, she asked him, "What are the safety checks?"

"Fuel. Thrusters. Strings," he repeated.

"And?"

He looked to Nia for help, but she only lifted her shoulders.

"Gears and sails," Vaila finished for him. "Memorize it. They're important." And with a swipe she opened the console window and showed him how to unfold the wings.

The year of learning began with observation. This came naturally to him, for the Quiet Ship had trained him how to be a shadow on the wall, and to anticipate the needs of those he served. In a sounder's outpost inflicted by red influenza, he attended Royvan with a box of fresh gloves before the next round of patients, as he once did the Mistress Cellist with her rosin. Listened to the doctor as he ran through his list of questions for each patient; of when the rash first sprouted, and how bad was the itch, and was their perception of color more or less vivid than before.

During landing and departure, he was in the cockpit, observing the intense knit of Vaila's brow and the aliveness of her eyes as she razed the strings of the cat's cradle, and kicked the *Debby* off the ground. He learned much about her, even though she spoke little. Could see clearly that this was where she was happiest, manipulating the *Debby*'s strings. The rumbling detonations of the thrusters felt through their shoes.

Sonja, dropping an unloaded rifle into his hands, telling him to acknowledge the weight of its power, and to recognize how false that power was. "Any idiot can squeeze the trigger," she said. "Smart one knows most of the time they don't need to." He sat by her, the both of them cross-legged on the blue tarp, and he listened to the click and the slide as she took the power from his hands and dismantled it, piece by piece, until she had returned the rifle to its true form, which was nothing.

He and Em sat on the bench before the ticking gears of the fold-core, the pulsing light in the throne of glass, and counted out the healthy beat of the drive, the six-eight of it. "It's like a heart," the engineer told him. "Once you start to hear the rhythm, not hard to figure out when something's wrong. Just have to listen. Put a finger to its throat and count." He opened a panel beneath the core and showed Ahro the veins of the ship. Showed him how the lights worked, the order of automation. The skein of wires whose purposes were impossible to decipher by color alone.

Sartoris gave a lecture on the first woman who ventured into Pocket Space, a long time ago, and how she was caught in the Vivacious Current and returned to Earth twenty years later, believing she had left only yesterday. This was the first traveler. "History is context," he exclaimed. "We understand only through context!" And when the lecture was done, and he was given his free time, Ahro sat in his quarters and played his flute for the two hours allotted to him, feeling that dance along his scalp as he rehearsed the song of homecoming—afraid of that feeling, of what it might mean. Intrigued. He spiraled the song off into other forms, new songs, so accustomed to the resonance that he was unaware that it was growing in strength and amplitude.

Nia stuffed his days with things to do, as if she knew what it was he wanted, and feared what would happen had he the time to search for it. He was no longer allowed to wander through the settlements and cities of the worlds they visited, with Sonja as his bodyguard—was instead by his captain's side as they looked for work in the travelers' bureau, overwhelmed by the raucous crowd in the pit; the spittle that flew from the shouting of desperate mouths; the elbows that knocked against his head; the loud and angry charge to this dark arena. He tried to hold Nia's hand, desperate for comfort, only for her hand to slip out of his grasp, a fish through his fingers, because, as she told him afterward, no one hires a captain who looks weak. He stood with her in the mass of people fighting for what was theirs and tried his best to take note as she shouted who she was, and what she could do, up to the balcony of employers, with her sig-card held above her head. For the rest of the day he was shaking out the ringing in his ears, and the memory of the concerto days, when the violin strings would slice the corridors of the Quiet Ship as his arm was placed on a table, the breaker's wand applied to his radius. The snap of bone. Being in the pit ignited an adrenaline that lasted all the way to the night, where in her quarters she told him why she did or did not accept a job, and where to place one's trust. "I learned the hard way," she told him. "You get the benefit of my own years of lessons." He did not tell her of the triggered memories—he knew how much it saddened her to hear those stories. All he did was listen.

Contracts were signed, and jobs accepted. He observed. And then he made his gradual participations. He carried the water and the bag of tools. He fell asleep on Sonja's shoulder during a long night relieving a guard post, bumped awake by her elbow as she told him sleep was for later. He learned to drive behind the wheel of a rented truck, a lesson that ended quickly when he crashed into one of the bouncing posts along the dock. He shriveled in his seat as Nia rubbed her temple. He tipped backward when he misjudged the weight-bearing of the loader, turtle-struggling to get back up while Em cackled above him. He reached for Nia's hand in the travelers' pit, and was shrugged off.

"Tell me why you can't hold my hand."

"It makes the captain look weak."

His free time was given to him in pinches. He spent it exhausted in his quarters, playing his flute, haunting himself to sleep with the same repeated melody. The invisible sparks dancing above his head as he grew more certain of what was happening while he played the song of homecoming, and asked himself, as the resonance shook his body, where that other world was, and when he would find it, and why he yearned to.

There was so much about himself he did not know.

But he came to know the fringe. It was rock and sea, and unending desert. Boundless space punctuated by exclamations of people. It was outposts and rare cities that bloomed like wild gardens on the other side of black mountains. Most of the worlds they visited were uninhabited but for the cluster of spires on promontories, the bubble buildings in the jungle clearing. There were people, some of them curious about these travelers, most wary and withdrawn. Barely placated by assurances that they were not Allied associates, and had not come to acquire. He was curious about these people. But he never had a chance to speak to them—to share a meal by the fire and learn what it was like to live beneath a sky chandeliered with green crystalline clouds—the majority of them warned off by the sight of Sonja's rifle. The people kept their distance; left a path wide open for him to follow Nia to the next job. On one oceanic world he caught in his periphery the divers who came back from the water with their fresh catch, the light of the water sliding off their broad shoulders in a way that ignited him as he tried to focus on washing the *Debby*'s sails, the black pool gathering at his feet and staining his boots as he peered at them from the corner of his eye. One of the men smiled at him, the spark briefly a flame, until there was only smoke, when Sonja appeared from behind the *Debby*'s landing strut, the Buffoon smiling wide in warning, and the man was gone.

Sometimes there was no work, and few supplies. Sometimes there were nights when the meals were small and they went to bed with angry stomachs and restless dreams. But these nights he didn't mind. He knew hunger long before he met Nia—was in a strange way comforted by the old sensation, safe in the knowledge that, at least here, there was no one who woke him up with the steel toe of their boot, no broken bones. The hunger was useful in its distraction. It stopped the other thoughts he had before bed; thoughts inspired by the men coming in from the shore with bodies like eels and sharks, and what it would be like to sing with them the song he learned on the moon of dogs. On the nights when there were no such distractions, he fumbled with himself in the dark, pretending he was not alone; an arm, wrapping itself around his waist; a finger, tracing his lips; nights that ended in frustration, his face pressed against the pillow as he reminded himself that it was late, and time to get some rest for the next day of work.

But first he played another song.

Saw, in between the notes, the vision of a black ocean.

The more reliable he got, the more the crew saw him as their equal. There was no child left to be coddled. They opened up the parts of themselves that still hurt; the names they carried with them. As they tightened the straps that hugged the crates to the floor of the cargo bay, Em sang stories of his life back on Galena. The scrappy jank of the boxtown he called home, where he lived with a two-tailed cat named Nanda, and where, every other night, he would visit the bedroom of the violent black-market queenpin Morissa Algernon, who would briskly tell him after their midnight tussles that if he ever disappointed her in bed she would have him killed, even though it was common knowledge that he was her only lover. Whether she was joking, he never learned. "I still don't know if she liked me," he said with a rare shyness.

Jogging through an empty glen, Sonja told him between gulps of air the story of the man who saved her in the gas fields of a Resource World. They were snuffing out a farmers' rebellion, she explained, stalking the pipe-rows and stomping on the ground in search of hidden hatches, when a nervous fool tripped a party mine wedged under the lip of an argon valve. The light of the explosion was like a flower. Wiped out half the squad in a single rapturous blink. She was blasted onto her back. A slim crack running down her visor. The neurotoxins whistling in. At this part of the story she stopped jogging. She looked away from him when she shared the moment she would never forget—how the man saved her by removing his own mask and forcing it onto her head, his last sounds that of manic, red-veined laughter as the toxins squeezed his brain into a pea. "Norrin," she said. "He was a kid. Not much older than you."

They were names of people who had passed on, and who lived only in the regret of their whispers. The patient Royvan had failed, the death that ruined his career. "Justine the Supreme, queen of your wet dreams. Immortal, until she wasn't." He poured out the last of the wine, until the red drink beaded over the rim of his cup. "Not everyone can be saved," he said. "Some people just die. And it doesn't matter how hard you try, because dead is dead. Dead is dead." He drank deeply, his teeth a red smile, and he whispered that name, Justine, as he met Sonja at her hatch, and disappeared into that unknown and forgiving dark with her.

As for Vaila, the stories she shared had everything not to do with the name she carried with her. These were the stories of the other people; the woman who drafted the first fold-accelerator, and the man who made art of the Thrasher military viper. Stories of other times. Her nervousness the day of her flight examination and how she almost crashed into the observer's tent. She never spoke the name of the one she loved, but she didn't need to. That story was in the clench of her ladeum beads and the days she went speaking to no one, trapped in fantasies that were for her alone. And so it was that he learned the names of Nanda, Morissa, Norrin, Justine, and Fumiko. And Deborah—the name that Nia whispered, after lights-off, when it was just her and him in the captain's quarters. The sister she had left behind, to start a new life outside the debts of her gambling father. "My mother had this series of books," she said. "An Old Earth collection. First edition. They were priceless." She chuckled mirthlessly. "I sold them for the price of one ticket. And even that was cheap, compared to prices now." He listened as she confided in him the old regrets—the friends she missed who were long gone, Nurse and Durat and Baylin, the names from another life whose faces were a blur in his memory, but for her seemed as sharply resolved as yesterday. And he was there for her to hold as she spoke aloud all the things she wished she'd done a different way, the words she had held back out of pride, and he smiled out of understanding the mornings after, when she apologized for how she'd behaved and told him that her comfort was not his responsibility.

"The only person you have to take care of is you," she told him.

He did not tell her about the music.

What was happening to him.

The work wasn't bad. He liked being useful, and feeling like a part of their company. There were days when it all clicked; when the work and the lessons made him the happiest he had ever been in his brief but eventful life. And there was the day he truly felt grown-up. Finally allowed to don one of the spacesuits in the locker, he left the ship with Nia into the float of space, their umbilicals making sines behind them as they climbed the rungs to the hull, their magnetic feet thumping along the roof of their home, to the place above the cockpit, where she showed him the emergency beacon and how to prop the antenna open by hand, should it come to that. And when she had finished her explanation, there was a silence as they both realized at the same time how vivid the stars were, the dappled swirl of the fringe, a paint splatter, a piece of art in progress. Everything far away, nothing important, nothing but the two of them as they smiled at each other through their visors and she held his hand and gave him permission to switch off the magnets of his feet, to float above her like he'd once done many years before in the kitchen, with the warm certainty that he was safe and that she would not let go, and the dark wondering of what if she did, and where he would find himself if not for the hand that gripped his.

On the job he watched the strangers his own age wander down the darkly lit alleys of the larger cities, beautiful in their almost feral energy, howling as they headed toward a world he would never know. He dreamed of howling with them. Dreams that were interrupted by Nia's nudges, Nia's hand on his wrist, Nia's calm yet insistent reminder that they needed to keep moving.

"The work waits."

They were always leaving.

Fuel. Thrusters. Strings. Gears. Sails. By year's end he was one of them. On his own he unfurled the sails by hand and rewelded the snapped conduits; applied suture gel to the superficial cuts along Em's arms after he was bit by the sharp brass teeth of the core gears, and made his own splint from materials he found in the medica when Vaila sprained her ankle coming to and from the cockpit, which she thanked him for a few folds later, presenting him with a rosary she had carved from many different-colored rocks. When he and Sonja walked out on a mesa, and she positioned an empty bottle on a high rock, far enough that it looked like a speck, he shattered it with one round of the gauss rifle, a feat that made him sick and proud. And by year's end, the pit no longer made him nervous. Nia beamed as he elbowed his way through the people, their smoke, and he held up the *Debby*'s sig-card, and shouted, "Captain Nia Imani! Barbet Transport Ship! Doctor Trained in Gracilius Med! Soldier with Ten Tours' Experience! Three-Day Limit! Captain Nia Imani! Barbet Ship! Experienced Crew of Seven! Ready to Work! Yes! You! This way!" and gestured for the employer to follow him, follow him back to his waiting captain. Another job, another outpost seen from behind Sonja's broad back. Tired and heavy at the end of the day. His eyes shut and his mind between worlds as he pressed the flute to his lips and felt the spark that would soon bloom into a flame, not long after his seventeenth birthday.

They celebrated with his first pipe smoke. The pipe was lit under a green sky scattered with white balloons that measured the materials of the sky. The smoke swelled his brain and inspired his fingers as he played his lyn, and his flute, and palm-tapped his drums, all the instruments he'd collected along the way. He played the songs he composed in his head during the work; a ballad for Sonja and Royvan, who danced together slowly, their relationship no longer an open secret, while Em made drunken twirls behind them. And as Nia and Vaila played a game of cards on an upturned box and foldout chairs, Ahro slowed the play of his lyn, and he glanced at Sartoris, his teacher, his thoughts bubbling about love. "Have you ever been with someone before?" he asked casually.

The old man opened one of his eyes. "Do you mean in the romantic sense?"

He strummed, nodded.

"Then yes," he said. "I have." Both eyes were open now. "Though my relationships were different from what I suspect you are thinking of. I was with a group of like-minded people. We lived together for a number of years, shared everything but our physical selves." He smiled, distantly. "I learned much from them. It's a rare day when they do not cross my mind."

"What happened to them?"

The man's head moved side to side, as if to say *this and that*. "The last I heard they were still together, with some new additions. But if you're wondering why I am not with them now . . . suffice to say I was young, and handled things poorly." It was a smile without joy. "I was cruel."

"I can't imagine you being cruel."

He chuckled. "Whatever you might think, I am but a mere mortal, and it is startling how easy it is for mortals to be cruel when they are afraid." When he let out a great sigh, it occurred to Ahro that he had never seen the man look so sad. And then, as if aware of how he was coming across to his student, Sartoris straightened up. "But I hope that doesn't dissuade you from learning your own lessons on love," he said, "whenever that may be. It should say something that despite my regrets I still stand by its recommendation. I would do it all again if I could, even with its lackluster ending."

In his periphery, Ahro saw Nia leaning back in her chair, her hand of cards facedown—knew that she was listening. "I don't think I'll have the chance," he said to Sartoris.

"What makes you say that?"

All Ahro had to do was give him a look.

"Right. Our situation." There was pity in Sartoris's eyes, and an unconvincing lightness in his voice, as he said, "There will come a day. One day."

"Ahro," Nia said, standing up from her chair. "Come help me with the bottles."

He put down his lyn and followed.

The cargo bay was dark, all the lights in the *Debby* switched off. There was only the light from the fire outside, which threw their shadows forward as they made their way to the bin under the catwalk steps. She kicked open the lid, and one after another they tossed the empty bottles in, to be refilled later at the next outpost. Because of the backlight, he couldn't see her face, her expression, when she said, "Things are good, right?" Saw her stand very still. "Not perfect. Nothing is. But I think we're doing okay."

He nodded. He placed the last bottle in the bin, the glass clinking against its brothers.

"You can talk to me. If there's something on your mind." Her head turned toward him, the concern in her eyes slowly resolving in the dark. "Is there?"

He hesitated.

"No," he said, smiling. "We're doing okay."

"Everything I do," she said, "the choices I make, I know it can be frustrating. But it's all to keep you safe. To make sure you can take care of yourself if I—if no one is there to help. Do you understand?"

He said nothing.

"This is all for you," she said.

The flute song that night was plaintive. It drifted through the vents, the hatches, and the corridors; past the rooms where the crew slept soundly, satisfied with their dreams, and through the hull, out of the ship itself. The notes of the song fell into the vacuum. Into the mythic constellations of the first travelers, and deeper still, until the song was caught in the pull of the black ocean, and disappeared, out of view. He put down his flute. Tapped it against his chest. There were some lessons he would have to learn on his own.

And so he decided to leave. Not for good, only for a night; a night of his own.

See what might happen.

One month later, an opportunity. They had landed in the docks of the Painted City, where the walls were murals and the people celebrated the lunar alignment of Dyack, Rohindra, and Essex. Like a crow in the rafters, he waited until the crew were well into sleep. And he snuck out—slipped out the escape hatch nestled in the ceiling, between the cockpit and the captain's quarters. Climbed down the rungs of the ship. Walked out of the docks. A nervous smile as he joined the cheering crowd in the streets. Above, the three blue moons telescoped outward, like three heads of smaller sizes stacked one atop another. There was enough of a glow that the streets were day-bright. He walked among the people—the old man draped in many fine cloths who called out to him from some crooked alley, the woman with beads in her braids and long fingernails scored by digital glamours—and he gazed across the street at the ones his age, the ones he never had any cause to speak to, the air around them intoxicating, so different from the older men and women of the *Debby*, crackling with languages he'd never heard. And he followed them, despite Nia's lessons; accepted the consequences as he went deeper into this city, and saw where the people went. And there he found himself.

It was an open park where they danced under electric moons to pounded drums. It was between the blown-out façades of old buildings, and among bone-white trees that helixed into the sky. He slipped into the dance, past the idle smokers and the lovers whispering into each other's ears, into a crowd like the travelers' pit but with bodies that moved in time with one another, muscles captured by the current of the music. Fell into this world, that old sensation, that resonance, as he breathed in the smell of the bodies and the sweat, and stepped into the movement toward the place where sound met sound like two whitecapped waves colliding. He grinned as a man bumped into him with a smile of his own. He held his hands up like everyone else. Shouted at the Essex moon. Colorful streamers scored the sky as he let himself be swallowed by the new; the limbs moving him toward the center, where the music was loudest. Where the electricity was like a finger traced up his spine, and where the world waved and warped as he clutched his swimming head, the resonance making a diamond shatter of his thoughts, shifting him into delirium as he felt the heat crescendo.

And he remembered it all. All of the memories withheld from his conscious mind. An impressionistic rush of images of his last moments on the Quiet Ship—the how of his escape. The force with which the Kind One threw him into the escape pod. The final farewell, in the form of their gloved hand on his cheek. A touch, before the other Musicians found them, charged forward, and parted them violently. The snapping of bone as they cracked the Kind One with their wands. The Kind One broken, their body a gibbering splay. Then terror, as the masks turned toward the pod. His cowering form, curled by the controls, wishing himself away. That terrified wish made manifest by that bright and violent spark. A spark that crackled as the grip of the Musicians' many hands dragged him out of the pod. The heat rising off his back. His robes flashing to ash. The smell of leaving.

He knew exactly what this was.

In the plaza of the Painted City, below the triad moons, his eyes rolled back and his hand clutched his chest and he let it take him. He gave his body up to the dancers and the moons, the black ocean and the roar. Time inhaled its breath and stopped the movements of this world. The dancers were pinned to the air and the drinkers held in their kingly repose of goblets tipped into open mouths, while above them all the glittering streamers were glued to the sky, his last thought a guttural recognition of how beautiful it was, this frozen sea of love and action, before the power within him, that old stranger, returned, and upon a blast of light he fell away from this world; his body gone, between the celebratory beat of their drums.

8
Home

And then he woke up.

It was dark.

Cold.

His entire body was numb; the limbs unable to rise; the brain's synaptic firings at a lazy and distracted crawl as he stared listlessly upward at the blanket of black above him. His eyes blinking once. Twice. Convinced in an unbothered way that he would not move again for days, or centuries.

It was a slow awakening. The details of this place leaked in like gas whistling through a crack in a wall, poisoning his lethargic ease. The movement of leaves, twittering above him on thin, skeletal branches. The irregular surface of the forest floor under his back; the wet mulch, the sharp twig that poked his rib cage. The chill of the mist that carpeted the ground, and curled its gray tendrils over his naked body, leaving behind trails of dew on his chest and thighs. He realized his nakedness. The leak of details became a pour. Leaves rustling like broken nails against a wind that shrieked through the branches, while among his hands and feet the nauseous skitter and click of insects and the slick tickle of small, many-legged things brushing his skin as they dove in and out of the leaf bed. And slowly, the awful dawning that it was not the wind that shrieked but something else altogether, borne on its sharp currents; the shriek of something man-made, and hollow, and—if the chorus of it was truthful—of large number. And underneath this uncanny shrieking, the faint tremors in the ground that steadily grew in force and volume, signaling the thump of something large and heavy in swift approach, a creature in rampaging gallop, letting loose a baritone howl so rich in death that when he heard it, the old, rusted lock within him was shaken off its latch and he snapped awake, transformed, the coddled adolescent of the *Debby* sloughed from him like old skin, and was now, once more, the small, hard thing in the shadowed halls of the Quiet Ship, whose body knew only one verb.

Survive.

He had jumped to his feet and dived into the leaves piled against the trunk of a smooth-skinned tree when, but a moment later, the tree was hit—the beast colliding with it with such speed the tree was no longer a tree but an explosion of wooden shrapnel. He remained corpse-still despite the shower of splinters that rained on his exposed head, his breath held in the fist of his throat and his eyes viciously wide as the pale, leathery hands that were unnervingly human in shape and joint, but large enough to hold an adult in its palm, stampeded to the left of him, and to the right, the creature's body swaying above him as it recovered from the daze of its impact with the tree. Its great snout whiffed the air; a guttural snort that caught the trace of him, as the snout tilted toward the leaf pile in which he lay. His heart kicking his chest, as he made what could've been his final calculation—to run, or be still.

The choice was made for him upon the shriek of a whistle, which hit the beast like a sonic wave. The beast staggered to the side, and—here, with distance, Ahro had a chance to witness its aged face, lit up by a beam of red moonlight that lanced through the canopy—it snapped its sagged jowls. Thick threads of spit flew out, dropping heavily onto the leaf bed in long, viscous loops.

From behind the tree a young woman appeared. She wore a one-shouldered red robe, and had a wooden whistle in her mouth, which she continued to steadily blow as she approached the confused mass of flesh in a lethal crouch, a wooden spear gripped tight in her hands. The beast gibbered against the sound she created. More whistles pierced the air, and from the mists the others emerged; men and women garbed in similar attire, and armed with whistle and spear. There were five of them in all, each of them injured in ways that would require days of attention. They were all tired, and scared, their feet dragging through the leaves, and their spears jangling in their hands. They circled the beast, trapping it in their pentagram of sound, and the beast, which reminded Ahro of a confused old man ten times the size, pulled and stretched with its long fingers at the loose and hairless skin of its head, as if to tear the sound out from its own brain. It curled into itself. The closer the men and women got to the quivering thing at the center of the clearing, the more Ahro believed it was over.

But then, a mistake.

The young woman broke rank and sprinted ahead. The others stared at her, horrified. And when she dug her spear into its distended belly, the tip sinking into the flesh like a finger through soft cheese, the beast swelled, and, with one of its eight arms, it backhanded her. Even from his distance, he heard the crunch of her bones and the strangely silent disturbance in the air as she was flung out of the clearing. The moment so sudden, a few of their number had stopped whistling, the whistles dropping from their parted lips, hanging limply by the cords around their throats. The moment was all the beast needed. It flung itself at them, its howl shaking the canopy, snapping the red and auburn leaves from their perch, scattering them through the mists. The great hands swung through the air. The sandaled feet crunched across foliage. The hunters ran in circles around the behemoth and dodged its wild whipping. One of them too slow. The humph of punched flesh. A scream.

As the battle ran its course, two voices were at war within Ahro, shouting in opposition across the aisle of his heart. The first voice was that of the shadow. It was the voice that for twelve years kept him alive through the worst of the Musicians' dealings. It was the voice that stayed his hand as he watched from around dark corners as others were beaten and broken, and thought him lucky. And it asked him now to take this rare opportunity, when both the beast and the strangers were too occupied to notice him, to run.

But the other voice said differently. It was still nascent, still maturing. Nurtured in the hatch and common room, the cargo bay, and fed on the lessons of his friends. It asked him to follow the trail of disturbed leaves to where the young woman's body had flown.

To help her.

She's probably dead, said the first voice.

To which the second replied, *Then do not let her die alone.*

He prowled across the forest floor, through the brush and the shadows. Silence was second nature, as was his calm. He followed the markings and signs of the forest, and found her beside an old and stunted tree.

He crouched next to her hiccupping form. She was not so much older than he. A handful of years at most. She looked up at him not with confusion but with a naked need he knew, just by glancing at her wounds, he could not do much to address. He tore strips of cloth from her robe and tightened them in loops around the gashes in her arms and her legs to stop the profuse bleeding, and balled a cloth against the torn hole in her abdomen, and held it there, feeling along the bones in his arms the pulse of life slowly leaving. Her impact with the rock had dented her chest, her breath a quick and empty wheeze. But despite the difficulty of her breath, she spoke, the words in a language beyond him and delivered in a rush so overwhelming he drowned in them. In the worst of his nights, when he lay with his head in Nia's lap and described to her in whispers the violence in his head, she did not tell him it was only a dream, that it was over, and there was nothing left to worry about. She spoke no lies. All she said was that she was sorry, which was all he ever wanted to hear; it could've been from a stranger, and it would've been enough to end the night. And it was these words that he now gave secondhand to the dying woman before him.

"I'm sorry."

But if she heard him, she made no sign of understanding. She stared past him, at nothing, everything, as the words frothed out of her mouth and down her sallow cheeks.

The beast let out its final bellow. And then it stampeded away, chased briefly by one of the men before he was called back by his fellows.

It is over, they seemed to say.

Let it go.

The woman stopped. He felt it before he saw it—the stillness, where his hands met the cloth on her abdomen, when the last of the air wisped out of her lungs. He gazed at her lax face. The waxed stun of her eyes. Her mouth, open, as if mid-thought. He did not cry. This was not his first body. He wiped his bloodied hands on his thighs and did as he had always done back on the Quiet Ship when he encountered on his daily routes a body slumped in its own spoils. He sat with her, and he kept her company, until someone came to claim her.

The men and women approached their fallen sister like cats. He moved aside, and for the time being, he was ignored as they attended to the corpse, standing in a loose circle around her, their heads bowed, and one by one spoke what he supposed were their goodbyes. He tried to parse their language, the texture of it unnervingly familiar to his ear, but his mind was too frayed to make any worthwhile connection. He waited for them to finish their business.

When the last words were given, the men and women turned to him, their bodies strong and coiled, as if ready to pounce. He covered the bareness of his body with his trembling hands. They gathered around him. A small-nosed man poked him with the butt end of his spear. They spoke in quick, fierce tones. He remained silent and small.

It was when they noticed the cloth knots he had made over the woman's wounds that their expressions softened, knowing now that he had tried. After some deliberation, the tallest of the hunters, a woman, removed her clothes and slipped him into her one-shouldered robe. She smoothed the dirt from his cheek, and shouted at the others. They began their march out of the forest, heading in the opposite direction of the beast and the tree-snapped trail it had left in its volcanic wake.

He walked among their numbers, his nerves stripped, no more energy to consider how familiar their magma-red robes were, or the musical cadence of their speech; no energy to wonder about his location; not until they finally emerged from the forest into morning, where the mist cleared with startling quickness, and he was delivered the last telling detail of this place.

By then the red sun had risen above the valley. From the hill they stood upon, the dhuba fields were in full view. They were as purple and unending as in his memory, and blazed now like stalks of gold in the dawning light. An awesome sight, which only served to tighten the dead knot in his chest, as he realized just how far he had gone.

* * *

They stopped to rest a few kilometers down the road, where there was an indentation in the hill, a cradle of warm grass. While the hunters whispered to one another, Ahro sat down and attended the soles of his bare feet, torn up by the walk. He winced as he drew a thin blade of wood out of his heel. The hunter who had given him her robe held out her hand and passed him two slices of withered jerky and a satchel of water. He chewed the meat slowly as he watched one of the men crouch by the slain woman's corpse, the face of which was covered with a square of dark-blue cloth. The man held in his hands two of her fingers, rubbing her cold knuckles with his thumb as if to warm them. And then he began to cry.

The colors of the sky were coming into focus with the dawn, the red as deep as an open wound. There were still stars out, though they were dull, and quickly fading, and Ahro felt nothing as he gazed at them—the inverse to what he had experienced in the Painted City, those overwhelming sensations below those three moons so distant from him now it was as though it had happened to another person, even though he knew that it had happened to him, surrounded as he was by the proof that he had moved from one world to another.

Long ago, when Nia had first told him the purpose of their journey, mere days after they had left Pelican Station, he did not know how to react. It had seemed so strange to him at the time, the notion of instant travel, that the information slipped right through him without hold, helped along by the fact that not even Nia herself believed what she said, her mouth a wry twist of a smile when she asked him if he understood their unique situation.

The meaning of the Jaunt had little purchase in him at the time because he had yet to have any true understanding of distance. His life had been a small one, worn into the dark grooves and corridors of the unchanging Quiet Ship. It wasn't until he traveled with Nia, and lived through the slow weeks of transit, and experienced the uncanny and dislocating feeling of returning to a changed world years later, that his notion of the Jaunt acquired a magical quality. But even then, it was a notion of wish fulfillment; an idle fantasy that made him sigh and smile as he drifted off to sleep in the *Debby*'s warm quarters. He once thought there would be unbounded joy, if the day ever came that proved the impossible possible; pride, even.

But now, as he observed the strangers around him, the empty set of their gazes, and the man who wept over the corpse of his friend, he felt only fear. Fear for his friends. For Nia. The ones he loved, who would not know where he had gone to. Fear of the hard choice they would make, when, after searching the streets of the Painted City in vain, they would inevitably find no sign of him, and leave.

Fear that they would not meet again.

He curled up, his chin meeting his knees, and he sat in this child-like pose, wondering, and fearing, until the leader of the group rose to her feet and signaled with a nod of her head that it was time to go.

The gates of the village opened upon the leader's whistleblow, the doors swung open by the strength of three men, and like a parted curtain, the thatched homes of the Fifth Village revealed themselves to him, along with the hill-raised streets. He listened to the crow cry of voices as the villagers greeted them in the plaza, and the somber quiet as the body of the fallen hunter was revealed. It was odd to him—as far as he could find things odd that day—that for a place he could barely remember, the sound and sweet smell of it could bring him to such emotion, as if some silent part of him were aware of a lovely secret that it could only communicate to his conscious mind through welling tears.

What followed was a ceremony it was clear he had no part of. He stood to the side as the hunters greeted the line of six old men and women who had emerged from the crowd. When the leader of the hunters bowed, the others followed suit.

With a strained voice, she seemed to relay the events of the battle to the old ones, who listened with faces flattened of expression. It was the sixth old one that Ahro took notice of; a woman so tanned her skin was the texture of beaten leather, her body short, and, un-like the others, she had a spine that was unbent, her poise startlingly youthful for one her age, as her gaze cut through the people and trained on him like a bird of prey, as if she knew him, and hated him.

The leader was still in the midst of her story when a cry broke out from the crowd, and the people were parted by five men and women who barreled into the ritual clearing with a cloud of dust on their heels. Middle-aged adults whose faces wore what Ahro recognized as the wrath of grief. His attention parted from the old woman, and he watched with hair raised as these five interlopers shoved the hunters aside and fell at the corpse's feet. They had the choked cry of baby birds. And though he knew no words of their language, he knew the tone of denial, and demand, as the stoutest of the men shouted at the leader of the hunters. With eyes downcast, she firmly answered his spat-out questions. The old ones, and a number of the crowd, tried to talk him down, but this served only to make him puff up. He pointed at the corpse, as if in accusation, while he prowled toward the hunter. He pointed at the corpse again, as if to show her in no uncertain terms her failing. The air turned to glass and all the people in the plaza into ice as he shouted once more. With a cold reserve, the leader of the hunters raised her head and met his eyes, and what she whispered next, whatever words of defi-ance, made a vein pop in his forehead.

He punched her in the gut. The fist thrown with such force that Ahro flinched in sympathetic response. Her eyes flew open. And as she fought for breath on her hands and knees, her fellow hunters dropped on the man, and like that, the second fight of the day broke out under the unyielding heat of the red sun. Through the hard smack of limbs and the terrible howling for the lost, the old woman's eyes never left Ahro, not even when his arm was grabbed and he was shown roughly out of the plaza by the only hunter who had not joined the fray, and three other men he had not yet met. The group of men pushed him up the hill, away from the brawl, toward the large house that overlooked the village, and even as they went, he could still feel her, the old woman, watching him.

The sun was directly above them as they walked up the hill. Noon shadows were cast by the houses and unattended objects they passed. An upturned bucket. A rake leaning against the wall of a shed. Their shadows like hard black slices that, in the redness of the day, made it seem as if the world had been cut by these shadows, and was now saturated in its own blood.

One of the men shoved Ahro forward.

The house up ahead, where once he had stayed with the kind old man and his wife, now loomed. And after the men had banged on the door and the governor came out of it, Ahro knew he would find no more kindness here, for in the governor's eyes he saw only suspicion as the hunter whispered in his ear. They questioned him in that yard. Questions he could not answer, even if he knew their language. He was below an ocean, watching all of this abstractly. As if it were the light that broke on the surface of the water. As if it were all just shapes.

He did not know for how long they questioned him, only that they were not satisfied when it ended, and that he was very tired. He did not struggle as they showed him down the hill, into a house with old wooden steps that led below the ground. He just stood there, in the middle of that basement, that square of light, looking up at them, as they shut the door, and locked it.

*   *   *

The darkness was total. He could not see his own hands. And when he heard the sound of his own quick breath, he was transformed once more that day—less a transformation than a reversion, as the small and hard thing from the Quiet Ship made his exit and left behind a child, lost and afraid.

He scrambled up the wooden steps, tripping in the dark on his way up, slapping his cheek against a hard edge. He tasted blood in his mouth.

He staggered forward and banged on the door. He clawed at it and shouted. He screamed Kaeda's name, the name coming to him only now, too late, in this dark pocket where no one could hear him and where he might never leave, shouting that he had been here before, and that he was a friend. He shouted for what felt like hours. When no one answered this plea, he shouted her name, believing for one stupefying moment that Nia was just behind the door, and that if he screamed loud enough she would hear him and release the latch. He shouted until he could not shout, his voice a sponge wrung of its moisture, shriveled by the dry heat of the basement. He drew his hands away from the door, and felt his way back down the steps, retreating to the far corner of this makeshift prison, where he curled into himself by a large, empty pot. Too tired to even keep his head upright, he rested it against the hardened mud of the wall, and re-membered Nia's secret lesson; the form of the poetry she had taught him one lonely night. *It won't save you*, she told him. *The bad dreams will still come.*

But it helps.

He counted the syllables on his fingers, while from his dry, hoarse throat, he whispered,

"I am far away.

I don't know how to get back.

She will come for me."

Whispered,

"It is dark down here,
My feet hurt and my head too,
She will come for me."

He whispered the haikus to the empty pot, to the wooden steps, the dust. The locked door of the cellar. And his body settled against the words he drew out of himself.

"Nia Imani,
The captain of the *Debby*.
She will come for me."

Elby, daughter of Jhige and Yotto, and of once-governor Kaeda, Mother of Hunters, was disappointed. "He is twice your age. Of the few punches he'd seen fit to throw, nearly all were drunken, and aimed at his children. You can call Chur many things, but you cannot call him a warrior." She glanced from the tea she was preparing, at the woman who now sat at her table, and who grimaced as she nursed the growing bruise on her belly. "How did you let that idiot hit you?"

"I didn't think he'd do it."

"Then you've learned nothing."

The woman—Taya—dropped her gaze, and bowed slightly when Elby placed the steaming mug before her. She cupped the tea but did not drink it, not until Elby splashed it with some hard stalk-liquor. Her cheeks warmed from the drink. And she muttered, "I'm sorry."

Elby grunted. She sat down opposite her.

"Tell me what happened."

Taya drank again before she began, the liquid beading on her chin, unnoticed. "We had gone to South Lantern Forest, searched there for easy game. I followed your instructions, the only thought in my head was to break in the new ones with sure victory. Show them the Mondrada patterns, what trees they like to nudge against. I wanted them to find one. But the woods were empty. The animals were gone and I heard nothing but the bugs. I knew something was wrong. I felt it, all the signs were there. So I told them that we would leave. Return some other night, or to some other patch, but Gede . . . she would not listen."

Upon hearing the name, Elby's grip on her mug tightened. "You were her senior. Why did you not control her?"

"She was determined not to return without trophy. And she is— was—good with words. You know that as well as anyone. You wouldn't have known it was her first time in the woods, with her confidence. And the way she spoke . . . it was a mistake, and it is a mistake I will never forget till my last day, but I let myself be swayed by her. I told them we would go no more than an hour deep." She shut her eyes. "It wasn't long until the Butcher found us. When we heard it coming, I told them to run. I did. We could've made it. But they were too scared. I was too scared. I didn't have time to tell them to ready their whistles before it grabbed Rej."

"You did not bring back his body."

"There was nothing to bring back. It swallowed him whole." She was very still, apart from the twitch of her finger on the lip of the mug. "It was horrible. But we fought. And in my eyes each of the new ones that night earned their status as hunter. It was a miracle that we hurt it enough to make it run."

"It tried to escape?"

Taya nodded. "But Gede chased after it. We had no choice but to follow. It was that, or abandon her. In a clearing we surrounded the Butcher. If we had attacked as one, maybe, maybe it would have fallen and Rej would be the only one we lost that night, but Gede, damn her. She was not ready, for any of it. She had no wisdom. Just hunger. She went forward on her own, I think to claim whatever glory she saw for herself there. And the beast slapped her away. Like a doll." Taya smiled, not out of joy, but as if something had broken in her. The face left to determine its own expressions. Her voice hollow. "She should not have been there."

"You blame me for that."

"I do." She said this swiftly, without thought. "You knew her best. Her passions. Her youth. And still you—"

"Your failure of leadership astounds me," Elby said, interrupting her, and Taya flinched, as if slapped. "I sent out a beginner's expedition, under your charge, and you return to me with two less your number, no meat, not even an herb to spice a dish with, and a volley of blame aimed at those who were not even there. Gede was young, but I was younger still on my first hunt, and miraculously, I returned to this village alive and unbroken. A dead long-ear in my bag. Do you know how I did it? It wasn't skill on my part, or luck. It was because I did not have a weak fool for a leader. Taya. I would have let Chur beat you to death in that plaza if I had no more need of you. I would have smiled as I picked up your teeth."

The words reduced the woman to a child. Elby waited impatiently for the sobbing to stop. It did, in time, Taya murmuring, *Tell me what to do, tell me what to do* as she tried to compose herself with the napkin her mentor tossed her.

"The boy. Tell me everything."

Taya breathed deeply through her nose. Her eyes were red.

"None of us saw him approach," she managed finally. "After the beast escaped, we found him sitting next to her body. He was naked. We thought he was one of the vile ones from the Eighth Village. We were rough with him at first. I still do not know where he comes from, but it was clear that he posed no harm."

"Clear how?"

"He had tried to save her." Elby's eyebrow raised imperceptibly as Taya continued. "Clumsily. He'd stopped some of the bleeding with the bandages he'd wrapped, but the wounds were too deep and too total. He looked more confused than we were. He needed help. That's what I thought. So I gave him my robe and brought him here. But I think now that was my last mistake today."

"Why."

"Noro. On our way back, he shared some whispers. A story his mother had told him, of a boy who fell from the sky. That he was an ill omen. That it was because of him the crops failed the following year." She smirked ruefully. "You're right. I am a bad leader. I've lost two hunters and I've cursed the village."

"The crops failed because of the poor mists and a hot season. They failed for boring reasons that do not make for good stories."

But Taya, who had inherited her mother's thirst for such stories, said nothing.

So. Noro knew the tale. Elby was disturbed as she remembered who had taken the boy from the plaza—Noro, and his idiot friends, headed for the governor's house. She rubbed her temple. Nothing good came of a gang of fools trying to tease out a mystery. She wondered if the boy was even still alive, or if the grunts had by then administered their own form of misguided justice. There was nothing left for it now but to see the results for herself. She dismissed Taya with a wave, and went to empty the pot out the window. The last of the water had dripped from the spout when she noticed that Taya had not left, but stood dumbly at the threshold of the door. "What is it?" she asked.

"Are you going to see the governor now?"

"Yes."

"Everyone is at Osan's, preparing Gede for last rites. They cannot finish without you."

"I am aware."

"They will be waiting for you."

"And after I meet with the governor, I will join them."

"You will have them wait?"

"She's already dead. What's an hour more?"

There was a moment that passed, where Elby could read with painful clarity the thoughts on Taya's face. But unlike in the plaza, with Chur, she did not speak aloud her defiant thoughts; that judgment. Instead, she simply said: "Before we found the beast, as we walked through the woods, she spoke about you. Your past hunts. The stories you told her."

Elby listened, without looking.

"She intended to make you proud," Taya said.

"Is that so."

"Yes," she said. "It is so."

And she smiled emptily before she opened the door.

The truth was Elby intended to postpone her visit to Osan's for as long as possible, though even she, the bullheaded sort, did not dare interrogate herself on why this postponement was necessary. Thoughts of emotion—especially those of her own—made her uncomfortable. Whatever went on in her mind she was more than happy to let continue without investigation, or oversight. It was much easier, she found, to simply do.

It was late in the afternoon when she made her way up the hill. The shadows of the village were long fingers by then, cast by roofing and ropes and spear poles left unattended against walls, and fences. The fingers draped over the road, as if readying to strangle it. And it occurred to Elby as she struggled onward, her lungs burning and her ass eager to sit, that she never liked this place. Her sister, Yana, had a deep and unyielding affection for every detail of the people and the roads they walked, a love that Elby had no access to, and because she had no access to it, assumed this love to be a flaw in her sister's character.

She let out a reflexive hum, a spare note of her inner music, as she thought of her. She thought of them all as she entered the gates of the governor's house. Of Jhige and Yotto, laughing together on the porch as they shared a cup of something strong; indulging in that enviable friendship of those who had known past intimacy and were at peace with intimacy's end. And Kaeda, standing by the window, looking at no one but the sky. He was, and remained to his last day, a mystery to her. It was the mystery of those who walked in their sleep; an otherworldly logic at play as they paced alone at night, in their empty hand a cup, which they drank from deeply. She could speak to him for hours, about village concerns, about hunting supplies for her people, only to discover, at the end of it, that she spoke only to a body. The mind elsewhere but for those rare moments when he would snap awake, and smile with them.

No, she thought as she knocked on the door. That wasn't true.

There was a period of time when he was fully awake.

She remembered everything from that night—the sound that shook the walls of the village, and the line of fire in the sky, clear and graceful in its delineation, as if it had been drawn by the steady hand of a sky-bound artist. She had come into her own as a hunter by then, and had led her scouting party into the fields on Kaeda's command, proudly so, unprepared for what she would discover at the impact sight. The naked child, unscarred, in that slight crater, among the strewn black wreckage. She reeled from profound vertigo, as if she were standing at the edge of a gulf where what she believed to be possible in this world was cleanly divided from the concrete proof her eyes beheld, and was overwhelmed by the dizzying distance between them. She remembered carrying him back to the village. How light he was in her arms. A small bag of leaves. The fleeting instinct she had, during the walk back, to snap his little neck, because wouldn't it have been easier for everyone if all they had found that night was a corpse?

Even now, as she waited for the governor to answer the door, she believed the answer to be yes. But as much as she loathed this place, she had a wolfish love for her family, and though she was distressed by Kaeda's off-putting fascination with the child and Jhige's learned fondness for him, and was dismayed to hear that Yana had begun to visit weekly to listen to his flute song, still she cradled their desires within herself like the last bright flames she would ever know, and accepted him as a part of their story's fabric. And now she would do as they would no doubt wish done, if it was them who still ruled this village.

She would see him home.

The door opened.

"Shouldn't you be at Osan's?" were the first words from Governor Jhoal's pursed mouth as he stared down at Elby.

"As much as you should have been in the plaza today to greet the returning hunters. But like you, I assume, I have other things to attend first. Are you going to invite me in, or are you going to make me stand?"

"What do you want, Elby?"

She looked at him. Looked at him till he knew.

"He's not here," he said, after an "ah." "Unlike my predecessors, I am not so . . . I would not keep a stranger of gray purposes in my home. I had him put away, for both his safety and ours, until things settle."

"Put away."

"To be taken back out, when matters are clearer." Jhoal was a tall, broad-shouldered man. She suspected that was why he was elected to this position. It was certainly not, in her eyes, his capacity for problem-solving, or his courage. His tone became gentle—the faux gentleness of a river's still surface, and the violent currents below. "Elby, please. You really should go to Osan's now. I know it is hard but—"

"Where did you put him?"

He sighed. "The Dawara basement. Under lock and guard. And please do not ask me if you may see him, you may not. Not today. By week's end, maybe. He was resistant to our questions, and by my judgment, had a look about him that speaks of trouble. I want him alone for a good while, at least till he's more compliant."

"He will not be compliant. He doesn't speak our language."

He shrugged. "There are other ways to communicate."

"You cannot possibly believe him a danger."

"I know that he has been here before, and that despite being sent off with the best of our labors, he has returned. I think that is reason enough to be wary." He leaned against the threshold. "People are still recovering from the river murders. Land disputes with the Fourth Village are getting worse. A failed hunting party returned today. Two are dead. Soon the others will be nervous about their food. It is a blessing that Noro brought the boy to me before he was truly noticed. The fight in the plaza could have turned much worse. It has been a hard few weeks for everyone. It will not do to add him to our problems. Not yet."

She shifted her feet, uncomfortable from standing in one spot for so long. *Bastard could have given me a chair at least.* "I have a plan. It would be prudent to act sooner than later for it to work."

He held up his hands, palms outward.

She said, "We both agree he does not belong here. But our Shipment Day was only last season. The ships from above will not return for another fifteen years. None of us want him to stay for fifteen years."

"So far we have common ground."

"But the villages on the other side of the water have yet to have their Shipment Day. Theirs will not come for another three seasons yet. The journey from here to there is just as long. We must send him there, now, before the ships leave. We must send him with a guide, or with proper instruction, and letters of reference for the villages he will need aid from. He will be one less problem, and you can continue doing . . . whatever it is you do in here."

"That is a long walk you would have him take."

"It is a longer wait if he does not."

He nodded. And he thought on her suggestion for all of a few seconds before he dismissed it with another shrug. "And who will go with him?" he asked. "I'll not lose an able body to this expedition. We need every last man and woman. And leaving aside the fact that we cannot give him directions, or spare the supplies, I will repeat the most important point, as I believe you will not hear it: We do not know what he wants. No one visits the same place twice without intention. With so little information at the ready, we set him free at our peril."

"You cannot hold him in that basement for fifteen years."

"Less if he behaves."

"It will be too late by then."

"Then it will be too late, and we will proceed with our lives in safety. But today, Elby, we do not act, because we have nothing to act on. I will let you speak to him. In time. But beyond that I make no promises. And right now, it is only you who are in danger of being late." He looked at her as if even he could not believe the coldness of some people. "How long will you make them wait?"

It was the smell she hated. It was one of those rare hates that could be traced to one specific point in time, a moment she was changed irrevocably. It was when she was young, a girl of five, and she was with her mother, visiting the halls where they pounded the dhuba into paste—visiting an aunt, or her mother's friend, she could not remember, could only remember her startled terror when a pair of large and callused hands hoisted her up from behind, and perched her small body on the rim of the long trough so that she could better see the working of the seed. And how she reached for her mother, who was on the other side of the hall, in deep conference with someone, anyone but her, before she tipped over the side, and fell face-first into the mash. Her nose broke against the hard cake of the paste. The sound like a finger snap. And in that panicked and dizzying inhalation, there was a revolt of the body, a complete shuddering, as her senses were overwhelmed by the purple sick sweetness. The curative of Jhige's embrace not enough to halt the pain or the nausea. Her lips curling, from that day on, at the sight of the pastry come dinner, or at the smell of the fields that infiltrated the village on the hands of farmers, the northern breeze. She loved her family despite the smells they carried of this place. And when they were older, and Yana embraced her after a long week's work in the mash halls, Elby would grasp her purpled hands in her own, and be overcome with the desire to clean away that stain, that filth, which, to Yana, was nothing less than the finest perfume.

She smelled the dhuba as she made her way to Osan's, on the other end of the hill. The halting breath of it in the air.

Like flowers bursting from the mouth of the dead.

"You." The others tried to hold Aska back, but she pushed them aside. Nothing, it seemed, would get in the way of her and Elby. "Two hours we waited for you, you selfish demon."

"And now I am here," Elby said.

"Yes. Now you are here. She would never have gone out there were it not for your stories. Your little words. There is no pride to be had in death. You were a fool to teach her that, and— No— no—you cannot come inside, you do not deserve her."

She stood in Elby's path with hands outstretched, as if that were the only way to stop the old woman and her force of will. The family members who remained outside watched the standoff. Elby walked toward Aska until they were a leaf's distance apart, and though she had always been short, and was shorter than Aska by two heads, history compensated for the height—all she had to do was stare at her niece, and say nothing, until Aska tsked and stormed back inside.

The crowd of family members, many of whom Elby had spoken to only once or twice, parted for her. In the heat of Osan's long hut, she observed the body on the table.

Here she was. Yana's granddaughter.

Gede resembled her grandmother in so many of the particulars, it was always a revelation to Elby. It was not just the pointed nose or the arch of the eyebrows or the smallness of her chin. Or the stubborn pride misdirected. The eager fire. It was everything. And it was the reason why Elby plied this young girl with her glorified stories of spilled blood in the forest—those nights by the fire when with relish she scared and delighted the girl with her dark descriptions of the Mondrada's howl under spear point; she wanted Yana again. A Yana untainted by sick love for the village, but a hunter in the woods, like her, where they could both enjoy the clear smell of the mists in the right season, and be silent together in the brush as they waited for the shadows to move and the animals to cry.

The clean robe that Gede was dressed in was parted down the middle, revealing the oiled skin of her chest. Elby pressed her thumb in the bowl of soot and pressed the soot into the skin above the girl's stopped heart, where she left her fingerprint, beside those of the many others; of aunts and uncles, nieces and nephews, and the lover Gede had only recently taken.

She bowed.

The body was burned in the grave fields, on a mighty pyre. It was Aska's duty as her mother to throw the first torch, but when it was time, she stood before the pyre, paralyzed, a helplessness so total she shucked away her hatred that night and asked Elby with her eyes for help. Elby gently took the torch from her niece, and she threw it without hesitation. The flames steadily ascended into great tongues that licked and spat against a rising wind. And Elby smiled, for love came in many shapes, and hers was jagged. Her arms were not meant to hold soft things, her hands born with calluses ready to grip the hunting spear. There was no grief in her heart as the fire consumed the body. There was only pride and envy and a profound gratitude to the spirits of this world for blessing her grandniece's death with this beautiful day; that impressionable youth who, on the worst and the best of days, was Yana's doubled shadow, and was as lovely, and as painful, to behold. Her smile spread as the flame devoured both wood and flesh, and she bid Gede farewell, praying that her last journey would not be long—and that tonight, she too would join her, and her mother, by that riverbank.

After the ashes were tossed into the moisture pits, and those willing went to indulge their grief with drink, and those exhausted by the day's events went to bed, Elby returned to her small home at the edge of the village and prepared for the long night to come. It was a warrior's preparation. The unclasping of her spear from the wall and the sharpening of its point. The removal of her cold-weather robe, and the dress of her old one-shouldered hunter's garb, the leather and freckled skin of her arm exposed for the first time in a long time; she breathed deep its familiar cool. She packed one bag, stuffed it with the food from her storage, enough jerky, enough greens and bread and water to last the few days' journey to the Second Village. She drew a map of the roads one would need to take to get there. She did not know the roads beyond. Knowledge would have to come upon discovery. And finally, she wrote out a simple letter on barkskin parchment, signed and drawn with her insignia.

To Uvay, Mother of Hunters of the Second—The young man who carries this note with him carries my protection, alongside the aid of my friends and colleagues, in total.

He does not speak our language, and does not know our ways. At any cost, he is to reach the villages on the other side of the Water, before their Shipment Day arrives. His journey is a long one, so please stock him with what supplies you can, and draw for him a new map that will lead him from your village toward Water, and write for him a letter of your own, like this one, for the next Mother.

It was true midnight when she knocked on the door of the old Dawara house, long since abandoned by its old members, and now used for whatever makeshift purposes the village required of it; a storage house, a prison. The guard who opened the door was Seeva, a hard-eyed little man who seemed confused by the old woman dressed in full hunter's regalia.

"Is it just you here tonight?" she asked.

"Yes, Mother," he said warily. "It's late. Should you not be in bed?"

"I'm here to see the boy."

He shook his head. "Forgive me, Mother. No one but the governor is allowed inside."

"You misunderstand." She looked up at him. "I am going to see the boy."

A hard thwack of the butt end of her spear tossed him to the floor. She stepped over his unconscious body and stood in the main room, listening to the sounds of the house to ensure that he had told the truth. When she was certain no one else was there, she crept down the corridor into the back room, where, tucked in the corner, was the square of wood with unmatched grain. A latch, with a hook, easily undone from the outside. She threw open the hatch, and with the candle that Seeva had made use of in the main room, she made her way down the old steps, into the dust and dark of the basement.

She discovered him behind the large pot, cowering in shadow, every muscle in his body taut.

"You do not belong here," she said.

Slowly, he raised his head, and she remembered those eyes, as wide and haunted as the forest itself.

Away from the torchlight, where the world was a dark road that curved around the hills and the red moon gazed over all with its tired eye, the two of them fell into their true nature. The hunter and the young man from the Quiet Ship did not speak as they walked, neither given to words that night, and perhaps that was the very reason why they both felt comfort in each other's presence—this mutual understanding that there was no need to explain themselves, or their next step. The road explained itself.

It was at the third curve of the road where Elby stopped. She gazed down the hill, where the land bubbled into the forest they called South Lantern, for fairy-tale reasons to which she had never given much thought, her life concerned with the practical, and the blood. She turned to the young man. The look she gave him made it clear that this was where they would part ways, and though he seemed not to know why, he knew that there would be no arguing the matter. With the end of her spear she made pictures in the dirt. A long curved line that swam around triangle hills and crossed the parallel lines of a river and rambled across the dotted plains. Beside these simple directions, she drew the sun and the moon, and made three tally marks. The young man understood. It was a three-day journey to the Second Village. She handed him a slip of parchment, a letter written in her language, with a name writ in bold on the flap, along with a copy of the map she had just drawn for him. She acted out what she wished him to do—that once he arrived, he was to hold that letter up to the guard, and be shown to her friend. Her friend would keep him safe. He nodded.

"I never knew why Kaeda was so taken with you," she said. His head perked up, recognizing the name. "It was difficult for my sister to hold his attention for more than a few minutes. With me we spoke of work. But for you, he gave his entire days. All of his music. I never understood that. Why he was called to a stranger." He didn't move as he listened to her speak to herself, the whisper heavy. "At the time it frustrated me that he never answered when I asked him why. But it doesn't frustrate me anymore. I've made my peace. I know now how difficult it is to explain what we are compelled by."

She nodded at him, and then, for a reason even she was not entirely sure of, she knelt down, licked her thumb, and pressed it into the sandy dirt. She then pulled at the angle of his robe to reveal his chest, where she pressed the thumb against the skin above his rapidly beating heart, and left behind her fingerprint. It was a ritual he had no concept of, but the act of it was enough that he was only a little scared of the road before him.

And then she left.

She walked into the forest alone, following the hunter's trail through South Lantern Forest, in search of the broken trees, her road to the Butcher's mouth. Prowling through the mists was not the same as when she was young, her legs tired too quickly and her eyes unable to distinguish shape from shadow. But she continued anyway, with spear in hand, because despite the complaints of her body, her heart had never been more certain of its course. She walked to her death that night with no regrets, not even for the days she let slip by without telling all the ones she loved how much they had meant to her. Like Kaeda, her life had been spent in a willful dream, and it was only now that she had awoken, and knew where it was she was meant to walk. Away from the village that was never her home. And away from the sweet stink of the fields' aurora. Her place was here, where the trunks were snapped in half and the air was thick with blood. It was the place between the trees, and through the pillars of red moonlight. She blew into Gede's whistle, calling out to the ones who had passed before her, and who, in their passing, had taken with them her home.

She heard in the distance a howl; with a quiet breath, she drew her spear.

Soon she would see them again.

He heard her whistle song in the distance. He listened for a time before he shouldered his pack and followed her directions down the long road, through the night and around the hills. His view was of the mists that rose from the forests like cold breath, lifting up toward the sky that did not call out to him. The small stones in the path chewed through the soles of his sandals as he walked. He ignored the scrit of movement from the trees and the hungry howls. His life had taken a turn into the surreal; he knew there was nothing to fear from a dream. The worst had already happened to him, years ago.

And it was so good, to be out of the dark.

The road sloped down the hill and rose again in the distance—a pattern that would repeat itself for many hours, according to the old woman, before he reached the river crossing. Up and down the hills he went, the fear settling against the routine of his steps, and, as people do when the road is long and there is little else to occupy his thoughts, he began to wonder about himself. What elements composed the ability that had left him here, and what it was about this world that called to him time and again. Questions with no answers. And as his surroundings shifted from forest into wide tracts of dhuba stalk, he was unnerved by the nostalgia that reached out from a time before his first visit to this place. An echo of an echo, the true message lost in the bounce, its source a memory he had no access to. Twice now he had come to this world; the beginnings of a pattern he did not understand, but could only detect by the troubled surface of his subconscious. But without a key, or even a lock to put it in, he pushed aside these wonderings and he moved on. Wiped away the spring of tears as he looked up at the red moon, and past it, searching for her coordinates.

She shouted his name down streets lit by the vibrant glow of the streetlamps, shouted till her throat was red and raw. The lamps beaded paths through the darkened city like so many colorful necklaces, and led her through its alleys, in circles. She ignored Sartoris's pleas to return to the ship. "Nia," he said, catching up to her. "We need to go back."

"We will when we find him."

"We need to go back and collect ourselves."

"He's out there. He's alone."

"The Haus will dispatch guards in the morning. This city is too large for you and me alone to search. Nia," he said again. "We need a better plan than to wander heedlessly."

A window from on high snapped shut. A small animal prowled around a bag of trash. She had no idea what street they were on, or how far they were from the port. "Go back to the ship," she whispered. "I'll meet you and the others soon."

"Nia—"

"That was an order. Not a suggestion."

Sartoris asked her once more to reconsider, hands held out with palms up in pleading, before she gave him her final answer, and he, defeated, returned to the ship alone. Nia continued on through the dark streets, the side streets, the crowded streets, along shadows that seemed to stretch from nothing. Walking down empty alleys with her hand rested by the pocket pistol Sonja had lent her. She had never shot a person, but in this moment, she believed she could. Each muscle in her body articulate and ready to strike. When she heard a crash, she flashed her torch on what she thought was movement by a darkened threshold—it was a small girl, wild-eyed and startled, who sprinted away.

Her torchlight flickered. She gave it a few hard shakes, and as the light of her torch blinked on and off and on again, Morse-coding the alley she faced, it occurred to her, without fanfare, that maybe he had Jaunted. That Fumiko was right, and now he was gone, was now far away. The sky was black and starless from the light pollution, bleached of signposts or direction. A map with no key or continent. Maybe he was gone. She slammed her palm against the torch until it stopped flickering, and searched another alley, for she knew that no matter what had happened, all she had was the search, which went on for fruitless hours.

She returned to the ship empty-handed. Through the cold corridors she walked, the place that was once home now a foreign thing to her, a collection of metal and wire. The crew was in the common room, listening to Sonja, who detailed the search plans for the next day, the sectors where they would inquire. Nia would be debriefed later; for now, she would be alone. She soon found herself standing in his room. The room itself had a long lineage. There was Yvon, who'd painted the walls with her family tree, which was many-branched, and took as long to chip off as it had to compose. And there was Ponchi, who kept his treasured pipe beside the bed, smoking himself to sleep, his ecstatic dreams recounted in loving detail the next lights-on, during breakfast, to no one's amusement but his own. And then there was a time when no one lived in this room, when it was just a space, empty, waiting to be filled.

It was filled now with music—a dozen varietals of instruments from the worlds they visited. An orb that played different tones depending on how its surface was massaged. A toothed metal twanger. A tautly wound drum that she and Sonja and Em had built together for Ahro's fifteenth birthday, the skin from a hunted beast on a desert continent, and the wood whittled down by Em's expert hands. She remembered how Ahro's eyes brightened when he was given the drum, this dumb, treasured thing, and the days he played it under dual suns.

The flute.

She picked it up, her thumb pressed into the engraving of his name. She did not know why she lifted the mouthpiece to her lips and played; why it was vital to her, to remember the notes, the sound of him, at that moment.

On Umbai-V, the young man stopped walking.

Heard, in the far, far distance, the note.

The sound of her.

She knew few songs.

This was the easy one.

A lullaby.

It was like an itch in the back of his mind. It came from a place at once outside of and within himself. The breeze roared into a wind and kicked up the dust on the road. He could hear the music coming from above—the plucking of stars. Something beneath his heart, an ancient instinct, coaxed his eyes shut, his mind quiet. The world beyond him narrowed out, the road and the fields and the forests, until he was suspended in empty space, like all those years ago when the Grav had failed, and the food flew, and he let out his first bright laugh. And then he saw the path—a current that arced up into the sky; a current of many colors, shifting, not true colors, but something beyond the realm of the senses; as if it had been waiting for this moment to reveal itself.

He rode the current off that world, through the nebulae, through the asteroid motes and gas giants, the stellar rings and mythic constellations, he an ancient and new creation, breaking through the laws of this reality, crashing through the established walls, the cans and cannots on his way back home, flying past the thousands, millions of other lines that spread out in an infinite network, old paths traveled, and new paths yet to be walked. He flitted past all of this, until the Painted City spun toward him, gaining in terrifying scope, he an infinitesimally small thing crashing toward it, toward the smoothstone spaceport, through it and its materials, the layers of metal and lastique and tamed quarry rock, slower now, drifting down, down through the quiet dark of the docking bay, toward the *Debby*, through the *Debby*'s charred hull, ancient hull, hull that had spent countless ages in transit, carrying with it thousandfold stories, and down, gently, into his hatch, the world flexing, and pulsing, before returning to its original, solid shapes.

There he was; and there, all his things. His bed. His clothes. His instruments. His joy too big to name. He brushed the ashes of the burnt robe off his body and dressed in his old clothes, hands shaking, for he had jumped through space, he was infinite, with no walls to restrict him, no distance denied. He felt he must shout this power from rooftops, but first, he would shout it to his family.

He ran out into the empty corridor. He heard the mumble of conversation from the common room. A giddy smile on his lips, he walked up to the doorway, took in a breath, and made his grand entrance. Vaila screamed. Sartoris, startled, dropped the cup in his hand and spilled the blue contents on the rug. Nia ran up to him, scooped him into a fierce, almost violent hug.

"Where the hell were you?" she cried. She pushed him away. Shook him, hugged him again. "Where did you go?"

He almost told her, almost, but his throat constricted and stopped the words from exiting his parted lips, his body aware of the truth of things before his mind; that this was his home, and he would have none other. Once he told them what he was able to do, how the impossible was in fact possible, the job would be over. They would return to Fumiko. And then, what would come next, he did not know—only that it would be over. He would lose these people. This home. And there was still so much to do.

So he told her a half-truth. That he had been lost. And Nia stared at him, into him, with that same searching look, only this time profuse with all of her anger, confusion, and happiness. "Goddammit," she whispered finally, smoothing his cheek with her thumb. "Goddamn you."

That night, he composed for them a story. He told them of the people his age that he had met. He told them of the spirits he had drunk. The dancing. A night of revelry carried away as they drove him to a distant outpost, and the morning when he woke on the couch in a house he did not recognize. He described his long day of wandering. The kind person who helped him return. He knew to keep the story vague; he claimed that because of the drink he could remember little of it, even made a show of a headache. Nia stared at him from across the table, but she said nothing, nothing other than how glad she was that he was back. And when the story had ended, all of them, exhausted by the long day, went to bed, each of them making some small gesture of how happy they were to see him. He thanked them all, and he apologized. He made art of his apologies while, inside, a small smile lingered in his heart, believing he had gotten away with it all.

It was only later, when he was back in his room, surrounded by all of his things, that he felt the guilt of what he had done.

The simple, hollow thump of it.

The guilt was a hard apple in his throat. It choked him when Nia would out of the blue touch his back, as if to remind herself that he was still there. But with time, he learned to cope. And it wasn't long till the guilt was subsumed by delight, now that he was certain he was as special as Fumiko claimed. Who else had true concrete evidence that they were so extraordinary? Delight would bubble up during his lessons with Sartoris, inspiring in the boy peals of laughter, much to the old man's confusion; laughing because, finally, he knew something that they did not.

In time he began to practice his newfound power. He waited a month, when Nia no longer demanded that he sleep in her room during their planetside visits, and when his every movement was not scrutinized. That was when he would sneak away from home, out into the dark, and test the limits of himself.

These were the months of his discovery, these night routines.

9

Night Routines

He walked alone across the vast on-off fields of BlackFlower and GreyWheat on Mondrian while the crew slept in the inn, oblivious to his disappearance. In a place where he was sure no one was watching, he stripped naked, knowing the clothes would burn away on his exit. Barefoot on the frosted dirt, his nerves gone numb, he narrowed his focus down, quieting the winds around him, the sensations of his smell, his taste, his touch, until all was dark, and still. And when he had done this, he heard the distant swell of music, detected the invisible currents, and was soon gone from that world. Time stopped as high and bodiless above the planet he followed the myriad currents that cat's-cradled outer space, funneling down a path that dropped him into—

The whirling dervish of a gas giant, free-falling through the wretched and toxic air, red-veined as he gagged and choked, borne along wind currents so rapid they would've ripped apart any other body not charged with the kinetic energy of a fresh jump, and he in his dimming consciousness thought this was it, he was going to die, why had he been so stupid—but then, the ancient instinct—a fishing wire that hooked his heart and yanked him out of the hemisphere-wide hurricane, lobbing him across the galaxy, till he dropped through the red sky of Umbai-V.

The burnt stalks beneath his body cracked as he stood back up. Dizzy, he clutched his head, steadied. Once he had reoriented himself, and saw where he'd landed, he dimmed the sensations again, and rode the currents back to the planet that lay claim to the *Debby*, landing with a sickening thud beside the clothes he had left behind, in the black square of the Mondrian field, his back arched as he reeled from the incredible, starry-eyed pain of whiplash, violent coughing. He dressed. He limped back to the inn a cowed dog, not ready to try again that night. He comforted himself with the fact that now he knew for sure—when he was in danger, he was always returned to Umbai-V; he did not know how, or why, but there it was, his safety net.

He got better with practice. In the icy drifts he stripped, and jumped, and learned that passage to safe worlds, breathable worlds—worlds that wouldn't rip him apart once he had quit the jump—was identifiable if he listened to the tone of its music. It wasn't music, not as he once understood the term; it was more the music's marrow, the stuff that would pour from a song's cracked bone; a rhythmic current; a melody sung not with the mouth but the body. His body sang past the stars, and dropped into a forest glade, dappled in sunlight. Some floral creature sped away at his sudden approach. The delirium once experienced during his first few jumps was lessened, now a dull ache that soon subsided. He grinned, and leapt back up the line that left the forest glade, warping to the other side of the planet, onto a rock promontory that overlooked a large valley whittled down by a silvery lake at the bottom. He pointed up at the highest ridge he could see; a ridge that narrowed out to a thin point in the green-tea sky. Now he wanted to see how exact he could make his jump. But his jump was still being tamed, still inexact in its landings, and his stomach gulped as he missed the ridge by a good foot, and fell at a dead drop so swift he had no air left to scream, the hard ground spinning toward him, sure he was dead before the ancient instinct woke and carried him up the currents, up into the sky, away from death, falling back into the purple crop fields. From there, back to the snowy drifts, barefoot but standing upright. And then his legs gave out.

"Are you sleeping all right?" Royvan asked at breakfast, reaching out to touch his forehead. Ahro played along and told the doctor he had been coughing all night. He was given water to drink, and told to stay in bed for the rest of the day. Nia poked her head into his hatch every other hour to make sure he was doing as he was told. He worried that these periodic checks were ones of suspicion, as if she was ready to catch him in the lie, but nothing came of it except more water, more hands measuring his temperature.

He swam in untouched lakes and let loose full-throated howls as he fell through swirling pink clouds. He rested in the forked branches of trees hundreds of meters tall as he gazed out into the misted horizon. He did what he pleased.

"Where are you going?" Sartoris whispered one night from across the hall.

"For air," he whispered back.

He lived in flight between worlds. There was freedom in these uninhabited places, where it did not matter how he behaved, or how he dressed, or not dressed. Pissing where he liked, bowels loosened from great heights, forbidden words shouted into the air—he listened as they bounced like stones off the faces of sheer cliffs. He said silly things into the ears of grobin birds, and sang into a great black pit his secrets, the fantasies, the wet dreams he ached with. He laughed, alone. Those were his animal days. And they were good.

But as happens with enough time, he soon grew tired of his count-less, empty Edens.

He wanted people.

He had been making a point to avoid the inhabited worlds. From listening to the currents he knew where the people were, could tell from the tempo and fury of the song; the music was always raucous on those worlds, discordant. He avoided them because he was afraid he would be discovered, or worse, captured. But the temptation was too great. Soon he stood atop curvaceous man-made dollops, look-ing down at the populated streets below and leaping from ship to ship, the pilots detecting minor fluctuations in weight before he was gone again. And as his talent became more exact, more precise with its locations, he leapt into people's homes, ate a pastry from their kitchen, and leapt out with them none the wiser, they wondering what that sound was from the other room. He slipped through cul-tures. He listened to the songs of New Tides. He went where the priests climbed trees by shimmying up the trunks with tough cloth ladders to be closer to their gods. He listened to the din of people far below, always too far to make out the words. And then he walked among them, stole clothes where he could so that he could blend in, close enough to see the subtle articulation of all their faces, the grains of their beards, their eyes red from drink, and the smell of their morning bodies.

But of all the places he had visited, all the vistas he had seen, nothing would ever compare to Kilkari, the sunbaked city where he stole a pair of breeches and an olive shirt off a drying rack and walked the clay stairs. Kilkari, where he dragged a careless finger across the blue-painted walls, and down the coast where the calm waters lapped the dock struts. Where the fishermen in the distance tossed stasis nets into the clear water, dragging up stunned creatures from the deep, creatures that whipped about as they were dumped into holding containers. Kilkari, the newly acquired city of Allied

Space, where as he stood at the edge of the quay and watched the easy waves, a voice from behind said, "Sanpa?"

It was a Kilkaran word, sanpa. It meant both *Hello* and *Have we met before?* It was a word, among many others, that Ahro learned that day from the boy who approached him on the quay, who said, again, "Sanpa?"

The boy was a little taller than he, with eyes cut from cold jewel, and a nose just a bit off-kilter, as if it had been broken many times, but never properly set. He was looking at Ahro now as if he were an old friend. He said that word again.

"I'm sorry," Ahro said, startled. "I don't understand."

The boy's smile fell. "You speak Station."

Ahro nodded. "So do you."

"Most of us do," he said. "But not by choice." He brushed this thought off with a flick of his thin wrist as though it were a trivial annoyance—a smooth gesture that Ahro found compelling. The boy bowed. "Your clothes confused me. I had thought you were some-one else. My apologies." But before he could go, Ahro told him to please wait, and the boy waited, with a look of impatience, what-ever warmth there had been before now gone. "Yes?" he said.

It was Ahro's first time speaking to someone his own age, and his first time interacting with a stranger without Nia or Sonja around. It was not a moment to squander. "What's your name?"

"Oden." The boy eyed him. "Why?"

The question caught him off guard. "I don't know," he said—then, feeling foolish for saying so, he offered his own: "My name is Ahro."

"Okay, Ahro." He said his name like a joke, and then he was gone, walking up the steps that led out of the quay without looking back once.

Ahro watched him go. He wondered what he did wrong. Of all

the lessons the crew had taught him, making friends was one they had never gotten around to. And so he continued his stroll down the pier by himself, whispering, "Sanpa," liking the way the word felt in his mouth, how the last syllable sounded like a small breath let out between parted lips.

With hours yet before he had to return, he wandered around the city, which seemed to be in perpetual sunset, the sun remaining just above the ocean's horizon, trapping Kilkari in the amber of its light. He watched a woman open an eel with a knife. The ease with which she pulled out the cartilaginous bones. An intense familiarity with the eel's body, her expression casual as she gripped the spine and popped the bones from the flesh. He was mesmerized by her work, until he heard shouting down the street—the sound of a crash behind him, and a blur of movement, rushing out the open flap of a building. Oden. Ahro saw him sprint into an alley, chased by an older man who, properly winded, fell short of the alley's entrance, shouting at the top of his lungs words that Ahro presumed were curses. The man stomped his foot, his quarry lost. The woman Ahro had been watching snorted at the sight before grabbing another limp eel from her basket and chopping off its head.

It didn't take long to find him. A few streets, to an open park in the middle of the city.

"You again," Oden said. He was collecting himself behind an auburn tree that sprouted angrily from the cobble. Sweat beaded down his face as he breathed in and out. "What do you want?"

"Are you okay?" Ahro asked.

"No." When Oden's breath had steadied, he stood up, glaring in the direction he had come from, where, in the distance, the man was still shouting. "No, I am not." He then glanced back at Ahro. "Do you not have a ship to be attending to? A captain who needs your service?"

Nia's face flashed in his mind. The time was fast approaching when he would have to leave. But he wasn't ready. "I don't have to go back yet," he told Oden, who gave him a measured stare. "Do you need help?"

Oden laughed. "And what help are you offering? How do you plan on solving my problems?"

Ahro remembered the Kind One on the Quiet Ship, how they had asked him what he needed, and how impossible that question was to answer; like trying to unearth a root dug too deep into the ground. He remembered the arrogance of them, how he wanted to tell them—but did not yet have the words—how little they knew, and how out of their depth they were when talking about his life. "You're right," he said to Oden. "I don't think I can help."

"No. You can't." But Oden's expression softened a little. "What is it you want?"

"Someone to talk to."

The words came out with little thought. He knew how pathetic he sounded, knew he deserved the laugh that Oden let out—but it was a laugh less harsh than the one before. It was laced with some amusement.

"Sahave," Oden muttered, wiping off the last of the sweat. Then, "See that hill?" He pointed up, toward the mountains that jutted out from behind the clay buildings like rising fingers. "I'm climbing to the top. Come if you want." And then he began to stride so fast that Ahro had to decide in a matter of seconds whether he should take the boy up on his offer. He knew Nia would be disappointed that he chose to follow this stranger out of the gates of the city, but she wasn't there to stop him.

They spoke little as they walked. Any questions Ahro posed to Oden were rebuffed with vague nonanswers, even simple questions like *What do you do for fun?* "That depends on the day," he answered.

"What about today?"

"Today, for fun, I walk up a hill with a kid who likes to ask many questions." He reached out his hand to help Ahro up the steep rock face, help that Ahro ignored as he leapt up with ease. Oden stared at him with appraising eyes. "And you?" he asked. "What do you do for fun?"

Ahro grinned. "Today, for fun, I walk with a kid who doesn't like to answer questions."

Oden's laugh was nearly a growl.

He was composed of hard edges, and walked like he was shrugging water off his back. Ahro was at once comfortable walking beside him, and wary, every nerve of his body awake whenever their elbows brushed, and whenever he caught Oden assessing him with his stark green eyes. Ahro kind of liked this—the agony of not knowing what the person beside him was thinking, but hoping that maybe he did.

They rounded the bend of the hill, and after climbing another steep incline, they arrived at a cluster of clay-textured homes along the edge of a bluff. The bluff overlooked the city proper, many meters below. The buildings here were sparer in their construction, the walls more cracked, and the roads that ran between them littered with trash, embedded in the ground like steel flowers. It smelled like mud. "Do you live here?" he asked Oden, but again he was answered with a shrug and another vague reply: "I live in many places." For the next hour, he followed Oden like a stray while the boy made various stops at different buildings, some more run-down than others, handing off a package to a small old woman, poking his head through a window and speaking in his language to people Ahro could not see. It was like Oden had forgotten he was there, like Ahro had turned invisible and was now observing this stranger's routine. People liked Oden. Their stony expressions broke into smiles when he came around, but the things they talked about were beyond Ahro—sometimes the person would cock their head with a curious yet wary gaze in his direction and ask Oden something, and Oden would do that flicked wrist gesture of his with a perfunctory statement, saying something to the effect of *He's just some guy who won't stop following me* or *Don't worry about him, he's irrelevant.* This went on for a time, until they had visited most of the houses, and whatever routine Oden was performing had ended. He looked Ahro in the eyes for the first time since they'd arrived at the bluff. "You are very patient," he said, not for flattery's sake, but as a simple observation. "Are you tired yet?"

Ahro had never been more awake. "I can keep going."

They walked out of the village in the opposite direction from which they had arrived. Here, the path continued to steepen; Ahro sweated as he navigated the footholds in the rock, wondering if maybe on this world there were hills that never stopped rising, no tops to reach. His theory was proven wrong an hour later, when they climbed the last of the ridges and fell onto the peak, which was mesa-flat and pimpled with black boulders. The sun was still at its perfect meridian while they scrambled up one of the rocks that jutted off the cliff. With a heavy sigh Oden slumped into a concave section of the boulder, his rear slotting into the groove as if it had been worn in by the years of him sitting here, whiling away the days staring out into the ocean distance. Ahro found a perch a meter above him. Even from way up here, he could still smell the salt of the sea and hear the crash of waves below. He squinted against the amber light. "When does the sun set?" he asked.

Oden chuckled. "It doesn't. Not for a few more of your Standard weeks." He said "your" as if it were Ahro who had come up with the system of standardized time. He wanted to correct him, explain he had no allegiance to Allied Space, but knew by instinct that Oden wouldn't listen to him, or believe him. The other boy looked up at him. "I'm surprised you don't know this. Most traders do."

"I'm not a trader."

"Then what are you?"

"Just visiting."

"No one just visits. Not now." He spat off the promontory, the ball of spit making a perfect arc off the cliff. "We are the newest 'Resource World of Umbai,'" he said with mocking pride. "The ships allowed to dock in our port are Allied caravaneers."

"You don't like the Allies?"

Another spitball. "They bought us. Then they blocked our access to the Feed. That's what Reeda said they would do, and they did."

"Who's Reeda?"

But Oden's mind was elsewhere. "She said they lie when they say they want to protect our culture. That what they want is to hobble us. They've taken most of the schools. Soon all we'll know how to do is fish those *shavevan* eels so that you traders can ship your rare inks." He sighed. "She was right, every word of it, but no one listened."

Ahro wasn't quite sure what to say. He'd learned from his time on the *Debby*—and from Nia in particular—that there were times when people needed to vent their frustrations, and the best thing to do was listen. Listening was safe. There was much he did not know about Allied acquisitions and culture stasis, those particular lessons from Sartoris often flying over his head, and he didn't want to appear stupid to Oden with a careless remark. So when the boy was done venting, all Ahro said was "I'm sorry."

The words were acceptable—Oden grunted, and then was quiet.

The weeks-long sunset made Ahro's skin glow, warmed it like stoked coals. He lowered himself onto the toasted rock with eyes half-lidded. He knew that time was running out and he would soon have to return, but it was nice here, beside this stranger. *Another minute*, he kept telling himself, *another minute here and then I'll go home.* Aloud, unprompted, he said,

"The sun above us

Does not do what it is told.

It will not go down."

He turned his head a little. Caught the way Oden now gazed at him.

He smiled. He wasn't sure how much time had passed when Oden climbed up the rock to where he sat and crouched above him, his face inches from his own; could've been hours, minutes. This close, he could see how one of Oden's eyelids was lower than the other, as if too heavy to hold all the way up. He could see the particular shatter of color in his eyes—the green cracked with gold. "Trader," he said, his voice deep, as if he were forcing it down an octave, "I have a proposition for you."

"I'm not a trader," Ahro said again.

But Oden continued regardless.

"My body for yours," he said.

There were many ways to keep time on the Quiet Ship. Metronomes of various make were in every room. Some metronomes were trapezoidal, with windup wands that conducted beats in rhythmic arcs; others were small disks imbedded with bulbs that blinked the beat in silence, one, two, three, four. Ahro was not sure why he thought of metronomes as he kissed Oden between two standing rocks. Maybe it was the rhythm of the thing. How they swayed back and forth like a needle, keeping time.

Oden breathed into his ear. He told Ahro to sit, and Ahro sat. There was a rough command to his voice, but the roughness was curbed by the nervousness of his hands. Ahro swallowed when Oden grabbed the front of his pants and undid the lace. The movement was at once quick and slow, the lace snapping from the belt loop like a snake's tail. Oden jerked Ahro's pants from his legs.

"Don't be loud," he said before he went down.

Ahro's back arched, and he heard shapes in his head, and felt color and warmth. But he did as he was told. He was quiet. He had years of practice being quiet. He gripped the earth, winced from the teeth but said nothing, afraid that all it would take was one word to break the spell, and for the pleasure to stop. Bore the graze of incisors, and swam against the tongue, Oden's hand pressed against his chest, lowering him until his back was firm against the rough rock.

This is happening, he thought.

I am here.

One of his favorite metronomes was the automaton hand owned by the Mistress Cellist. On one of her kinder days, she allowed him to wind it up. He was dazzled by the crafted index finger that twitched the beat, like it was scratching some invisible itch. And while behind the gauze curtain the Cellist prepared for bed, he sat by the metronome and watched that finger scratch the air, worrying away the seconds.

"Tell me what you want," Oden said.

Ahro thumbed the spit that hung from Oden's lips.

Oden laughed.

He often wondered who had made that automaton hand; what old tree it had been whittled from; the hours of care it must've taken to coordinate the many little gears within. He wondered why the metronome was a hand and not a foot. Why it was not just a box with a blinking light, like the others, and what was the purpose of its shape, and what did its beauty serve?

No purpose, he thought with a hand in Oden's mussed hair.

It just was.

Neither boy spoke as they descended the hill. Their sweat cooled in the dead amber light. Sometimes their eyes met, and their mouths quirked into smiles, but soon the city was in full view, the walls dividing the sky, and they were again in its shadow. Ahro knew he would not see Oden again. Felt the need to make some gesture of goodbye, something more personal than just words, but when he reached out to touch him, the other boy stepped away.

"Time to return to your ship, trader," Oden said. He wore a pained smile. And then he ran through the gates and was gone.

Ahro walked back into the wilds alone, at once full and empty; discomfited, pleased. He smiled as he remembered the feel of Oden's tongue, and hoped that his own tongue felt as good; if there was more he could've done, should've done. He rewound his memory, relived it. The hand that gripped the back of his neck just enough that he could feel the pressure. And he wondered if he might return to this place and find Oden again, after the *Debby* had folded to the next world; if Oden would remember him in a few months' time. Ahro stopped at where the trees began and considered turning back. But he decided not to press his luck. He knew Oden had spoken true: it was time to go.

In the wilderness of rock and wood, he jumped. He followed the currents off of the world, high and bodiless in space and time, thinking of the warmth of skin, and Oden's startling eyes. So distracted were his thoughts, he did a double take when the trip was over, surprised it had gone so fast—that already he was back on the *Debby*'s planet, standing on the mossy ground beside the folded clothes he had saved for his return. In a daze he dressed, the pants first, and then the loose shirt. Grinning. He didn't notice the man who sat on the rock behind him, not until he spoke.

"Hello, Ahro," Sartoris said with a sad smile.

10
Stopwatch

They woke Fumiko when they arrived at the moon. A gloved finger dialed up the temperature of her stasis chamber, and her eyes flitted open and regarded the evaporating mist, the concave wall of the metal coffin that encased her gowned body. She once felt delirium when awakened after cold sleep, but she had long since become accustomed to the process; now she woke sober, listening to the beep, unceasing, like a bug in her ear.

"Good morning, Fumiko," the doctor said after the shielding had been lifted and she was exposed once more to the harsh glare of the chamber. He helped her up to her feet. "How was your sleep?"

She stretched her toes. Her neck.

"Time?" she asked.

"Year 3320. Tuesday, 0800, standard time. We'll be landing on Stopwatch in three hours." She did not know what Stopwatch was. Perhaps the confusion was evident on her face, for he explained, "Stopwatch is your private research base."

Now she remembered.

"Stopwatch is my private research base."

"Yes, Fumiko," the doctor said. "There is no need to worry. Your memory will be returning over the next few hours."

He showed her to a furnished bedroom, where she dressed and waited for the ship to land. She wore a fitted black blazer and slacks, and tied her hair up in a tight, constricted bun, all of this done in the haze of routine as her mind collected itself. *My name is Fumiko Nakajima. We are about to land on my private research base. The base is on the lip of a crater. It is where I do my work.*

What work?

"Good morning, Fumiko!" someone said from the doorway, her demeanor bright. "Can I get you anything to drink?"

"Water," she said without thinking.

She closed her eyes. From the time she woke up to the moment the airlock irised open, three hours had passed, almost all of it gone from her memory. This did not worry her. This was the effect of prolonged exposure to cold stasis. A fritzed head. Clipped time. She knew this. But still it was unnerving.

Strangers welcomed her as she walked out of the airlock, down the steps, onto the landing pad. A handful of men and women and others. One of the older men led the pack. He was wearing a thick coat, an ID badge on the chest, but the badge flitted in the wind, and she could not read it. He was eager to speak with her, though she did not know why. She did not know him. "It's a pleasure to see you again," he said.

Maybe she did know him. "Who are you?" she asked.

For a moment, his smile wavered. "Hart Solumen," he said. "Lead scientist of the Stopwatch Research Group." He bowed. "I'm glad to see you back safe, Fumiko."

The crowd waited for her to speak. From the look in their eyes, she was meant to give some meaningful speech.

"I'm cold," she said.

Over time, the world resolved itself into understandable shapes and notions. This was Stopwatch. She had established this place many years ago, her time. What was once a collection of modular buildings along the lip of the crater was now a vast complex that dug deep into the chalky flesh of this blue satellite; a private place away from the eyes of Umbai. The man who knew her, whose name now escaped her, guided her from floor to floor, each more cavernous than the next. A place decades in the making. Whenever they entered a room, the movement of the workers would slow to a halt, and they would gaze at Fumiko with hushed excitement. The older man spoke eagerly about all that had been accomplished since her last visit, the new lightweight alloys that would better slip through the pressures of Pocket Space, but she did not care. Though Fumiko's memories were a broken spiderweb, she knew that what he told her was irrelevant in the grand scheme. "And has there been word from the *Debby*?" she asked, interrupting him.

"We're still waiting for the latest report from Sartoris Moth," he said. "It should be coming in, in a matter of hours."

"Then there is little else for us to talk about," she said.

He opened his mouth, closed it, as if in reconsideration. "Of course." He bowed. "Is there anything I can help you with in the interim?"

"Yes," she said. She pursed her lips. "Where is my room?"

A woman. A woman on a bench by the pier, with a spoon of curry in her mouth. That was it; a simple, unadorned dream that she was woken from when the alarm went off by her bed, and she remembered that it was the year 3320, that it was Tuesday, and she was in her private research base named Stopwatch. She had taken a nap before the welcome dinner, which was to be held in the amphitheater. The fact that this place had an amphitheater was surprising to her. She supposed it was a construction unauthorized by her, as she couldn't fathom its use in a research facility. As she bathed and dressed for the second time that day, she thought about the woman in her dream, tried to remember the particulars of her, but the details eluded her; a blond haze in her memory, a haze without a name.

"Purple eyes," she whispered as she clipped the last button on her dinner jacket. "She had purple eyes."

She smiled, unsure why this detail pleased her.

There was a knock on her door, and then time clipped, and a glass flute that bubbled with sparkling wine toasted hers, the sound of the toast ringing clear across the amphitheater. The low rumble of a hundred conversations died out as the man who knew her raised his glass in toast to Fumiko Nakajima. "For affording us this place of study, for providing us this opportunity to research unchained from the strict, business-driven demands of Allied-Umbai Incorporate, we thank you. To Fumiko!"

"To Fumiko!"

A sea of glasses glinted under the bright, clockwork chandelier. It was when the room broke into song, wishing her a happy birthday, that Fumiko remembered she was seventy years old. No. Seventy-one. In the wall-length mirror to her right she observed herself. Her artificial youth, purchased by Umbai. She ran her finger down the smooth skin of her arm, the muscles that were revived and rewound to a younger version upon each awakening. Seventy-one years old, this body was. Seventy-two would not be far. She was always celebrating birthdays. A long, unending string of birthdays.

She stuck her fork into the well-seasoned, vat-grown meat. Blood pooled from the punctures, and soon the meat was gone, and the people were up on their feet, in clusters. Clustered around her. Speaking to her. One worked in the hydroponics lab. Another was a maintenance worker. One was a teacher in the school one tram ride away, at the three o'clock of the crater. Another worked in the shafts, where they hollowed out the rock, to clear the way for yet more floors, to make room for the new families. As she listened to them explain their occupations, it occurred to Fumiko that she had by accident created a miniature civilization. And then she remembered she'd had this same realization before, during her last visit—it wasn't a concrete memory, just a thumb of a feeling. The people shared with her their names, but the names were already lost on her as she excused herself from the conversation, feeling claustrophobic. On her way out of the amphitheater she was intercepted by the man who knew her. He told her he hoped that they could speak in private about her future plans for the base, but Fumiko lost the thread of the conversation as she was struck by the memory of this having happened before. A moment similar to this. Maybe. *I was at a party—a reception—and I wanted to leave—and then I met her—and she said . . .*

"I feel that I haven't acquitted myself well today," the man said with a gentle smile. "But if you can find the time to sit down with me, I think we can—"

"Has the *Debby* contacted you?" she asked.

"No," he said. He looked away. "If Sartoris's report does not come in tonight, it will arrive by tomorrow morning at the latest. He has never sent a report later than that. Are you sure you wouldn't like to stay longer?"

She stared at him until, with a broken sigh, he stepped aside and let her pass.

The sound of patter, like rain on an umbrella. A spring shower.

Spring.

Children ran past Fumiko, laughing on their way down the corridor, chased by an older child who smiled as if in apology before speeding back up, calling out more names Fumiko had never heard before. Strange syllables. They disappeared down the curved corridor. *So there are children here too*, she thought. There was a boy, somewhere, in the back of her mind. He was holding out a cherry blossom. *For me?* Fumiko touched her cheek, and slapped the tear away before hurrying back to her room. Waking from cold stasis was always a trial for her, but she couldn't recall a time that it was this exhausting—or maybe it had been this hard before, but she just couldn't remember. It was better after she had showered, her skin warm from the water, her muscles relaxed by the mist, but when she lay in bed, she did not sleep.

This was another symptom.

Reaching back for the headboard, she switched the virtual display on the window from a dark, limitless field to that of an Old Earth city skyline. She dialed up the background noise until she could hear in the distance the thrum of a train, the honking of taxis, a soundbed of nostalgia to drift away to, but this did little to help. She entertained the idea of returning to her ship, to the cold-stasis chamber, then thought better of it. It was a bad idea to go under again so soon. So she dressed for the third time that day and went for a walk around the base; went from floor to floor, looking for nothing. At this late hour, there were still people working at their stations. People bowed when she passed, and waved at her from behind glass partitions. The brave ones attempted conversation with her, and she entertained them for a few recited lines before walking away without giving any prior signal that the conversation was over, leaving them stunned mid-sentence. She was aware of the murmurs behind her back. She did not care.

It was perhaps inevitable that she ran into the older man again. He seemed to be everywhere, or maybe, she thought, the world was that small.

This time he was on the patio that overlooked the vast blue crater below, a cigarette in his mouth, flicking the ash off the railing, into the nothing. Above, Fumiko could see the gauzy skin of the pseudosphere that kept the air in, and the poisons of the moon out—the pseudosphere was like a giant wet eye that blurred the stars and made the sky look like it was melting. When the man noticed her, he offered her a cigarette, which she declined. She knew her body was too sensitive to the smoke.

"Is it the side effects?" he asked. "The reason you're awake?"

"I believe so."

"It wasn't this bad the last time you woke," he said.

She stood by the railing, placed a hand on its smooth sheen. "I don't remember this patio. Strange that a research base would have such a thing." She looked around at the empty tables. "It's like a hotel."

He looked at her, almost with pity.

"It was always here," he said. "You wanted this place to feel like a home."

"You've reminded me of this before."

"I have."

She withdrew her hand from the railing and clasped it with the other behind her back; looked out at the crater, the big blue spoon; tried not to make it known how disturbed she was that he knew more about her than she did. "You really don't remember me," he said.

There was no point in denying it. "I do not," she admitted.

He wore a hurt smile. It amazed her, how easy it was to break his heart.

"There are ways to hold on to the memories you lose in cold sleep," he told her. "Memory extenders. A hard drive they inject right here"—he touched the back of his ear, where there was a small loupe of a scar. "They hurt for a little while, and sometimes you get unwanted flashbacks, but they do the task. You never forget again."

"Some memories aren't worth keeping."

"How would you know this, if you don't remember them?"

"Intuition. I've lived a long time."

"We both have," he said.

She looked at him, surprised. But she never had a chance to question him, for it was then that the alert went off—the wail of the emergency sirens, and a call, to each of their devices, that an Umbai warship had folded out of Pocket Space, in orbit of their moon.

The man dropped his cigarette into the dark.

"They found us," he muttered.

The swell of excitement in her breast. She found it pleasing as she and this man ran together through the corridors, the way the blue lights pulsed hypnotic along the carbon-steel panels, and the rush of movement as bleary-eyed workers emerged from their dens to the sound of coming danger. It was the delight of chucking a rock at a beehive, and witnessing the explosion of movement after. It was a splash of cold water to a sleeping face. The man who knew her noticed her grin but said nothing. It was clear he was not as appreciative as she was of their situation's aesthetics.

In the amphitheater, they studied the projection of the system map, the red dot signaling the location of the Umbai ship. It was when she saw how close they were, how close she was to losing everything, that something sparked in Fumiko—the memory of the plans she had made, in preparation for such a day.

"Call coming in from the ship," a woman shouted from an elevated platform.

"Send it through!" the man who knew her shouted back.

A dead voice echoed throughout the vaulted room.

"This is the warship Euphrates. *As she is in breach of contract, we of the Umbai-Pelican Fleet have come to discipline Fumiko Nakajima, and collect the intellectual property of the company. Compliance will be met with peace."*

"Send the families down to the basement," the man said, then joined Fumiko's side, the stylus he held slipping from his grasp with all his palmy sweat. "We don't have the power to fend off the *Euphrates*," he told her. "We have to let them enter."

But Fumiko was not paying attention—she was still scratching at the calcified memories, unearthing the actions her past self had done, the fail-safes she had installed.

Another voice from across the room shouted, "Just received message from the *Debby*!"

"Read it!"

"Start. Fumiko, the child has exhibited the ability to jump. We are ready to return. Requesting rendezvous coordinates. Signed, Sartoris Moth, end of message."

The message silenced the room; the operators and the scientists, the guards all wordless. Fumiko's smile sharpened into something frightening. The lark was real. There it was, after all this time.

The Jaunt.

All she needed now was a way out.

Why, darling, we've wired the whole place with explosives.

And then she remembered the fail-safe.

"Open a line with the warship," she said.

The woman confirmed that the line was open. The man who knew her looked at her with begging eyes.

"Warship *Euphrates*," Fumiko said into the microphone. "Embedded in Stopwatch Crater are YonSef explosive devices. If your warship does not fold away, I will speak the command word and destroy this base, along with the intellectual property you have come to collect. You will lose decades of vital, progressive research that will change the course of your history. I repeat, fold away, or we create a second crater."

The man stepped away from her, his hand to his neck. "Is it

true?" he asked, choked. "The YonSefs? When did you—Fumiko, there are two hundred families on this base!"

She ignored him. "Umbai, confirm that you have received this warning."

"*Confirmed,*" the voice said.

The line went silent.

Then,

"*Your proposition is denied.*"

"This is not an idle threat," she said into the microphone, heart beating at a pace it hadn't in a long time, her brow cloaked in sweat, the world zeroed-out, the world the microphone, her voice, and the warship *Euphrates*. "Fold within five minutes or I will speak the key command. Do you—"

She heard, from somewhere far off, the sound of a hollow thwack. It took her a moment to realize that the sound was that of something hard, struck against the back of her head. She staggered to the floor. The man who knew her had hit her with the butt end of a torch. The last thing she saw was the disappointment on his face before it all went black.

No sound. No alarm when next she woke. There was only the plain-faced man who sat beside her bed, in his hands a packet of paper, which, when he saw that she was awake, he read from without affect. "This partnership agreement is made this Wednesday of February 2132 and between the party of the Umbai Company and Fumiko Nakajima." She fought to control the doubled vision in her eyes, and the multidirectional throb of her brain. Her mouth was dry, her lips chapped to the point of bleeding. "And unless the context otherwise requires, the word or words set forth below within the quotation marks shall be deemed to mean the words which follow . . ." She tried to touch her lips, but her hands were restrained with magne-ties to the bed railing. "All research and creative endeavor performed by Fumiko Nakajima under the purview and collaboration with the Umbai Company will be in perpetuity considered rightful ownership to said company . . ." She lay there as he spoke, for hours it seemed, until he arrived at the ending, the mistake she had made so long ago. "Signed here by one Fumiko Nakajima." He showed her the jagged heart attack of her signature. "Do you acknowledge that this is your contract, and your signature?"

"What purpose is this question?" she asked, her voice empty of force.

"Do you acknowledge that this is your contract, and your signature?" he asked again.

"Yes," she said.

"Thank you." He took a drink of water from a metal cup. His pronounced Adam's apple bobbed with each gulp. Fumiko found this grotesque. She wanted to tear the apple right from his throat. "Fumiko," he said. "You know why we're here, don't you?"

There was hair in his nostrils. She wasn't sure why she was so fixated on this, but she was. "To 'discipline' me."

He nodded. "Your Allied citizenship credentials have been revoked, as have any degrees earned from secondary learning institutions. While you were unconscious, we've taken the data from the storage banks, the research from the primary, secondary, and tertiary labs, the ships in the landing pads, as well as the strong majority of raw materials in the subbasements. The computers have been dismantled, and the generator plant in Station B has been drained."

"You've been thorough."

"*We* have been thorough," he corrected. "Please understand that I am the executor, not the judicator. The specifics of the disciplinary actions have been decided beforehand, by the Pelican-Barbet-Thrasher-Macaw Tribunal."

She laughed. Her own birds were against her.

Fine.

"Is that it, then?"

The man sighed. She was startled by the amount of feeling in that one sigh—startled that he felt anything at all. "No," he said quietly. "There are two more actions that need to be taken. First, once everything has been settled, you will be left here. Alive, and unharmed. But we cannot take you with us into Allied Space. The tribunal has decided this place will be your banishment."

So dramatic. "And the other thing?"

"Your subordinates." He drummed his fingers. "They will be let go."

"'Let go.'" She found this euphemism hilarious, but had no energy to laugh—could only muster a weak smile. "Killed."

He hesitated. But whatever correction he planned to make he restrained.

"I was willing to blow them up an hour ago. What difference does it make now?" Fumiko sighed. She did not relish the idea of more than a thousand people dying because of her, but it was worth it, the callousness of her response, just to see the surprised expression on the man's so-average face. It was all out of her hands anyway. That was what she told herself. But the façade didn't last, her voice small now, as she said, again, "Fine."

"The tribunal has also ordered that you observe the terminations," he said. "So that, in their words, you may 'understand the consequences of breaching your contract.'" He stood up, not looking at her. "I'm sorry," he said before he left the room.

The pain of her dry lips was excruciating. But when she reached up for her glass of water, she was stopped halfway to the bed stand by the cuff on her wrist.

She had never wanted anything more in her life than that water.

She licked her lips with her sandpaper tongue as they escorted her out of the medica. The termination was to be performed in the subbasement, a room the size of a warehouse that smelled of dried clay. What used to house the raw materials with which the research base was expanded was now filled with the 2,590 residents of Fumiko's little toy city.

There were adults, and there were children. None of them moved, not a sound from their mouths, as though they thought that if they continued to obey the orders, and stood very still, the bullets would go around them. The Yellowjackets had Fumiko stand in the center of the firing squad, as dictated by tribunal orders. From the odd way the soldiers acted, she supposed this was not a normal course of action; that even they were startled by the harshness of such a discipline. But they complied anyway. Fumiko swallowed. She made herself watch. Told herself this was only another cost of business, and that after all the years she had passed through, all the lives she'd seen end in the passage, she had learned that life was cheap refuse to be discarded over her shoulder. Refuse without names, without faces and—

The mag-rifles raised on the lieutenant's command. As if pushed by a great, invisible wave, the people fled into the opposite wall. Amid the riot, this fresco of hell, she saw the man who knew her; the one who had knocked her unconscious. He stood his ground, straight-backed and sweating. He stared at Fumiko in a way that beguiled her. It was without anger, without warmth.

And then she remembered how she knew him, and where they had first met.

It was the same coldly neutral look he had given back on Old Earth, more than one thousand years ago, when she had found him outside of his mother's cabin, chopping wood for a fire—a look that said, *Oh. It's you.*

She had always wondered what had become of the man whose career she had ruined after she had deconstructed his sloppy work on the whiteboard of the Cybelus conference room; wondered if the rumors were true that his newfound infamy moved him to suicide. "It didn't," he said, nestling his ax into the stump. "But I haven't left this plot of land in three years." He unsheathed his gloves. "A boy from town brings me groceries."

The plot was in the middle of a North American forest, on the rise of a hill, peppered with skeletal pine trees with roots dug firm in the black dirt. It had taken a while for her to find him, but she needed to do it before she rode the Ark away from this world— needed to close the last of the loops. "I never intended for that moment to go viral," she said.

He shrugged. "If you're here to apologize, don't bother. I've made my peace with things."

She nodded. "I'm glad to hear that."

That would've been the end of it—she would've gotten back in her car and left him to his solitude, had he not stopped at his front door, and, after running his hand through his thinning hair, asked her if she wanted some tea. Her time was limited, for there were still many preparations to be made before she rode the Colombian Elevator the following week, but she accepted his invitation anyway.

She sat on a homemade stool that tilted to the right while he put on the kettle. He told her about his life. The mundane details about his day. The pot noodles he liked to cook, the weekend fishing in the tributary a few miles east. "Trees make for good company," he said, apropos of nothing. He told her that he still worked on his mathematics skills. That he was no longer the arrogant young man in the viral video. He said this with pride. It was obvious to her that he was lonely, that the mere act of talking was enough to make his hands shake. She knew lonely, and knew that, however inadvertent, it was her actions that had created his loneliness; that was why she interrupted his life story and asked if he would like to board the departing Ark with her. Hot tea dribbled from his mouth as he told her yes, God yes, and she saw in his eyes how she had turned from Specter to Savior; the gimp pelican, spreading its wings into transcendence; an intoxicating sensation that she would chase for centuries.

Hart was her first loyal bird, among hundreds more to come. There were days when he was her only friend in the universe, and it was just the two of them in a conference hall, sharing their memories of Old Earth. Without hesitation he synced his cold sleep with hers, and followed her through the dregs of time. She supposed he loved her. A kind of love, one that she could not reciprocate, but still appreciated, for it was better than no love at all.

In the depths of the crater, in the vault of screaming, she remembered him. She was about to shout his name when the triggers were squeezed. She flinched from the percussive blasts of the rifles, but kept her eyes open as they killed her people, and the friend she had forgotten.

The plain-faced man was the last to speak with her. The soldiers were boarding the transport ship on the landing pad as the man told her they had left behind the foodstuffs in the storage area, enough to last one person a lifetime. When he was certain they were not seen, the man stepped close to her and pressed a pistol into her hand. "It's empty," he whispered, "but I left a cartridge in the amphitheater." And then he turned and boarded the ship, and with a boom he quit the moon. She was alone.

What she had witnessed in the subbasement was too vast to comprehend. The trauma came in rounds, crippling her to her knees as she walked down the steps of the base, tightening her chest to the point of breathlessness as she walked the corridors. It took time, and effort, to gather enough composure to make it to the amphitheater, where she discovered the truth of the plain-faced man's words; the computers had been destroyed, and there was no energy in the circuits, no lights but for the torch she found in the emergency cabinet in the central staircase. Anything that would enable contact off-world was dead. And there, on the round table, where Hart had knocked her out, stood a cartridge for her empty pistol.

She left the cartridge where it was for the time being. Spent the next few days searching the base with the small sliver of hope that Umbai had missed a crucial component that her past self had anticipated. But every fail-safe she had installed into the guts of the base had been found, and stripped. The isolated scramline terminal. The backup communications chips for the ships. Even the old radio transmitter. Without access to the amphitheater consoles she had no way of searching the ship logs to see if there were any that had left and were due for return, but she suspected there were not, certain she had seen a full roster in the bay when she first arrived. She knew in her heart that all of the pilots were in the subbasement with the others; that they were dead, like she should've been, a long time ago.

Her vain search for salvation ended, she returned to the amphitheater and sat in the chair by the round table, where she gazed down at the plain-faced man's parting gift. The only tool she had to leave this moon. Her hand wrapped around the cartridge and guided it into the pistol with a satisfying click. She did this slowly, drawing out the movements as she imagined what was to come—the great wind that would blow her troubles out the side of her head, like dirt cleared from a pipe. When the gun was loaded, she hesitated— thought she could smell curry from down the hall, thought she could hear the patter of rain on a café window—before these sense memories evaporated with a shudder.

She raised the gun to her head.

It was the movement that did it. The way she tucked the nozzle against her right temple, until the nozzle became a cherry blossom, tucked behind her ear by a blond woman with purple eyes, and the pistol slipped from her trembling hand, clattering to the floor, as did her knees, as she wept, for after centuries, she remembered Dana's name.

* * *

The floodgates were broken. Over the coming days the memories rushed in, filling the hollows of her mind. The true memories, of a bench by the pier, of ribbons of curry, of Dana's foot touching hers under the table in that café while outside it rained; a dirigible drifting against a parchment moon. They arrived like drops of water on a dry tongue. She was sustained by them. The museum exhibit. The canals. Images delivered fresh from her past life. She even had it in her to smile when she remembered her mother's calorie counter, for like the other images, it had happened to her. The pistol soon forgotten, as she was entertained by the stoked embers of her mind, and the mystic shapes she caught in their smoke.

Two weeks passed before she gathered the strength to venture down to the subbasement. The first time she entered, she almost fainted from the overpowering stench, and she returned wearing an air-filtration mask so that she could walk the field of corpses. Hart was easy to find. His was the only body in the center of the room. She snapped the bloodstained name tag from his chest and dropped it into her bag—did the same for the thousands of others who were congregated on the far side of the chamber, rolling bodies over, moving limbs aside, so she could collect their names. The children were without name tags, but the parents were easy to find, their arms wrapped protectively around the small bodies. The work took many hours, and when she was certain she had all the tags, she returned to the upper levels of the base, to the dormitories and family suites, and followed the names to the appropriate homes. On twin beds and kings and child-sizes she laid the tags to rest, sometimes guessing which name had slept where. This was the only action she could take, for the elevators were dead, and she could not lift each body up the many flights of steps. Once the names were given to their homes, she spent the next few hours sitting in one of the living rooms, picturing the day in a life on Stopwatch. *He showered first.*

Then he dressed, here, before he went to the kitchenette. Three soy packs in his fridge. He halved one, and mixed it with the ricemeal. Gave it a pinch of sweetener before he brought it to her in bed. And when night came, and it was time to sleep, Fumiko lay in her own bed, her body still, as the memories from long ago continued to return to her, and with those memories the flash pain of what she would never experience again; the way Dana would cock her head to the side when confused, the smell of her hair. The crushed lilac of it.

There was no more Pocket Space, and no more cold sleep. Fumiko was forced to live through real-time again, and had no choice but to let the days come and go, slowly. She marked the days in the pages of a notebook and continued her routine of visiting each of the dormitories, and giving the dead a few hours of life in her mind's eye as she learned about them from their records, and imagined how they moved through their spaces. The routine became ritual. She repeated their names as she walked the base, and their stories, like mantras. Jayne, who worked in the tertiary lab. Cardet, who was a gardener. Cardet's daughters, Sufa and Delon. There was no folding away. No way to pass the time but to acknowledge the bodies. This was her new life—the rediscovery of the old.

Hart, who followed her through time.

She spent her nights in her room on the thirty-third, where it was still warm, but never warm enough, and she shivered as she read books by candlelight. The candle was made from her own improvisation, from the tub of tru-fat she found in the central kitchen. The light of the candle wavered, and was not the most reliable source to read by, but she preferred the dull orange glow to the harshness of the torch. Often she would stare into the finger of fire, tranced by it. She would recall Dana's work with the bioluminescent lightbulb, her gift to those the Arks left behind on Old Earth. *She was right that day*, Fumiko thought one night, when she remembered their conversation in the café. *Not everyone gets to leave.*

She licked her fingers and pinched the flame.

In her dreams she walked toward the dark shore, past the food cart, to the benches by the docks, where the one she loved waited for her, with an empty seat by her side.

"Don't," Dana said when Fumiko was about to sit. "Not yet."

She asked her why not.

"Because you're not done yet."

Fumiko told her there was nothing left to do, but Dana shook her head.

"We wired the whole place with explosives, remember?" She smiled with teeth, and placed her hand on Fumiko's. "If we can't have our world, then no one can."

Her heart stopped. She threw off the blankets. Remembered the last fail-safe. The YonSef explosives she buried in this crater long ago—how she could reverse-engineer them into workable power sources. Somewhere in her mind Dana was cheering her on as she searched the construction site in the lower levels for the rudimentary equipment Umbai had not bothered to take or destroy. There was a drill without batteries. Crowbars and tubing. A pickax. The pick in hand, she continued her descent, flying down the steps as she flipped through the banks of her memory, hoping she had the right of it—*right here*, she thought, pressing her hand against the concrete wall of Substrata D; one hundred feet from here, into the rock of the crater, the YonSef waited.

Dana materialized behind her. Fumiko knew she was not there. That she was only a projection, and in all likelihood the first sign of her insanity. But still, she was glad to see her. "Are you sure it's there?" Dana asked.

No, Fumiko was not, but she raised the pick anyway, and began her assault.

11

The Last Stop

The others were just beyond the hatch. Nia knew their ears were pressed to the door so as not to miss a word of what she or the boy said, despite the fact that she had commanded privacy. But she did not throw open the hatch and shout at them to scatter, for they were in a place beyond protocol, beyond even her command—the impossible place where mirages were real, and where one-thousand-year-old women were correct in their lunatic speculations; the place Nia feared as she looked down at the boy. Her stranger.

He was seated in her desk chair, where she had told him to sit, his head hung low as he stared at his feet, unable to meet her eyes. This was just as well. She knew she would find no truth in them. "When did it start?" she asked.

When he did not answer, she made her guess.

"Was it in the Painted City? When you went missing?" His whole body was still, his chest barely rising at his breath, as though he hoped she would forget he was there, if he simply willed himself into stone. "That was it, wasn't it?" she said. And she felt a rock drop into her stomach when he confirmed her suspicions with a nod. "Ahro." Her voice was strung out. "That was four months ago."

He curled one foot behind the other.

"Four months you lied to me."

His shoulders trembled.

"What am I supposed to do with that? With you?"

As he cried, she opened a drawer and pulled out a box of tissues. She yanked out a ply and handed it to him. He blew his nose.

"I don't know anything about your ability," she said. "All I know is that I can't stop you; whatever your power is, I can't command it." She crouched before him, hard-eyed. "So I'm just going to ask you once. Just once. Will you stay until the job is done, and the contract is finished?"

He nodded, his face covered in the napkin.

"I need you to say it. Say you agree."

"I agree," he said with a small, cracked voice.

She stood up.

Opened the hatch.

"Go to your room," she said. "We'll talk later."

He ran out. She caught a glimpse of his puffy-eyed face as he turned the corner and disappeared. "Sartoris!" she shouted. The little man stepped out from behind the hatchway, hands clasped before him, his eyes betraying his utter discomfort. "Have you sent the scramline to Fumiko yet?"

"They sent us rendezvous coordinates ten minutes ago. We'll be ready to depart as soon as Vaila returns."

"And where is Vaila?"

He held up his empty hands. "She said she forgot something back in town. She was no more specific than that."

Nia attacked her scalp. "Tell Em to spool the drive. Once Vaila's back on board we lift off. Not a second after."

"Yes, Captain." He turned to go, but paused at the hatch, sparing a worried glance at her before she snapped, "Now!" and he rushed down the causeway, chased by the footsteps of the others who had been listening.

And then she was alone.

She picked up the empty cup on her desk. Held the cup in her hand like a glass egg. Felt the weight of this object, in this impossible place. No more than a few ounces. She studied its hexagonal faces. How it refracted light. Too real to be a dream. But there was only one way to know for certain. She smashed the cup into the floor. It exploded—the shards skittering across the room, and glinting like sand against the lamplight. It was all real, she thought as she fetched the broom from the closet and swept up her mess.

Vaila returned a half hour later, panting. She had sprinted all over the colony searching for the ladeum beads she had dropped, a story she related to her captain even though Nia made it clear she didn't need to hear it; that all she needed from her was to get the ship off the ground. The hands in the cat's cradle kicked the thrusters to life and the *Debby* quit the sky and folded into the Pocket. It would be a two-week trip down the Chimerical Current to the rendezvous point—enough time for Nia to gather the words she would say to him.

For days they avoided each other. His chair was empty at breakfast. She left it to Sartoris to bring him food from the kitchen. On her walk down the causeway, she caught a dash of movement in her periphery, the lav door shutting behind the blur, but she did not wait for him to emerge. She continued on. She was not ready yet.

The crew was just as lost. The *Debby*'s corridors and hatches were stilled by their silence. When they spoke to one another it was in a whisper, for everything about him was suspect, and they could not be sure of the limits of his perceptions, what he could and could not hear. They listened to Sartoris as he recounted what he had seen in the plains—the wavering air, the sudden materialization of his naked body, like a thought, solidified—and they asked one another, and themselves, how this power could be possible, and what it meant.

It was on the second day that Nia heard one such conversation. She stood outside the cargo bay, and listened to the carry of voices as her crew volleyed thoughts to one another in the far corner of the room.

They were all there. Everyone but Vaila.

"I haven't slept yet," Em said.

"How can anyone?" Royvan asked. "There's a god on our ship." He said the word with a laugh. A half joke.

"I think we're safe though." She heard Sartoris pace around. "The power seems to be harmless."

"Can you be sure?" Royvan asked. "There's so much we don't know—so much the kid might not even know. Remember the report? How he was found in the dhuba field surrounded by rubble? What if he Jaunts and the ship . . . reacts? Pulls us with him. Turns the ship, and us, into char. It could happen at any moment."

"That is a lot of what-ifs."

"What-ifs are all we got, Sarty."

"Has anyone talked to him?" Sonja asked.

Sartoris sighed. "He wouldn't speak to me when I brought him his food. I think he'll only speak to the captain."

"Whenever that happens."

"She will," he said. "Eventually."

A pause. "It's crazy," Em said. "'Side from Fumiko, I'd never been this close to someone this important. He might change the course of human history. Make folding obsolete."

"No more lost time," Sonja said.

"Can't even imagine it," Royvan said.

"What do you think Fumiko'll do with him?" Em asked.

"I suspect she will try to find a way to duplicate his power," Sartoris said. "Disperse it. That's if her research is fruitful. It might be a long while till anything comes of the study. It could be years."

"But our job is over," Em said.

"Yes," Sartoris said. "It is."

They were quiet.

"Feels like we just left."

Nia stepped away from the entrance.

In her room that night, she sat at her desk and thumbed through the pages of her old notebooks. The entries she had written along the way, the poems inspired by the small things they had done together. And then, she thought of them. Deborah and Nurse. Imagined the conference these two women would have with each other, about her—there, sitting side by side on her cot, each of them smirking at the other, sharing a private joke that was beyond her. And it occurred to Nia—no, she was reminded—how easy it was, to miss the chance to say the important things. She put the notebook down.

It was the next day, after lunch, when she knocked on the boy's hatch. By then her thoughts on the matter had settled.

"I'm coming in," she said.

The room was dark. It took her eyes a moment to resolve the shadows and see his small form, buried underneath the blanket. She asked him if he was awake and took the subtle movement of what she guessed was his head as an affirmative, and walked over to the bed, tripping over one of his discarded boots. She sat down beside him. The mattress gave way a bit. The body under the blankets did not move. It hurt her, to see him breathe. The fragility of it. She needed him to understand. "There's not enough time," she said. "I need to be angry with you. I need you to understand what your lie has cost, could've cost, but there's not enough time. Maybe after this is all done, and we still— I'll scream. I'll show you how furious

I am that you broke my trust. But that day might not come. We have so few days left, and I've wasted so many, Ahro." She coaxed the blanket off him. Revealed him, knuckling his wet eyes. Her hand gripped his shoulder. "Listen to me, Ahro. I love you. Do you hear me? I don't care what you are. I love you."

"I'm sorry," he sobbed. His head was in her lap.

She stroked his hair.

"I will always love you," she whispered angrily. "Always."

He explained to her that it was like he could feel a breeze no one else could feel. A breeze he could see, and follow, wherever he wished. A breeze of music, of time.

He explained his jumps. The first, in the escape pod of the Quiet Ship, and the second, in the Painted City, when the moons were in alignment, and the music was loud. Loud enough to shake loose the door in him. How he found himself back on Umbai-V, where he was helped by an old woman with a spear, and where, beyond the purple fields, he heard Nia's music. Told her shyly that the music had led him back to her, her beginner's string. He did not know why. Why Umbai-V or why the music. It just was. He shared with her the many places he had visited. The icescapes and mountaintops and wild cities. The breathy span between stars. And he told her, hesitantly, with care, of his time with Oden, picking which details to share and which to keep for himself.

She listened. By the end of it, when everything had been shared, she sank back in her chair, amazed. "You've lived a whole other life," she said. She let that fact sit there for a time while she rubbed the back of her head. "What was your favorite part?" she asked.

"Coming home," he said.

She stared at him.

"Bullshit," she said. "It was Oden, wasn't it?" When he started laughing, she pointed at him. "I knew it! You little liar. Coming home, my ass. You think sweet lines like that are going to make me forget everything?"

He smiled, sheepish. "Did it work?"

"A little," she conceded. She leaned back in her chair. "Just a little."

He spoke to the others over the days, apologizing to each of them for drawing out the contract for longer than he needed to. For lying. But they were more interested in his worlds-shaping power than his apology, and he did his best to address the thousands of questions Sartoris threw at him, their teacher-student dynamic now reversed as he tried to describe the music and the lines that bound the stars, as they drank DanSen Tea in the common room. Sonja burst into laughter—the booming kind, her hand slapping the table—after learning of Ahro's physical status upon finishing a jump. "What on earth is so funny?" Sartoris asked, annoyed.

"It's perfect," she said, palming tears from her eyes. "Naked bastard flying about."

He sighed. "Can we elevate our discourse? This is the harbinger of the New Age."

But Ahro was laughing too.

It was a good trip. Royvan, the most wary of them all, soon came around and stopped avoiding him. Amid all the excitement, no one noticed Vaila's self-imposed solitude in the cockpit, intoxicated as they were by the fact of the boy, and the fact that, after many years, the job they had taken on would soon be over, eleven years earlier than expected. It was Sartoris who observed that what they were experiencing was the best-case scenario. The statement went undisputed.

Ahro was nervous about what was to come with Fumiko and her plans that were still a mystery, but he tried not to think about that—focused instead on the better things that might wait ahead. About Oden. Alone in his hatch, he stared at the ceiling, as he remembered all he had felt between the two standing rocks. His hand traveling past his navel to take care of what was necessary as he relived the feel of Oden's hands, his mouth. The eyes on his eyes, pinning him to the center of nature. Maybe once all this was done, and Fumiko had figured out what made him go and no longer needed him, he would take some time to himself. Maybe he could visit Kilkari again. Stand by the docks until he found him again. While away a few more hours on that mountaintop.

But most of the time, his thoughts were on the ship. On the last night of the trip, he walked the *Debby*, wishing to absorb all that he could. His stomach full with all the food from the crew meal Royvan had cooked earlier, the fruity greens and wild beans, the ample glass of spirits Nia allowed him, he swam the echoed space of the cargo hold, where they stretched before each emergence; the medica, where Royvan would tell him stories from his hungover school days as he performed his monthly diagnostics. He sat at the kitchen table and remembered the sweet rice. He flipped through books in the common room. The adventures of the warrior queen Nia had read aloud to him. And then he went up to the cockpit, where he sat in the copilot's chair and placed the headset on his ears. Listened to the white noise of the Pocket. Why he always returned here to this chair, to these sounds, he did not know. Maybe Fumiko would know the answer. He sighed. It didn't matter. Regardless of explanation, something elemental within him communed with the noise and quieted him to sleep, which was what he did that final night; slept soundly in the head of the *Debby*, while around him played the songs of the universe, unaware when the woman entered the room with the syringe in her pocket, until the dream was snapped as she locked his head in her arms, and stuck him in the neck, his consciousness dimming out with these last thoughts of terror as she depressed the plunger, and whispered, "I'm sorry, I'm sorry."

* * *

There was no going back.

Down the dark causeway Vaila went, her footsteps quiet, the soles bare as she padded along the cold grating with his limp body in her arms. Down the steps into the cargo bay, to the lockers beside the airlock, where she laid him down and dressed him in one of the spacesuits. Fitted the helmet over his doped-up head, and propped him up inside the locker. She had slammed the door shut when a voice called out to her from the entryway. Every nerve in her body prickled.

"What are you doing?"

It was Em.

"I couldn't sleep," she said. She patted the locker door. "Thought I'd just—I don't know." She laughed. "You?"

He nodded.

"Same," he said. She watched him walk to the center of the bay, where he gazed up at the shadowed catwalks. She joined him there. He shook his head. "Hard to believe it's over."

"I know."

"Still. You must be happy." He grinned at her. "Fumiko will be all over you, I bet. You deserve it after all this time."

"No," Vaila said. She smiled as the tears streamed down her cheeks, and left Em confused on her way back to her room. "I don't."

Morning. Nia stretched in the small space of her room, folding herself in half, her hands gripped around the balls of her feet, her muscles aching from the whiskey of the previous night. When she was limber again, she dressed and went to the kitchen to make breakfast for Ahro, pouring out a few glasses of water for the coming dehydration. Normally she had him make his own food, but today, the last day of their trip, she would make an exception. She smiled as she sprinkled sugar over the bowl. She would spoil him rotten.

She made him his sweet rice on the stove element, along with a cup of spiced tea; placed these things with care on the tray and bounced to his room. But when she knocked on his hatch, there was no answer. Again she knocked. Supposing he was still asleep, which was unsurprising considering all he had eaten and drunk the night before, she walked back to the kitchen and left the tray on the counter for him to discover when he later emerged. She finished off her tea as one by one the crew entered. Conversation was light, yet charged; same as all those years ago, when she finished the Umbai job and they all had the great sense of impending.

The intercom let out a burst. Vaila's digital voice told them the ship would soon be unfolding. They all went up to the cockpit to watch. Nia frowned when she saw that Ahro wasn't there in the cockpit, but when she asked them if anyone had seen him, no one had an answer. "He wasn't up here when you came in?" she asked Vaila. The woman shook her head without looking away from her controls. Nia sighed.

Again she knocked on his hatch, her stomach worried into knots. She'd never known him to sleep in so late.

"Ahro?" she said. "You awake?"

Still no answer.

"I know it's scary," she said to the door. "Being at the end. But like I said before, I won't let anything happen to you. Okay?" She placed a hand on the hatch, the cold metal of it. "Come out when you're ready."

"Is he still asleep?" Sartoris asked when she returned.

"I think he's scared," she said. "Can't say I blame him."

"What's he scared about?" Sonja asked. "If Fumiko's a problem, he can just get the fuck out. And it wouldn't even matter at all, 'cause we'll still get paid." She almost broke into a jig. "Still working out what I'm gonna do with all that money."

"Like open a hospital on a City Planet?" Royvan suggested.

"Or buy our own City Planet."

Nia laughed.

"We're here," Vaila said. She turned to Em. "Can you?" He nodded and ran down to the engine bay to flip the core. Nia regarded Vaila as she manipulated the console, the woman's jaw worked into a rictus, tension vibrating off her body; supposed this tension was rooted in their shared anxiety of the coming end.

"All right," Em said over the intercom. "Let's do it."

"Leaving," Vaila said.

The world flexed. Nia felt a slight tingle in her guts, but nothing more. She smiled when she saw Sartoris rubbing his thumb along the tines of an old comb. And then the flexing stopped. The viewport shutters rattled open.

Nia squinted against the sudden blast of light. They were facing a blue-green sun. She reached up and adjusted the tint on the screen. Blinking, she saw that the sun let out great bands of light, like swords. In one of the swords, suspended in the blue-green beam, was a small black dot, almost invisible to the eye were it not for the gilding of light that described its shape. "Is that a ship?" she asked.

"Maybe it belongs to Fumiko?" Sartoris suggested.

"Open up the comms channel," Nia said. "Vaila?"

"I've had a surprisingly beautiful time with you," Vaila said. Before Nia could ask what had come over her, she flicked the comms link and left the cockpit, with Sonja asking, "Where the hell is she going?"

Something wasn't right. "Hello?" Nia said into the headset. "This is Captain Nia Imani of the commercial transport ship *Debby*. Who are we hailing?" There was no answer. Just static. Again, she repeated, "This is Captain Nia Imani of the *Debby*. Who are we speaking to? Does this vessel belong to Fumiko Nakajima? Hello, is anyone there?"

Then.

"This is the Umbai warship Euphrates. *We have come to collect our rightful intellectual property. Please allow the Umbai representative on board to exit unharmed with said property. Comply or we will be forced to perform disciplinary action. Compliance will be met with peace."*

"What do we do?" Sonja asked.

Nia punched the intercom. "Em, we need to fold. Now."

No response.

"Em?"

And then they heard it, the sound from the other side of the ship. A balloon popping. A cork exploding. These were Nia's first associations, though it was obvious it was neither of those things—that it was, in fact, the resolve of a triggered pistol.

What happened next occurred within a three-minute window.

There was a third pistol shot; the lights flickered; a tingling sensation Nia was very familiar with overcame her—she had enough wherewithal to grab the console's edge before her feet left the floor. Unlike her, Royvan and Sartoris had never experienced a malfunctioning Grav unit before—or a sabotaged one—and they scrambled in the air as Sonja grabbed one of the wall railings and asked Nia what she wanted to do. Nia shouted, "We're going!" and she kicked herself from the console and through the hatch to the causeway. Together she and Sonja climbed the rungs while messages looped through her brain, *Keep the boy safe, Keep him close, Keep him safe.* She waited as Sonja slipped into her hatch and emerged with two rifles. With one hand gripped around the rifle, she propelled herself down the causeway with the other, blood coursing through her veins, pounding at the gates of her head. They passed the common room. She stole a glimpse inside, saw a sea of books and chairs. A lamp suspended, tipping orange light into the kitchen. Sonja stopped at the stairwell down to the engine room. "I don't think she's down there," she said, reading Nia's eyes. "No exit." Which meant she was in the cargo bay, the airlock. "Em?" she asked.

Nia doubted the engineer was still alive.

Don't think about that now.

"The boy comes first," she said.

They frogged down the rungs to the cargo hold. It was a strange experience, to maneuver through her inverted home, turned as it was ninety degrees to the right as she clambered along the wall. It was lucky she had stretched that morning. She thought it funny that she was even thinking about that. It was the adrenaline; a calm in her head that allowed the grace for these extra notions. Sonja held up a hand when they arrived at the portal to the cargo hold. She peered around the lip. "I see her," she said. "In the airlock."

"Go."

They propelled themselves down into the wide space of the hold, gripping the straps on the floor that once restrained the crates of dhuba seeds, the floor now a high wall that they clung to like rock climbers, their rifles trained on the woman in the spacesuit who floated in the depressurization chamber of the airlock, a second body in her grasp held hostage. The woman was about to shut the interior hatch and open the exterior doors when Nia shouted her name.

"VAILA!"

And then the woman, as if on instinct, held the boy in front of her like a shield and shoved a pistol through the crook of his arm and fired twice. One shot ricocheted off the wall behind them, but the other snagged Sonja in the shoulder, the momentum spinning her away, Nia watching her fly, unable to shoot Vaila, afraid she would hit Ahro—all she could do was let go of the rifle and propel herself forward as the woman punched the button and the hatch shut and Nia slammed against the metal surface, banging against it, watching wild-eyed through the window slit as the exterior door was opened and the woman jumped out into space, propelled by the spine jets of the suit, dragging the boy behind her, their bodies all but invisible in the blackness as the exterior door shut behind them.

"The suits!" Sonja shouted from across the way. She was slowly twirling, suspended in the middle of the hold, clutching her bleeding shoulder. Blood escaped between her fingers in thick globs. With her rifle hand she pointed at the lockers.

Nia footed the window slit of the airlock and leveraged herself up until she could reach the wall rungs again, and as she climbed her way up toward the lockers and yanked the door open and wrestled an extra suit from its hook, Vaila, jetting through the vacuum, sent out a ship-agnostic transmission blast, picked up by both the *Euphrates* and the *Debby*.

I'm outside the ship with the boy. They're going to follow me. Do something.

In the cockpit, Royvan heard the transmission, and knew what he had to do. He grabbed Sartoris by the collar, kicked himself off the old man's chest, and fell into the console. With a sweep of his hand he switched the intercom and shouted his warning to the others.

"They're going to fire! Hold on to something!"

Nia and Sonja looked at each other.

On the bridge of the *Euphrates*, the captain sighed, and said not to destroy the ship. "No need to punish them too much for being misled," he said. "A slap on the wrist should suffice." He nodded at his chief gunner. "Fire a concussive round."

The gunner spooled the wheel and a small, beveled cannon emerged from the starboard side of the warship, like a thumb between fingers.

Nia stopped struggling into the suit and pulled herself into the locker. Her hand was about to shut the door when she looked out at Sonja. The vet was still suspended in the middle of the bay, holding her bleeding shoulder, nowhere close to safe purchase. Nia shouted her name. They traded one last look. There was a sober quality to Sonja's eyes. A cold realization. She nodded. "I'm sorry," Nia shouted before she shut herself inside the locker. With a click, the cannon fired its payload. The discharge was invisible. Composed of materials too minute to be seen. A wave of kinetic energy that traveled thousands of miles in the span of microseconds and smashed into the *Debby*'s hull, the slap on the wrist pirouetting the ship into the black, the G-force slamming Nia into the locker's wall, cracking something in her body, she wasn't sure what, couldn't be sure, for her world was spinning out of control, the breath squeezed out of her lungs as it spun away from her, all the food in her stomach, and the thoughts in her head.

Her eyes blinked open. Three straps pinned her to a bed. That was all she could tell through the blur as the man who floated above her—Royvan, she realized, distantly—said that he was sorry, that he had to do it. She fingered the latch of the strap with her right hand, the cold metal. Her left arm was bound to her chest in a wrap. He told her it was broken. She nodded, half understanding, before she drifted out again.

Thirteen hours swam by, each of them dreamless, before true consciousness returned. Her skull was tight, her brain a grape in its fist. Her eyes were sore. Light was dagger-sharp. There was no moisture in her mouth. Royvan gave her water through a straw, and time to order her thoughts, before he informed her of what had happened to the rest of her crew, his voice shredded as he told her that both Sonja and Em were dead. He found Em by the folding core, drifting among tendrils of cabling. Vaila had shot him in the back, twice. He bled out a few hours before she woke. As for Sonja, he couldn't tell her that eye to eye. He had to look up at the ceiling. When the ship spun, the floor had hit the vet's body. Killed her fast. Most of his time since had been spent cleaning the mess. He smiled as he said this. Like he couldn't believe it. Her body was with Em's in the cargo bay, wrapped in tarp. "I wanted to wait for you to wake up before I . . . sent them off."

Nia didn't know what to say.

No words came to mind.

"Ahro?" she asked.

She knew the answer, but her heart still withered when Royvan shook his head. "They're all gone," he said.

All but Sartoris, who was in the medica, bound to an improvised stretcher of Royvan's creation. The stretcher was hooked to a wall railing. A tube disappeared up the old man's sleeve, feeding him with nutriments while he gargled for breath in his coma. Half his face was bruised to the point where he was almost unrecognizable, his skin a wrath of swollen berries. Nia thought he might pop if she stroked his cheek. "I don't expect him to survive the week," Royvan whispered.

"Yes," she said, her finger grazing Sartoris's smile lines, "probably not." She turned away. "Where are the others?"

The bodies were hovering before the airlock doors, each of them wrapped in tarp and bound by rope. Nia put a hand on both of them. She gave Royvan time to say goodbye; waited outside the airlock as he hugged Sonja's form, the tarp crinkling as he whispered things the veteran wouldn't have understood even if she were alive, choked as the words were. She and Royvan suited up, and they carried the bound forms out through the airlock and pushed them into the black. Royvan clung to a railing and watched them drift away as she jetted up to the hull and surveyed the damage her ship had taken from the concussive round, her gloved hand touching the warps along the hull. The back was broken. If they folded, the ship would disintegrate. She was numb as she recognized this.

There was only one hope. Outside intervention. With Royvan's help she opened the panel above the cockpit, twisted the handle, and activated the SOS beacon. The small blue light blinked as the beacon pulsed a looping emergency broadcast message; the ship's designation, its coordinates; pulsed the message past the blue-green sun, out to whoever might be listening.

The nearest inhabited system was a three-week fold away on the Irresolute Current. It was a six-month wait in real-time. The two of them settled in for the long wait. Their bodies moved on autopilot. Basic survival. Royvan counted their rations in the storage bin and the kitchen cabinets while Nia checked the water recycler. There was enough food to last them four months. Five months for water. But none of this mattered.

They had only one month of air.

As the beacon pulsed, the days became listless, powered only by the inertia of routine. They ate the freeze-dried stuff and drank the spheres of water that thought-bubbled from the faucet. They went to the bathroom in emergency vacuum bags and ejected the bags through the engine filtration system. They were not always successful using the vacuum bags, and would argue about the messes, shouting from across rooms about smells, particles in mouths, their bodies drifting past each other, close to strangling the other, until they would remember that air was scarce and they would fall quiet again, clutching their chests, heaving. There was no choice but to live with the sick film on their tongues.

They changed Sartoris's sheets in silence.

* * *

The days were interchangeable. There was little else to do in those dark corridors but revisit old spaces. She and the doctor went from room to room, and back again, until the rooms no longer resembled rooms but boxes briefly inhabited. Nia wondered if this was what Nurse did when she was stranded in the fringe, and wished she could ask her old friend what the best way was to pass the time when one had nothing left.

There was a day when Royvan touched Nia's arm. They were passing each other in the causeway when he reached out. It was an invitation of sorts, Nia could tell that much from the desperation in his eyes. But she brushed him off, in no mood to entertain, and she swam into the next room, not looking back to see his shamed expression.

Breath was a struggle.

With each day it was more difficult to concentrate.

Royvan pulled the suits from the lockers and they used the spare oxygen tanks to breathe. They hooked Sartoris to a mask. The oxygen would prolong their survival for a little while, but they had only so many tanks.

Time was marked by the emptied canisters, and their bodies. Royvan's beard grew into a wild bramble. Nia's hair returned to the thick afro it once was when she was a child. Neither saw the point in grooming anymore. Or talking. As the number of canisters dwindled to the single digits, the two of them spent less time together. They found their own quiet spaces in the ship, where they could retreat into memory in private. Nia stayed in the boy's hatch, floating above his unmade bed, his blanket wrapped around her as she shut her eyes against the familiar warmth and smell, while Royvan stayed in Sonja's hatch, remembering the lights-off they spent together, the rough tumbles, and the hours after, when he would open his eyes and discover that she had never fallen asleep but had stayed awake all night, whispering the names of those she had lost in war. He had never understood the exercise. It seemed to him a pointless self-haunting. But it was only now that he realized the use of it as he said her name, again and again; it was not a haunting at all, but a call for company. A way to let her know that he would be there soon. He sighed. Hooked Sartoris to the last of the oxygen canisters before he prepared two syringes. He made one for himself and one for Nia, should she decide to follow. He slid the needlepoint into his arm, hesitating for a moment before he flooded his veins with the cocktail, the chemicals flipping the switches in his brain, one by one, bringing down the curtains, with Sonja's name the whispered encore on his lips. Nia did not leave the boy's room. She never learned of what Royvan had done, not as she drifted among the clothes and linen and instruments, and groped at the last handfuls of air left in her suit, her thoughts of the boy who fell from the sky, until she saw it coming—the long road that led out of her body. Her brain now singing a high-pitched tone.

Let this last leg be easy, she prayed.

A quartet of men and women levered open the airlock and flashed their torchlights into the dark of the causeway. They found the two survivors, both of them unconscious, and pulled them from the ruin.

It was not luck that brought the salvagers, but Vaila, who had made a second call the day she warned Umbai of the boy's power. She knew with grim certainty that the *Debby* would not emerge unscathed from the encounter, and so, as a final gesture of goodwill to her soon-to-be-former captain, she notified the Kerrigan Salvage Fleet of the possibility of a derelict that could be found at these coordinates, at this date, and that they would have to act quickly if they wished to find the ship before the other salvage fleets she had notified found it first. The Kerrigans saved what was still of value. The cache of rifles. The fine wooden desk in the captain's quarters.

The musical instruments from many planets. A shirt from a bureau that one of the salvagers thought would look good on his partner back with the fleet. The rest of it they left untouched, and they dialed up the temperature of their scoring blades and swarmed the derelict until the whale carcass was a skeleton, and all of its flesh, that valuable metal, was bound and brought back to the hauler, which folded into the Pocket, its destination the home fleet.

It was in a private booth of an unfamiliar medica, where Nia woke with a light in her eyes, and a voice asking if she could remember her name.

When she was able to walk again, the Kerrigans brought her to the requisitions office and presented to her what they had saved—the last of her effects. She was silent as she walked past the paltry collection. The gang of rifles, a haphazard pile of shirts and tank tops, a few dress pants. One wooden desk. She stopped before the musical instruments. Crouched till her knees touched the floor. Weeping, as she held in her hands the wooden flute, bought for five iotas, from a small shop on Macaw.

III

12
The New Resource

His name was the first thing they took. He was the same as the eel inks and dhuba seed that they extracted from their Resource Worlds; he was an Acquisition. That was what he was named, before they took his body.

They did this in the vat. They lowered Acquisition into the translucent orange fluid, the body suspended as the hair drifted like seaweed. On the other side of the window, the surgeon fitted on his hands the conductor's gloves, which were white, and patterned with the black lines of circuitry. The gloves were the masters of the vat's fluid. The fluid did as the gloves commanded. When the surgeon dragged a vertical line through the air with his index finger, the fluid unzipped Acquisition's belly, from sternum to pelvis. When the surgeon moved his hands as if parting a sea, the fluid spread open the incision, and revealed the many working organs beneath the skin. The gulp of the heart. They did not worry about losing Acquisition—they could keep the body alive through most anything. With his gloves the surgeon gestured toward himself, and coaxed the insides out. The stomach and the spleen. Unspooled the intestines. These things no longer organs but objects to be scrutinized under the rays, in search of the properties of the new. The body was divided into a series of frames. The skin, the skeleton, and the nervous system, which fractaled out from its locus, the brain, the last piece that was brought forth to the bank of windows by the surgeon, who steepled his hands, then spread the fingers apart, opening the folds.

And as this last part of him was opened, Acquisition heard a hum, like a zipper opening, in the far place in his mind. He followed the hum through the muraled streets of the Painted City, and across the on-off fields of black spice. Followed it through the shower of playing cards and the band of musicians at rest on their stools in the concert hall—followed it past the red curtains, into the wings of the theater and up the ramp that led into the cargo bay, where the hum was loudest.

She was there, standing beside a crate of seed.

"Did the noise wake you?" she asked.

Acquisition nodded. He looked around; it was coming from above.

"It's nothing to worry about," she said. She knelt beside him till they were eye to eye, one hand pointed up at the catwalk. "See there? That panel?"

"Yes."

"Behind that panel is where we keep the machine that recycles the air we breathe. Every five days the machine has to clean its filters, so the air stays clean. That's what you're hearing right now." She smiled. "Not so scary anymore, right?"

"No," Acquisition whispered. "Not scary."

She was confused by his worry. "Come on," she said, wrapping an arm around his shoulders. "Are you hungry? I'm hungry."

Acquisition nodded, tears in his eyes.

"Yes," he said. "I am very hungry."

He leaned against her as they walked down the causeway, used her for strength. He thought he could walk forever like that. But the hum was getting louder. It didn't matter how far they were, he could always hear it. A needle in his ear that became a drill. In the kitchen she said something that was lost on him, it was so loud. He wanted to warn her that something was wrong, but she didn't seem to hear him, or notice the plates that danced on the counter or the cabinets that were flung open, smiling as she mouthed words he could not hear but could read by the movements of her lips, she was telling him it was okay, that he was okay, and then the light bloomed, and the ship flipped on its side and he hit the wall like it was the floor and all the change spilled out of the cup, each coin a name that fell through the dark grates, the place where Sonja and Em and Royvan had gone, along with the dumb jokes in the cockpit and the food in the air, the metronome hand on his chest that beat the time, the lips on lips, these thoughts like birds startled from their perches, crashing through the window, taking flight into the cloudless sky, heedless of wind or gravity, until they were gone, the room empty, leaving behind only broken glass and bloody feathers.

They made a home for Acquisition. The home was a tube that was long and wide enough to fit one body. Nested inside this tube were wires and port-jacks and lights that blinked in sequence. The body of Acquisition was adjusted to better fit inside this tube. The fingernails were removed to allow the aleph/wiring a better angle of insertion, and long incisions cut along the arms and at the nape of the neck to allow the entry of the judiciary ports, which were thick, and blunt, like thumbs. They wove the body into this machine until the body and the machine were synonymous. And then they shut the door.

The work was for the most part done. Umbai Labs made their

preparations before going public; tucked Acquisition away in a place where no one could reach it—a private eddy in the dark of Pocket Space, where the capsule could drift outside of time itself, safe from interference but still able to perform its good works. They thought they had done a thorough job scrubbing Acquisition's mind, making it compliant to instruction, but there was a place they could not reach, for they did not know it existed—a pocket below the ancient instinct, where the water was black and lapped gently against the cool sands of the beach. An island outside of time. That was where he slept as he waited for the song.

A song that began with the beat of sharp metal on rock.

13

The Grave of Birds

The impact echoed throughout the dark, cavernous space of Substrata D—a sharp *crack* as the tooth of the pickax bounced off the rock and was brought back down again in rhythmic arcs. Each strike made a tuning fork of Fumiko's arm. The sensation once unnerved her, but over the past few months of digging she had become accustomed to it, and even found pleasure in the dance of muscles. She raised the pick again and chipped away at the wall before her, smiling as she worked.

She had been tunneling since dawn, and though it was now early afternoon, she had no plans of stopping. Her body no longer demanded rest like in the beginning. She wore a work shirt with the sleeves ripped off. The jagged sculpt of her biceps squeezed and stretched. She was strong. When she went to the bathroom and caught herself in the mirror, it amused her how powerful her upper body had become, and sometimes she would flex for herself, and pretend she was on the stage of one of those Old Earth competitions; a small vanity she was unaware was within her until now, as she nurtured the sculpt with protein mixtures and vitamixes from the upper-tier kitchens before returning to her work in Substrata D.

Crack. A break was in order, but like most activities she took part in, it was hard for her to stop when she found her rhythm, never failing to find that addictive quality in the work. The percussive impact of the pick on rock. The hypnotic repetition of the swing. The keen awareness that every inch she broke off was another inch closer to her goal—the YonSef explosives she had once buried when she first erected this base. Every inch of concrete was another inch closer to restoring power to her base.

"You're so close," Dana whispered.

Close, she thought as she licked the sweat off her lip, *I am close*. She raised her pick like a fiery sword.

Crack. The sound of a cork popping out of a bottle. Flutes of bubbled spirits toasted, the connection echoing throughout the brightly lit cathedral space of the banquet hall on Pelican. The hall was empty but for the two people seated at the end of the long table. It was a lonely celebration. Only one of them drank the sparkling wine that was served, and ate the many fresh fruits in the glass bowls dolloped with true cream. The other sat silent in her chair, with no appetite at all, her hands folded in her lap and her eyes cast toward the bank of windows that looked out over the unfolded expanse of Schreiberi Wing. It was a familiar view to her. She had been in this banquet hall once before, many years ago, back when she was still an accessory on Fumiko's arm—back when she had a different definition of love.

"Do not hold back, M. Jenssen," the representative said as the cakes were carted in. "You've earned every bite of this dessert."

Vaila pushed aside her plate. She refused the cakes and the sweet words the representative plied her with, the medals he offered up to her, and as he spooned the cream onto his fruit and went on about how proud she should be, she slumped in her chair and zoned him out, praying for a quick end to this tiresome dinner. She took what pleasure she could in denying every effort the representative made to please her. "I'm not hungry," she told him when he offered her a slice of gelatinous strawberry cake, the dessert wiggling when he set down the plate, and let out a restrained but still audible sigh.

"Then what is it you *would* like?" he asked.

There was only, and ever, one answer.

"Fumiko Nakajima," she said.

He dropped his crumpled napkin on his plate. "As I told you before," he said with a tight smile, "the moon is blackballed. I do not know the coordinates of her base, and even if I did, I would be unauthorized to hand them over to you. M. Nakajima is in exile for crimes against Allied Space. Even if she somehow still lives, she is allowed no visitors."

"Am I not the reason for your victory?"

"A victory for which we are grateful," he said with an obligatory nod of his head. "But there is no negotiation on this point. The tribunal has made this very clear. My hands are tied. Please, M. Jenssen, let her go."

Vaila swirled her glass. "What about the boy?"

"The Acquisition," he corrected.

"Is the boy still alive?" she asked.

"M. Jenssen," he said. "Your service is complete. Your responsibilities to the traitor Nakajima and to the crew of the *Debby* have ended. As of this moment, you are in a position most Allies dream of—a life of easy retirement, if you so choose. Do not think of the past. Think of tomorrow. Tell me what the company can do to make your tomorrow a satisfying one."

"Fumiko Nakajima," she said again.

She could do it all night.

The representative breathed through his nose. "If you cannot think of something reasonable to request," he said, "then you will be given the standard package."

It was the standard package that they ended up handing her, in a small, sparsely attended ceremony on a noble's balcony, where she was bestowed high rank in the Allied government: Custodian-Aerie of the Thrasher Fleet. The consul gave her a small gold pin, which bit into the lapel of her tailored jacket, and wished her congratulations on the new appointment. The position had no real power, but it paid well and had few responsibilities; a meeting every few days, if Vaila so chose to attend, and some console-work assignations her assistant was more than happy to complete on her behalf. She attended the meetings on a lark every now and then, when she had difficulty being alone, and would blink through the long and meandering talks of future expansions, startled alert when on the rare occasion a lieutenant would turn to her and ask for her thoughts on the latest Resource World acquisition. It was not long before they stopped extending her these invitations, and distracted her instead with a private schooner, with near-limitless access to stations and planetary bodies; everywhere but the place she desired to go.

This was Vaila Jenssen's well-earned vacation. Long days of schooner-skipping across City Planets, lounging on the many well-lit balconies that overlooked the noble-owned beaches, and smoking fruit-laced pipes, alone, in her private alcoves. She baked under suns both real and artificial, drifting in and out of noncommittal naps on her lazy chairs, and she grimaced when inevitably those naps were interrupted by the memory of the gun in her hand; the weight of it, as she pointed the muzzle at Em's back, and the percussiveness of the trigger—one shot—two. The sound of the sudden crumple of his body. Her eyes would snap open, her shirt stained with sweat, nothing for it now but to lean over the balcony railing and gag, nauseous from the blood she smelled in the perfumed City

Planet air, even on this cold night, as if the stars themselves were wreathed with iron flowers.

It was easy to ignore the smells at first—the savory waft of curry and the perfume of cherry blossoms—as were the voices she heard, the low murmur of boardroom meetings and university panels. These were only small fractures. But once Dana appeared, and spoke to her with a voice so clear it seemed impossible she wasn't real, Fumiko accepted that her thousand-year-old mind, without cold sleep or neural supplement, could no longer keep the real and the imagined separate. She worked through the breaks in reality, continued her tunneling as Dana talked about the things she'd done that day—that terrific biography she read, about the architect who designed the waterborne Ashgala Stadium—and never stopped tunneling, even when the rooms themselves began to change, shifting into the places from her past. She was in the central kitchen brewing her morning protein mixture, her spoon in mid-swirl, when she realized suddenly that she was standing in her mother's living room, the transformation having occurred without fanfare—Aki on the couch, watching her old vids on the wall screen, swooning to the younger version of herself; her mother asking her if she had ever seen this one, telling her how underrated the vid was at the time of its release. Fumiko told her that she had seen it, many times, and not by choice, and as her mother glared at her, she finished off her drink in three large gulps and left the room, peeking back through the door, at once glad and saddened that the living room was gone and the kitchen had returned.

"You think you're losing your mind," Dana said while Fumiko tore off another chunk of rock with her pick. "But you're not scared."

"No. I'm not."

"Why not?" she asked.

"Because it will happen regardless." She rested the pick on her shoulder. Smiled at her. "And because I don't mind it."

She did not fight the transformations. She let them come, and slipped through these concrete memories as she plowed through the crater, stopping only sometimes to enjoy the visions. The cherry blossom trees that sprouted through the walls of the staircase, coating the steps with their pink petals. The SeaTram windows that appeared along the carbon-steel corridors, affording glimpses into the Pacific waters of Old Earth, and the cities swallowed by its tide, while in her seat, a young girl took advantage of her mother's absence and doodled the bucket beak and splayed wings of a pelican in her Handheld. The closer she got to the YonSefs, the more vivid and frequent the fractures became, until it was rare that she saw the base at all, and the last real things in her life were the tunnel, the taste of her meals, and the weight of the pick in her hand as the metal tooth tanged off the rock.

The work was slow, but thorough. With the databanks they extracted from Stopwatch, the Umbai Company created a map of where Fumiko had perched her loyal birds. Vaila had access to their progress. She read up on which of the loyalists had been killed that day, and if she knew them. Many of the names she did not recognize, and she felt only a numbing weariness as the number climbed into the hundreds. These were not the deaths that weighed on her mind.

When the Kerrigan Fleet Command informed her that Nia Imani had survived the encounter with the *Euphrates*, she smiled, thinking it was just like her former captain not to die. She paid the Kerrigan Command a small fortune to care for Nia and Sartoris, who were both at the time still locked inside their comas, adrift in their reconstitution pods aboard the *Joplin*, the fleet's main cruiser; the two of them unaware that she, with her power as Custodian-Aerie, had their records absolved of any associations with Nakajima. In the bedroom of her hotel suite Vaila prayed on her ladeum beads, reciting the prayer of sustenance and health in their honor, aware that these small acts were only cotton balls for the gaping wound she had created, but not knowing what else to do with the guilt. These days of prayer were interspersed with her continued scramlining of the *Joplin*, checking in with the doctor to ask about the progress of their healing. But when the day came that they informed her of Nia's awakening, she never called again, because they had asked her if she wanted to speak to the former captain, and Vaila was afraid that she would give in to temptation and say yes. There was no walking back what she had done.

It was on that day that she stepped out onto the hotel balcony, and stood on the platform under the bright City Planet sun. She observed the perfect day—the vines that curled in pleasing loops along the railing, the tour ship that cut the emerald sky with its white contrail—and she knew there would be no better image to leave by. She stepped up to the railing.

And she jumped.

The drones caught her before she hit the ground, but still, it was nice to pretend for a few wind-rushing moments that it would end here, the ground so close before their suspension cables ensnared her, dislocating her arms. A bright, happy pain shot through her and made her gasp with laughter as the drones floated her back to the building proper, to the medics who waited in the lobby, the gurney already prepared, a placid smile on her lips while they brought her to the mental moderator, who, in an office designed so bland it was uncanny, told her that what she was feeling was normal, and that one could not simply erase years of Nakajima's indoctrination. It was nothing they had not already told her before. She puttered around the curvaceous spaces of the clinic where the company suggested she should recuperate, dressed in a feather-soft evening robe and nothing on her feet, the polished floors warm enough to render slippers unnecessary. She did not speak to the other residents, her mind preoccupied by the salvager's description of the *Debby*'s wreckage. The story of their final days was easy to piece together with the clues available; the funeral that must've occurred for Sonja and Em before their bodies were pushed out into space, and the long stretch of weeks as the doctor and the captain waited out the dwindling oxygen. Royvan's corpse in the medica. The needle in his arm. And Nia, in the boy's room, cloaked in his blanket, surrounded by his instruments and his music; a vision of Vaila's own creation that she whipped herself with in the dark of her clinic bedroom as she prayed on her beads for the chance to take back the pain.

And as she prayed, Fumiko suffered her own haunts. She was on her way up the stairs, headed for the kitchen to prepare lunch, when she felt the cold Icelandic winds blow through the door on Level 32. She opened it, and a chill crawled down her spine as she witnessed through the portal the last day she ever saw Dana.

It was the year she was to leave on the Umbai Ark. Like Hart, she wanted to find some measure of reconciliation with Dana before the long sleep, but whatever words she planned to say were stopped in her throat when she arrived in Reykjavik and saw the ripe swell of Dana's belly under the duffel coat. What she saw now was their meeting in the city park; the two of them seated on the lip of a stone fountain, watching a street dancer twirl on his head to the pulsing remix of Haydn scales, looking only at him and not at each other. Dana's hand on the bump of her coat as she asked Fumiko, hesitantly, if there were any more seats on the Ark—if she could find it in her to use her influence with the company to procure three tickets. One for her, one for her wife, and one for the baby that would be arriving any day now. Watching them from the stairwell door, Fumiko's hand gripped the handle tightly, remembering the impotence she had felt that day, the vague promise she had made to the only woman she had ever loved; how she didn't even fight Umbai when they told her no, that Dana's wife had affiliations with certain protest groups they found undesirable, and because of this, both Dana and her prospective child were compromised. She could have convinced them otherwise, wielded her influence like a sword and cut out a path, but she did not. She only nodded in assent and later told Dana she had tried, and listened over the Handheld as the woman with purple eyes was silent, for a minute, maybe two, before she thanked her anyway. Spelled by this memory, Fumiko did not move from the doorway until the other Dana appeared and guided her back to the substrata—her last chance to make amends.

Vaila spent her days in the clinic by the windows that looked out into the courtyard, where an old prince massaged his grief into holographic sculptures on the verdant lawn. She felt a kinship with him as she observed his process; the intricate creations that he would delete just before the piece was finished, the hours of progress gone with a sad smile as he went back inside for his meal. She knew the immense catharsis of sweeping one's hand across the table and destroying all that progress, for no reason greater, or lesser, than to stick a thumb in the eye of the one she loved—a shout so loud Fumiko would have no choice but to sit up and pay attention. But now she saw that the shout was in vain, and that there would be no response. Nothing to her name but a title, and a catalogue of regrets written in bold on the floors she walked, with no way to undo the deletion. She stayed in the clinic for a month before she decided there would be no peace gained there. On their last session together, she told the mental moderator what he wished to hear: that she knew that one day she would be fine with how the pieces had fallen. He smiled and told her that he believed she was on the verge of a breakthrough. By then the rumor had begun to spread—the labs had decoded the Acquisition's properties, and would be presenting a prototype of the new technology in the coming year. A firestorm of anticipation on the Feed that she could not share in, the news only underlining for her the boy's fate. She crawled into bed, the only place she could ever think to go, and with the aid of some meds, passed out—asleep, when Fumiko brought down her pick, and finally, after all these months, completed the tunnel, and broke through the rock.

She had expected more fanfare, for the reality distortions to reach their climax and present her with an orgy of spectacular visions as the people of her past congratulated her on a job well done. But there was only the small whistle of wind escaping into the hole she had made, and the stillness of the tunnel that stretched behind her. She attacked the opening with her pick until it was large enough to climb through, and she stumbled forth, leaning into the crevasse, lighting up the darkness with a torch. Nestled within this small pocket was the YonSef. It was of spare construction: a silver orb, with a port connected by wire to a briefcase terminal. She scrambled inside, the soles of her shoes cut on the sharp rock, and cradled the explosive device in her lap, stroking its smooth surface with her callused fingers.

"You did it," Dana said.

"I did it," she said, exhausted.

It was a days-long process to siphon its volatile energies and route the jellied paste from the YonSef's nut into the generator's combustion vat; days of holding her breath, afraid that her hands would slip and blow away the progress before her success at week's end—the heating elements in the floor vibrating again, the lights switching on, level by level, and power returning to the sole working console in the amphitheater, which booted up with a trill of piano keys.

Stopwatch was awake.

She entered the amphitheater, which to her spelled eyes was now the meeting room in Cybelus Chicago. It was the long table popu-

lated by coworkers and interns that she walked past, to the head of
the room, where Hart waited by the console, pulling out a chair for
her to sit. The room hushed, the eyes watching her as she accessed
the public Feed; planetary news and gossip, and billions of multi-
media entertainments, and, with the aid of the many back doors
she had installed over the millennia that Umbai had never found,
she learned of the death of her birds. She read aloud each of the
names as her coworkers performed her emotions, the room flooded
by their weeping. Their shouts to the ceiling of apology. And as they
wept, Hart asked her quietly, "Do none still live?" and the weeping
was stilled by fury when she discovered that only one did: Vaila
Jenssen, promoted to Custodian-Aerie. Her hands went rictus while
the coworkers brandished their chairs and attacked the walls and
cracked the windows, the fluorescent lights above them flashing red
from the betrayal—the anger curbed when she accessed the messenger log of Vaila's neural and learned of the woman's many rebuffed
requests to visit this hijacked moon, and the plan materialized. The
people quieted and sobered as, with some hours' effort, she pene-
trated the new encryption systems and dove into the neural-network
Friendly Messenger System. Sent out her clarion call.

Message +1

Vaila was still half-asleep, groaning as her left eyelid blinked
blue, her neural flashing her an emergency update.

Message +1

She shifted. Winced the muscles around her eye to shut off the
notification, cursing the assistant who messaged her about details
she did not care about. She shunted the message aside, but it persisted, poking her until she deigned to lift the fold. Scowling in the
dark, she sat up and stretched her neck—a pop—and opened it.

She is alive.

That was all the message said.

In the attachment was a series of UCS coordinates. The message had come from a scrambled address. When she replied, requesting their identity, there was no response. It was once she input the coordinates in the schooner's console, and learned that the numbers led to a remote moon beyond the boundaries of Allied Space, that her suspicions, her hope, were confirmed, and with trembling hands she prepared for her mission of redemption.

Her plan was this: find Fumiko and, together, save the boy, thus earning her former captain's forgiveness, or at the very least her begrudging neutrality. Re-create what she had destroyed. Rediscover a good night's sleep. An unlikely outcome, but she needed to try anyway, because however unlikely it was, it was the only plan she had, and if there was anyone who could accomplish the impossible, it was Fumiko Nakajima. With steps light and urgent Vaila procured rations for the three-week fold and armed herself with the pistol that had taken Em's life, should Fumiko prove resistant to listening to her. And then she visited a configurations shop. Had her hair cut short and dyed blond, and her irises sugared into purple confections, for when she met Fumiko again, and explained her actions, the reasons of the heart, she needed Fumiko to see it on her body: the mask that had warped her.

She folded out of the system. For those three weeks of travel down the Gallant Current, she was understudy to her future self, practicing the speech of contempt and reconciliation she would deliver to Fumiko, at gun barrel's end if need be. Fumiko, submissive for once in her life as Vaila would explain to her, in detail, the agony of being abandoned by her.

Three weeks of rehearsal that were a year for Fumiko, which she spent unearthing the last of the YonSefs, a task made easier by the restored power, and the working drill that cleaved quickly through the rock.

The isolation of the schooner sharpened Vaila's mad resolve. She practiced her speech on the empty pilot's chair, holding up her ladeum beads for emphasis when she told the empty chair how every prayer was for her, had always been for her. She shaped the cadence, the emphasis of choice words, like "betrayed" and "broken." And when she was certain the speech was the rhetorical bullet she hoped it would be, she whispered the lines to herself as she ate her meals and sat on the cot with eyes focused on nothing, the words her new prayer as she thumbed each of the ladeum beads in turn.

"What will you say to her?" Dana asked Fumiko.

"Nothing," she said, cradling the last of the YonSefs. "There is nothing left to say."

There were five orbs in total. It was enough to evaporate an ocean. She placed them into a stasis bag, and for the remaining months she had left, spent her time on the terrace, which was now a café. She sat with Dana at the table by the window and lived there, in her favorite of all the memories, when it was only the two of them, sheltered from the rain.

That perfect week, years ago, which shaped Vaila in ways too numerous to account for—that was where she lived during that journey. That week she was Fumiko's consort, and the joy she felt when Fumiko told her she was perfect, and the weightless quality of the Canopy Deck as they danced, twirling like flowers thrown from a balcony, only the two of them in that dome in the stars, as if Pelican had been built for them, and only them. And between the rehearsals of her speeches, she sat in her pilot's chair and wondered if there would be another day like that.

"Did any of them look like me?" Dana asked. "Your consorts?"

"They resembled you. But none of them were you."

"But you still used them." Dana shut her eyes. "She loved you, and you used her."

"I know," Fumiko said quietly.

"And you're still going to go through with it?"

Fumiko nodded. "It's the safest option."

"I suppose you're right."

And then the year was up. The schooner unfolded. With hands in the cat's cradle Vaila guided the ship through the blue moon's atmosphere, fire licking the viewport, her heart palpitating as she made her descent on the landing pad along the western rim of the crater. Fumiko sighed as she watched the landing through the screen of her console. The schooner's feet thumped onto the pad. Beyond the viewport Vaila could hear the buffeting winds, and saw the frost that bloomed on the glass. Fumiko sprinted up the steps of the base, bounding over the roots of the cherry blossom trees. Vaila bundled herself in a thick coat and stepped down the schooner's ramp, her teeth chattering, shivering from the cold, and the anticipation. Level ten, level nine, the numbers flying past Fumiko as she ascended. Blond hair whipped by the gale as Vaila sprinted for the elevator doors, and then, after the button let out an empty click, to the stairwell doors across the pad. Level three, level two. Vaila dragged the door open, was greeted by the backdraft of warm air—grinning now, her nerves alive with sparks—and she pulled her torch from her belt to light the darkened stairwell but had no time to click it on, for by then, the bullet had blown out the back of her head.

Fumiko lowered the gun. She ran up the stairs and stepped into the wind, crouching over the body to make sure the woman was dead. She brushed aside her bangs, revealing the hole in the forehead. The false freckles. The eyes still open, the iris an unnatural shade of purple. With her thumb she rubbed the purple dye until it was gone, and saw that the truth was chestnut.

"You were right," Dana said. "She didn't look like me at all." She sighed. "She was much more beautiful."

Fumiko picked up the body, and she descended the steps of the base that was not a base. Walked through the park strewn with cherry blossoms, and the long tunnel that spanned the risen ocean, past the blown-out buildings. Made the long journey to the sub-basement, where the other bodies were, and where she would lay the last body to rest, the path tracked by the blood that dripped from blond hair. Fumiko entered the subbasement and felt the heat of the California sun, which broke through the glass enclosure of the bird preserve. She squinted against the light and gazed out into the false river, the gully, and the trees; the land strewn with the corpses of her birds. It was by the river where she placed her.

The Pelican slipped from her hands, onto the ground.

Its wings limp.

At the door, she offered the preserve one last bow, and made her way back to the schooner, picking up the bag of YonSefs on the way.

They were all there, waiting for her on the dock of the canal. Aki and Hart and M. Toho, Vaila, and the other thousands she had known. None of them spoke to her, or smiled. They only observed her in silence as she stepped down the dock and boarded the boat with her bag of vengeance. She sat beside Dana, took her hand, and told the ferryman their destination. With his wooden oar he pushed the boat out, and as it rocked down the flooded canal, Fumiko spared one last glance at those she was leaving behind, and held up her hand before the boat rounded the corner between buildings, out of sight. And so it was that, for a second time, Fumiko Nakajima disappeared; gone in the Pocket for a trade of years, while Umbai finished its development of the Fast Travel Chip.

14

One Thousand Fires

A man from City Planet Buestana was chosen to lead the people into tomorrow—a poor child from the substrata streets who signed up for battle and made good in a resource war in an asteroid belt few people knew the name of. The man was at once notable and un-noteworthy. And though he was honored when Umbai chose him to pilot the prototype viper, he was afraid. Afraid that they had chosen him because of his anonymity; that if something went wrong in this first flight, and he dematerialized into ash, there would be little uproar; that he was a safe risk, and that this flight would be his last. And so, the night before the Fast Travel test, outside a neighborhood bar beyond the walls of the military base, he spent that fear in drunken joy-shouts while his friends held him above their heads like a sacrifice to the sky, and chanted his name, the chosen one. He carried that exalted moment with him to the cockpit of the viper, and held his friends' voices close to his heart as he flipped up the comms, and told the judiciary that the ship was ready to jump.

Many were in attendance the day the man from Buestana warped from Barbet Station to Thrasher in the span of one-quarter of a second. The onlookers at the Canopy Deck windows gasped when the viper dematerialized in the view of their spyglasses. It was difficult for them to fathom what they saw, even after they replayed the proof from their recording neurals; how once a ship was there, and then it was not, in one-quarter of a second. The news spread like wildfire over the Station Feed, and the Feed of Allied Proper; an electric current that skipped from neural to neural, and opened the eyes of the people who then realized life had irrevocably changed. The news arced to the Obsolescence Fleets, the ships of the Kerrigan, where it became excited chatter in the *Joplin*'s mess hall, and over their mash the metalworkers muttered to one another what this news might mean, some of them wary of the coming change, but most unable to deny that in the long run, this was a good thing. The doors of the frontier would soon burst open.

Only one of their rank remained silent. The former captain of a commercial transport vessel who sat alone at the end of the far table, not touching the food on her tray as she listened to the mess-hall chatter, annoyed by their jovial obliviousness. To her, they didn't have a clue what the price was for tomorrow. As she thought of the boy she had lost, her hand curled around her fork as if to bend it. Few of the workers noticed when she abruptly stood up and took her leave. The ones who did spared her only a glance, surprised that not even the biggest news of Allied Space could inspire a smile or even eye-widening curiosity on that broken woman's face, before they returned to their burning conversation.

Nia strode down the light-blasted causeway, her step wavering as she went. She had to lean against the wall to stop from falling. She ignored the young woman who asked if she needed help, her focus entirely on the feel of the cold metal on her shoulder, and the rage that coursed through her veins.

"He's dead, isn't he?" she whispered that night in the medica.

Sartoris shifted his head toward her. His body was still pinned to the bed by protective casts, his movement restricted to tight head turns. He had woken up only a week ago, the flesh of him still withered from the long sleep, his once precise attention now dulled and prone to drifting when they spoke; his words slurred, as he said, "You look very familiar."

She said nothing to this. With a defeated sigh, she leaned back in her chair and gazed up at the ceiling while she listened to the plaintive beep of his heart machine and his incoherent murmurs. She stayed with him until he fell back to sleep and then returned to her quarters, where she lay in bed, awake, waiting for the next day of work. The hours in the dismantler with her heat blade, rendering metals into shippable quantities with the arm that was never quite the same since the attack on the *Debby*, the shoulder joint flaring up when she lifted a heavy container, the throb not leaving until the post-work group showers, when she would sigh under the spouts of cold water while always in some far corner a couple made themselves at home in each other, their moans inspiring nothing but frustrated glances from Nia as she tried to disappear within herself. She took her meals alone. Moved the mash around with her fork as she asked herself, over and over, why she had not just escaped with Ahro when she had the chance, why she had even bothered returning to Fumiko when all she wanted was already with her, aboard her ship, until the mash was a soupy swirl and the dining hall was empty.

All she had now was the metalwork, and Sartoris. Her visits to the medica were at the end of the day, when only a sole technician was stationed in the front of the room, his face lit by a silent entertainment on a scroll-screen. Nights when she and Sartoris sat in silence, her heart breaking when he smiled at her with polite confusion, wondering why this stranger kept returning to his bedside, but not minding either way. Her attention remained on the flute in her hands. Her thumb on the name engraved at its base as she thought of his song and was haunted by the worst of her imaginings. Of what pain he'd been subjected to, what surrender, with him alone in some dark corridor, reaching for her. And how soon it would be till she joined him there.

"I know you," Sartoris whispered, with a smile. "You are a captain."

She breathed out.

"I was," she said.

Of all the losses she had endured in the past year, the loss of her former title stung Nia the least. There was comfort in no longer being in charge. To coast on a river of someone else's orders, the items of the day, accountable only for the tool in her hand and the disassembly of metal. She lost herself in the rhythm of the work, the tactile pleasure of the blade parting sheets of hull like a finger through wet mud, safe in the knowledge that there was a ceiling to the consequences should she mess up; a slip of the heat blade, maybe, but even that was a comparatively small cost in the grand scheme of things. Now, after all she had been through, she could survive the loss of a finger, or a hand, as long as it was hers, and no one else's.

She was the first to arrive in the workbay, and the last to leave. She was silent, entertained no side conversations, and was reliable with her quotas. With each week and month that passed, she became more of a ghost. Willed herself into a state of transience. Even those who worked alongside her were unsure what her voice sounded like, or what her name was, referring to her in asides as "the former captain," or simply "the woman." But despite her effort to remain unnoticed, the floor manager quickly keyed in on the quality and consistency of her metalwork. Favored her with breaks she did not take. And on the anniversary of her tenure, when her temporary contract was almost up, offered her a more permanent position on the *Joplin*. "Best Kerrigan ship to work on, in my very biased opinion. Five-year contract with upward mobility, which wouldn't take long for you," he said, "considering your skill. Includes room and board for you and yours." He was referring to Sartoris.

"How long do I have to decide?" she asked, with her hands in the pockets of her jumpsuit, staring out at the flying sparks of the bay.

The manager shrugged. "Say, three months. Around about when the payment your benefactor gave Fleet Command runs out." He picked up his board, nodded at her. "Take your time. Think about it, Imani. But say yes."

He left her standing there, by the burnt-out shell of a cockpit. She gripped the handle of her heat blade and walked back to her station, wondering if she could do it; if she could forget, and start again.

We know where this path leads, her sister's voice said.

Nia flicked on the blade and shouted that she was ready for the next load. The scrap metal rolled down the conveyor. And like yesterday, and the day before, she set to work.

It is a circle.

First it was given to the military crafts and noble schooners, then the company transport ships and large commercial passenger fleets. With time, the FT Chip made it all the way down to the ramshackle bussers.

Demand was high. A line of hopeful pilots kilometers long spilled out the doors of City Planet Ustinov's Port Authority, curling down the ramp outdoors, the streets, all the way to the elevators that led to the district tiers. Busser pilots, waiting for the chip's distribution, many of them having waited in suspense for weeks on end. At the head of the line was a woman who had camped outside the requisitions office for a month, sustained on the food and drink and colostomics her daughter brought her each morning, waiting for her share of the future. And then the office opened, and she was gestured to the desk. It was the second proudest day of her life when she was handed the chip; her sig-card registered, the crowd outside applauding her as she held the box above her head, and her daughter—her first proudest day—running to meet her. Together they returned to their busser to install the new technology. The installation took the better part of three days, for most of the woman's savings had gone into the purchase of the chip itself, and there was little money left to hire someone to do the work for them. Carefully following the vid-instructions, they reconfigured their busser's engine, stripping out the fold-core, replacing it with the black box that held the chip beneath its smooth, impenetrable exterior.

Neither the woman nor her daughter opened the FT black box. Their curiosity was not strong enough to risk voiding the warranty. Others did, retrofitters and pirates and simple hobbyists, who shared their findings on the Lower Feed: how within the FT circuitry was nestled a small glass ball, and inside that ball, a red prick of blood, fine enough to stand on needle-point. There were questions about this blood, but Umbai was silent on the matter, protected by the intellectual property code. There were some protests, people who worried about the source of potentially unethical tech, but Umbai's stock was unharmed by these meager outcries, which rarely made a dent in the public consciousness. Like most people those days, the woman from Ustinov did not understand these protesters. To her, one prick of blood was a small price to pay for the future, though she did have her moments of wondering, such as when, one drunken night, a fellow busser played devil's advocate and asked her what if it were her own daughter's blood that fed the chip. She fell silent before stating, resolutely: "I would never let that happen." She knew this was a nonanswer, but still, it satisfied.

Hers was one of the first quick-service public bussers on Ustinov.

It was a good life at the start. While her daughter collected fare from the passengers and served them drinks in suc-pacs, the woman hailed the judiciary from her cockpit, and requested authorization for the jump.

She lived for the moment authorization was cleared. When she could hear the hushed anticipation in the cabin, and the shouts and cries when in one-quarter of a second they arrived at their new destination. That new City Planet sky. In those days, most people had never traveled offworld, the price—both financial and temporal—too high a price to pay. But now, families that had not met in generations were reconnected, as well as old friends and older lovers. Money flowed into her open hands. In a twelve-hour period she finished thirty routes, the demand for travel so high she and her daughter got little sleep, exhausted by day's end, kept awake only by the adrenaline tablets and the pleasure they got from the stunned rapture of their passengers, who upon landing would fall to their knees in wonder at how far they had come while thanking the woman, her daughter, trembling as they shook the hands of these generous queens, along with all the other pilots who were in those days treated as gods.

The woman from Ustinov and 322 of her colleagues, proven loyalists to the company cause, were chosen to be the chip's ambassadors to the neutral fleets that had yet to sign loyalty contracts with Umbai. She was notified of this mandatory civil service by a young Pelican representative, who presented her with the parchment declaration signed by the hand of the head consul, a declaration that she had framed and nailed to the front of the cabin beside the beaming portraits of her parents and blessed aunts.

Their charge was the Kerrigan Salvage Fleet. They departed a week later, the woman humming as she hailed the neutral fleet and entered the dock of the *Joplin* along with the twelve other assigned bussers. She told her daughter to ready the refreshments.

If all had gone well, it would've been the third proudest day of her life.

The corridors were empty. The heat blades left to cool on the tables. The loaders in the abandoned grind halls unmanned. Every worker congregated in the vaulted docking bay, cheering the arrival of the Allied bussers. Jumpsuited men and women on the catwalks and the staircases and shoulder to shoulder in the entryways, elbowing one another to get a better view of the approach of the FT-capable ships.

Nia stood on one of the back benches to see over the sea of heads, while beside her Sartoris sat with his hands propped on his cane, looking about the crowd with a placid, bemused expression, as if not sure what the commotion was for but charmed by it all the same. Waves of cheers rippled throughout the hangar when Fleet Command and their coterie cut their way through the crowd and greeted the pilots of the bussers. After a brief introductory speech, which Nia could not hear from her distance, Command and their coterie boarded the ships, which then eased out of the dock, the applause slowly quieting as the last ship left. For thirty minutes the entirety of the dock was in a hush. Murmured wonderings of how long it would take. If they should not be back by now. Someone asked Nia if she could see anything. And then, an explosion of cheers when, one by one, the bussers returned, and Fleet Command stepped out and gave their salute of approval, the roar so fierce Nia was nearly swept up in it before her jaw tightened and she reminded herself how all of this was possible.

In rounds the workers were allowed to board the bussers and experience the jump for themselves. They pushed forward, eager for their turn, until Command blew their horn and the crowd immediately organized themselves into single-file lines. Nia did not join the lines. She sat on the bench, believing that to ride one of those bussers would be a betrayal to Ahro's memory, her participation a tacit acknowledgment of the company's feats, and of the few things she had left in this life, it was his memory that she held most dear.

And yet, when she looked at those bussers, the celebration of them, there was something beneath her righteousness and her boiling anger as she observed how every worker who returned from the bussers did so in reverent silence, offering only dazed shrugs to those still in line who asked them what Fast Travel was like. Nia was infected by the curiosity of the impossible. The dark wondering of why-not.

When the last round was called three hours later, she stood up.

"Do you want to come?" she asked Sartoris, and after he nodded like an eager child, she helped him to his feet.

They were shown to the last busser in the line. With his arm entwined with hers, she brought him to the empty row in the back and held his cane while he eased himself down into the window seat. Buckled him in as a young woman walked the lone aisle of the busser pushing a cart of company-sponsored drinks, handing the two of them suc-pacs of Umbai Ale. While Sartoris gingerly sipped his ale, Nia strapped herself in. She winced at the tug of the strap around her waist, the feel of something sharp poking her hip. She drew the flute from her pocket. Laughed. She had gotten so used to the feel of the thing in her pocket she'd forgotten it was there.

The intercom flicked on and the cabin went quiet.

"Welcome aboard O'Daja Departures Busser. I hope you are enjoying your refreshments, compliments of Umbai-Allied Associates. As I am sure you are all aware, today's flight will be a preview of the proprietary Fast Travel Chip. Once we are cleared we will be jumping to three different systems: Averyn, Palau, and San Osha, in that order. We won't be pausing for long at any of our destinations, so please keep your eyes toward the windows if you wish to see the effects of the passage. We should be back home in thirty minutes. Please enjoy the flight."

Everyone looked out their portholes at the sweep of ships that composed the Kerrigan Fleet, the dozens of ships that dotted the Red Nebula like black pepper on a splotch of blood. In all her year-long stay here, Nia had never left the *Joplin*; never seen what the fleet looked like from afar. This was not her home, but still her skin goose-pimpled as the pilot counted down from five, her hand gripping the flute, as she mouthed, to no one, *I'm sorry.*

. . . *two, one.*

Nia braced herself.

But there was no light. No spectacle.

The stars simply shifted position. The nebula, and the fleet, gone. Through the window she saw only empty space. The transition was so sudden that for a moment she thought it a trick of the eye, a skip in the frame of some cheap holo, the jump imperceptible but for the slight stutter of her chair. Almost laughable, until she followed Sartoris's gaze toward the bank of windows on the other side of the busser, and saw why his eyes widened—saw the spindles of an Umbai City Planet in plain view, the bleached spires glowing against the sun it orbited like a sea urchin in a drift of volcanic light.

No one spoke.

"We've arrived at City Planet Averyn," the pilot said with a smile in her voice. "You'll see it on your left. Take it in. We'll be jumping again in five minutes."

Wordlessly Nia stared at the City Planet. Here it was: vivid and concrete proof that they had moved across the galaxy in one-quarter of a second. She pressed herself against the back of the chair, tears beading her eyes, rivering down her cheeks. One-quarter of a second. Not even enough time to sign a shipping contract, or to utter the first syllable of the sentence "Ready to fold." No time at all.

She curled her arms over herself, pressed the flute to her chest. All the years she had given up to the Pocket. The sacrifices that were now irrelevant. There would be no more lost time. No more derelicts stranded in the fringe without hope of rescue. No more last goodbyes to old friends. No skipping across the entire lifetimes of forgotten lovers. It was so beautiful, and so horrible, she couldn't breathe.

Sartoris's hand fell on her shoulder. Through wracked breath she told him she was all right, even though she knew she would not be all right again.

She wiped her eyes and looked down at the flute in her hand, the cheap wooden thing. She decided to play a song. A final song, here, in memoriam to the fold, and to all the people she let it take from her—a song for Ahro, who felt close now, everywhere, wherever there was a ship that could leapfrog the stars. A song for his blood price, and the smile of his she desperately missed; the slap of sandals down a Barbet class corridor.

A sound she could hear even now. She found her fingering and pressed her lips to the mouthpiece. With nothing in her heart but the crater of her love for him, for all of them, she trilled the first few notes and, on her first note, that clarion call, the veil was pierced, and in the place below ancient instinct, a small flame bloomed on a dark shore, where the young man woke with a gasp as if punched in the chest, not knowing who he was, or where, or for how long he had slept; only that the dark was broken by some sudden light—a campfire, just a few meters away, small, but bright enough that he had to look away as he crawled toward it, dragging himself across the textureless sand and over the log benches, all the while feeling like he knew this beach and that dark water and even this fire, but not knowing from where, haunted by this ember of a feeling as he crouched before the campfire's leaping flames and listened to its crackle, the sound of it familiar, the whisper-snap of a woman's voice . . . a voice that coaxed him forward with its promise of love and safety, compelling him closer to the red-white heat, close enough to singe, close enough for her to hear him as he opened his mouth

and with all the air in his lungs called out to her in a great shout—
I'M HERE!—and the busser jumped with unexpected force, like a
hand slapped to the back of the head, the passengers winded by the
protective hug of their seatbelts, their suc-pacs of ale thrown into
the air like confetti, the young server falling forward into the aisle
with her ankle caught in an armrest with a twist, the shouts in the
cabin at once sharp and guttural, before droning into a chorus of
dull groaning as the lights rattled back on and the hull trembled to
a stillness, the ship settling, while Nia, dazed, gripped the pulled
muscle in her neck and held her hand out to Sartoris, touching him
to make sure he was still whole, her friend's face scrunched up as he
pressed his palm to his temple, which he had banged against the
window. She asked him if he was all right. With a grimace, he nodded. The cabin was quiet as everyone collected themselves. They
were so preoccupied with gathering their wits that no one noticed
the morning flare of the white sun that broke through the starboard
windows, not until someone screamed and pointed as if in accusation at the sight of the jagged mountain of this unknown planet. The
cold white cumulus. The coarse wind that wobbled the glass.

The world that was not Averyn.

The pilot confirmed their suspicions, her voice shaking as she
said, "I—we jumped. I'm going to hail the judiciary, see what's going
on. Thank you for your patience."

The people were not happy. The magic was gone, and now the
workers shouted at the young woman in the aisle who was still
nursing her ankle, demanding answers. And as they shouted, Nia
felt the ground for the flute she had dropped, grasping at the instrument that had rolled under her chair.

"What happened?" Sartoris asked.

"I don't know," she said, rising up, making sure the flute was not
broken.

And she didn't know, the pieces in her mind, the vital clues, not put together until the busser jumped again, by Umbai's command, and they arrived at Thrasher Station. Technicians and Yellowjackets waited in the Thrasher docks, ready to determine the cause of the glitch. The passengers were corralled into the port security offices while the woman from Ustinov stood by her ship and watched helplessly as the Umbai technicians stripped her livelihood apart. Nia and the others were body-searched in separate rooms for contraband belongings, of any evidence of tampering with the FT system, the Yellowjackets finding only lint balls and playing cards and twizerine screwdrivers in the workers' pockets, and, mysteriously, a flute, which a pair of gloved hands studied under the harsh light of the interrogation chamber. And as the light flooded the holes of the instrument, and the inspector peered through the tube, and blew into it to make sure nothing was hiding inside, Nia was graced with her first suspicion; a simple connection in her mind like two meeting fingers. A dared hope of cause and effect, one that would infect her thoughts after they returned to the *Joplin*, and she, holding the heat blade limply in her hand, would for the first time in many months allow her mind to drift from the work, and remember what the boy had told her before he was taken; a memory of the music that had once called him home when he was lost.

Come workday's end, she met with the floor manager and told him she would not be signing the new contract; that, in fact, she would be gone by the end of the month. He did his best to convince her to stay, but in the end was only able to grunt and wish her the best of luck in her future endeavors.

She ate in the mess hall with purpose. And she strode down the corridors, to the room that she and Sartoris shared, her gaze ahead steeled as she worked out the beginnings of her plan.

No one was sure what had provoked the unscheduled jump, but they were determined to find out. For ten hours the Fast Travel network was shut down while the labs resurfaced the capsule from the Pocket and scrutinized Acquisition's wiring and automated health utilities, the body that lay in the heart of the machine, the history of its heartbeats. A diagnostics check, interrupted by the movement of Acquisition's body.

It was his eyes. They shot open, the pupils dilated, staring blankly at the domed ceiling of the capsule. Tears tracking down his cheeks.

None of the technicians moved, frozen by the fear that one of their number had messed up with the drug doses, and that the boy was about to escape on the wings of his power. But the open eyes were only a reflex. "It's fine," the head tech said, holding up his gloved hand. "He's still asleep." Once the heart-stopping moment had passed, they dialed up the sedatives, and the eyelids shuttered to a close. And they sent him, and his capsule, back into the Pocket.

But the technician was not entirely correct. A part of him was awake now. He had seen the piercing light, and the crooked bend of shadowed people standing over him, before the new load of drugs submerged him further into the dream. The cold water rising over his face as he was dragged through the black water and crawled back onto the nighttime shore like a protean thing, back to the small, wavering fire on the beach. He heaved himself onto one of the seating logs. His muscles sore. A fist of needles in his head that pricked against the movement of his neck as he looked around at this place below the ancient instinct, knowing now that this place was not real. Not really. Not the silent tree line to his right, with rustling leaves that soundlessly rubbed against one another in the breeze, or the water to his left, the small waves described by the strangely bright light of the moon. He didn't know what this place was, but he knew that in truth he was elsewhere. He held his hand to the throb in his head.

A dread feeling overrode the pain of his body when he glanced out at the limitless water, and saw a figure approach. The figure was a black silhouette against the smooth white moon, walking above the waves as though they had no weight at all, their body cloaked in a robe that reflected no light, and their face covered by a mask of cold porcelain, pale and unforgiving.

The figure stepped onto the beach, making no footprints in the sand, and, after circling around his fire, regarding for a curious moment the young man, they sat on the log opposite his.

"You're awake," they observed.

The young man trembled as the cold water dripped off his skin. Beyond the feverish shaking, the needling pain in his head, there was a chime; the small brass bells of recollection; the memory of the mask this person wore. He had seen it before. The disturbing smoothness, and the dark eye slits angled as if in anger, or laughter. "You are the Kind One," he said. He was unsure where the name had come from, or how he remembered it; like the beach and the black water, it was as though the name had always been there, in some secret pocket in his mind, waiting to be reached for.

Somehow, even though there was no mouth, it looked as though the mask were smiling. "They cut so much from you, but not everything, it seems," they said with their many voices. "They still believe memories are citizens of the mind. But memories also live in the bones, and the blood." The voices were a genderless whisper-rush, asynchronous, some voices dragging behind the others, disturbing the clarity, each voice a cold-warm tendril in his ear. "Do you know where you are?" they asked.

The young man looked around. "No," he said. "But it feels . . . familiar."

"As it should." Their gloved hands met, and rested in their lap. "You celebrated a birthday here, once."

He winced. There was a knot in his head—a knot of memory that he could not undo. A haze of someone asking him to play another song on his flute.

What flute?

"Don't worry yourself about these things," the Kind One said. "They are no longer relevant. All that matters, is that." They pointed at the water from which they had come with their gloved hand. And then the waves stilled, and the ocean seemed to the young man a solid thing, the light of the moon a path that ribboned across its valleys, into the black horizon. "That is the way out from this place. The last road."

"Where does it go?"

"To a long overdue rest."

They stood up and held out their gloved hand, which was gray leather, and stenciled by the light of the silent fire. There was a pull, a coaxing, that the young man felt for that hand. And he knew by instinct that to take that hand, to follow the Kind One across the water, would mean the end of pain. Of everything.

But something else was pulling at him. The fire he sat beside. The voice that had come from it. The yearning he felt, to hear that voice again.

He hugged himself, and snubbed the Kind One's outstretched hand.

"Not yet," he said, staring at the fire.

"You know you are dying," they said. "They are burning through you like my brethren did in the Quiet Ship. Using you up." They sighed. "Young One, your end has been written. I am sorry for that, but this is truth. But what has not yet been written is how you arrive at this end. From here there are two paths. Stay, and let the birds peck at your body. Or leave, with me, and deny them their stolen meal."

But the young man's eyes did not waver from the flame.

"Not yet," he whispered again.

The Kind One withdrew their hand, stared at him through their eye slits, their thoughts beyond him. They sat back down.

"It is up to you," they said simply. "When you are ready."

"Thank you," he said.

And on that quiet and darkened shore, he did his best to ignore the steady flare of pain in his body as he waited with his shepherd for the next whisper from the flame.

Beyond the place of ancient instinct, in Allied Space, FT traffic resumed as it had before the glitch. In the report sent to the judiciary, the technicians explained that due to the array of inputs and drugs that were fed into Acquisition's system, it was inevitable that there would be the occasional involuntary reflex—a random jump, perhaps, that would leap a public busser from City Planet Averyn into the atmosphere of a border-fringe world. There was little they could do to combat these "system kicks" but to amp the drug cocktails, and hope. Any further action was not advisable, for one glitched jump out of thousands was not worth the cost of its inquiry. The judiciary agreed with the report. It was in the company's financial interests to instead address the more pressing matter of the increasing load of FT-capable ships.

They called it the Bottleneck. They had but one Acquisition, which could service only one ship at a time. From ship authorization to the jump itself and then the post-confirmation, one service job took three to five seconds. As more planets and fleets signed contracts with Umbai, and more ships became FT-capable, the daily authorization queue reached into the hundreds of thousands, inflating the time between request and jump into tens of hours, sometimes days. The Feed swelled with complaints concerning the absurd wait times. Jump schedules were coordinated in advance by weeks. Some unlucky bussers jumped only once a month, which meant ticket prices rose to combat the scarcity of flights. Umbai continued its steadfast optimization of the process, shaving fractions of seconds off the authorization loop. And to satisfy their investors, the company established the Preferential Hour; a one-hour "fast lane" during the Station Standard Day, when jump access was restricted to corpro-government ships and any civilians willing to pay the substantial admission fee, the ships able to come and go as they pleased; a law that, transparent to all, was meant to aid the noble fleets, and few others.

For Umbai, these were good problems to have. Their coffers were lined with iotas made from the distribution of the chips, the toll tax, the Preferential Hours, and the loyalty contracts of neutral galactic powers. Profits jumped by exponents. City Planets multiplied. Each newly installed chip, each jump, like a nerve peeled fresh from Acquisition's back.

The room was unfamiliar to Sartoris. He did not know these beds, or the chair by the desk, or the dark view of spires from his window. He touched the cold glass. He did not know how he got here.

It had happened again.

Things were always slipping from him. He thought he was getting better, had a better grasp of time. But sometimes, like now, he would turn around, and forget. Circumstance gone in a finger snap.

He paced around the small room, his cane thumping along the coarsely fibered carpet as he went to the door, and then back to the window. He looked out again. Swallowed dryly. He did not know this place.

He was alone.

Hand trembled against cane head as he sat down on the chair by the desk. Something crinkled in his pocket. A sheet of paper, torn fresh from a notebook. Words written on it, a scrawl jotted down in haste. It took him a while to divine the words.

He had gotten better, but words were still difficult.

Sartoris, the note said. *This is Nia. You are in a hostel on City Planet Galena. We rented the room for the night. It is ours, so please do not leave. I left at 1600 hours for the substrata, and will be back before midnight. Something down there I need to get. I will tell you more when I return. Try to get some rest. There are snacks in the bag by the bed if you get hungry.*

Don't worry.

You are safe.

He flattened the sheet on the desk. Ran his fingers over the words *You are safe*. Muttered it to himself as he stood back up and returned to the window.

"I am safe," he muttered as he looked up at the unfathomable heights of the City Planet spires, and down to the dark, limitless depths. "I am safe."

Words whispered in frantic prayer as life moved on without him. A flow of people traffic in and out of the strata elevators. Down into the underbelly, where the stars could not be seen, and where the people made their own light with broken crackle-sticks and fires fed by trash chuted down from the higher strata. The streets were thronged with crowds, and in the midst of all of them, a child smiled as she crouched in the gutter and relieved herself, waving at the four members of the citizen militia that patrolled past her with their strapped rifles. And nearby, a body, limp on the ground, its throat opened by a knife, while around the corpse people peddled to passersby pairs of knock-off neurals, orbital necklaces, and a fine gem diadem once worn about the head by a forgotten queen of a generation ship. This was the path that Nia walked with a rifle of her own—an old gauss that had once belonged to Sonja—past the boxtowns in the alleyways and the eyes that trailed her without affect before those eyes returned to their listless gazing at the holo-light adverts thrown against the walls, adverts that proclaimed the expensive miracles of new Umbai Company products. No one asked why she was there. They received many visitors from the higher strata, and knew they could do nothing but hope that these visitors too got swallowed by this place.

Every City Planet had a substrata, but there was only one where Em had grown up. More often than not, Nia tried not to think of her old crew, but there was one memory that was necessary to dredge up despite the pain: her former engineer's stories of growing up on Galena. The violence he'd known. And his connection to a woman who had a finger on the pulse of the black market.

Morissa. All Nia remembered was the first name, but after a few hours of cold calls to the countless Morissas who lived in the substrata, she finally found one who recognized Em's name—and more important, the name of Em's cat.

Speaking Nanda's name won Nia the woman's trust, and directions to her belowground apartment complex; to the door at the end of a long hall, lit by harsh fluorescents, and walls graffitied in languages unknown to Nia, for down here, even Umbai could not standardize everything. When Nia knocked, she was greeted by the looming silhouette of a man with a half-burned face, the scars crinkling when he smiled and asked if she would please wipe her shoes on the mat first before entering, as he had only just cleaned. It was a warm home. The kind found in a fairy tale, rich with pillows and curtains, and a table made of real wood, adorned with teacups and a steaming kettle, where an old woman with a severe underbite welcomed her with a surprising hug. Fragile arms that wrapped around Nia's body, held her close, with a whisper in her ear: "I loved him. And I will do all I can to help his friends. But I need to know now, before I give you what you came for: Are you a slaver?"

"No."

She parted from Nia, hands still on her. "This is the truth?"

"Yes."

She nodded. "It's not so difficult to tell these things," she said. "But still. I had to ask." She nodded at the man with the half-burned face, who then left the room and returned with a package wrapped in crinkled foil. "One license scrambler," she said with a touch of pride. "Should confuse the judiciary enough to let you go unnoticed. But space out its usage. Keep the time between jump requests random. Don't let Umbai pick up a pattern, or before you know it, they will swarm you."

Nia accepted the package. "How much?" she asked.

But Morissa held up her hand. "Not many captains remember the name of their engineer's old pet." She smiled. "A good memory should be rewarded."

When Nia returned to the hostel, Sartoris was in bed, asleep, the note she had written him clutched in his hand, the paper crinkled so that the only words she could make out were *Don't worry*. She touched his shoulder, then placed the scrambler in the bag. And then, on the hostel's terminal, she made the call to procure a ship—to Toral Anders, former captain of the commercial transport vessel *Solus*, now head of Solus Bussers Incorp. He blinked in surprise when he saw her face through the vid. "I can't believe you're alive," he exclaimed. "Baruk was certain you'd passed in the fringe. Where the hell did you go?"

"It was a job. A long job." She went into no further detail. She looked at her old colleague. Toral was noticeably older, but not so much so, a decade maybe. He had only stopped using the Pocket a few years ago. There were bags under his eyes that betrayed how exhausted he was, but despite that, he was still handsome. "It's good to see you," she said.

"You too, Imani." There was a lost quality to his eyes, like he was staring at a ghost, or a shimmer. It was clear by the tentative smile on his lips that he still remembered the night they had spent together. "What can I help you with?"

"Acclimation," she said. "I left the fold a few weeks ago, only to discover that things have changed while I was under."

"Isn't that always the way. But I bet you weren't expecting the upending of interstellar travel."

"That's the thing. Now that folds are obsolete, I'm looking to reorient my business. I heard the busser movement is strong. Was hoping with your position you had leads on a cheap vessel for me. Something I could start on."

He nodded. "I'll send over a list. Should warn you though, bussing isn't an easy market. It's crowded with hopefuls, most of them failing by month's end, and with the new taxes, it'll be a while before you make it in the black. Umbai's about to open up some Resource Worlds for tourism. Proud to say that Solus Bussers Incorp won the bid on one of those routes." He smiled. "I can make an opening for you, if you want to work with us."

If Nia had no plans of her own, plans that needed to stay secret, she would've considered his offer. "Appreciated. Truly. But I'm going to try on my own for now. I'll come running if it's as bad as you say."

"I hope you do," he said.

She could tell he meant it.

The list he sent her was comprehensive. The names of a few hundred prospective sellers on Galena alone; the histories of the ships, and the offers made and pending. While Sartoris snored on the other bed, she flipped through the list until she found a busser in her price range and to her liking. She called, and then met the seller in the Port Authority. He was a younger man with the drowning look of someone who'd never had a break in his life. He showed her to his busser; a small thing, as squat as a brick, at home in the less-guarded docks of Galena. It was a twenty-seater, and smelled of a sour incense. The back room was crowded with bags of trash, which she threw to the side while the younger man threw out apologies and complained about his lazy fool of a brother, but she paid him little attention. She didn't care about his brother or the trash or the smell. In the engine room she placed her hand on the black box. The Fast Travel Chip. After a test jump, she traded the iotas for his key and sig-card, and he thanked her profusely before running down the dock, as far and as fast as possible, as if afraid she'd reconsider, and renege on the one fair deal he'd known. He did not know that for Nia, there was no reconsidering. That there was only forward.

She tossed the trash out of the busser's entrance.

In the morning, she showed Sartoris inside their new ship. Strapped him to the copilot's chair, and, with her hands in the cat's cradle, guided the ship from port, away from the City Planet. The hull rattled and there was a whisper-sound of air that leaked through the cabin doors, but she was used to old ships. Preferred their marks of history. She smiled once they were outside of orbit and floated in space, far away from all things. She peeled the scrambler from its wrapping, opened the hatch in the floor of the cockpit, and set to the wire work. "What is that?" Sartoris asked from above her, but before she could answer, he shut his eyes, said, "No. Do not tell me. I can remember."

Half her body inside the hole in the floor, she waited.

His mouth hesitated into a smile. "License scrambler," he said.

"That's right," she said with pride.

"So they cannot find us."

"If the theory holds," she grunted, snapping on the last node. She pushed herself back out and ignored the cut on her arm as she withdrew the flute. "Do you remember this?" she asked him.

After a beat, his smile widened.

"It's his," he said.

She winked as she brought the mouthpiece to her lips, and played—

—and like a finger plucking a web, a pulse of music ran down the veins of Pocket Space, a spark through the swirling currents, into the border between, to that dark shore hosted by memory, where a second fire bloomed down the coast, a fire that, though far away, he could see, and hear, even from where he sat: the whisper-voice in its crackle, that voice that hugged him from behind, and the Kind One observed him through their dark eye slits as he sprinted to this second fire, nearly tripping over one of the logs that surrounded it, on his knees before it, shouting as he did before and the busser jumped and City Planet Galena was gone.

They were in deep space now.

There were only stars outside the busser's viewport.

Nia lowered the flute from her mouth, her hands trembling, unable to bottle the vicious swell of emotion, the dared hope now certain, for finally she knew that he was listening.

The jump hadn't taken them far; a single-planet system that neighbored Galena. In orbit of the blue Jovian, Nia paced up and down the busser's aisle, her fingers wrestling with one another, nerves electric, while Sartoris followed her circuit from his perch on one of the passenger seats and listened to her theories. "The way I see it, there are two possibilities," she said. "One. He's alive. Somewhere. And he heard the song, however that's possible, and he reacted. The jump was his way of reaching out. Or." She slowed her walk. Fingers stilled. "He's dead. That what happened with the flute was some . . . reaction to whatever part of him was left behind in the system, and all we did was dance with a shadow." She stopped. "What do you think?"

"Please give me a moment," he said with his hands on his temples, as if rubbing out an ache. "Apologies. This is all a bit much for me. Thinking is somewhat trying. Where are we?"

"Sledge." She sat down beside him. "It's one system from Galena."

"Hardly enough to establish a pattern, is it? Perhaps you should play the flute again, and see where it takes us next."

"Not yet. Morissa warned me to be careful of timing. We should wait a few days before we jump again."

"Terrific. Plenty of time to draft up a plan of action. Let me get something to write with." He fumbled around in his bag for his notebook. But when he pulled the notebook out, he furrowed his brow, returned it, and rummaged some more. He chuckled. "It's around here somewhere."

"You're looking for your notebook," she reminded him.

"I know," he muttered. He pulled it out, along with his pen. Opened up a fresh page and began writing *Our Plan* in slow, trembled letters.

"Maybe I should write," she said.

He ignored her. *Step one. Play flute.*

Drops splattered on the page as he wrote.

Tears.

"Sartoris."

"I need to learn again," he said, writing through the blurred ink. His wet cheeks. "I need to get better."

"Okay," she said.

"So. We have our first step." He cleared his throat, his pen ready. "Now, what is our second?"

For the duration of their three days in orbit of the Jovian swirl, they discussed the plan; what they knew, and what they still needed to learn. The busser was without bedrooms, so at night they slept in the rows of seats, with Sartoris near the front so that he could access the bathroom, and Nia in the back, near the engine, where she was closest to the FT Chip. They knew the chip was responding to the flute song, and they knew the chip itself was in communication with an Umbai capsule that lay somewhere in the Pocket—this was known rumor, but what time-stalled eddy the capsule swirled in no one knew. The information was useless to Nia regardless. She was not a soldier. She couldn't storm a company ship even if it was in real space, and she was unwilling to risk the fold, not even for a day, not one more second of time. All she had was memory—their last

two weeks together on the *Debby*, when he told her of his power—
that when he was lost, it was her song that guided him home. That
was the plan. Guide him home.

"And if he never returns?" Sartoris asked, at night. "If possibility
two is correct, and he is no longer with us . . . what will you do
then?"

"Then I will keep playing," she said. "Until I come to him."

They spoke through the night, while in the place below ancient
instinct, the young man sat on the beach and watched the two fires,
both of which were occupied by his shadow selves, shouting silently
into the flame. The sight of the fires comforted him—enough even to
distract from the nausea he felt, his belly full of knives. The throb in
his head like the gentle nuzzling of a hammer. "More ships fly on
your blood each day," the Kind One, who stood beside him, said.
"They are draining you. Soon there will be nothing left but a husk."

"A husk," he whispered.

He was tired.

"Your death is certain. Nothing will change that. You only prolong the pain with your stubbornness. Unless you can break the sky,
what use is there in remaining?"

A third fire bloomed down the shore.

The young man understood.

"Then I will break the sky," he said.

Umbai made the obligatory gesture of forming a small task force to
keep tabs on the situation, but they knew the task force would in all
likelihood emerge empty-handed. The ID that popped up on the
judiciary was scrambled, untraceable. One in thousands. An itch to
be slapped at but not fussed over, for as ever, they had more pressing
concerns.

They were in the process of creating the New Tourism industry.
The people demanded new places to go. And so the Resource Worlds

once isolated to protect the harvested commodities were opened up for public consumption.

But first, preparations had to be made.

On Umbai-V, in the house at the top of the hill, the governor's son stood behind his bedroom door, listening in on his father's conference with the offworlders in the main room. He strained to understand the words, the sharp yet controlled inflection of his father's voice. The boy was proud of his father. Everyone knew him as a very brave man. But that day, with the unexpected arrival of the offworlders, he was different. Like a cornered animal. And as the boy peeked around the door, he saw his father, slumped in his chair, his face pressed into his hands as he asked the five strangely dressed others if there was no other choice in the matter.

"The contract was signed well before your time," one of the women said in her doubled voice while small jewels floated around her head like stars; the boy tamped down a powerful need to snatch one of the jewels and toss it back into the sky where it belonged. He kept out of sight. "As for your other choices, there is but one alternative. A long and involved process, one that you or"—she glanced toward the boy's room and he hid behind the door—"the others would not likely see the end of. Do you understand what I am saying?" The boy pressed his back against the wall. He did not hear his father say yes, but he supposed he nodded, for then the woman said, "Good. Here is what is going to happen."

It happened like she said it would. The following week, when the ships returned, he asked his mother what they were building in the fields beyond the village. She told him with some wariness in her voice that they would be having many visitors, and that large house was where they would arrive. She held him tighter than she had ever held him before and whispered that it was called a Port.

There was agreement among the adults that the Port was a bad omen, though there were those who never cared for working the fields or milling endless containers of dhuba, and saw in this new construction a chance for a better life. These differing opinions filtered down to the children, who parroted the arguments of their parents and guardians among themselves in the yellow fields, shouting at one another with the ferociousness of those uncertain what they were fighting about, while behind them, the great machines installed the last of the landing pads. The governor's son, like his father, remained quiet. After the Port was finished, and with it the tall building called a Hotel, which blocked the eastern view of the river delta with its glass body, the first of the visitors came. They came on strange ships, wearing strange clothes, with guards that wore outfits a nauseating yellow. He stayed glued to his father's hand as these visitors approached the village, until his father shook him off and smiled for the first time since he spoke to the representatives, and welcomed them, the offworlders.

The governor's son was young enough that he would one day forget the strangeness of these new quantities. In time he would no longer remember the unease as the tourists walked the roads of their village, looking at everything, his home, as if in wonder at how anyone could live like this. Nor would he remember his anger when one of them was offered a bowl of unsweetened, unworked dhuba, and after thumbing a taste, spat it on the ground, making a sour face as his friends laughed at him; or the embarrassed joy when one of them crouched in front of him and asked him with a kind smile what his name was. One day, his memory of these first visitors would evaporate, and he would believe that they had always been there; that of course they would march through the stalks, disturbing the soil, to ask one of the startled farmers if they could try a swing of her machete. That was what they did.

Life adjusted around these people, with new buildings erected to accommodate their growing numbers. The representatives suggested that the people of the Fifth Village learn Station Standard. Some of the visitors stayed and taught the children. By the time he was eight, the governor's son had basic fluency, which made his father and mother proud, or so he at first thought. He never understood why they would forbid him from speaking in Station Standard when they sat down to eat. They never told him the reason for this rule, but there were times when he thought he got it—when he saw his father look at him as if he were a stranger.

The boy did as he was told. He kept the new language to himself. And he absorbed the new teachings, unaware that his life was beginning to split in two, right down the sternum. There was little else for him to do but adapt.

Change was coming regardless.

Change approached on the wings of music. Nia played her flute, and he chased the fires. The third flute-jump brought them to another neighboring system. The same with the fourth. And the fifth. Sartoris wrote his observations. *There is no*—"What's the word for when two things are related?" he asked her. "Correlation," she told him—*correlation between the song Nia plays & our destination. The same notes bring our busser to different stations or no station at all. The dead spot between stars. Our end points are random. We skip on reflex. Her note is the hammer on the knee. The jump is the leg twitch.*

Fires sprouted down the shore, from nothing. The woman's voice doubled and tripled, and was carried on the sea breeze that made the hairs on his arms stand on end, as if the hairs too were listening. The Kind One watched him impassively as he threw himself at these new fires and shouted into the flame. But the response never changed—there was always the static, the waver, as if she were asking a question with words that were beyond him. All he could do was shout louder.

Tenth jump. *The only pattern that we can detect is that the more we play, the farther our jumps go. Instead of neighboring systems, we skip over the stars. But there is no shape to our journey—nothing that can give us any direction other than to keep playing, with the hope that the increasing distances are a sign in our favor.*

Twelfth jump.

Nia says it is like having a one-sided conversation.

She could feel him just beyond the door, but the door had no key, not even a lock, only a jammed knob. And while Sartoris slept in his cordoned section of the busser, his body draped across a row of seats, she crouched before the busser's engine, the black box, her hands pressed against her forehead as she asked for a clearer sign, the black box remaining silent, unaware how on the other side, the young man walked the necklace of fires with the Kind One dogging his step, ignoring the ache in his chest and in his head that grew in strength each hour as he waited for the next whisper.

"Nothing will come of this," the Kind One muttered.

Fortieth jump. *We are poor. The funds Nia had earned on the Kerrigan have dwindled, forcing us to return the busser to its original function.* In the desert flats beyond the sounder's outpost, Nia threw down the last stroke of white paint. Sartoris glanced up from his book and read aloud the name she had painted on the side of the busser. "The *Ahro Imani.*" He cracked a smile. "A bit obvious, isn't it?" She flung paint at him. *Now we scuttle passengers between the recently acquired fringe worlds, where there is less competition, for the City Planet plans are still being drafted. I serve the drinks to our twenty guests, suggesting the pairings with our frugal selection of snacks, while Nia pilots us to the next world.*

They made their routes in the days between flute jumps. It was an involving job, and sometimes swallowed entire weeks with its menial upkeep and bureaucracy. Once, a whole month lost when the busser was suspended pending a "thorough" safety inspection, when a passing Allied inquisitor decided he did not like the rattle of its thruster. They brushed the chairs of crumbs and cleared out their makeshift beds before the passengers boarded. Switched off the scrambler before hailing the judiciary for authorization. Endured the long wait in the queue, which would more often than not span the better part of a day. Sometimes authorization would spring up at random; there was no choice but to hole up and wait. To placate the restless passengers who were without neural entertainments, they scattered objects around the cabin that would pass the time. Packs of Tropic Shuffle and pipes and books. A long-necked lyn from Suda-Sulai, which Nia ended up playing more than anyone else, for she could not play the flute when they had company, and the lyn was the closest she could get to being in his company.

She sometimes plays music for our guests. Strums simple chords to the popular songs of the day.

Sixtieth jump.

She has gotten quite good.

Eightieth.

She makes her own songs now.

As she played, in the place below ancient instinct, by the light of the hundredth flame, the young man could hear it. Her song. It was faint, all but a feeling. But still he could hum along to the notes, and remember the words of homecoming. And it was as he listened that the Kind One placed their gloved hand on their mask and removed it, revealing the face of a woman, tall and strong, who looked at him like he was brighter than the fire itself. A woman whose name was just beyond his tongue.

She held out her hand.

"Come with me across the water," she said.

He felt himself unspool when he stood up, and left her. Fought the temptation to turn back as he tracked the static whisper to the next light—the one hundred and first, at the end of the fiery chain that rambled down the shore, and to the dozens, and hundreds, that followed.

It was a long march on feet with soles pricked by a directionless pain. He bore through it. The Kind One shadowed him on this march, appearing before him at the next fire without taking a single step, the beguiling mask always there to greet him, and tempt him with that final route across the water. Three hundredth fire. They tempted him with faces. They would remove their mask and show him the faces from his past. The hard-nosed veteran, the doctor with the immaculately trimmed beard, and the engineer who made a habit of glancing over his shoulder at the imagined shadows that were behind him. Four hundredth fire. The bald teacher with generous eyes, and that young man from the mountaintop, whose shattering eyes pinned him into place and flared his heart, along with the long line of fires behind him, the shoreline bright with his desire. The people he cared for, speaking now with the Kind One's voice, telling him to let go. All of them tempting, but none more than the woman he now remembered was a captain, and who once sold her mother's prized books for a ticket offworld. Difficult, but comfortable. A kinship in the hard-won lessons. Tacit understanding of each other's hurt. A friend he once feared would leave him, but who never did, for where else would she go, with eyes so fierce with love? These were the faces the Kind One threw at him, always with hand outstretched, beseeching him to give in. Five hundred fires now. They were just behind him, asking why he did not stop. Could he not bear the pain? Umbai showered his blood onto the FT Chips of the Personal Flyers, each release of these ships, and each jump, a prick on the young man's skin, a pluck of a nerve that tripped his step. Did he not know that this road led to the same end? Six hundred. The swarm of stings built to a crescendo, and Umbai smeared his blood onto the heart of the Pelican and jumped the massive station down the galactic arm, proclaiming their dominion on the black ocean, and his body. His heart seized, doubling him over onto the sand. "Your body will only withstand so much," the Kind One whispered, crouched beside him. "You are a glass bird in a vise, and that vise is squeezing. You will crack. You will shatter." They shook their head. "You beg to return to a world that has beaten you. A world that even now is siphoning the life from you so that it can grow large enough to swallow all cardinal directions. Why do you waste your time walking this shore? Why attempt this return?"

He gritted his teeth and pushed himself back on his feet, his hand clutched to his chest as he drag-stepped to the next fire.

"Because she is waiting for me," he said.

And she was, even as she grew older over the years of her music, and all that she had seen and lived through now made their witness marks on her body; the happy wrinkles hardening into crows'-feet, the joints going rigid, and the hair sprouting new and varied grays. Through age, she waited. Some days she was hot, very hot, to the point of claustrophobia, as if a blanket had been smothered over her body. Those were the days when she sat on the roof of the busser and played her lyn, cooling herself off on the lip of a wind-blown canyon. A week spent landed on the last of the fringe worlds, the last of the rocks not stamped by an Umbai spire. No strata in sight. Only the ache in her arm as she held the lyn and pulled from its strings her songs while, below, Sartoris listened to the tribble of notes through the opened busser door.

There are things missing in my memory—residual gaps from my coma. She tells me stories of the crew that we once traveled with, but their names are gone. It is only when I hear her play these songs that I can grasp it—the blur of faces.

Faces of old friends.

Nia played for the shadows that gathered around the busser. The dozens she'd once known, their ghosts come for the performance.

At the head of them, Deborah, and Nurse.

Old friends that slip away when I reach for them. The shape of them like paper cutouts. A play of one act, before the curtain is drawn, & they are gone again. I wonder why my brain bothers to retain these abstractions. What use is it to me, to hold on to these half-formed memories? Where am I supposed to put them? What pocket?

"I'm not going to stop," Nia told them, for she had long since learned her life's purpose. Accepted the nature of herself: that she would always, and ever, chase after what was just out of reach. Even if it was, in the end, a shadow.

Nurse smiled, and Deborah nodded.

We know.

Maybe it's enough that they are there at all, he wrote.

The shouts rang past time and location. Six hundred fiftieth jump. There were nights when it almost ended; when she lay beside the black box, howled, and raged, and when the Kind One almost convinced him the pain was not worth the process, and he would look into the dark water and think how tempting it was, to walk that distance.

Seven hundredth jump. But always there was another fire in bloom, and a new chance to shout his coordinates. She would play her song, and he would find that new flame, and together, they would add another voice to the choir. Eight hundredth jump. Even when their bodies went ragged and age clawed its way down her back and made it hurt to sit upright, and the new fleets dragged the air from his lungs and he shivered in the dark, they continued. Past the nine hundredth jump, the nine hundredth fire. Time leaping from their fingers and their tongues as they chipped away at the wall, her music and his shout; his many shadow selves his chorus as their cries echoed through the flames and down the vaults of the Pocket, and made the bonfires erupt and dance. Their music was an assault. It was the moment itself. The unshakable feeling that they were working toward something, together. A finger, in some distant capsule, twitching to the beat. Both of them with hands held out as they whittled away the years, until one day, the music stopped, and the interstellar dance then ended.

Here: the year and hour when Umbai jumped their first surveyor ship to Andromeda, the distance between galaxies, and the farthest anyone had ever gone before.

It was the last great act. The company had pulled the string to its breaking point. When that surveyor ship made its leap from out of the Milky Way, the last of him was torn from his chest. Life's energy fluttered out parted lips. His legs gave. And in a silent humph, his face met the sand.

He knew he would not rise again.

The Kind One lifted him up into their arms. Their voices were gentle as they told the young man, "There is no shame in this."

And in the sad and sweet tones of their voices, he knew that they spoke the truth. He was limp. He would not move again. They carried him past the line of bonfires, and toward the water. There was nothing left in him. "Some roads go on and on," the Kind One said. "And some roads end before their route. But no road goes on forever.

"All of them are half-finished circles," they said.

The Kind One's feet touched the surface of the black water. Their steps made no ripple as they began the long walk to the other side. The young man pressed his face against their chest as they journeyed across the water, and the shoreline shrank, the fires small now, the rage of their burn dying. The farther he went from shore, the less important it all was.

He pressed his hands to himself. He was shaking. It was surprising to him, how tired he could be, and still so scared. As if reading his thoughts, as if being his thoughts, the Kind One squeezed him against their chest, just a little, just enough to feel it. And in that moment, he knew that he was ready to let go.

"You tried," the Kind One said.

I tried.

"That's enough for anyone to be proud of."

Be proud.

He relaxed in their embrace, and was borne on their floating walk across the water. I am proud, I am proud; these words his last prayer, as they voyaged from that brightly lit shore to where the tired ones go to rest.

"They took so much from you," the Kind One murmured. "Take comfort in the fact that even if you emerged today, it would have likely been your last."

The young man recognized this truth. He could feel it in the cracked bone and the turned-out flesh of him. But the words also stirred in him another truth—a deeper one, pinned to the lyrics of an old farmer's song.

"They could take my day," he said—leaned forward, just a bit— "but I'd still have the night."

He was not sure where those words had come from. Like the shore, and the Kind One themselves, it was another thing unearthed. Woven into the fabric of him. A hint of the first parting he could not remember. And when he looked up, he saw it: the hairline crack that ran down the latitude of stars. That fissure of light above the coast that had been slowly unraveling itself, all this time, like the loose thread of a sleeve by an agitated thumb—ready now to be torn open.

It was then that he saw the birth of a new flame. The thousandth of her fires wavered like a star before dawn, weak but still living, beyond his reach, and calling to him from the end of the shore.

In the cockpit of the busser, she played on, to no response. Sartoris watched her fluteplay, the frantic madness of notes, his face sagging as he accepted what she could not. Hunched in his chair, his whole body resting against his cane, he whispered the truth.

"I think that's it," he said.

"I'm sorry, Nia," he said.

But after fifteen years, there was too much momentum to stop her. There was no choice but to play to a leaving audience. She did not stop playing. Even after Sartoris had returned to the cabin, she did not stop. Even after the busser went into standby and the lights switched to dreamer's blue. Even after she knew that it was over.

As he was drawn deeper toward the heart of the cold water, it struck him, this sudden and wretched ache to be near that last fire's warmth. He demanded that the Kind One take him back. They sighed, and stopped their walk on the tip of a frozen wave. "If that is what you wish," they said. They brought him to the thousandth bonfire, the last bonfire, and laid him beside its crackle, its still-audible whispering, and it was there, by the sound of her voice, calling to him, where the young man let out his final shout, and completed the circle.

The busser jumped. It settled against the wind currents of the new atmosphere. And something in Nia's heart stirred as she gazed through the viewport at the purple fields of Umbai-V.

An old ache.

The world had changed with new industry. They sailed past the cluster of hotel spires, the bridge port, and the large factory beyond the fields, landing in the outskirts of the Fifth Village, where few things were still recognizable from the time when ships traveled the long way around. There were fold-out capsule homes shipped from Umbai-Fac to accommodate the growing population, stacked atop one another in looming towers. Children from windows high up watched her and Sartoris pass through the crooked streets. Some shouted at them in Standard. *Look at me. Pretty, pretty. Why are you with that old man?* They walked on. Few of the homes were still constructed from dhuba stalk and the wood from the nearby forest, and as far as Nia could tell, no one lived in those.

"Why do you think he brought us here?" Sartoris wondered.

She couldn't say.

Today was a break day for the Fifth Village. There were no tourists walking the roads. The two of them were the only visitors, and were for the most part ignored, while the residents prepared the main plaza for an event later that night. Tables were carried out and propped open. Freestanding torches were dug into the ground, circling the perimeter—in the center, the collection of wood for a great fire. Nia caught the attention of one of the men preparing the tables, and asked him if this was all for Shipment Day, to which he answered with a blank stare. *Of course it isn't,* she thought, feeling ridiculous for even mentioning it. The man and his friends stared warily at her. Seeing no graceful way out, she offered to help stack the wood for the fire they were building. They accepted, almost out of sheer surprise that it was offered to begin with, and she worked through the burning pain in her shoulder, glad that she had found some use for herself here. Once the last of the timber was dropped into the pit, they invited her and Sartoris to stay for the celebrations. One of the men asked her for her name. She told him it was Nia, and that it was an Old Earth name, and when he smiled, she thought he was going to make a pass, but he only nodded and walked away. She laughed at how disappointed she was that she had not found another Kaeda; was glad she still had the capacity to expect such a thing, and to want it. This was no longer the world of her memory.

That world was gone.

The event that night was a birthday party for one of the governor's sons. While Sartoris admired the spread of food on the long table, she leaned against the wall, feeling a keen déjà vu as she watched the young people dance. The governor's son fumbled his arms around the hips of a woman who was unaware of his presence. Is this why we're here? To watch kids grope each other? She tipped her cup and drank. She felt impatient, but she didn't know what for. Something about the youths who held one another around the heart of the flame agitated her, the nervous energy of them reminding her of the time in her life she was given to dancing, and the sway of men. The memories did not make her happy. She needed to be alone.

"Where are you going?" Sartoris asked, breaking briefly from a conversation when he noticed her stand up.

"For a walk," she said. "I'll be back soon."

"Would you like company?"

"Not tonight." She touched his shoulder. "Stay, old man. Enjoy the fire."

He smiled up at her.

At the edge of the plaza, she looked back at her friend with great fondness as he regaled the table with old busser stories, his words finally returned to him. She left Sartoris where he was always meant to be, holding court over good drink, and bribed the guard at the gate to let her through. She walked down the dark and rutted road at an ambling pace, her way lit by the torch in her hand, and she journeyed past the black looming structures that were the new citizens of the fields as she searched for the reason why her heart was compelled toward these outskirt hills.

Fumiko sensed it; the change of direction in the air. Her eyes opened against the sunlight that cut between the tops of the buildings and gilded the languid waves of the waterway. Dana's legs were stretched out along the passenger's bench, her eyes half-lidded like a pleased cat as her hand draped over the side and grazed the calm water. At the head of the boat the oarsman guided the vessel around a curve. He nodded at Fumiko. And Fumiko understood that her long route through the Pocket was almost ended.

"We're close," she said.

Dana followed her gaze upward. The sun was gone, and the clouds had begun to darken. The canal waters rippled with small detonations. Together they watched the breaking of the sky in silence. Both knew that nothing more needed to be said.

It was time.

And while in her delirium Fumiko accepted the inevitable and fast-approaching end, Nia continued her walk through the outskirts of the village, listening to the quiet of the rolling hills, and the subtle buzz and flip of night bugs. The wind that whistled through the rows of dhuba. By then she was a kilometer from the village. She spotted a nice hill from where she could get a view. It was a surprisingly steep climb up to the top. She winced against the complaints of the body, but made it undamaged over the last rise. She looked out at the dark fields, and their tough, unyielding stalks. There was something about this place. Something important.

In the place below ancient instinct, the young man and his Kind One gazed up at the fracture in the sky. The light from which they could hear the memory of a song.

They waited.

Once in a rare while, there is an alignment. Moments that, to some, reveal the workings of God, and to others are simple fortune. But there is no known explanation for this communion of events.

It only is.

And then she remembered what this place was. The fine hairs on her neck standing on end as the memory unzipped itself.

Below that hill and behind that rock was where she and Kaeda first embraced. She flashed the light of her torch on the grass by the rock, and she remembered how long that night felt; long, in a good way, like a walk for walk's sake. She remembered the feel of her head lying against his chest, and the song he hummed for her—the vibration she could feel through her cheek when he sang the words.

The notes were coming back to her; notes to a song with a name she could not remember. To her, all it was, was the song of her youth—one that was leaving, as quickly as it had come, its notes fading from memory before she pulled the flute from her back pocket and caught it.

It was a song many years old, from the time before the harvest. The song the mother sang to her newborn son in the quiet dark of morning. The song she imbued into his flesh and bone, its melody and its lyrics, before the people of the Quiet Ship came and took her son away, on a journey of suffering that would stretch past her lifetime. The song she would hum to herself in the long years after he was gone as she held her hand up to the sky and imagined him reaching down to take it.

It was the song that was passed down the generations of this world. The song the farmers chorused when the work was done and it was time to return to the village, wheeling behind them their purple harvest. *Take my day*, they sang, *but give me the night. Feed the hearth and ready the brew, for I am coming home to you.* It was the song he heard when he first returned to this world, as he sat with the old man on the top of the hill and witnessed the return of the farmers; the sweet pastry in his hands forgotten as he listened to this song and was captured by it; the words foreign to him yet somehow familiar, unaware that the words were in his blood, woven into him decades ago by a mother who missed him.

It was the song that now inspired the fires along the dark shore of his ancient instinct and bloomed them into tornadoes of flame.

Flames that whipped into the broken night sky of his opiated dreams and ripped through the black veil, the light let in through the open tear, along with the memory of his name. The name he had chosen for himself with the help of the Kind One, who, with the kaleidoscope of faces of all those he loved, now picked him up and lifted him toward the shattering fracture, into the widening hole of light, until,

he opened his eyes.

Dry eyes that needled in pain as he tried to focus beyond the drugs still coursing through his system. He was awake, but only half so; a tether on his mind, urging him back to sleep. Through half-lidded eyes he looked around, and he listened. It was quiet in his capsule. He could not hear the commotion on the other side of the door and the observation window, where the technicians on duty were frantic as the screens alerted them of his sudden consciousness; was unaware of their flurry of movement, the scroll-screens and vitality drinks tossed aside as they dialed up the dosage beyond safe levels to stop his escape. He dove back into sleep.

Fell like a rock into the black.

There was a rising hum in Nia's throat, as if she were possessed by something other than herself, something greater, as she let loose from the flute this song of homecoming. She played the notes that rippled throughout the currents and pinged her coordinates.

His skeletal hand twitched in its restraint. His eyelids fluttering while in the dark spot of his mind he swam upward against the narcotic drift, reaching for the constellation of notes above him. The drugs like a hand on his ankle, dragging him farther downward.

"Get the needle!" the head tech cried as he keyed the code and opened the door to the capsule's chamber.

He clawed toward the light of her fevered music. The system pulsed in time with his quickened heart, and in sympathy the FT-capable ships throughout the galaxy leapt randomly and beyond control of the judiciary, millions of them, the bussers, vipers, and personal flyers dancing around the stars, the binary planets, the giants, the spiraling systems, the nebulae, the red dwarfs, the rainbow-stained gas columns, everywhere, no one sure what was happening, ships lost, then found, then lost again, the hundred stations warping to random points. Pelican Station, gone from its perch in the controlling sector of the galaxy—now leveling under its great weight a pinewood forest as the birds quit the canopy in its wake.

The tech bit the cap from the narcotic pen. Raised it like a stake, aimed for Acquisition's chest as he waited for his partner to open the capsule and the chance to deliver this finishing move.

The lever was halfway pulled when she arrived.

Fumiko's schooner broke from the Sibilant Current and joined this eddy in the Pocket, at the center of which the capsule swirled, like a rubber toy dancing at the drain of a faucet. She wore neither smile nor frown as she pulled the strings of the cat's cradle toward her chest and opened the starboard sails, and careened her ship down the eddy's centrifuge toward her fated target. There was only the strict jaw of focus, the clarity of eyes that saw the entire route of a life and had made peace with all of it, determined now to finally meet the end of a thousand-year journey. It happened quickly. The nose of her ship accordioned against the wall of the capsule station, and her body flung forward from her seat. Before her head met the viewport and it all went black, she could swear she heard the high, piercing note of a song—a note that gave her peace before the schooner crumpled and, between the mash of metal, the YonSefs detonated.

Fractures ran across the capsule's spherical hull in the space between seconds, chased by the light. A bright ball that hiccupped and swelled. Vaporized in an instant the corridors, the bunks, the mess hall, the console theater; the techs at work, and the techs at play, none of them aware of Fumiko's arrival, or her exit, before they

were swept away by her last willful shrug. And in this space between seconds, before the iridescence of the YonSefs' light swept
him away too, Acquisition's eyes snapped open, the old instinct
awakened against the approach of danger; the bow of him drawn.

The arrow let loose through the stars.

It was when Nia had sliced off the final note of the song that she
heard it. The rumble in the clouds.

The crack.

The object punctured the sky. She watched as in the middle distance the object crashed with a bloom. And she ran. Ran down the
hill, throwing off the sandals that slowed her progress, ran through
the stalks, soles cut on fibrous shards that jutted from the dirt, and
ran with lungs on fire, her hands on knees when she arrived in the
charred clearing the explosion had made, stumbling past the blackened chunks of metal, the ground hot under her feet, nothing in her
lungs at all when she saw, in the epicenter of this small crater, the
smooth capsule the size of a coffin. Hands shaking as she reached
out and touched the capsule and burned herself on its knife heat.
She grabbed the capsule's handle, her body beyond physical sensation as she gritted her teeth and forced the lever clockwise, her nostrils filled with the smell of her cooked palm skin, until the latches
released and the capsule door sighed open like an oyster's mouth.
Cold mist curled past her feet as she stepped toward the opening
and looked inside, her breath stopped when she saw what lay within
the capsule, nested among a medusa of black cables.

The naked body of a grown man. His limbs long and emaciated.
The skin of his face taut around the skull and the skin of his body
crisscrossed with scars both faint and vivid. A story of pain. She
peeled away the tubes that pockmarked his body and drew out the
long, clear vine that was snaked down his esophagus. Pressed two
fingers to his thin throat, relieved by his turtling pulse. And she
picked him up, carrying him away from the crash, trying not to

think about how his body was as light as paper. The two of them crashing out of the fields, out into the road, where on the dirt she sat down, exhausted. Holding him in her lap as she wheezed. Her chest diving deep to swallow the air while he stirred in her arms, murmuring incoherently from his dry, cracked lips. "Don't talk," she said, smoothing the sweat from his forehead. "Save your energy." But he disregarded his captain's order. He lifted his head. And when he opened his eyes, she was glad that, despite the years, his eyes were still those wide, dark beauties. That time had changed nothing; not even the music in his voice, as he whispered, "I heard you."

Acknowledgments

Countless people helped in some small way, but space is limited and memory unreliable, so I'll stick with who comes to mind today. The last year of this project was hard on me. Matt Johnson and his awful dad jokes were bright spots, as was the company of the wonderful Merab Okeyo and Nouria Bah, who since high school liked to remind me of the world outside my bedroom; and of course the funny and talented Oscar Mancinas and Doug Koziol and our unending and sorely needed phone calls. Thank you to my readers, Anthony Martinez and Prof. Jessica Treadway, for their comprehensive and useful perspectives, and my main reader, Erin Jones, whom I bombarded with drafts and endless questions and general neuroses that she, in her supernaturally gracious way, accepted and addressed, and always left me feeling better than I did before. My thesis adviser, Prof. Kim McLarin, for her generosity of spirit and time, and her effortlessly insightful feedback, without which this book wouldn't be half as good—her students are fortunate indeed, for she's one of the best. Shout-out to my agent, Hannah Fergesen, and my editor, Sarah Peed, both of whom have given me phenomenal support through the publishing process. Thank you, Hannah, for believing in this project, and thank you, Sarah, for sharpening it. It is a privilege to have such a formidable team. And lastly, my family. Mom and Dad. My brothers, Quinn, Kane, Garth, Sebastian, and Nicholas (Farrah and Clarissa), and my sister, Sara. It is a rare and lucky thing, to not only love, but to be fond of everyone you're related to, and to enjoy their company; rare, and lucky, and mine.

Read on for an excerpt from Simon Jimenez's
next standalone novel,

The Spear Cuts Through Water.

Before you arrive,

you remember your lola, smoking. You remember the smell of her dried tobacco, like hay after a storm. The soft crinkle of the rolling paper. The zip of the matchstick, which she'd sometimes strike against the lizard-rough skin of her leg, to impress you. You remember the ritual of it. Her mouth was too dry to lick the paper shut so she had you do it, the twiggy pieces of tobacco sticking to your tongue like bugs' legs as you wetted the edges. She told you it was an exchange. Your spit for her stories. Tales of the Old Country; of ruined kingdoms and tragic betrayals and old trees that drank the blood of foxes foolish enough to sleep amongst their sharp roots; any tale that could be told in the span of one quickly burning cigarette. "It was all so very different back then," she'd begin, and you'd watch the paper curl and burn between her fingers as she described the one hundred wolves who hunted the runaway sun, and the mighty sword Jidero, so thin it could cut open the space between seconds. Her words forever married to the musk of her cigarette and her bone-rattling laughter; so much so that whenever you think of that place, long ago and far away, you cannot help but think of smoke, and death.

When did she first tell you of the Inverted Theater?

You were thirteen, you think; it was around that age that she often seemed startled by you, offended even, her lip curling whenever you came into the room, as if an untoward stranger had just tripped into her on the street. You thought her distaste was because of your body odor, your oily skin, your shy hunch, but the truth was she was just surprised by how quickly time had passed. Your youth wounded her. It made her want to protect you, and to kick you out the door.

"Sit," she said, when she saw you passing the kitchen. "Listen. I have a tale to tell."

The warm, breeze-blown night came in through the propped-open window, playing at the sheer curtains and the smoke from your lola's fingers, as she told you of the theater that stood between worlds.

"Once, the Moon and the Water were in love." She lingered on that word, love, just as the smoke lingered in the air. "You can imagine it was not the most convenient affair. One was trapped in the heavens, the other the earth. One was stillness itself, the other made only of waves and tempests. But they were happy for a time. The Moon would bathe the Water in its radiance, and the Water would dance, with its ebb and flow, to the Moon's suggestion. And though they occupied different spheres, they were able to visit one another through less direct means, for there is no barrier in this life that love cannot overcome. The Water would send up to the skies plump storm clouds, swollen with its essence, its cool mist and salty breath kissing the Moon's dry and cracked surface. And the Moon, when it wished to visit the Water, would cast its reflection into the Water's surface, and in the Inverted World that lies suspended below our own, in glass and still water, they would meet, and dance, and make love." Your lola paused, and stared at you from between curls of smoke, in study of your expression. There was a time when you would be squeamish at the mere hint of intimacy in her tales, but not this time; this time you simply sat in rapt attention—a sign of maturity that both heartened and depressed her. "Anyway," she said, after a rasped inhalation. "It was in that world of reflection where they built the theater that is the locus of our tale.

"Being the patron gods of artists and dancers, the Moon and the Water both loved the stage, which is why they created their own: a pagoda so tall its height cuts through the heavenly bands, within which the performances of the ages would be hosted. The telling of tales beyond even my knowing." She coughed. "Even after the Moon and the Water parted ways, the theater remained, run by their love-child, a being of immense beauty who took to inviting even mortals such as us to come visit their arena."

You asked her how mortals could reach such a place.

"Through dreams," she said, the cigarette butt ash in her hand. "A deep sleep, in waters deeper than your dreaming spirit has ever swum before. That's all. Dreams, and luck. And when you arrive, you are told a tale of the Old Country; the right tale at the right time. And when you leave—when your body comes up from that deep slumber—you will feel satisfied, whole, though you will not remember why, the memory of your visit forgotten, slipped from the mind like soapy water, the way any good dream might the more one tries to recall it. You will try to remember it. With great effort." She smiled, wistful. "But you will fail."

Your lola began rolling another cigarette.

"Perhaps before the end," she said, "I'll finally remember my own time there."

There was giggling from the other room. As your lola worked the tobacco through the rolling paper, you leaned back in your chair to better look at your brothers, who were listening to the radio in the living room. All nine of them were crowded around the radio like stray cats at a butcher's shop—a leg draped over the arm of the couch—a head lolling off the side of the love seat—chins propped on fists on the coffee table as the weekly serial neared its climax—*all of the inquisitor's men aiming their rifles at the church windows, ready to shoot Captain Domingo dead, wondering as they aimed down their sights why the jackal dared to smile at the hour of his death—the reason clear, once the good captain revealed with a wink the detonator in his gloved hand*—and as you looked at your brothers, you felt both envious that you were not sitting with them and also glad that you were apart from them. That you could see them all from your chair in the kitchen. That you could hold them all in your eye and keep them there.

"We might try to go back," your lola said, staring out the window with her large, wet eyes, "but we only get one turn. One invite. So do not waste it. If nothing else, remember that."

The night air came in through the small kitchen window. A horn from an old car blared down the road. Your father would be home soon with the day heavy on his shoulders. The table still needed to be made. But your lola was unconcerned with time, her drags deep and unhurried. "You will not know the Inverted Theater has called for you until you are already there," she said as she let the paper burn, and the years burn with it. "It is a place you cannot plan for." The shutters trembled against the coastal breeze. "And when you arrive, dream-tripped and unexpectedly, in that amphitheater, the best thing you can do is sit, and watch, and listen, for you are not there by accident."

She sucked on the paper, the tip now an orange rose. The cigarette was just about finished when the front door slammed open.

Your brothers scattering from the radio as your father came inside with his mood and all the outside world—your lola gripping your wrist, before you too could go to greet him.

"The tale is for you," she said.

The tobacco burning in her lungs.

"So let the dreaming body go."

She exhaled.

And the smoke, blown in from the dark, envelops you until all you can see are the curls of gray matter swirling around you, the thick fog seeming to lift you, to cradle you, bearing you gently downward until you light upon a smooth, hard surface, and the smoke clears— the memory of your lola in the kitchen fading as day does to dusk, before you find yourself standing before the very place she had once spoken of, all those years ago.

Welcome to the Inverted Theater.

You step out of the smoke and you see it: the towering pagoda on a still lake at night, its reflection in the water perfect, its many levels at once rising high above you and, in its watery likeness, falling end- lessly below. Lanterns hang off its curved eaves like earrings, light- ing up its ornate facade against the darkness of the black-carpet sky. The structure looms, made up of an infinite stack of balconies, each one painted a different color. From a purple balcony high up a her- ald leans over and shouts that the performance is soon to begin, to please enter and take your seat.

A stone path begs you to cross the dark water. As you begin your crossing, you realize you do not walk alone. You walk amongst a river of other dreaming shades, who pass through you like gusts of wind, their thoughts coming in and out like radio signals. They are thinking about work. About lost loves. The hours they wasted in rooms darkly lit by stubbed tallow candles. *I was keeping the books for a madman. I knew I needed a new job, but I couldn't risk the downtime—who can risk the downtime?* Some you understand, others are beyond you. They speak in languages you do not recognize, or in terms that, stripped of context, mean nothing. *Thread-ripping down the runner of stars, was in the midst of my third weft, fast a-tumble in my sleeper's mitt, when my dreaming self was coaxed here, to this dark lake shore.* Shades of people from everywhere and everywhen. Faceless, out of focus, loud. And as you cross this lake, their noise comes all at once and overwhelmingly, sounding like nothing less than the vast ocean's roar—a collective hum, breathed out by the mouths of thousands, indistinct and infinite. An infinity in which you now sit.

Eighth row, dead center.

You blink, and you are here—in this many-pewed theater space, lush in drapes and blackwood flooring. The theater is styled from an era long past and almost forgotten. You are seated on a bench that has been reserved for you. You knew this was your seat before you even laid eyes on it. Called to it. Certain of your destination.

You are less certain about other things. As the others find their own seats and the attendants run up and down the aisles with lit candles floating behind them, the tall shade sitting beside you leans over and asks you where you are from.

You struggle to answer.

This moonlit body comes to your aid. With a gentle nudge of the toe, it unfurls the parchment of your people's history, this toe running along the battles and the treaties, the dispersals and the reunions, until it finds you here: in the time of trains and steamships, when cathedral radios crackled from the open windows of the dockside town in which you lived.

There is a war, you tell the shade.

The shade nods in grim understanding.

You are from a time of posters and propaganda. When news of the war effort fluttered down the painted walls of crooked alleys. Sun-draped and salt-scented ocean views disrupted by the silhouettes of warships in the blue distance. Wounded soldiers sometimes boated into town. The war is everywhere, but if you were awake tonight—this night, now—and you turned the dial of your radio, you would not hear the staticky voice of a slick man sharing news of the front but instead the crooning warble of Dorrado "Chilo" Semina, whose voice has captured the hearts of most lovesick listeners across the Unioned Continent—but alas! Tomorrow morning, when you wake, you will have to lie to your compatriots when they ask you if you stayed up to listen to his new single, and you will have to pretend to sing along with their delighted chorus, mouthing the words you shamefully have yet to commit to memory, because right here, right now, as the people of your town swoon to the pop signal, your body lies in deep slumber in a room once shared by you and your nine brothers.

That is you. A merchant's child. But one of many. How old you are outside this dream is irrelevant; in this theater you are as you feel—a youth, deep in your adolescence, and, like all youths, lonely in your own unnameable way. Fearful of your father and hounded by your lola, who was uninterested in the developments of your body, or your roaming interests, as she sucked smoke from a wrinkled cigarette and explained to you the land your family had come from and the tales that had come with them. "There is no preparing for the Inverted Theater," she had said. "It greets you when it chooses."

All of this you say to the shade, and it nods, satisfied, before it turns away to other business. You wonder if you should ask it where it is from, but the shade seems very much done with you, so instead you look about this Inverted Theater with a lost expression, your awe for your surroundings mixed with a deep longing, and unanswerable confusion, as you try to divine for what reason you might have been summoned here.

"There is always a reason."

You begin to suspect it might have to do with the object you only now realize you are holding in your hands.

This spear.

You know it well; the blood-red tint of the wood; the red tassel that chokes the gleaming and deadly point; the strange grooves and etchings that travel the length of the weapon in esoteric patterns. Ever since you can remember, this weapon has dutifully hung on the family room mantel, ignored by all in your house as but part of the scenery, for it was too expensive, too ancient, and too useless to interact with. You and your brothers once caught holy hell for playing with it in the courtyard when you were very young. One of the housekeepers informed your father, and your father, who never hit you but knew other ways to make you feel small, spoke to you and your brothers, one by one, in his office, and never again did you touch the weapon, much less look at it, which is why you feel an illicit thrill to hold it now, whether it be the real thing or merely a dream of it.

"It has traveled far to get here," your lola liked to say, "with farther yet to go."

You notice the other members of the audience, the other shades, stealing furtive glances at your weapon. *We were wondering why this shadow was armed.* And they are wondering why the weapon looks so familiar. Why you have brought it with you to this sacred place. And if you intended to use it.

But such questions would have to wait.

For it begins.

The performance that you have been called to witness. You hear the beat of a drum. A polished wooden stick rapping against taut, oiled skin. Thrum. The drum punches through this dark space. Thrum. It strikes you, right there, the middle of your chest. Thrum. *It made us shiver to hear it.* You listen to the heartbeat of this building. Thrum. The swelled, anticipatory breath of the people around you. Thrum. And you lower the family spear, you let it rest at a slant against your side, forgotten for now, while you and the other audience members all turn to the stage with not a breath released, your unblinking eyes watching the drapes begin their soft and silent lift up into the rafters, revealing, like parted wings, the stage.

Thrum.

This moonlit body stands before you. And though this is your first meeting, all of you recognize this body immediately. *We had seen the renditions, the statues, the friezes.* The depictions of a figure of broad back and narrow hip, with skin the color of a blue summer sky and eyes that shine like light on silver. You have seen the artists' dreams of this moonlit body, with its sea-green hair that sways as if underwater, and as you see this body now, bowing at the head of the stage, you realize that all of the dreams of its beauty were true. Somewhere in your memory, your lola is sighing in a yearning way as she looks up through the small kitchen window at the star-rich swirl of night. "And should you one day find yourself sitting in that theater, lucky enough to watch those curtains rise, it is the child of the Moon and the Water who will greet you. That creature born of the dance between the lunar wane and ebbing tide, now cast in their role as the eternal performer of the Sleeping Sea. Forever imbued with the strength and grace of the most accomplished of dancers."

She smiles.

"A beautiful, moonlit body."

And you look upon this moonlit body with surprise as it breathes in through its nose so deeply its belly distends, pregnant with wind. This body's feet braced on the boards of the stage before it releases in one long exhale all that it has taken in, the gust from its pursed lips blowing out all the braziers in this theater, whipping the fire into smoke until the room votes in favor of the dark and all that is visible to your eyes is the last of the lit braziers onstage—your pupils narrowing on this ancient and raging flame, as this moonlit body stands before it and, like a magician at some unholy font, conjures from its crackling hearth the voices of the ancient and the dead, *our tale soon to be told—of that week of blood, that week of chaos,* the rush of whispers filling the theater, for some tales are too large to be told by one voice alone.

This is the tale of your land,
And the spear that cut through it.

You hear a charge of horses pouring over some distant hill as dancers now swarm the stage, their footsteps a chaotic syncopation. The flames leap, the walls blasted with light and shadow, and in this dreaming theater you swear that you can see the scene as it is, as this moonlit body's movements, and those of the dancers, carve out of the air that land far away and long ago—a place once known to you only through your lola's descriptions, now springing to life in the deep root of you, as if it had always been there. The deep valleys and old forests, the staggering black mountains that cut the clouds, and the carpets of mist that rise from the gulches between sheer cliffs. *This is the land where we lived, and where we died.* The Old Country, your lola called it, but there were other names too. Names etched in runes and woven in tongues long lost to your history. Tonight it is the Land of the Moonless Night. Tonight it is the land that sweats under the Endless Summer—and as the fires of this theater rage, you feel the unblinking sun on your back. You smell the dried grass. You see the dead brooks and the curling fingers of roadside corpses thick with flies that scatter as the riders gallop heedlessly past this parched landscape bearing the banner of their emperor.

This is where our tale begins, with a band of warriors performing a royal inspection of the country, the dancers' feet stamping into the boards of the stage as might a brigade of fearsome riders across a dust-beaten land, and you see with clarity the rider at the head of this royal charge—a man who lifts his laughing face into the air and breathes deep the smells of the country, his birthright, while he leads his warrior-sons west.

"Listen," your lola would say as she lit her cigarette.

Listen, this moonlit body says as the bloodied sun lifts into the parchment sky to the bone-snap of drums.

Listen to the Brigade of the Red Peacock.

The sound of distant thunder in the bright and cloudless day. Thunder between the ache of the rolling hills and the green burst of forests. Thunder that scared the animals into their burrows. The people turning their worried ears to the sky. *We heard them before we saw them.* The thunder of the royal stampede.

The villagers put away their scythes and turned over the feed buckets as the pebbles danced and the terra-cotta eaves trembled. The children held close as the horses crested the nearby rise, two score in number, their riders garbed in red; a gash on the noon horizon. Warriors vicious and without mercy, their faces tattooed with their namesake, their sharp cheeks and hungry eyes framed by red beak and feather; a sight feared by any wise traveler, by anyone who heard the stories, for of the many brigades and bands and gangs that haunted the valleys in those days, it was the Red Peacocks who were deadliest, led as they were by one of the princes of the Throne, a man who had well earned his title of the First Terror.

Across the land, the people lined up to greet them. It was the eve of the Emperor's Holy Pilgrimage, and the brigade was charged with the sacred duty of preparing the land for His Smiling Sun's arrival.

They did so with great pleasure.

"Soon," the First Terror said to the weavers and the quarry workers, the fishermen and the farmers, "in but a matter of days, He will arrive, and in His generosity of spirit, He will visit you all over the course of His five-day journey to the eastern coast. You will present Him with the finest offerings of your craft or your harvest. Your pearls of rice grain, your fresh salted fish. Your richest tapestries. The spirit of your hard work. And He will take these offerings with Him, and He will cherish them, as He disembarks to visit our colonies across the Great and Unending Sea. His visitation, the greatest honor of your life. In later years, you will recall it to the children at your bedside. Squander this moment at your peril." During these speeches the Peacocks slapped open doors and rummaged through dressers and kicked at loose floorboards, searching for evidence of dissent. Chickens were chased out of coops. Sharp knives taken to grain sacks, to linen sheets. The people listened to the ransacking of their homes *but we did not dare turn to look, for we all knew the consequence of turning away from a prince.* "When His caravan passes through this way, you will hear a drum heralding His arrival. You will line up, like so, across the entrance to your village, facing the road; every man, woman, and child. And you will bow. You will bow low, so He cannot see your face. Every head that does not bow for our Smiling Sun will be added to our collection," he said, pointing at the fly-strewn cloth sacks that hung from the horse saddles, the cloth black with dried blood.

In one of the villages, there was a loud clatter—a crying girl dragged out of a small house.

"This rat was hiding under the boards, Father!" the Peacock shouted.

The villagers took in a collective breath. *And we glared at the girl's parents, who in spoiling this child had doomed us all.* The girl's bare feet trenched the hot dirt as she was brought to the prince for judgment.

One of her parents fought against those restraining her.

"She was scared!" the mother cried. "Forgive us! She was scared!"

The father quiet, his head bowed low.

The First Terror drummed his fingers against his waist. He lifted the shivering girl to her feet *and then he looked into her eyes, and we could feel the wind begin to whip and rise and we were certain that this was our end, that the prince would not forgive this rudeness and all of us would be tossed into the pit of Joyrock. That we were spared that day was a fortune beyond measure.* What feeling of grace prompted the Terror to send the girl gently into the crowd, into the trembling arms of her parents, would remain to them forever a mystery. The unnatural wind dying down. An easy smile on his lips. "Let it not be said that the Throne is without its mercy," he said. "But on the day of His caravan's arrival, should any transgress beyond their station, do not expect such forgiveness."

Then they left. The horses rearing not long after the Terror finished his address, the people left in stunned silence, a few of them coughing in the stampede's dust wake. The mother clutching the girl to her breast as the father looked on them helplessly, having given up his daughter for dead. *And never would my wife let me forget the shame of that day. Never again could I meet my daughter's eyes.*

Never would we understand why we were spared.

The reason was a simple one. It was the same reason that the First Terror was in such high spirits during the tedium of his tasks, in those weeks of his inspections. Why he spurred his horse at a quickened pace, so eager to return to the palace without delay or incident. A reason that came vividly to his mind when he looked into that little girl's eyes and saw they were the same color as that of his beloved son.

Of Jun.

"For six months I have been parted from his company. He serves the Throne with pride; I recognize this. And I recognize the importance of his mission. But I cannot help but wish he did not have to perform his duty. That he was riding by my side this day. It has been a great difficulty, waiting for him to be returned to us."

The commander of Badger Gate, a small man with a smudge of hair on his chin, poured tea for the Terror, as was protocol, *doing my utmost to not show the tremble in my hands; my utmost not to soil myself.*

"You are a caring father," he said with a servant's smile, placing the polished-clean teacup before the royal prince. "May all the sons of this country be so blessed, to have a parent like you."

Sycophantic words, nonetheless true. The First Terror wept with his sons and he laughed with them, *and in turn we gave him our unwavering devotion, riding with him to the ends of the country, killing anyone who needed to be killed.* But he had a favorite. And he was not shy about who that favorite was.

"To Jun," the commander said, raising his cup, hoping to please his guest, a social tactic that played excellently, as the Terror toasted him with moist eyes.

"To Jun."

Their cups clapped to Jun Ossa, the twenty-fifth Peacock, who had for six months been guarding the fabled Wolf Door beneath the palace mountains, the sole protector of the empress. The Terror wiped his eyes, moved by this imagined scene: Jun's six-month rotation, spent alone in the cold and the dark of that deep mountain cavern with nothing but one's blade, and one's thoughts, and a locked door to protect, to keep one company. This image weighed on him for the rest of the day, until later, at camp, his other sons placed hands on him in comfort, *and we told him it wouldn't be long now,* the prince then smiling at his boys, grateful for all of them.

Horse spurred onward, they journeyed west and completed their assignment, uncommon mercies spared for those they passed, the Terror's mind split between duty and family. As he made his inspections, as he flipped through poorly kept records and questioned an endless parade of perspiring commanders, he thought of his son. Of Jun the Beautiful Knife, who slit his first throat at eight years of age. Jun the Red Shadow, who alone had tracked the infamous Dorogo Bandit Clan into the vagrant woods after their raid of Lady Panjet's sacred vaults, none of the bandits aware they were being hunted that night, not even as they were bled dry in the dark, one by one, throughout their premature celebrations. Jun the Torchbearer, who lit swaths of grain fields on fire in search of the traitorous dogs who had ambushed the Swan Road patrols. *From our houses we watched our harvests burn and the men we hid burn with them as that little demon lobbed his torches.* Jun the Many Titled, these honorifics bestowed upon him by his doting father.

"I remember the last time I passed this way," he said at Eagle Gate to a quiet crowd of sentries, "some seasons ago . . . my son Jun noted that there was an unacceptable level of indolence amongst your sentries. A disorderly mess hall, an unkempt barracks. Jun is quite adept at such judgments. He rightly shamed you for your lack of discipline, and at the time you had promised to tighten the loose threads of your command. We believed you." His finger sliding all the while across the wall of the barracks, holding up to the sweating creatures who awaited his judgment a print of dirt and dust. He did not have to say anything. The sentries and even their commander fell on their knees and polished every inch of the barracks and he smiled, for though the emperor would not care about the dust, much less see it, it was good to see that the people were still well under control despite rumor of the growing rebellion.

This was how he made the last stretch to the capital; with news for his father that the land was well groomed and tamed for his journey, and with the anticipation for the long-awaited reunion with his prized son. The sun burst from behind a dark cloud. The western mountains known as the Jaw rose ever higher to meet them. And the First Terror howled into the air, and his Peacocks howled with him when the city gates unfolded to their arrival. But whatever triumphant return the Terror might have been expecting come his riding through the steep roads of the Palace City, those expectations were not met, the mood subdued and tense. An unusual alertness to the guards posted along the mountain road—so distracted these men were they took no notice of the bags of severed heads the Peacocks had brought home that day. *We were less concerned with those coming up than we were those coming down—there was a culprit in our midst, readying their escape.*

The Terror sniffed the cold, high-altitude air. He detected a sourness, like rotten lemons, and he knew his father was in a bad mood.

When they had crested the last rise, one of the attendant generals rode up in greeting, and it was from him the prince learned why the mood of the Jaw was so grim. The general wore the painted mask of a tusked boar, for it was the custom of the court to cover one's face entirely when in the emperor's presence—the boar's eyes appropriately wide and panicked as he breathlessly explained the situation.

This is the tale of the end of the Moon Throne.

And it began here.

PHOTO: © SIMON JIMENEZ

SIMON JIMENEZ's short fiction has appeared in *Canyon Voices,* and 100 Word Story's anthology of flash fiction, *Nothing Short Of.* He received his MFA from Emerson College. This is his first novel.

simonjimenezauthor.com